WILD DOGS

WILD DOGS

MICHAEL TRANT

BANTAM
SYDNEY AUCKLAND TORONTO NEW YORK LONDON

BANTAM

UK | USA | Canada | Ireland | Australia
India | New Zealand | South Africa | China

Bantam is part of the Penguin Random House group of companies
whose addresses can be found at global.penguinrandomhouse.com

Penguin
Random House
Australia

First published by Bantam in 2022

Cover photography courtesy of Shutterstock and Silas Manhood / Trevillion Images
Cover design © Christabella Designs
Typeset in 12.5/17 pt Adobe Garamond Pro by Midland Typesetters, Australia

Printed and bound in Australia by Griffin Press, part of Ovato, an accredited
ISO AS/NZS 14001 Environmental Management Systems printer

 A catalogue record for this
book is available from the
National Library of Australia

ISBN 978 1 76104 677 3

penguin.com.au

AUTHOR'S NOTE

This story is set in the Murchison and Gascoyne regions of Western Australia. I acknowledge the Traditional Owners of those lands and pay my respects to Elders past and present.

While there are remote Aboriginal communities situated in that beautiful part of the world, Jakob's River and its inhabitants are fictional. Any similarity to actual people or events is unintended and purely coincidental.

ONE

She lies perfectly still, listening in case they draw closer, in case these strangers come for her. Listening for the telltale click that precedes the thunder, the whine of something hot and the pain that follows. Listening for the roar of things that would chase her at great speeds through fallen branches and dry scrub, never losing their breath, never slowing down, never stopping. But most of all, she listens for the Men to leave.

High up on this rocky ridge, sheltered in her den from the day's fierce sun, she had been sleeping when the machine arrived. These metal monsters were not new to her; she had heard them before, had run from them before, but never this close to home. Is it here for her? She does not know.

She creeps forward, silently, cautiously, and peers out into the bright midday glare. Already she is panting, both hot and nervous. The machine stops, the roar settling to a low grumble. It carries the stench of death and decay. She hears the voices of Men as they climb from its belly. Perched on this granite outcrop she sees two approach. One stinks of fear and looks hurt, and she shuffles back into the shadows, for it is never good to be seen by Men.

There is the click, and then the thunder. She ducks as it booms, shrinking back even further. The smell of hot blood wafts up,

1

filling her nostrils and making her long for tonight's hunt. More sounds from below, a dull thud, and then the machine rumbles off to wherever it is such things come from.

The dingo sniffs the air once more and returns to her den. She will sleep, and later inspect the area, removing any trace of the intruders' scents with her own. This is, after all, her territory.

TWO

It's the slow burn that gets them, Gabe decided. Not like floods or fires; they all happen too fast. You don't have time to dwell, or to hope, you just deal with the shit as it pours down and worry later. But a drought? Those bastards linger.

He could see it in the station owners' eyes, earlier that day as he passed through. The season was going to break soon – it *must* break soon. Gabe had nodded in mute agreement with them, seated on the old homestead's verandah as he sipped his coffee and ate the dry fruit cake they'd laid out for him. What else could he do? Everyone knew it would rain again, it was only a matter of when. He'd heard it before, from each property owner or manager along his run, some relying on experience to form their judgement, others on the blind faith that comes from not wanting to consider the alternative. Besides, it always rains after a drought.

Not that it was a drought, not technically. Just a bloody long summer that happened to follow an extremely short winter. Dry, but not dry enough to attract any attention beyond the region. No well-meaning city folk buying a bale out here just yet.

He shifted his weight, easing the pressure on his knees. The hessian bag under them was not there for comfort, but to catch his scent. Fresh tracks showed in the surrounding dirt. The owners had said there was at least one dog watering nearby, and Gabe suspected it might be about the only thing drinking in the area.

The sun was at its peak, beating down with relentless force and continuing to suck away whatever moisture still remained in the earth and surrounding scrub. His hands sweated under latex gloves, and tiny black flies danced at his mouth and nose, dodging the sharp puffs he blew at them from pursed lips. All around a hum echoed, a mixture of fence wires singing along the track he was on and the incessant chirp of cicadas, interrupted only by a *thunk* as his mattock bit into the ground. But it was easy digging and his efforts soon ceased. Just a small hole was needed.

Gabe wondered how these people could do it, with nothing but hope and resolve keeping them going. He knew what it was to be trapped with your thoughts, and it wasn't as though they could just stay busy to take their minds off things; the dry was everywhere you looked. Country cried out for a drink, and bare dirt greeted his eyes all through this area, the carpet of red broken by poverty bush and mulga trees doggedly hanging on. Any other palatable shrubbery had been eaten down to woody stumps by what stock was left. He'd passed a small mob of sheep shortly after leaving the homestead, all hips and ribs, their heads either down searching for the last skerrick of grass, or skywards, straining to trim back the curara trees even higher. They could have well been looking for rain. God knows everyone else was. Hindsight said the stock should have been sold off months ago, but months ago it was going to rain soon, wasn't it? Slow burn indeed.

The hole was the right size. No surprise there; he'd done this a hundred times before. Gabe laid the steel trap in its new home, keeping his hands clear of the rubber-coated jaws, particularly the one with deadly strychnine powder wrapped under black electrical tape. He checked the foam beneath the trigger plate one last time, sifted dirt back over the trap until it was buried, and scattered a handful of crushed twigs and leaves onto the disturbed earth, covering all but a patch directly above the plate. A single dried dog scat from the container among his other gear was placed under the bush behind the set, at arm's length past the trap, and a final drop of pungent liquid from his brewing bottle finished the lure nicely.

This was the perfect spot, funnelled in by broken branches on either side. Any passing dog deciding to investigate the foreign scents had no choice but to walk across the trap, and the only spot to lay a paw without fear of prickles was the bare ground over the trigger. *Bang. Gotcha.* Another happy station owner, another bounty claimed. One down, hundreds more to go. Gabe stood to admire the work, his knees cracking like gunshots, and he rubbed his hip, knowing that the dull throb would not go away until later when the whisky bottle came out.

He gathered his gear and carried it back to his LandCruiser, a khaki four-door model all kitted out for bush living, and stowed it in the large white upright toolbox mounted inside the tray's canvas canopy. A second, older toolbox took up the rest of the left side of the tray, this one silver, dented and adorned with all manner of warning stickers. There was a place for everything. Gabe had spent considerable time and thought getting his dog-trapping outfit precisely the way he wanted it, though it had come at a price.

He returned with a hand rake and scratched away at the dirt in front of the trap; just another old dog marking its patch. A leafy branch was swept over his tracks as he walked to the ute for the last time, removing any trace of him ever being here — so far as the next mongrel who trotted down this fence was concerned, there would be nothing suspicious around save for signs of a strange dog invading their territory. He had considered setting two traps but decided to save the second for where he knew the quarry roamed in larger numbers, and where he would have to be much more inconspicuous in his work.

He closed and locked the silver toolbox, the one that held the business end of his trade, the one that he did not want to leave open for prying eyes and curious fingers. Removing the latex gloves, he wiped his hands on the towel hanging from the tray rail. He would wash them properly once away from the set, not wanting the scent of soap to potentially spook any wary dogs. *Leave no sign, leave no trace.* That was his rule.

Gabe kicked off his sneakers, tucked them into their designated pocket on the tray, and lowered the mesh security cage surrounding the canopy's steel frame, locking the panels and zipping up the canvas flaps. He padded around to the driver's door and, once inside the cab, slipped on his work boots. Stained with kangaroo blood, spilled diesel and all manner of giveaway scents, these never saw the ground within cooee of a trap site. Traces, and all that. Plus, he knew of a station owner whose labrador had been unwittingly poisoned after licking contaminated boots. The inept dogger who had kicked off his footwear by the kitchen door was lucky she hadn't force-fed him his own baits in return.

He started the engine and rolled a smoke while waiting for the air conditioner to begin its battle against the heat that had built up in the ute like an oven as he worked. Others left theirs running, he knew, keeping their cabin sanctuaries cool for when they returned. But others didn't catch as many dogs as he did, and sweat was a small price to pay for a bounty.

6

Reaching back into the Engel, he retrieved a beer, glad to finally have his hands on something cold. The fridge took up most of the rear bench seat, with a canvas bag containing a few changes of clothes and a tub with his dry stores occupying the rest of the rear seating. He hadn't bought the Dual Cab model for passengers, he had no need for that, but the extra enclosed storage space was handy. A second, larger Engel resided on the tray, stocked with a mixture of store-bought and bush-caught meats, and, more importantly, extra beer. Save for fuel stops at lonely outback roadhouses Gabe had no real need to deal with civilisation for a while yet, and that was fine by him.

After a long draw of beer, he retrieved a GPS unit and record book from the overhead console. His fingers brushed the rifle concealed inside, the one pushed back deep, away from the same prying eyes he didn't want looking too closely at the locked box emblazoned with *Danger Poison* stickers. He figured most times anyone asking would be focused on the .223 sitting close to hand in the gun rack behind his head. That one he had papers for.

If the drought doesn't get us all, he mused while the GPS booted up, *the bloody paperwork will.* The book was filled with dates, notes and locations, all meticulously recording each and every trap set since he began this contract. Some had details of dogs caught, others merely stated *Nil.*

He marked the new position on the station map stapled inside, then completed the entry with the coordinates from the GPS. No doubt some boffin down in Perth would have a field day with the data once he sent it in, along with the slivers of ears taken from his previous catches, each nestled in its own little specimen tube, labelled, numbered and ready to be paired with Gabe's entries. All to create the latest DNA map showing just how far the dogs had moved since the last report was compiled.

Gabe didn't need a map to know they were moving in; the phone calls from property owners served well enough.

Clerical duties completed, Gabe stowed the bureaucratic bullshit back in the overhead console, tossed the empty can into the bin bag hanging from the passenger door, pulled a second one from the fridge and set off down the station track. There were still a few hours before he was due to meet his friend, but Gabe was in no hurry, knowing they would wait for the goods he carried. And such things were best done under cover of darkness.

THREE

The road stretched on, rising up and over the horizon. An orange dust cloud ahead signalled an approaching vehicle. Probably a station ute, since tourist season was finished, thank fuck. No more dumb shits pulled over on blind corners, snapping away at flowers or dead roos or whatever the hell else brought them out here in their pristine caravans. He didn't blame them for coming, though. The wildflowers were spectacular – when it rained, that is. And it's a well-known fact that red dust tends to get into every-thing, including your blood.

The two vehicles drew closer. Gabe saw headlights flash and recognised the police troop carrier. *Beauty.* He slowed down and rolled to a stop – not bothering to pull over, what with traffic amounting to stuff-all out here – and tried to ignore the slight flutter in his stomach. *Relax,* he told himself, pushing the two empty beer cans deeper into the bin bag. *Nothing to worry about.* He took a swig from his water bottle, rinsing his mouth in case they felt like dusting the cobwebs off their breatho, and rolled a smoke while he waited.

The troopy pulled up alongside his LandCruiser, the two vehicles effectively blocking the road. A young constable Gabe didn't recognise lowered the window.

'Afternoon, sir.'

Gabe eyed the man, clean cut and easily young enough to be his son, if he had one.

'Afternoon.' Gabe looked past him to the older passenger. 'Sarge.'

'Gabe,' Sergeant Aaron Parker said, leaning forward as he unbuckled his seatbelt. 'Good hunting?'

'Couple of big bastards back on Lister.' Gabe watched as the two officers exited their vehicle. 'Just started the rounds a day ago.' He jerked his head towards the constable. 'You got an apprentice now?'

'Sure do. This is Constable Matthew Jefferson.'

Gabe reached through his window and shook the man's hand. He seemed a little awkward and out of place, continually brushing at the flies descending on his untanned cheeks and the corners of his eyes. Gabe saw those eyes linger on his own face where a scar ran down his temple and disappeared into the silver stubble covering his cheeks. 'City boy?'

The eyes shifted back to Gabe's. 'Yes, sir.' Jefferson grinned, somewhat sheepishly. 'This is my first rural posting.'

'Jesus, who'd you piss off?'

The two policemen chuckled, and Gabe relaxed a little, wondering how this greenhorn would go with his first taste of a pub brawl. Probably taser his sergeant by mistake and faint after shitting himself, which would be a lucky thing for the brawlers. He knew Parker did not muck about if push came to shove, once famously subduing two blueing shearers while off duty in the Meekatharra Hotel before returning to his meal without so much as washing his hands first – or so the story went. Gabe had no reason to doubt it; he and Parker had been crossing paths for years, though thankfully never in any official sense. Not yet, anyway.

'No, I requested it,' Jefferson explained. 'Wanted to get out of Perth.'

'Can't blame you for that,' Gabe said. 'Shit of a joint.'

Parker grinned. 'We're doing random vehicle inspections. Don't mind, do you?'

Gabe minded a lot, but shrugged.

'Right, off you go then, Constable,' the sergeant said.

'Yes, sir.' Jefferson pulled out a notebook and began to speak in a very official tone. 'Good afternoon, sir. I am Constable Jefferson and this is Sergeant Parker. We are conducting a routine vehicle inspection today. May I see your licence please?'

Gabe passed him the requested card, watching in the mirror as Parker walked around his ute.

'Thank you, Mr Ahern. And where are you headed today?'

'Up towards Mount Augustus, cut through station country to Carnarvon, then meander back down to Gero again.'

'That's quite the trek. Got plenty of fuel and water? Communications?'

Gabe pointed to the two-way radio in the dash and held up his satellite phone. Gabe thought that one was overkill, but the pen-pushers in Perth wouldn't let him work for them without it. Safety first, and all that. Gabe figured, should he accidently poison or shoot himself during the course of his work, he'd have just enough time to let them know where to find the body.

'Excellent,' Jefferson said, making some notes. 'So you'll be going through Jakob's River?'

Gabe was already reaching for his permit to travel through the Reserve.

'Thank you. Carrying any firearms or alcohol?'

Wouldn't you like to know? Gabe patted the Ruger above his head. 'Just this one,' he said, handing over the appropriate card before being asked. 'And there's two cartons of beer and a couple bottles of whisky in the Engel.'

'Are you planning on calling into the township? You know it's a dry community now?' Jefferson asked. Was that suspicion in his voice? 'You always carry that much?'

'It's too bloody expensive outside of Gero,' Gabe grunted. 'Gone a long time and I get thirsty. Wasn't planning on sharing it. Not really one for chatting with the locals.' *Or nosey coppers,* he thought, keeping one eye on the sergeant in the passenger side mirror.

'Right, well, leave it in the fridge. So long as you don't open anything you'll be fine. Exemptions apply for tourists or passing travellers in this case. The restrictions were a community initiative so they get to decide the rules, otherwise you'd have to take a really long detour. And there's no hunting on the Reserve.' Jefferson gave him a friendly smile. 'But I'm sure you know that.'

Gabe did, which is why he planned to stay off the main road.

Parker returned to his charge's side. 'Got a nice set-up here, Gabe.'

'Bloody want to be for what it cost me,' Gabe said, taking back his papers from Jefferson. He didn't feel like thinking about what it had cost him right now. That would come later, as it always did.

'Must be good money in dogs.'

Gabe scoffed, pushing back the memory. 'Barely. And you got to catch them first, Sarge.'

'Same as us. Right, Matty?'

The young officer nodded, agreeing wholeheartedly with his superior. Gabe got the impression that happened a lot.

'Fire up that aircon for us, Constable. I'll join you in a second.'

Here we bloody go, Gabe thought, watching the young officer almost leap into the cool of their troopy.

Parker rested his arms on the shooter's rack strapped to Gabe's door frame, and leaned in closer, lowering his voice. 'So, how are things, really?'

'Same as usual.'

'That good or bad?'

'Not bad.'

'But not good either?'

Gabe shrugged, but didn't answer. Parker's eyes flicked to the bin bag hanging from the passenger door. The top of Gabe's last can poked out just enough to be clear it wasn't Coke, and Parker raised an eyebrow.

Gabe shrugged again.

'People worry, Gabe. It's okay to feel—'

'I'm fine, Sarge,' Gabe said, a little sharper than he meant, and softened his tone. 'I'm alright. Really. I've got three weeks out bush with nothing to bother me except flies and dust. Being out here helps.'

The lie was almost convincing enough to make him believe it, but the reality was while being out here felt like coming home, it also carried all the painful reminders of earlier times. But it was better than being stuck in suburbia, if you could call Geraldton suburbia. Parker clearly wasn't buying it either, studying him before giving a drawn-out sigh.

'Righto, Gabe, just . . . shit, just look after yourself, yeah? Touch base every now and then? Like you used to.'

Gabe said nothing, having no intention of touching anything other than another beer once these two boys in blue got out of his hair. Parker meant well, but Gabe wished he'd stop bringing it up. It had been four years now. Funny how people fond of suggesting moving on never took their own bloody advice.

'Okay, well, we won't keep you. Sorry for the hold-up. Safe travels.'

The two officers carried on their way. Gabe watched the dust in the mirror, and, once satisfied they weren't coming back, he opened another beer and drove onwards. It was a hundred kilometres to his camp site, and he wanted to get there before the sun got much lower. Long shadows and blinding light through dirty windscreens made for dangerous road conditions, as he well knew. And, more importantly, he wanted to be set up and ready before the others arrived to collect their goods. Goods that, if Sergeant Aaron Parker had discovered them, would have led to a very different parting conversation.

By the time Gabe reached the clearing, it was almost dark. He had nearly missed the obscured turn-off, but caught it at the last second and guided the vehicle between the trees and over gutters formed from long-gone rains, doing his best to avoid broken branches and sharp granite. He didn't feel like changing a tyre; he felt like a good feed and a stiff drink. His hip was beginning to ache from sitting for so long.

Gabe parked in the usual spot and killed the engine, allowing the immediate stillness to swallow him as stars emerged one by one in the late dusk sky. A kangaroo regarded him curiously from the opposite edge of the clearing, and with practised speed the Ruger was in his hands, sights on the animal, a round chambered. He needed fresh meat for baits, so why waste the opportunity?

His finger had already tightened around the trigger when the animal ducked down. Gabe peered over the rifle and saw a young joey scramble into its mother's pouch. He raised the barrel, ejected the unspent cartridge into his hand and stowed the rifle again. There would be others, ones without joeys. He glanced up at the stars once more. *Happy, Valerie?*

The stars didn't answer, and the kangaroo casually hopped away as he climbed out and rolled up the canopy sides to expose the mesh cage that encircled his tray. No one got into his ute without his permission or a damn good set of bolt cutters. He unlocked the latch and the panel sprang open on its gas struts, exposing another upright tool chest on the right side and the second Engel. Like the sarge said, he was well set up – driver's side for living, passenger side for working, and the two never mixed. He began to make camp and decided to light a fire, since you can't sit under the stars, beer in hand, without the crackle of flames. Just wouldn't be right.

Thirty minutes later, a steak and half an onion were sizzling on the steel barbecue plate while a couple of potatoes did their thing in foil amongst the coals. Gabe sat in his camp chair, occasionally prodding the fire with a long stick, while a bottle of Johnnie Walker – cheap and effective – rested beside his battered pannikin on the table, along with bread, butter and salt. So far as Gabe was concerned, he had all the five food groups here – never really considered himself much of a camp cook. Not like Valerie; she could knock up a good feed out of anything. Gabe could picture her now, standing over the camp oven, stirring away, nattering on about some bloody thing while he admired her backside and . . .

He stopped himself, willing the memories to disappear lest they overwhelm him before the others arrived.

Apart from the flicker of flames and the dull moonlight, he sat in darkness as he ate, the silence broken only by the fire's crackle.

In his mind he went over tomorrow's plan: check the traps, inspect that breakaway ridge again for sign, and carry on towards Mount Augustus. Simple enough. He should probably top up the ute's water tank tomorrow as well, and call in to the community on the way through. Would've had to anyway, even if he weren't taking back tracks through the Reserve, so there would be no suspicions raised at his unannounced presence.

Despite the sun being long gone, heat still radiated up from the ground. He decided not to bother with his swag's tent cover tonight. He could catch what little breeze there was and the view was much better without it. The rooftop tent mounted above the canopy was only used when he was staying put for a few days to scout a new area on his quad bike. But he'd left the bike and its trailer at home; this run was a simple check and reset, and the bloody tent wasn't worth the effort for one night. *This is living,* Gabe thought, pouring a drink and settling back.

He heard them soon enough. Sound travelled for miles in the still night air, and when he turned his head towards the crunching branches and rumbling engine, he saw a spotlight cut through the sky. He rose and flicked on the LandCruiser's floodlights in case they sent a bullet his way by mistake. The crashing stopped, as did the strobing light. Moments later, a gunshot echoed, followed by a thud and a cheer. Seemed the boys had bagged something.

When a battered troop carrier emerged through the scrub, Gabe had to shield his eyes from the harsh glare of its headlights. It was a similar model to the police troopy, though in much worse wear. An impressive-sized kangaroo lay strapped across the bonnet and bull bar, its head lolling over the wheel arch where blood ran down and mingled with the red dust.

'Bloody big roo, hey Gabe?' said the driver, an older Aboriginal man who had seen just as many musters as Gabe, probably even more. Gabe had known Bobby for years; they'd met as young jackaroos on northern cattle stations.

'Good size alright – who bagged him?'

Bobby tossed his head towards his passenger. 'This here, my nephew, Darren. On a break from the mines. Said he'd give us a hand.'

Darren offered him a little wave.

'Fuck's sake, Bobby, I told you, no strangers.'

'He's not a stranger, he's family,' Bobby said. 'You worry too much.'

'You don't worry enough,' Gabe grunted back. 'Passed the coppers earlier, and they stopped me. Random vehicle inspection, they called it.'

'That new fella's still pretty green, hey? Reckon I met backpackers with more clue than him.'

'He might be, but Parker's no fool. He gets a whiff of this and we're both fucked.'

By now Bobby and Darren had climbed out of their troopy. Gabe led them to the work side of his ute and unlocked the large silver toolbox with the warning stickers plastered on it.

Bobby watched him cautiously. 'You sure none of that shit spills? I seen what it does to them dogs you catch.'

'I'm sure,' Gabe said. This was the business end of his trade, the nasty part, the bit you really didn't want to muck about with or spill on your boots, or you'd end up poisoning the station owner's dogs by mistake, or worse.

Inside one end of the steel chest sat a plastic tub containing various bottles, syringe guns, and packets of masks and latex gloves. At the other end of the tool box, dozens of steel traps were piled next to the tub. Strychnine powder, injectable liquid 10-80, some laced oats – this was where all the deadly shit lived.

He even had a few bottles of other stuff that you could no longer buy but was exceptionally effective. Which was why you could no longer buy it.

Gabe lifted the container and placed it on the ground. He reached back into the chest and grabbed a rope handle attached to the plywood floor the tub had been sitting on.

'Give us a hand with this,' he commanded, motioning to the other end of the box. Bobby grabbed the second handle and the two men pulled, lifting the false floor, and with it the traps, revealing the four beer cartons and half dozen liquor bottles underneath.

'Good hiding spot,' Darren said, watching the men work. He was a short, stocky young man, early twenties perhaps, dressed in faded jeans and an old orange high-vis shirt from one of the surrounding mines. The silver strips glimmered in the light as he moved. *Not exactly inconspicuous,* Gabe thought.

'It is, and you'll keep it to yourself,' Gabe growled. He hoisted out a carton and thrust it at him. Darren didn't reply and carried it around to the rear of their troopy, muttering something under his breath as he went.

Bobby handed over a wad of cash. 'When you coming back through?'

'Probably in a couple of weeks, maybe longer. Depends,' Gabe said, pocketing the notes. He pulled out the bottles and handed them to Darren as he returned. He thought the young man scowled at him, but it was hard to tell in this light. Probably wanted a different label.

'No problems. You let me know when you coming back.' Bobby helped Gabe lift the false floor back into the toolbox. 'Better go – boys will be wondering where their feed is.'

'Don't go doing anything stupid, and if you do, you didn't get it from me,' Gabe warned.

'Nah, we're good,' Bobby assured him. 'Any trouble-makers got gone when they shut down the grog. Only us poor fellas left, just wanting a beer after work, that's all.'

This time Gabe was sure Darren glared at him, the ungrateful shit.

The troopy doors slammed shut and the vehicle disappeared back into the scrub. Gabe finished reorganising his toolbox and locked it, then opened the passenger door and placed the wad of notes in the ute's glove box. While he was up, he retrieved his camper's bed and set it up in the middle of the clearing, then killed the lights, stoked the fire and sat back down. Off in the distance, the noise of his visitors faded and once more it was only the fire's crackle that broke the silence. He topped up his pannikin, took a sip and leaned back to study the stars, feeling the warm burn as he swallowed. A couple more of these and his hip would stop aching, his conscience would quit nagging and his mind would stop dredging up the past.

FOUR

He is driving back to camp, his mind elsewhere, thinking they should give the contract fencing away and find another gig. It's getting too hard on the both of them. Maybe shooting again? But that's night work. What about dogging? He'd always been good at that, and word is the government are looking for new doggers.

The dusty windscreen is almost opaque in the setting sun, but he doesn't worry. He could drive this road with his eyes closed, and he is in a hurry. The day has been hot and hard, and he's had no offsider. Valerie's on the stores run, but she should be back by now, and among her load of shopping will be his beer. She will have packed some in the Engel for him before beginning the long drive from Geraldton, and they will be cold and like cool nectar on his parched throat. Yes, they will look for some different work. Even with a pneumatic drill, digging strainer holes is no job for someone of his vintage.

His ute crests the rise. The sun, partially hidden behind the horizon, now flares with all the intensity of a welder's flash and—

Gabe woke, immediately feeling the bile rise in his throat as the morning light assaulted his eyes. He rolled and vomited onto the dirt, just missing the kicked off boots by the camp bed. Vomiting was good – a sure-fire way to erase the memory of the dreams. At least this time he had opened his eyes before it really began.

Gabe sat up, ignoring the pounding against his temples. That would go away soon enough; it always did. He ran the back of his hand across his mouth and spat into the dirt as he pulled on the boots. A smoke and coffee and he'd be right again, ready to pack up camp and find those traps. Nothing made you forget a hangover – and dreams – like a bagful of dog scalps. This could turn out to be quite the profitable trip.

Within the hour he was underway, seeking out the first site. Aided by his GPS, he found it soon enough and parked the ute under a mulga. There were no roads or tracks out here, just open scrubland, which required careful driving to navigate without spearing a tyre or bending an axle. Gabe retrieved the rifle from the overhead console and slung it across his shoulder. The M1 Garand was his father's, souvenired from the war, and had ended up in Gabe's possession when the old bugger finally died. He preferred it over his bolt-action .223 for this sort of thing; the semi-automatic M1 packed a punch, and if he came across more than one dog, he could drop them quickly. His sister had been all set to hand the thing in, but it was too good to be destroyed, so Gabe had walked out with the rifle and not much else from his father's meagre estate. Ursula never asked about it again and Gabe never mentioned it. Not that he saw her much anymore, or anyone for that matter, if he could help it.

He retrieved the trapping gear and headed off into the scrub on foot, GPS in hand. The set was a few hundred metres in and it was easier to walk. Safer, too; there was no hunting allowed on the Reserve. Wheel tracks might lead to curiosity, and curiosity might lead to trouble. Couldn't be too careful, even out here.

As he trudged towards the creek where the set lay tucked away against a bank, Gabe listened. There was nothing, only the crunch of his sneakers on dried branches, and the humming cicadas. Always the bloody cicadas. He emerged onto the narrow gully and, across the sandy bed, saw what he was looking for: the swollen, outstretched carcass of a large brown dog, its front paw pinned by the rubber jaws. Gabe's spirits lifted. *You bloody beauty*.

He crossed the dry waterway, placed the gear down on the ground and began to inspect the dead animal. Male, adult, a hybrid cross of some sort, probably sired by a town dog drawn out to the scrub by a dingo bitch on heat. His gloved hands prised open the trap; the tape and small piece of cloth carrying the deadly strychnine powder had been chewed away, resulting in the dried froth and fixed snarl that adorned the creature's muzzle.

The stench of decayed flesh was strong, but Gabe was used to it. He guessed the dog was caught a week ago, not long after he'd laid this set on his way home. Not for the first time was he glad he could lace his traps with strychnine to ensure a quick death and save having to check them daily. You could cover much more ground that way, and the idea of anything being stuck in a trap for days held no appeal for Gabe. He had little love for his quarry, having seen firsthand the torn sheep carcasses and the festering wounds on young cattle, but he wasn't completely heartless. And he did hold a begrudging respect for the dingoes. Trapping them took skill; in some ways it was a battle of wits, seeing who could outsmart who. A few times he'd arrived at a set to find a fresh turd waiting for him, placed so close to the buried trap that, had the damn thing gone off, it would have taken the bugger's nuts with it. A proper *fuck you* in dog speak.

But in this case, he had won. Fresh tracks peppered the ground around him – his instincts had been right once again; there were still a few more to catch in this area. He grunted contentedly and got to work. His hunting knife made no noise as it slid from its leather sheath on his belt, and he removed the scalp with ease. Later he would add this dog's details to an earlier site in the record book, one whose GPS coordinates would not cost him his contract and a fortune in fines. He doubted any station owner would begrudge him if they knew.

Gabe worked quickly, removing the old trap and setting three fresh ones around the carcass. There were another eight sites to check on the Reserve, none of which were easy to get to, and if this first one was anything to go by, Gabe had a busy day ahead of him.

It was midday when Gabe drove into Jakob's River. Two sets remained to be checked on the northern side of the Reserve. It had been a good day. Another eleven scalps were concealed in his toolbox, and tomorrow he would let them dry in the sun as he cleaned and re-laced the used traps, before clipping a DNA sample from each scalp and forging the paperwork. He could see no harm in that. The way the dogs were moving through, they would've ended up in station country sooner rather than later. They didn't exactly pay much attention to the permitted trapping zones marked on maps.

A group of kids on bikes rode towards him, with a couple of dogs dancing between them. They stopped to inspect Gabe as he drove by, and the older ones gave a friendly wave, recognising him. He raised a hand in acknowledgement but barely glanced at them as he passed. There would be no lollies handed out for them today. Hadn't been in four years.

Transportable fibro houses, a town swimming pool, a school, a nursing post, a community centre, a store and one small police outpost made up Jakob's River. The houses were mostly tidy, save for a few ramshackle buildings on the outskirts, but, in general, everything was well kept. The community leaders ran a tight ship, predominantly led by Elsie, an Elder, and a woman not to be trifled with. Gabe knew many tourists drove through here on the wildflower trail and the town made a tidy trade out of them, when it rained. He also knew if she suspected what he'd been up to last night, old Elsie would run him out of town herself.

Gabe pulled up at the store. All he wanted was to top up his water tank and keep moving, but he would need to ask Melissa for the hose first and buy something for the privilege. He stubbed out his smoke in the dirt and walked inside.

'Mel,' he said, giving the young Aboriginal woman behind the counter a slight nod as he headed towards the snack aisle.

'Back again, Gabe?' Melissa smiled.

He never answered, merely grunting as he went by, knowing if he looked back he'd see the same sympathetic expression on her pretty face that she always threw him these days.

The store had fairly slim pickings; Gabe assumed the delivery truck was late again. One limp lettuce and a bag of tomatoes that looked about a day from becoming sauce were the only remaining items in the vegetable rack, while the dairy fridge was all but bare.

'Milk's in the freezer if you need some,' Melissa called. 'Meat too.'

Gabe grabbed a couple of bags of jerky and went back to the counter.

'Just these ones, thanks,' he said, fishing a crumpled note from his pocket. 'And the water hose please.'

'Big spender today, aren't you?' She scanned the packets. 'You want a bag for all this or you right?' It was friendly sarcasm, but sarcasm nonetheless.

'No bag. Saving the planet.' He could do sarcasm too.

Melissa handed him the change. 'When did you come through? This morning or last night?'

'This morning,' Gabe said, not meeting her gaze. 'Camped up on Lister.'

'Pity you weren't here yesterday. Bobby left last night hunting kangaroo, if you're looking for him. Haven't seen him since.'

'That's too bad,' Gabe said, keeping his eyes down. 'Tell him I said hi. Can I grab that hose?'

Melissa reached under the counter and handed him the garden hose. 'Bring it back in, yeah? That's the third one this year. Bloody tourists, you'd think if they can afford them big caravans, they can afford a bloody hose too, hey?'

'That's people for you.' Gabe took the hose and went outside. He threw the jerky packets onto the LandCruiser's passenger seat and set about refilling the water tank nestled under the tray, gazing out across the street as he did so, and almost dropped the hose.

A young woman dressed in the blue scrubs of a community nurse emerged from the medical centre and walked towards the store. The last time he crossed paths with the nurse here the gruff old matron had lectured him on his smoking, his diet, his mental health and pretty much every other bloody thing while he stood talking to Bobby. He'd half expected her to bend him over and check the old prostate there and then, but fear of an impromptu rectal exam wasn't what startled him today. This woman wasn't the matron, far from it. He didn't recognise her, but at the same time he sort of did, and it was disconcerting to say the least.

'Good afternoon,' the nurse said, giving him a friendly wave as she approached. 'Bit warm, isn't it?'

She was quite short, with light brown hair cut in a bob, and looked to be in her late twenties, maybe early thirties, but he couldn't be sure. Gabe was finding that the older he got the younger people appeared.

'Is a bit,' he said. 'Don't reckon I've seen you around before.'

'Started last month. Do you come here often?' The nurse broke into a laugh.

Bloody hell, she even sounds similar. It was like looking at a younger version he'd never known.

'God, that's like the corniest pick-up line ever. I mean, do you drive through here often? You're not a tourist, are you?' She was eyeing his large roof-mounted spotlight and the padded gun rest attached to the driver's door.

'Dog trapper.' Water overflowed onto his boots. He swore, turned off the tap and began recoiling the hose.

'You mean dingoes?'

'Dingoes, wild dogs. Either or,' Gabe said, searching the lady's face for any reaction. If she was like most nurses who found their way out here, she would be from the city, where dogs were family, not pests.

'Interesting,' she said. 'So you shoot them?'

'When I can. Trap them mostly. And bait.' Gabe started to head back into the store.

The nurse followed him. 'Baits? Like poison?'

'Yeah. 10-80.'

'I've heard of that. It's pretty lethal stuff, isn't it?'

'Only if you eat it,' Gabe said. 'But yeah, it is. No cure. Tourists' dogs sometimes swallow one, then they drive for hours to the vet in a panic. Be kinder to just shoot the poor thing there and then.'

'Sounds grisly.'

Gabe shrugged. 'We buggered up the balance out here when we started sinking bores and providing free meals on four legs. Our dogs mixed with dingoes, wild dogs bred up, and now they need controlling. Someone's got to do it, might as well be me.'

The door tinkled as they entered the store. He handed the hose to Melissa, and the girl gave him a cheeky grin.

'Didn't take you long to chat up the new nurse. You watch him, Courtney. Sly old dog, this one.'

'Is that right?' Courtney said. 'We haven't even been introduced yet.' She extended a hand. 'Courtney Drage, RAN for the region.'

'Gabe.' He shook the offered hand briefly. 'I should get going. Sorry, in a bit of a hurry.' He turned to Melissa – 'Thanks for the water' – and gave Courtney a quick nod as he left. 'Nice to meet you.'

'Same to you, Mr Dogger,' Courtney said. 'I guess we'll see you again?'

'Bound to,' Gabe said as he walked out the door. Over the screech of the flyscreen swinging shut behind him, he heard Melissa.

'That old fella's not much for talking.'

She's got that right, Gabe thought. He reached his vehicle, climbed inside and opened a jerky packet, laying it on the dash. The small, dried chunks of meat reminded him that he needed to make some more baits later on today, if he managed to shoot a roo. He pulled away, keen to find the last two traps, get off the

Reserve and make camp. The sets were a fair walk into the scrub, and he knew by the time he finally settled into his camp chair for the night, his hip would be giving him curry.

And thanks to that familiar-looking young nurse, so would his dreams.

FIVE

Gabe was hunched over, halfway through resetting his last trap on the edge of a shallow creek bed, when he heard the vehicle. *Shit.* It came from the other side of the watercourse, so he doubted they would spot his ute parked a few hundred metres behind him. Locals on a roo-shoot perhaps, maybe even Bobby's mates with their newly acquired grog. That's all he needed: a bunch of half-cut shooters driving over his gear. Gabe lowered his head and kept working, listening for any sign they were getting closer.

The vehicle stopped and doors slammed. Voices echoed but he couldn't make out what they were saying; he wasn't even sure it was English, but somebody clearly wasn't happy. He guessed three, maybe four, men were arguing. Probably stupid fucking backpackers who'd gone and hired a tourer and then got themselves horribly lost.

Gabe swore in a low growl, spitting out the curse as he covered his trap. He'd have to go and find out what the commotion was about, point them in the right direction and send them on their merry way with a smile, a wave, and a good story to take back home about the friendly Aussie bushie they met in the middle of nowhere. *Stupid pricks.* He didn't have time for this shit, but the last thing he wanted was a search party stumbling onto his gear while looking for dopey bloody foreigners lost out here.

Gabe finished his work and packed the tools off to one side. He removed his gloves and briefly considered taking his rifle, which was leaning against the bank, but changed his mind. No point in scaring them; he probably looked like that guy from *Wolf Creek* as it was – he'd been told as much more than once, although maybe a good fright was what they needed. The arguing was getting louder and was definitely not English. German maybe? He couldn't tell, but started off in the direction the strange language was coming from. By the sound of things, it had gone from an argument to a full-blown fight.

The gunshot rang out as Gabe was halfway up the embankment, followed by a scream. He instinctively ducked, the shock of it stopping him in his tracks. *What the hell is going on over there?* More screaming peeled through the air, choused with panicked yelling. Gabe began to move forward again. *Some idiot's gone and set off their gun, probably blasted his toe away or something while showing off.* It was when the second shot silenced the screams that Gabe realised this was no accident.

His first thought was to get the hell out of Dodge, but he considered the consequences. Someone had just been shot. Shootings lead to coppers poking around, and poking around here could lead to him. His sets were concealed, he could hide his footprints, but the ute tracks would remain for a few days at least. There'd be a sign. There'd be a trace.

'Christ!' he hissed. Gabe clambered back down the embankment and collected the rifle, hoping he would not need it but checking the clip regardless, and turned to go back up the slope, cursing as he went, a small knot of fear developing in his stomach. *What the hell are you getting yourself into?*

At the top he peered through the scrub but couldn't see anything. The voices still carried towards him, and he figured there were three, all men. One was sobbing, the other two shouting. Gabe gripped his rifle tighter and crept forward, wiping the sweat from his eyes as he went. Not all of it was from the heat.

He saw the glint of the car's white paintwork before he spotted any people. It was parked on sheet rock next to the large ironstone ridge that rose high above the vehicle, a four-wheel drive Dual Cab ute with a well-body tray – a Holden Rodeo, or maybe a Ford Courier. Gabe couldn't tell, but, as he crept around a thick curara bush, being careful not to touch the needle-like leaves, it didn't matter. What mattered was the scene playing out in front of him.

Four men were beside the ute; two were standing while another knelt, facing them, with his hands held to the back of his head. A fourth lay motionless next to the kneeling man on the stony surface that surrounded the outcrop. From his position square on to them, Gabe saw they were of Middle Eastern appearance. The standing men wore casual clothes – slacks and polo shirts – and looked more suited to the main streets of Perth. The third, the one on his knees, was dressed in jeans and a yellow high-vis shirt. He stared up at the man standing over him, his eyes wide with fear and fixed on the handgun aimed directly at his head.

Gabe darted behind the knotted trunk of a mulga. It wasn't wide enough to hide him completely but was still better than nothing, and he didn't think they had seen him. The one with the gun was staring – no, grinning, he was grinning at his captive. Who holds a gun to someone's head and grins like that? No one good, that's who.

The man on his knees was still pleading, and Gabe didn't need to know what was being said to understand the conversation.

31

This was a scene straight out of a movie, with Gabe the unwitting hero. *You've got to be fucking kidding me.*

Gabe's ears pounded as his heart tried to jump out of his chest. *Christ, now what?* He stood there, both hands clenched around his rifle, breathing so hard he was sure the man with the gun would hear. He wiped his palms on his thighs, one at a time, in a futile attempt to stop them sweating, and did the same to his brow using his forearm. *Think, Gabe, what are you going to do?* The pleas escalated and Gabe knew they would soon be cut off completely. He took a deep breath, flicked off the safety and spun around from behind the tree, sighting down the M1 at the armed man.

'Drop it, or you're fucked!'

There was a moment of stunned incomprehension as all three men turned towards his voice, and then things happened very quickly.

The kneeling man dived at the gun-wielder, knocking him to the ground as the two grappled for the weapon. *Here we fucking go,* thought Gabe, and his eyes focused on the remaining man, who was in the process of recovering his wits and reaching behind the small of his back. Gabe was in no doubt as to what would appear in his hand.

'Don't fuckin' do it!' he roared, fighting the urge to dive back behind the tree. A hunter by trade, but never before had his quarry been as equally armed as he. Gabe saw the weapon being brought to bear. He fired and the retort echoed across the scrub like a thunderclap. The would-be shooter staggered when the 30-06 hollow point slammed into his shoulder, sending a spray of blood over the moulded tray of the ute as he toppled back. Gabe knew the bullet would've made mincemeat of flesh and bone; they were designed for bringing down large animals with maximum carnage. The man's gun fell to the ground with a clatter as it bounced off the shale surface, and his body slumped down against the wheel arch of the Dual Cab.

Jesus fucking Christ, I've just killed a bloke. Gabe stood there stunned, the rifle heavy in his hands. He looked down at it, at his fingers clenched around the stock, then at the dead man. *Is this shit really happening?*

A shout yanked Gabe from his stupor. The newly freed prisoner was on top of his captor, both hands clasped around the gun, while the man beneath him rained blows across his head with his free arm. Gabe trained his rifle on them, unwilling to fire lest he hit the wrong man, although precisely *who* the wrong man was in this scenario he wasn't sure. For all he knew, he might have just interrupted a citizen's arrest – but what citizen shoots one person and stands grinning over another? He began to move in closer and reversed his weapon with the intention of striking the gun-holder when the handgun suddenly fired in quick succession as the men struggled.

Gabe felt a bullet whistle past his ear just as he dived behind a termite mound. When the firing stopped, he peeked back and saw the hostage biting down hard on the hand still holding the gun. A slow scream emerged from the gun-wielder's throat as he resisted at first, then finally released the weapon. The hostage immediately whipped him across the face with it and rolled off, springing to his feet. He was spitting blood and flesh from his mouth as he raised the handgun at his attacker. Gabe took that as his cue to step forward. With much caution and his own gun at the ready, he tentatively approached.

SIX

'What the fuck is going on here?'

Gabe tried to sound more in control than he felt. There was no answer as the victor kept his eyes on his new captive crouched before him, cradling a torn hand and looking up at them both with a mixture of fear and rage. Gabe got to within three metres of them and stopped, this time levelling his weapon at hip height towards the one with the gun.

'Oi! Habib! Fuckin' answer me.'

'Habib' took four steps to the side, glancing back and forth between Gabe and the kneeling man, whom he kept his gun firmly trained on. The man on his knees shouted at him.

'*Kerim da basta khanadonet!*'

It sounded Arabic to Gabe, and whatever it meant clearly wasn't complimentary – it resulted in a kick to his face, shutting him up pretty quick as he fell back.

Gabe watched the standing figure, noting he held his weapon with both hands, one cupped under the other like a police officer would, not in the panicked double-fisted or one-handed way he might have expected. But still, the man was clearly shaken. Not overly surprising given what had just unfolded. Gabe realised he was beginning to shake himself.

'My name is Amin, not Habib,' the gun-bearer called back to Gabe, keeping his eyes on the captive.

Gabe figured he was right in his assessment of the man's ethnicity. He sounded Arabic for sure. He sported a short but messy beard and dark hair, and looked to be in his thirties.

'Who are you?' Gabe gestured at the man on his knees. 'Who are they?'

A sudden, chilling thought gripped him. He took a step forward, lifting the rifle butt squarely to his shoulder, and aimed straight at Amin, who noticed this change in his demeanour and turned towards him, also bringing his own gun around. 'You're not fuckin' terrorists, are you? Because so help me God . . .'

Confusion spread over Amin's face. 'Terrorists? No, I—'

A gunshot cut him off, the shock of it almost causing Gabe to trigger his own weapon. From the corner of his eye, he saw the man he'd shot and assumed dead still slumped against the ute, but with one arm raised and his gun wavering at them both. Gabe felt his stomach lurch as he spun to face him and wondered if he'd been hit, but didn't dare look down for fear of what he might see.

Amin reacted at the same time, sending two quick shots at the shooter just as Gabe fired. Neither missed, and it was clear the man would bother them no more. Amin turned to his prisoner, who was launching himself towards Amin in much the same way as had been done to him only minutes earlier. Gabe didn't hesitate and fired again.

It occurred to Gabe, as he watched the assailant collapse, that this would be nothing new to the vintage WW2 rifle. Who knows how many Fritz or Japs had fallen to the same barrel? Either way, thank Christ he had this weapon on him and not the bolt-action Ruger.

Amin remained standing, gun still pointing at the dead man. Gabe saw a dark stain start to spread on Amin's sleeve.

'Jesus, you're hit.' His ears rang from the explosions and his voice sounded muffled. Great, his hearing was going to be even worse after all this.

Amin stared blankly at the blood as though he hadn't realised. It began to run down his left arm as it dropped to his side. He brought his other hand to the wound, but didn't release the gun. Gabe lowered his rifle, though only slightly, still trying to figure out exactly what he had walked into, and breathed hard as he studied the man in front of him. Amin's eyes were searching back and forth, peering past Gabe, perhaps fearful others might be close by, before focusing back on him. So, maybe not a terrorist, just a terrified man.

'Who are you?' the man demanded, suspicion in his eyes as they returned to scanning the scrub. 'Why are you out here?'

'None of your bloody business,' Gabe answered. No way was he going to divulge anything to this stranger just yet. Amin raised his gun at him and Gabe suddenly grew angry – a reaction to the shock and adrenaline charging through him like an electric current. He'd never had a gun pointed at him before and now here he was, one levelled at his chest for the second time in as many minutes. His own gun came up again.

'Look here, mate,' he growled. 'I just saved your skin, and I've got no idea what is going on here, but you point that fuckin' thing at me again I'll jam it so far up your arse you'll be shitting bullets for a week.'

There was a tense moment of silence as Amin considered this threat, and Gabe wondered briefly just how much of it he understood, and if it had been such a wise thing to provoke a distraught man holding a gun.

To his relief, Amin gave a strained smile and raised his hand – and the gun – in a gesture of compliance.

'I am sorry, my friend. But we do not have much time.' He tucked the weapon into his pants.

Gabe relaxed, but only a little, keeping his rifle on Amin. 'We're not going anywhere until you tell me what the bloody hell is going on.'

'Please. They will kill my family if I don't find them first.' His eyes pleaded with Gabe.

'They? Who's they? Answer me, dammit!'

'These men, they have my family somewhere. We have to go before more men come.'

The idea of leaving appealed to Gabe immensely, but he wasn't going anywhere without some answers, and judging by the amount of blood pouring down Amin's arm, this man wasn't going far either.

He pointed at the wound. 'That looks pretty nasty. We'll have to get you to a hospital, call the cops.'

'No! No hospital! No police!' The man tensed, as if to flee, but Gabe suspected he had no clue as to where he was. Gabe held up both hands, one still holding his rifle, which now pointed skywards.

'Look, mate, I'm not real keen on getting the cops out here either, but there's three dead buggers over there, and if you don't get that wound cleaned up, it'll be four.'

Two of which I bloody shot, he thought, suddenly feeling a little light-headed. *Fuck me, now what?*

Amin didn't answer, instead squatting in front of the first body, the one that had already been lying in the dirt when Gabe arrived. Gabe watched him roll the man over, checking for signs of life, but when Amin dropped his head and closed the corpse's eyes, Gabe knew nothing could be done. He walked over, trying to calm his breathing to the point where he didn't sound too panicked when he spoke.

'You knew him?'

'Only for a little while.' There was sadness in his voice. 'Oh *miskin*; he seemed a good man.' Amin made to stand up but almost toppled before Gabe caught his uninjured arm. 'Thank you, friend, for arriving when you did, or I would be sharing Khalid's fate.'

Gabe surveyed the scene around him as he supported Amin. 'What the hell is going on here?'

Flies were already swarming, attracted to the sickly smell of fresh blood. Gabe knew in this heat the bodies would soon start to swell, and wondered what they should do with them. The insects were also converging on Amin's sleeve, where the blood continued to flow and drip off his hand onto the sheet rock on which they stood.

'Shit, we need to get you patched up,' Gabe grunted.

'I must have a drink.' Amin motioned to the mulga Gabe had been hiding behind. 'Let me sit in the shade of that tree. We need to move, but you are right about my arm. In the vehicle is some water, I think. Could you bring it to me please, sir?'

'Just call me Gabe.' He helped the man to the ground under the mulga.

'Thank you, Gabe. *Alhamdulillah Shukur*, I think the wound is not too bad.' Amin gave him a pained smile. 'God has smiled on me today.'

Gabe scoffed and looked about the parched landscape. 'God forgot about these parts a long time ago.'

He walked to the other side of the ute, avoiding the blood that had pooled around the three bodies on the cap rock.

It would soon bake onto the hot surface like some morbid form of bitumen. Gabe leaned his rifle against the wheel arch and opened the rear door. The smell of stale cigarette smoke and body odour filled his nostrils as he grabbed two plastic water bottles from the cardboard tray in the middle of the rear seat. Littered about the floor were food wrappers from roadhouses. Maybe they'd called in at the Junction, which meant somebody would've seen them, and most probably the direction they were heading. And given it's not often four Middle Eastern men in a ute would be seen in the tiny outback settlement, they would definitely be remembered. Gabe wasn't sure if that was a good thing or not.

He noticed two black hoods resting on the back seat, and realised Amin and Khalid must've been wearing these during the trip. On a whim he reached forward and opened the glove box. Some papers tumbled out, a box of .22 bullets and then he saw what he was hoping for – a small first aid kit. Gabe grabbed it, closed the door, retrieved his rifle and headed back to Amin.

The man was watching him intently as he approached. The handgun rested on a rock next to him, and he still held a palm over his bicep. Gabe crouched down beside him and passed over a bottle of water, cracking the lid first.

'My thanks, friend.' Amin took a long drink and then pulled up his sleeve to reveal his wound. He poured the remaining water over it, washing away most of the caked blood to reveal a ragged gouge across the outside of his bicep. The water was warm, almost hot, and Amin sucked in his breath as it hit his skin. Fresh blood began to flow, mingling with the water, and dripped onto the dust, where it beaded briefly before being sucked into the thirsty ground.

'I think it is just a scratch, *Alhamdulillah*,' Amin surmised. 'A little more to the right and maybe I would not be talking to you now.'

'Some scratch,' Gabe said. 'Looks deep. Bullet might still be in there.'

Amin twisted his arm, inspecting his torn flesh. 'I think not.'

'You've seen bullet wounds before, have you?' Gabe's tone was somewhat derisory.

'Sadly, yes,' Amin replied bluntly. 'Though never this close.'

Gabe shook his head in disbelief. 'Who are you?'

Amin beckoned for the kit.

Gabe passed it to him, and then stood back, gripping his rifle with both hands. 'Get yourself patched up, and then you've got some talking to do.'

SEVEN

There wasn't much in the tiny kit, but it contained enough for Amin to dress his wound. He rubbed down the area with the antiseptic wipes and motioned for Gabe's assistance. After a moment's hesitation, Gabe wrapped the bandage while Amin pressed cotton padding hard against his injury. Twice he hissed out what Gabe assumed was a curse.

'If we were closer to my ute, I'd offer you something to take the edge off,' Gabe suggested, and elaborated when he saw Amin's confusion. 'Whisky.'

'I do not drink, but thank you all the same.'

'Suit yourself.' The wound looked worse than just a scratch to him, and personally Gabe was more than ready for a drink. Anything to stop the tremble in his hands.

Amin gulped down two Panadol tablets and picked up the gun. He released the magazine, checked its contents, reloaded the weapon and tucked it into his belt.

'My thanks to you again, Gabe.'

'Yeah, well, not like I had much choice. Now are you gonna tell me what's going on?'

While Amin had been tending his wound, Gabe's mind had raced, playing over what had happened and planning what to

41

do next. All he knew was that he had just shot two men with an unregistered gun while illegally trapping on Aboriginal land. Not exactly good Samaritan material. How in the hell was he going to get out of this one? He had just killed two men. In self-defence, yes, but still . . .

Amin sat back down and took another sip of water. 'I owe you that much. And perhaps afterwards you will be willing to assist me further.'

Gabe rested his rifle against the tree trunk and took a seat next to Amin, in the shade. He flexed his hands again, trying to get the shaking to settle, but when that failed he wedged them under his armpits as he folded his arms.

'Start talking.'

'My name is Amin Tahiri. I am from Afghanistan, and, to answer your earlier question, no, I am not a terrorist.' He gave Gabe a wry grin. 'Is that all you think when you see a Middle Eastern man?'

Gabe shrugged. 'Only when they're trying to shoot each other. And me.' He jerked a thumb over his shoulder. 'So who were they and why were they about to blow your noggin off?'

'The first man I know only as Khalid. I met him in the work camp a few weeks ago. He too is from Afghanistan.' Amin shook his head with sadness. 'All this way just to be killed out here like this.'

'And the other two, the ones waving guns around?'

'I do not know their names, only that they are part of the people-smuggling group that brought myself and Khalid here. We thought they were taking us to our families, but they lied. I suspect they wanted to kill us because we threatened to expose their operation if they did not fulfil their promises.'

Gabe fumbled his tobacco pouch from a shirt pocket and

began to roll a smoke – no easy task with his shaking hands. He saw Amin eyeing his fingers and offered him the finished rollie, which the man accepted with thanks. He rolled another, lit it and tossed the lighter to Amin. 'Brought you here? What do you mean "here"?'

Amin was silent for a moment as he leaned back against the mulga, then sighed. 'I will give you the short version for now – we must get moving once I have caught my breath. We – my wife and son and I – were forced to flee our homeland, and we came here.' He smoked rapidly as he spoke, whittling the cigarette away between each sentence. 'We sold everything we owned to buy passage with the smugglers. The two dead men are part of the group that held us and sent me to work in a town on the coast. I cannot say the name properly, but it is far.'

Gabe could scarcely believe what he was hearing. Illegal refugees getting shot up out here?

'So they're holding your wife and kid somewhere?'

'Yes.' Amin's voice began to tremble as he spoke. 'The men said they would be told we had an accident. They said my wife would have to work for them or they would kill our son. This is why I must find them.'

A million more questions sprouted in Gabe's mind, but Amin spoke again before he could pick which one to ask.

'We should leave this place.' Amin flicked his finished smoke away and struggled to his feet. 'I do not know when they were expected back. We must go, though I am afraid I have no idea where I am.' Then, with sadness in his voice again: 'Or where I am going.'

'We're on Jakob's River, a blackfella Reserve.' Again, Gabe saw the confusion in Amin's eyes. 'Aboriginal land.'

'I thought it was all Aboriginal land,' Amin said. He started towards the smugglers' ute. Gabe could now see it was a Rodeo, as he'd first suspected.

'Suppose it is, in a way.' Gabe grabbed his rifle and followed. 'But you can't hunt or shoot here unless you're part of the community.' He took in the surrounds. The face of one of the bodies was almost completely obscured by black bush flies. 'Not that it helped these blokes.'

Gabe watched as the insects crawled in and out of nostrils and open mouths, and felt ill. He was no stranger to death. If it wasn't trapped or gunned-down dogs, it was the carcasses of emaciated livestock who'd succumbed to the dry, or a kangaroo he'd shot to make baits or for his dinner. *Maybe we aren't any different to animals,* he mused. *Our dead make us uncomfortable. Isn't that why you hang your dead dogs in the trees and on fence lines? To ward off the next one passing by?*

'What brought you out here then, Gabe?' Amin stopped by the first smuggler's body and began rummaging through pockets. He coughed and hacked as a fly, or maybe a dozen, found their way down his windpipe.

Gabe paused. 'Just a bit of sightseeing,' he said, watching on and surmising that perhaps the stubborn knot in his stomach was simply due to the fact that, had he arrived a minute later or not reacted quickly enough when the shooting started, it could be him lying on the bloodstained stone, baking under the sun while flies danced around him and some stranger went through his pockets. Gabe suspected this was the most likely reason.

'If that is the case, I am glad you brought your camera' – smiling, Amin gestured to the M1 in Gabe's hand – 'along with you.' He finished searching the first body, finding only a wallet, which he began flicking through. A thought occurred to Gabe.

'Hey, you shouldn't be touching all that. The police—' He never got to finish, because Amin whirled on him.

'No police! I already told you!'

Gabe stepped back, raising his hands. 'Alright, no cops. Look, honestly, that works for me too, but what about these bastards?' He pointed to the bodies. 'Anyway, why are you so spooked? You think they'll send you back?'

Amin made his way to the next body and commenced another search. 'They have people in the police. That is how they know when to bring the boats ashore.'

'What fucking boats?' It suddenly clicked. 'You mean you came here on a boat?'

'Yes. Hidden in trucks on the way to Pakistan, then a plane to Indonesia, and from there the smugglers put me on a fishing boat while my family waited for me to earn enough to pay for their passage here. After many days we swapped to a larger, much more modern boat and came ashore at night.'

'Bloody hell,' Gabe said. 'I thought the government stopped all the boat people. Sent them all to some island. Manus, or some fucking thing.'

'I don't know the details,' Amin said, still hunched over the body. 'But I do know the smugglers have changed their operation. I think they had to. But we can talk about this later. We must get moving before others come looking.'

'Shit,' Gabe said. 'We can't leave everything like this.'

'Why not?' Amin looked genuinely confused. 'Who would find them other than their friends?'

'Who knows? Anyone could pass by.' Gabe waved his arm in a broad arc towards the scrub line. 'I found you. Mob of locals could come past while shooting roos, or a tourist thinking he's the next Steve Irwin. A station owner flying over looking for lost cattle would spot that Rodeo a mile away. Who fucking knows? It's not as isolated out here as people think. Anyway, you can be sure as shit the cops will find all this sooner or later.' And that was the last thing he wanted.

Amin finished his search of the second body and Gabe helped him to his feet. He'd found another wallet, a mobile phone and the second handgun, which he checked over and tucked away in his belt. Again, Gabe noted the man knew what he was doing with the weapon.

'Then what do you suggest?' Amin held the phone up high. 'This is not working.'

'Won't until we get to the Junction or go back to the community. Not much signal out here.' To Gabe's surprise, Amin gave a chuckle. 'What's so funny?'

'At home I could get signal all the time. Even after the Americans had destroyed most of it.'

'Welcome to Australia.' Gabe gave a small grin, despite the seriousness of their situation, and then sobered as he turned his attention to the bodies.

EIGHT

'If what you say is true about other people finding this place, then we must bury them,' Amin insisted.

Gabe immediately shook his head. 'Not a chance. All this country has shallow cap rock under it. You'd only get a foot or so down, and besides, you're in no shape to dig, and I'm not digging a grave on my own.'

'Two graves.'

'What?'

'Two graves. These two' – Amin kicked at one of the smugglers – 'can burn in Hell for all I care. Allah will deal with them. But I will not insult Khalid like that. He was the same as me, simply trying to save his family.'

Gabe muttered a curse under his breath. His sense of unease was growing with each new bit of information Amin supplied. He didn't know much about people smuggling or refugees save for snippets he heard on the radio news, but he could already gather that what he'd stumbled upon was no small operation. Amin mentioned work gangs in a coastal town, and a large, modern vessel, plus they had cops working for them, or so Amin claimed. And the fact they were willing to shoot two men who threatened to expose them meant they had enough to lose to justify it. *Of all the bloody places to be, why'd they have to choose here?*

Something clicked.

'Amin,' he said. 'Why'd they shoot Khalid right next to the ute?'

'He tried to grab the gun when they told us our families were not here, and that we were to die for daring to threaten them. Why do you ask?'

'What do you reckon they planned to do with the two of you once you were dead?'

Amin scratched his beard, casting his eyes around the area. 'I don't know. I had no time to think of such things. Until we arrived here, we did not suspect they were going to kill us.'

'They've got no digging gear,' Gabe pointed out. 'Plus, this ground here is all rock. Pretty shit digging. And I'm fairly sure they wouldn't just leave two bodies lying around. So why come here?'

Amin shrugged. 'But this is where they wanted to be. They said so. "We have arrived," they said. I thought they meant to where our families were being held. But when our hoods were taken off we were not in any camp, and they were not here.'

'If they were going to kill you, why'd they bother with hoods?'

Amin thought for a moment. 'They always said the camp where our families are kept was a secret. Perhaps they feared we would be suspicious of something if they didn't. That would also explain why they did not bind our hands.'

'Makes sense, I suppose.' Gabe looked around. 'So, if they planned to get rid of you here but not to bury you, there has to be something nearby. Like I said, they wouldn't have just left you in the dirt.' He eyed the ridgeline behind them. The breakaway rose sharply, tufts of dried wanderrie grass sprouted between rocks, and a lone mulga had somehow rooted itself halfway up the side, barely clinging to life in the harsh surrounds. Further up, another tree had lost the battle for survival, and it was now nothing more than a wooden skeleton in between the boulders with an eagle's nest resting in the fork of the dead branches. Gabe suspected it had been long abandoned, like most of the countryside. Near the peak he could see a small opening in the rock – the perfect dog den. Were he here under different circumstances, he would probably attempt the climb for a closer look, perhaps throw in a few baits just to be sure. But he had more pressing concerns than wild dogs right now.

Further along the breakaway's base a dead curara tree lay between two jutting ironstones. The way it was wedged in seemed out of place. The trunk had been snapped off, yet there was no sign of any stump in the ground to suggest it had grown there and simply fallen into the gap.

He walked over, grasped the trunk and pulled. It wasn't exactly light but he managed to drag it out of the way, exposing a deep opening in the ground. Being very careful where he placed his feet, Gabe peered down into the darkness, but couldn't make out anything. The smell of death rose up to greet him. Normally he would assume an unfortunate kangaroo or billy goat had fallen in, but today he suspected it was not animals at the bottom of the hole.

Amin's voice startled him. 'Our intended resting place,' he said solemnly.

'Christ, don't do that to me. Jumpy enough as it is.' Gabe's heart had only just returned to a steady pace but was now thudding against his chest again as Amin joined him at the edge of the hole.

'It looks deep,' he said. 'Do you think there are others down there?'

'Well it's not fuckin' roses at the bottom, that's for sure.' Gabe picked up a stone and tossed it in the hole. It fell for a good three or four seconds, echoing up to them from the blackness before finally coming to rest with a clatter.

'Perhaps we could use this?' Amin asked.

Gabe rubbed his chin as he weighed up their options. What they did from here could have a massive effect on any chance they had of getting out of this shitstorm intact. In his mind he went over what Amin had told him. An illegal organisation was involved, one willing to kill if they felt threatened; they appeared to have done so before. Two of their members were now dead by Gabe's own hand, and sooner or later someone would come looking. The question was, would they know where, or was this a secret location known only by those whose task it was to get rid of 'problems'? The obvious solution was to dump the bodies down the hole and leg it out of here, pronto. But it didn't feel right.

During the course of Gabe's work, there were times when he relied on his gut instinct rather than skill. On more than one occasion, he had abandoned what at first glance appeared to be the perfect trap site because something felt off. He could never quite say what it was. Maybe the wind blew in at the wrong angle, perhaps the area nearby was too open, too exposed for a wily old dingo to venture out and inspect the lure. Gabe only knew that the few times he'd ignored the nagging doubt in the base of his belly, he never bagged a dog.

Amin was studying him. 'You are thinking something; I can see it on your face.'

'The only way any others would come here is if they knew about this spot,' Gabe said.

'True enough.'

'And if they know how to get here, I reckon they'd know about the dumping hole.'

'Why is that of concern?'

'Look, these pricks seem like they're happy to kill anyone in the way, right? So, if they get out here and realise you've somehow escaped, they might just find a way to have a good look down this hole. If they see their two dead guys sitting at the bottom and not you and your mate, your wife and kid might not be so safe anymore.'

Amin paled at this suggestion. Gabe could see him wrestling with his thoughts, and the look of resigned guilt on his face told him that the man was blaming himself.

You know all about self-blame, don't you, Gabe? Gabe ignored the little voice in his own head. Now was not the time for self-pity.

Finally, Amin spoke. 'Then what do you suggest?'

'Give us a hand to cover this hole back up first.'

Amin did as asked, helping where he could but restricted by his wound. The two men covered the crevice again and made their way back to the Rodeo. Gabe surveyed the area. The track the smugglers had driven down to arrive at the clearing could be seen heading into the bushland to the north. Their vehicle had not left much in the way of tyre marks on the flat stone that surrounded the ironstone, and the ground beyond where the smooth granite disappeared beneath the earth was a hard-baked clay, with only a faint impression of the Rodeo's wheels. He looked in the opposite direction and spotted the opening where the barely discernible path continued on, and Gabe thought he knew where it would end up. A plan began to form in his head.

'Can you drive?' To Gabe's relief, Amin nodded. 'Good. Because I think I know what to do with these two pricks.'

NINE

Gabe lowered the Rodeo's tailgate. 'There's a well about forty kilometres back that way,' he explained. 'They decommissioned it a few years ago when the state government bought out the station owners. Deep fucker too, but the windmill's knackered and the tank's collapsed, and because the property got decommissioned no one's bothered to fix it. I called in there a while back, see if there were any dogs sniffing about. Didn't look like anyone had been out that way since they shut the water off. Bit of a billy goat track to get there, probably worse now. But it'd be a good spot to dump the bodies. Reckon there's probably a few dead goats already down there.'

'You were looking for a dog?' Amin asked. 'You lost your pet?'

'What?' After a moment of incomprehension, Gabe realised this man from Afghanistan would know very little about the outback. 'No, wild dogs. Dingoes, or ferals – I hunt them. That's what I do.'

'Ah, I see.' Amin glanced at Gabe's rifle, now leaning against the ute. 'That would explain your "camera".'

Gabe walked around to the side where the first smuggler lay, the one who'd nearly put a bullet in him. 'Are you able to give us a hand?'

'I think so.'

Gabe grabbed the body under the arms and dragged it behind the ute. He tried not to get any blood on him, but it was impossible. His first bullet had completely blown the shoulder blade apart. How the man had gathered enough strength to have another crack at them was beyond Gabe. The second shot had torn through his abdomen, and Amin's had riddled his chest with holes. As they moved the body, the stench of stomach contents filled the air, thick and heavy in Gabe's nostrils and seeping through his clenched jaw into his mouth. Even Gabe's cast-iron stomach rolled a little, and he hawked and spat in an attempt to rid himself of the taste of death. Dead dogs were one thing, but a dead man's bile was another.

Amin, who had at first seemed unfazed by the corpses that surrounded him, had gone a shade of grey and a cough escaped him as he raised an arm to cover his nose and mouth.

'Sooner we get him in the back the better,' Gabe said through tight lips. The flies were covering him now, trying to make their way into his own mouth and nose. He shook his head, blew a burst of air at the determined creatures and looked at Amin, who bent down to assist.

'On three, right?'

'Yes. On three.' Amin grasped the ankles and Gabe gripped the body under the armpits as best he could. At Gabe's count they swung the body into the tray with a thud. Amin gave a sharp grunt as they did so, and his hand went to his arm.

'You okay?' Gabe asked.

'I will be fine. We need to hurry.'

Gabe spun the body around, dragging it to the back of the tray's well. It slid against the rear of the cab, leaving a red slick on the smooth metal floor. The tray was too short for the dead man and his feet hung out over the lowered tailgate. Gabe would fix that once they had the other two in.

The second smuggler followed. Gabe had shot this one square in the chest, so they were spared the nauseating smell of his breakfast as they positioned him next to his partner in crime. By now Gabe was panting hard. His shirt clung to his back as sweat dripped from his brow. While the men weren't overly large, with Amin hampered by his injury, Gabe had been forced to do most of the lifting, and his hip had begun to ache, which up until moments ago he had forgotten about.

'What about Khalid?' Amin asked.

Gabe took a deep breath and went to the final body. 'We'll have to put him in with them.' Amin started to protest, but Gabe cut him off. 'Nothing else for it. Can't put him in the back seat – too much blood. Might have to dump this ute at some point. And by the time we get to where we're going, he'll be stiff as a board and we won't get him out.'

With reluctance, Amin agreed. They hoisted the corpse into the tray, laying him as gently as they could on the first two bodies. Gabe itched to get moving. He could feel the eyes of everything watching them – the crows sitting hunched over in the mulga tree, the bungarra that had emerged from the scrub, tasting the air with its forked tongue. And he knew there would be a dog out there somewhere, lurking just out of sight, watching, waiting to see if these men left anything worthwhile when they moved on.

It was a struggle to close the tailgate with three sets of feet hanging over the edge, but the two men persevered and, after a bit of repositioning, managed to slam it shut. The Rodeo had no canopy or tonneau cover to hide the bodies under, and even after ensuring the corpses lay as flat as possible, Khalid's knees stuck above the well-body sides. Gabe supposed the chances of running into someone out here was pretty remote, which was probably exactly what the smugglers had figured. Just in case, Gabe opened the back door of the cab and retrieved another two water bottles. He threw one to Amin, took a mouthful from the other, then used the remainder to wash down the side of the ute. It wasn't the best job, but he managed to remove most of the blood, which had by now baked onto the white paintwork. If they did run into anyone, at first glance the red smear might look like dust.

Amin drank half of his water and offered the rest to Gabe, who shook his head. He had much colder things waiting for him in his Engel, but first they had to get there. Although his LandCruiser was only five hundred metres or so from where they stood, to take the smugglers' ute to his, they needed to follow an almost non-existent track. Gabe was certain it would cross the creek bed he had been working in before all hell broke loose and loop onto the track he'd driven along this morning. From there they would head to his ute and cover the bodies with the tarpaulin he used as a ground sheet at camp sites when he planned to stay in one place for more than a couple of days. Then he would get Amin to follow him to the well, and they could ditch the bodies. After that, fuck knows. He had to get himself out of this mess somehow, but was unable to think that far ahead just yet.

He emptied another bottle onto the bloodstained ground, and then another. Amin looked at him with some concern. 'Should you not save some?'

'Jesus, mate, do you think I'd be pouring water on the fucking ground if I didn't have any more? Got a shitload in my ute. I just need to make it look like I was never here.'

Amin's face flashed with anger for a moment. 'Just you? You are not going to hide my presence?'

Fuck's sake, this bloke asks some stupid fucking questions, Gabe thought, but replied with a sigh, 'I'm hiding the both of us. Now shut up and let me concentrate.'

Gabe inspected his work. The blood had diluted and fanned out further over the ironstone, the red blending in with the ochre and purple hues of the rock. Once it dried, it would be hard to spot.

'Stay here,' he instructed, and began scanning the ground. How many times had he fired? Once, then once again after that. The two spent M1 cartridges were easy enough to spot, but he could only find six casings from the two guns Amin carried. He wasn't sure how many were lying around; he'd been too busy dodging them to bother counting shots. It would have to do. He might spend all day searching and still turn up nothing. Hopefully anyone else looking would do the same.

He turned his attention to the tree they had sat under. His eyes, accustomed to scanning the ground for the faintest trace of a dog print, picked up their marks easily enough. A couple of hand prints, a scuff where Amin's backside had rested at the mulga's base, and the packaging from the wipes used to clean his wound. Gabe gathered the rubbish, and with a handful of dried wanderrie grass brushed away at the dirt. For added effect, he scattered some fine curara needles over his efforts. Not too many, just enough to blend in with the rest of the ground. He stood back and assessed his work. To him it stood out like a neon sign, but then he knew where to look. Maybe others wouldn't. *Leave no sign. Leave no trace.* It would have to do.

He made his way back to the smugglers' ute. Amin had seated himself side-saddle on the front passenger seat, watching with interest.

'You seem to know what you are doing,' he commented, observing Gabe wipe away their shoe prints and the drip marks from Amin's arm. Gabe's sneakers didn't leave much of a mark, but Amin wore heavy work boots, with deep ridges in the soles. Gabe was grateful the dirt here was hard.

'Dogs are cunning sods,' Gabe said, not bothering to look at Amin as he worked, bent over. 'Some of the older ones, the ones others miss, they get wary. You leave the slightest sign, the smallest mark or touch or scent, and they'll bolt.'

'And do many bolt from you?'

As Amin asked his question, Gabe reached the point where the flat stone rose from the dirt. He stepped onto it, straightened his back with a slight groan, and turned to his new companion.

'No, not often.'

TEN

Gabe drove, easing the smugglers' Rodeo away from the ridge and into the scrub, following the track as best he could. It disappeared once or twice on the hard clay pan, and for a moment he thought they'd lost it, until it appeared again, leading up a sharp bank, then down into the shallow creek line he had been working in earlier. He dropped the vehicle over the edge and stopped in the middle of the dry watercourse.

Amin looked around the landscape in concern. 'What is wrong?'

'Nothing.' Gabe pointed along the gully. 'Just got some stuff to grab from up there. Stay here.'

He opened the door and climbed out, leaving the engine running as Amin sat back and closed his eyes.

'Do not be long.'

Despite the air conditioning blowing in his face, beads of sweat had formed across the man's brow, and Gabe suspected he was in more discomfort than he let on, but closed the door without replying. There wasn't anything he could do in the short term. He just hoped Amin would be able to drive. Where they were heading was not exactly the smoothest of trips. He trudged around the front of the ute and set off up the creek, not looking at their morbid cargo. One of the smugglers' eyes had remained open and Gabe did not care for their dull gaze.

The creek bed comprised hard clay and washed river sand, deep and coarse, which Gabe avoided where he could. Where he couldn't, the loose sand did not show the tread of his footprint, just divots as he walked. An observant person might notice these marks, but with luck nobody would.

At the trap site he gathered his equipment, considered whether he should remove his trap or not, and finally decided against it. They were running out of day and he didn't have time to cover his workings again. If somebody did happen to pick up his trail down the dry waterway Gabe very much doubted they would find his set, unless of course it contained a dead dog.

Although, if a dog, or anything else for that matter, did set it off, it *would* give him an alibi as to why he was in the area. If everything turned to shit and somehow he was placed here and the cops – or worse, the smugglers – started asking him questions, there was no reason for him being anywhere near this place. By rights, he should have been on the main road, heading north, not out on some side track in the Reserve. That was what he had told the sarge and his offsider, who no doubt would have written it all down in that poxy notebook like a good little boy. But if they discovered his trap, he could use that as an excuse. If the police were the ones asking, illegal trapping would be much better than shooting two people with an outlawed rifle. And should he be unlucky enough to meet the people Amin was so concerned about, he could just claim ignorance of the whole affair.

The thought of Amin raised another question. What the hell was he going to do with him? Gabe was certain that if the police did get involved, Amin would not reveal anything to them for fear of reprisals, since he firmly believed the authorities were corrupt. Gabe wasn't so sure. In Perth maybe, but out here? Parker was alright, for a copper, but Amin wouldn't know that. He'd just see the uniform. His companion would keep his mouth shut, but what if it wasn't the cops doing the asking? That would change things.

An image from a movie he'd seen years ago, back when he occasionally watched the things with Valerie, crept into his head. Some poor bugger strapped to a chair while a guy went to town on him as 'Stuck in the Middle with You' played. Gabe shuddered. Up until then, he'd quite liked that song.

You're being stupid, he told himself. Maybe, maybe not. These blokes didn't seem like they mucked around. He and Amin would have to do some talking, get their stories straight in case things got out of hand. *Like they aren't already? You're about to chuck bodies down a well, for Christ's sake.*

Gabe reached his set, picked up the crate with his equipment and left, glancing back over his shoulder for a final check. It looked clear enough, with no discernible indication that anyone had been there. No sign, no trace. Satisfied, he carried on to the ute. He met Amin fifty metres from the vehicle.

'Thought I told you to stay put,' Gabe growled.

'You were taking too long. I was worried.' Amin looked at Gabe's load. 'What is all that?'

'Trapping gear. That's what I was doing when I heard the ruckus.' He kept walking and Amin followed.

'And this was so important that we had to stop?'

Something snapped in him. Gabe whirled. 'Look, mate, I didn't have to get involved in all this shit. I could've bailed the second I heard that shot. Christ knows that would've been the smart thing to do.'

Stunned by the outburst, Amin stared at him, arms folded. Gabe stared back, feeling a touch remorseful about his lack of tact. Amin had every right to be impatient.

'Ah, shit,' he cursed, and began walking again. This time Amin did not follow.

'If you do not wish to help, I will find my own way,' he declared.

'Good luck with that,' Gabe called back, not bothering to turn his head. 'You'll be lost in a heartbeat. Now hurry the fuck up.'

There was a moment when he wasn't sure if Amin would do so or not, and then he heard footsteps crunching through the deep river sand. They continued walking in silence until they reached the ute. Gabe placed his tools on the back seat and they both climbed in, saying nothing as Gabe drove the ute over the opposite creek bank, carrying on along the track for the next five minutes, still without a word between them.

Finally, Amin spoke. 'You were not supposed to be here.'

It was not a question, and Gabe didn't answer. Instead he lit another smoke, staring straight ahead. He didn't offer one to Amin.

'You said there was no hunting on this land, yet here you are with a gun and whatever it is you have back there.' Amin thumbed towards the equipment rattling on the rear seat.

'So what if I was?' grunted Gabe. 'Lucky for you I turned up.'

'I agree.' Amin cradled his injured arm as the ute lurched over a particularly sharp gutter. 'I think whether you should be here or not is of no concern to me. Thank you again for your help. You are a good man, Gabe.'

Gabe sighed, retrieved his tobacco again and passed the bag to Amin, shaking his head sadly as he did so. 'No,' he said. 'No, I am not.'

ELEVEN

They reached the road Gabe was looking for. This one was much more defined, though it still only consisted of two wheel ruts weaving between the low trees and rocky outcrops. It was seldom used, but as usual Gabe had driven his LandCruiser off the track and into the bush before setting off towards the creek line on foot, just to be safe. He parked the smugglers' ute under a mulga tree just in front of where his tyre marks could be seen veering off into the bush.

'Back in a minute.'

Gabe retrieved the rifle resting on the dashboard and followed his wheel marks across the red dirt. He had never really expected his vehicle to be spotted, but he was cautious by nature and didn't like leaving too much to chance. Stranger things than unexpected passers-by had happened before – today was proof enough of that.

He reached his ute, changed his sneakers to his boots, then walked to the rear of the vehicle where a small water tank resided under the tray, complete with tap and soap bottle. Gabe proceeded to wash his hands and face – partly to remove the remaining bloodstains between his fingers, but also to clear his head. Now that things had settled somewhat – if you could call driving around with three dead men settled – his mind had been going over their next steps after disposing of the bodies, and so far had come up short of ideas.

His hands cleaner but his mind no clearer, he picked up the M1 and headed back to the cab. With the door open, he worked the rifle's action, allowing the unspent cartridges to eject onto the seat, a satisfying *ping* following the last one as the empty clip sprang from the weapon. He reloaded the rounds, adding fresh ones from the box in the overhead compartment, and reinserted the clip. Checking that the safety was on, Gabe sat the rifle in the passenger's footwell, close at hand if need be.

He climbed into the LandCruiser, started the engine and pulled two beers from the fridge. The first can was empty in a flash, and he winced as the ice-cold liquid sent sharp bolts through his temples. The second one he drank a little slower while guiding the ute back to the road where Amin waited, though not so slow that it wasn't empty by the time he stopped next to the smugglers' Rodeo.

Amin had left his seat and was standing at the roo bar, waiting for him. Gabe jumped out, opened the rear door of his ute and fished about in the fridge for the can of Coke he knew was rattling in the bottom somewhere. He didn't drink much of the stuff, preferring his whisky neat, but occasionally would grab one when it was too early for a beer, even by his standards. He found the drink, offered it to Amin and grabbed another beer for himself.

'Get that into ya,' he said. 'Sugar will do you good, I reckon. There's a couple more in there, and some cold water too.'

Amin took the drink with thanks, and he must've been thirstier than he was letting on, gulping down half in one go before the fizz caught in his throat, causing him to cough and tears to well in his eyes. Gabe laughed. He was feeling much better already as the faint buzz of two beers in quick succession brought with it a small glow of optimism. Gabe had always been a happy drinker, for the first few rounds at least.

Amin also gave a small laugh, and then saw the beer in Gabe's hand. 'Do you think that is wise?'

'What? Havin' a beer?' Gabe was beginning to open his ute's canopy, seeking the tarpaulin stored inside.

Amin spoke carefully. 'I think we should be keeping our senses, given the situation.'

Gabe scoffed. He found what he was looking for and dropped it on the ground at his feet, along with a coil of rope. 'The current situation is the reason I'm having a fuckin' beer. Don't worry. It'd take a few more of these before I lose any senses.' *That's because you've had some practice,* he thought. Amin didn't look convinced, but said no more.

'Hey, you hungry?' Gabe wasn't, but he didn't know when his companion had last eaten. He reached into the canopy and opened the larger fridge residing at the back, remembering it contained a cold lamb chop, and then it occurred to him he may not have anything Amin could eat. Weren't they fussy about that kind of thing?

Amin nodded. 'A little, yes, but I think it can wait until we finish our business with the bodies. Thank you, but this drink will suffice for now.'

Gabe shut the fridge lid and closed up the canopy. 'Suit yourself. Give us a hand with this tarp, will ya?'

Amin finished his Coke and helped Gabe unfold the plastic sheet over the well-body of the smugglers' ute. Despite Gabe's careful driving, the corpses had slid around inside, and he was reminded of a time many years ago, in another life, when he had filled a trailer with freshly shot kangaroos bound for the pet meat factory. The men's eyes had a similar vacant expression and the tongues lolled exactly as the big boomers' had done when he'd dressed out the carcasses, with about the same number of flies crawling in and out of their open mouths. *Doesn't matter what we tell ourselves – in the end we all finish up the same, one way or another.*

He wondered if he and Amin might end up like that. They both very nearly had, but he pushed those morbid thoughts out of his mind. It was no use worrying. Worrying didn't change anything; it just distracted you from getting on with the job. And right now, the job was to get rid of this dead weight.

Threading the rope through the tarp's eyelets, he tied the cover down. Amin looked on, helping where required but for the most part standing out of the way. He seemed to be lost in thought again, and Gabe considered asking how he'd ended up in this mess, what had made him leave his homeland, but decided that would be best left for when they didn't have three rapidly bloating bodies to deal with. While the sun was sitting lower in the sky, the day had not cooled and the idea of throwing back the tarp when they arrived at the well, after their cargo had sweltered under the plastic during the trip, did not hold much appeal. He was going to have to give it a good wash before stowing it again. Or maybe he'd just burn it. That and his bloodstained clothes. His laundry skills weren't the best, and although he could easily explain away the stains as work-related, who wanted to walk around with another person's blood on their shirt? *Or on their hands, isn't that right?*

He stood back to inspect. Nothing suspicious here. Just a couple of blokes going for a drive, collecting a few . . . a few what? Wrong time of the year for firewood. He couldn't say it was kangaroo or feral goats under there; you weren't supposed to be shooting anything on this patch of dirt. For the life of him, Gabe couldn't think of a good explanation for the bulge under the tarp. They would just have to hope nobody questioned them about it.

'How long will it take to get there?' Amin asked.

Gabe retrieved his trapping gear from the back seat. 'Dunno, depends on the road. Haven't been there for a while. Might be an hour, might be two.'

Amin followed him around to the other side of Gabe's Land-Cruiser, the work side. 'So it will be dark by the time we arrive?' He was looking at the floodlights on the roof rack.

'Not quite.' Gabe opened up the canopy and his white toolbox, then unlocked the long silver one behind it. 'Should have enough light to do what we need to. If not, I've got torches and there'll be a reasonable moon too.'

He snapped on a pair of latex gloves from the cardboard dispenser in the white toolbox and pulled a trap from the crate on the ground, placing it with the others in the silver chest. He had taken two with him this morning but only used one. The spare was still laced with strychnine, so he rested it in the corner, away from the others, lest they rubbed against the tape and spilled the deadly powder everywhere. Then he began placing his tools into the white box – mattock, sieve, rake, hessian mat, adjustable spanner for the shackles and a set of pliers, all had their place – until the crate was empty.

Gabe closed the first toolbox and was about to do the same with the second when Amin peered in. 'This is how you catch the dingoes?'

'Yep.' Gabe pointed at the laced trap. 'Trap bites dog, dog bites trap, poison kills dog. Don't touch them. Nasty shit, that strychnine.'

'That is why you lock this box?'

One of the reasons, yes, Gabe thought. 'Yeah. Got other stuff in here you don't want to mess with. 10-80, injectors for making baits, all sorts of shit.'

'Baits?'

'Dried meat injected with 10-80, poison. Chuck them where I can't set a trap, or where I think a den might be to get the pups. Like that ridge back there. Perfect spot.'

He shut the lid, locked it and closed the canopy, then slid the milk crate under the tray, clipping it in place with an occy strap, and washed his hands.

'C'mon,' he said. 'We better get moving. Sooner we get this over with, the better.'

To his surprise, Amin shook his head. 'I must perform my afternoon prayers.'

Gabe was stunned. 'You must be joking. We haven't got time for that crap.'

Amin merely shrugged. 'It will only take a few minutes, and I think, given our situation, it would be wise not to neglect God. Do you have any water I can wash with?'

Gabe pointed to the tank and soap under his ute's tray. Amin quickly washed, then moved a little way from the two vehicles.

'Fuck's sake,' Gabe muttered to himself, leaning against the LandCruiser's bonnet while Amin began his ritual. 'Stuck out in bum-fuck nowhere with a pile of dead bodies and a bloody mussie gibbering at the dirt.'

He watched on, growing more and more agitated each time Amin seemed to kiss the ground, then stand, only to return to his knees again. Either Amin was praying quietly, or to himself in silence, as Gabe could not hear any words. He had been expecting some sort of wailing. Isn't that how it was done? He'd only seen snippets here and there of prayers on the news before. Usually after some nutter had blown himself up, along with a bunch of other poor sods. Not that he watched much news. The world had gone nuts and he was quite content keeping to himself out bush, garnering enough information from radio reports to know that things weren't getting any better. Hell, today only confirmed that even further. If shit was reaching out here, what chance did anyone have of keeping clear of it?

Before he could answer his own question, Amin finished and returned to the vehicles. Gabe eyed him as he approached. 'Did you get an answer?' he asked, barely hiding his annoyance at the hold-up.

'Time will tell, my friend,' Amin said. 'Come, let's go.'

Gabe snorted, flicked away his smoke and climbed into the LandCruiser, still not quite believing just how this day was turning out.

TWELVE

By the time they reached the abandoned well, the sun was almost below the horizon, casting an orange hue across the sky that faded to deep purple as the first of many stars materialised. It had been an anxious drive, Gabe leading the way in his LandCruiser, Amin following in the smugglers' Rodeo, along with the bodies it carried.

Gabe was reluctant to travel too quickly for fear of losing Amin in the dust, and knew the rough road they bounced along would be very hard on the man's injured arm. But his caution was tempered by the urge to get rid of these bodies as quickly as possible. Until that was done, any planning about their next step was futile.

So he drove cautiously, one eye on the side mirror watching Amin's vehicle creep over the gullies and washes that had once been a half-decent station track, the other looking out for hazards ahead, be they in the road or driving towards them. And while there were plenty in the road, they met no one on it, nor was there sign that anyone had been out this way in a long time. So far, so good.

Amin did well. Twice, Gabe stopped after a particularly sharp gully, expecting to have to tow the lower slung Rodeo through, but Amin had picked the correct path both times, and they carried on. Gabe supposed after years of having the shit bombed out of them, anyone from Afghanistan was probably used to driving over rough ground.

The well was indeed abandoned. A derelict windmill with most of its vanes missing straddled the square stone-lined edging, squeaking mournfully as the unbalanced fan tried to turn in the gentle easterly breeze, only to give up halfway and swing back down. How the thing was still upright was beyond Gabe; one of the three steel legs had all but rusted through, and loose stays hung from the tower framework. One good willy-willy and by rights the whole lot should fall in a heap, probably taking out the rest of the stone tank that stood next to it. The tank had already partially collapsed, constructed from large square granite rocks carted in from only God knows where, its ancient mortar finally succumbing to years of weathering and no maintenance.

Gabe wheeled his LandCruiser around to point at the well and shut the engine off. He grabbed the torch mounted in its charger behind the seats and climbed out, making a circling motion to Amin, instructing him to reverse the makeshift hearse towards the well. Amin did so and exited the vehicle. Gabe immediately saw he was in pain.

'You alright?'

Amin joined him at the Rodeo's rear where Gabe had begun untying the rope. 'I will be fine. The road and the gear changes were not good for my arm.' He winced.

'Once we get this shit sorted, we'll find a camp spot and set up for the night. Get you cleaned up and into some fresh clothes, take another look at that arm and have a feed, if you're hungry by then.' Gabe still wasn't and he doubted that would change any time soon, considering the job before them. 'Give us a hand with this tarp.'

They dragged the covering off to one side, sending a cloud of flies swarming around them. Gabe still wasn't sure what to do with it afterwards; the idea of using the thing again for any camp site didn't hold much appeal. The pile of bodies was just as morbid as before, but thankfully the worst details were difficult to make out in the dying light. Neither Gabe nor Amin had used their headlights during the trip, but it was getting to the stage they would need them soon.

He turned his attention to the well and removed the sheet of rusted corrugated iron over the opening, tossing the short wooden beams weighing it down to the side, and peered over the edge. The torch's powerful light reflected back at him from the water pooled below, casting shadows against the bare earthen walls. It was a long way down and the hole was interspersed with wooden crossbeams dug into the sides to carry the steel pump column that would've once dangled from the windmill. Some had since rotted away, others still remained intact, but Gabe was confident few would be left once the corpses crashed their way down, and with any luck the hole might cave in after them.

Amin stood next to him, also looking over the edge. 'I can see why you brought us here,' he said as the two turned back to the smugglers' ute.

'Glad you approve.' Gabe unlatched the tailgate and lowered it. The six dead legs that were leaning against it barely moved, and he knew what that meant. Rigor mortis had begun to set in. He cursed quietly, but there wasn't much to be done about it. Gritting his teeth, Gabe grabbed Khalid's feet and pulled. The corpse did not budge. During the journey, it had wedged itself between the other two, and now that they had started to stiffen, all three bodies moved as one.

'Christ's sake, give us a hand, would ya?' He pointed to where Khalid's arm had snared under one of the smugglers. Amin attempted to free the limb while Gabe continued to pull. When it still refused to move, Gabe lost his temper and gave an almighty heave. Khalid's body slid out in a rush. Gabe stumbled back as the corpse bounced off the tailgate and onto the hard dirt, and an explosion of gas erupted from both ends as it hit the ground with one long, drawn-out fart. The smell was sickening, and although he'd dealt with worse, Gabe finally lost the battle with his stomach. His throat burned as he hunched over, coughing up the three beers. Behind him, he could hear Amin doing the same.

The two men straightened and stared at each other until the shocking ridiculousness of the situation overcame them. Both started to laugh, slowly at first, until they were howling like fools at the huge yellow moon poking over the horizon. The madness they were undertaking was too much, and the laughter was the only thing keeping their panic at bay. It was some time before sense returned.

'Jesus Christ,' Gabe wheezed, wiping away tears. 'What a fuckin' shitshow this is.' Amin was breathing hard, and could only nod in reply.

Collecting his wits, he dragged Khalid's body out of the way and returned to the others. Fortunately, the first one came easily, and the two men manhandled it towards the tower. They leaned the body against the steel cross struts, grabbed the feet and lifted. Gabe felt his back twinge as the corpse tumbled over the strut and disappeared past the well's edge. A series of wet thuds echoed up to them, the rattle of loose dirt, what sounded like one of the wooden beams snapping off, and finishing with a satisfying splash. Amin picked up the torch and shone it down the hole. Gabe was pleased to see the back of a polo shirt floating at the bottom.

'One down,' he said.

The second corpse was a little lighter, but locked in an almost fetal position from lying squashed up in the tray for so long, and much more awkward to shift. After a great deal of effort, they managed to thread it through the tower and over the edge, only this time no splash came. Amin picked up the light again and shone it down to reveal the corpse hanging over one of the more substantial beams about halfway down.

'You've got to be fuckin' kidding me,' Gabe groaned. 'What else can go wrong today?'

He looked around, thinking there might be a length of old column lying in the dirt they could use to prise the body off, but another glance down the hole told him this was pointless; it was too far down to reach from the top.

Amin swung the light back up to the surface and towards the collapsed tank. 'Perhaps a heavy rock could knock him free?'

'Good idea as any.' Gabe spotted a piece of rubble that might work and motioned for Amin to follow him to the pile. The stone was a square slab of granite with a chunk of mortar still clinging to one side. It was too heavy to lift but Gabe managed to roll it up to the edge of the well, and after a bit of careful positioning, he sent it tumbling down. Both men watched in anticipation as it dropped, smashing through a beam before narrowly missing the hanging body.

They tried twice more. The last one hit the corpse on the leg, sending it teetering a little, but not enough to flip. Gabe knew it was no good. There was only one solution.

'Gonna have to go down there,' he said reluctantly. He had never liked wells. As a young bloke, he'd landed the job of bore runner on a cattle station, tasked with keeping the windmills pumping and water flowing. The only part of that job he hated was shimmying down the columns to change pumps when the leather buckets flogged out. It was quicker and easier than pulling the entire column, but he'd always felt like the walls were closing in on him while down there.

Amin shook his head in disbelief. 'You cannot climb down there, can you?'

Gabe started walking back to his own ute. 'Won't climb. I'll use the winch.'

'That is madness,' Amin protested. 'Just leave him. Who will come by? Who would—'

Gabe cut him off. 'I'm not leaving that rotten bloody corpse hanging there,' he growled. 'If we ever get out of this shit I don't want some fuckin' tourist finding it six months down the track when he decides to have a sticky beak in that hole while out looking for bloody wildflowers. I want those pair of pricks at the bottom.'

Amin didn't answer, and Gabe collected what he needed. Daylight was all but gone now, so he flicked on the floodlights and went around to the bull bar. He connected the winch controls, released the brake and walked the cable to the windmill. The canvas winching bag he carried held a snatch block, and Gabe threaded the steel cable through the pulley and hung the assembly from the wooden beam that ran above his head over the well. The beam would've once had the steel pump column clamped to it. Now it was going to support something else.

Using the rope they'd secured the tarpaulin with and one of the timbers that had been keeping the well cover in place, he fashioned a crude bosun's chair and hung it over the hook dangling from the winch cable. As a test, he pulled down hard on the chair. The beam creaked, but did not move. Gabe still didn't feel overly confident but at least the whole thing shouldn't collapse under him.

He fitted a small LED headlamp to his brow, took a deep breath and turned to Amin. 'I'll show you how to use the winch.'

Amin shook his head. 'No. You cannot go down.'

Gabe was about to lose his patience once more when Amin spoke again. 'I will go down.'

Now it was Gabe's turn to argue. 'Not a chance, not with that arm. And you've lost a lot of blood. What if you pass out?'

'And what if the winch should stick? What if, God forbid, you should fall? I have no knowledge of this land and would be stranded, with no hope of reuniting with my family.'

'Not much hope either if you're the one that falls,' Gabe said, but he could see Amin had a point.

'That is true, but you will be able to help them still.'

'Hang on a second there – what exactly is it you're expecting? Find this smuggler camp and storm in there like John bloody Wayne?'

'I do not know,' Amin said. 'All I know is on my own they have no chance.'

'Bugger me.' Gabe took a seat against the tower, pulled out his tobacco and rolled two smokes. The familiar action gave his hands something to do. 'So you're telling me if anything happens to you, you want me to go get your family? But I can't call the cops because they're bent?'

He offered a rollie to Amin, who slid down next to him, accepting the smoke and lighter that followed.

'Yes.'

'What makes you think I'd stick my neck out like that?'

Amin took a deep draw. 'I told you. You are a good man.'

'You don't know the first bloody thing about me,' Gabe retorted.

'I know you came to help a stranger when you could have remained hidden. I know you saved my life twice. I know you haven't just driven away and left me to my fate. And I know you are going to help bury a man when all logic and reason suggests Khalid should join those two dogs down the well so we can keep moving.'

Amin took another drag, savouring the smoke, perhaps fearing it might be his last once he stepped over the well's edge. 'And, you share with me your cigarettes. Any man who does that can't be all bad.' He smiled.

Gabe gave an exasperated sigh. 'I should chuck the both of you over the side and be bloody done with it. You know digging a grave is not going to be easy.'

'I know,' Amin replied.

Gabe shook his head in resignation. He stood and held a hand out. Amin grasped it and hauled himself up. 'C'mon then. No good standing here talking about it.'

THIRTEEN

Amin stepped into the crude sling as Gabe held it open for him, tucking the wooden seat firmly under his buttocks and placing his arms outside the rope, allowing it to run under each armpit. With one hand, he gripped just below the winch hook and then grasped the tower as he leaned back over the well like an abseiler about to kick off a cliff face. Gabe removed the headlamp and refitted it to Amin's brow, and then, after a nod from the nervous man, Gabe pushed the button on the winch remote. The electric motor whined as it lifted Amin until he swung out over the square stone-edged opening.

The tower creaked and Amin looked up at the beam from which he hung. '*Bismillah hirrahman nirrahim*,' he said.

'What does that mean?' Gabe asked. From the tone he suspected it was the equivalent to a Catholic crossing themselves.

A nervous smile accompanied Amin's reply. 'It means please do not drop me.'

'I'll try my best.' He handed the flashlight to Amin, who looped the band over his wrist and resumed his death grip on the rope. 'One flash means stop. Two flashes for down, three for up, okay? I might not be able to hear you down there. If I call and you don't answer and you don't flash, I'll haul you up straight away.'

Amin took a deep breath and gave a single nod. Gabe began to pay out the cable. The winch was highly geared, and the cable fed out slowly. Amin gradually disappeared down the hole, beginning a gentle spin as he did so and sending shadows in a slow dance as the headlamp lit up the walls.

Gabe peered down. 'You okay?'

'I am okay,' came the reply. Gabe watched as Amin pushed himself off the wall to clear the first crossbeam. It sent a scattering of loose dirt to the bottom. Only the top few metres of the well had been lined with stone; the rest was bare dirt. Gabe hoped nothing would fall onto Amin as he continued his way down.

The torch flashed up at him once, and he released the button. From his position it was hard to see what Amin was doing, but the light was flickering around much more, and Gabe could hear grunts and heavy breathing echoing up to him. There was a crunch followed by a loud splash, and then the torch flashed twice, this time accompanied by a muffled call of 'Down!' Gabe assumed Amin had kicked out another beam. The winch whirred again.

After what seemed like an age, the torch flashed once more. It looked so far away, just a small pinprick in the murky blackness. More sounds bounced around the well: panting, sharp words in Amin's own tongue and the occasional splash. The noises swirled, mingling in the confined space before escaping up to the silence that surrounded Gabe, who was kneeling anxiously over the hole. A triumphant cry suddenly burst out, followed by a loud splash.

Gabe could make out the words 'Bring me up' as the light flashed three times. He pressed the button and the electric motor took a deeper note as gears bit, hauling up the load. Above his head the beam creaked. Gabe watched on as Amin drew nearer to the surface.

'Stop!' came the cry. Immediately, Gabe halted the winch. 'I am caught on this wood. Let me down some more.' He did so, and again the light danced and grunts echoed as Amin struggled to free himself. 'Up!'

The winch wound over and Amin continued to rise. A scream shot out of the hole, startling Gabe so bad he nearly dropped the controller. He released the button again, but this only intensified the panicked cries.

'Up! Up!'

Gabe could see Amin flailing below, kicking away from one wall, only to bounce back off another.

'Stop swinging about!' he yelled. An ominous crack rang out from the beam carrying the snatch block as it bowed, and a sliver of split timber appeared along the base.

'There is a snake! Up! Up!' Amin was screaming at him now, but Gabe couldn't make the winch go any faster, and the flash from Amin's headlamp had momentarily blinded him.

'Hold still, for fuck's sake, or you'll bring the whole lot down on top of you!'

Amin's kicking ceased, but he was still swinging like a pendulum, each motion causing the wooden beam to creak alarmingly.

It seemed to Gabe the winch ran slower and slower as Amin inched closer to the top. He knew that the steel cable was plenty strong enough, but, should the beam break, there was every chance Amin would be thrown from his seat when he dropped the few metres as the slack was taken up, or the shock might break the rope he was dangling so precariously from. That was without the obvious possibility of being struck by the falling timber, or the chance that the rub of the cable on the well's edge dislodged some of the large stones lining the inside.

All of these scenarios ran through Gabe's mind as he watched Amin draw nearer, but there was nothing to hand he could use to prop up the beam. For a split second, a small voice in his head suggested that Amin falling would be the easiest way to end his involvement in this mess. Gabe immediately pushed it away. He might not be a good man, but he wasn't that cold-hearted either.

Finally, the bosun's chair emerged above the hole – first the hook, then the rope with Amin's hands white-knuckled around the coarse fibres. The flashlight swung back and forth from his wrist, much like he and his makeshift seat did from the beam above. Amin's head came up and Gabe held a hand to his eyes to avoid the searing flash from the headlamp strobing wildly as Amin searched for the fastest way off his unstable ride.

Gabe climbed outside of the windmill's framework and leaned against the strongest looking tower leg. He reached in with one arm.

'When I get you up, grab my hand and I'll pull you to the edge.'

Amin nodded, and as soon as his feet cleared the lip, his hand shot out and latched onto the offered limb with such force Gabe thought he might topple over. He braced against the steel and pulled. Amin swung towards him, and his feet touched the dirt just as a loud crack split the air behind him. The beam gave way, snapping in half and tearing its ends free of the bolts clamping it to the tower. For a heart-stopping moment Gabe felt his grip slipping, but Amin grabbed the steel leg with his other hand and hauled himself clear as the timber pieces and snatch block tumbled down into the well's depths. A few seconds later, a splash echoed up to them.

Gabe helped Amin out from under the windmill. They stood hunched over, breathing hard. 'Bet you won't be doing that again in a hurry,' he rasped. Amin looked up, and this time Gabe was too slow to prevent copping an eyeful of white light. 'Shit, gimme that thing before you send me blind.'

Amin slipped the headlamp off and handed it over. 'You never,' he panted, 'mentioned . . . snakes.'

Gabe took the lamp and switched it off. 'Yeah. Sorry 'bout that. Slipped my mind. Didn't get you, did it?'

He had been caught out by a sleeping reptile twice before. Once, standing over a shallow well pulling a column by hand, he'd reached down as the pump came up, not really paying attention, when a sudden movement caught him by surprise. There, wrapped neatly around the steel casing, was a small brown snake just rearing its head back to strike. Gabe had released the pipe in shock, sending the whole assembly crashing down to the well floor. Fortunately, after much fishing about, he was able to loop a rope over the protruding end and hoist it back up again, this time with no sign of the snake.

Amin winced as he straightened. 'No, but my heart may not survive another shock like that.'

Gabe noticed his hand had gone to his arm again. 'That okay?'

This time Amin shook his head. 'I think that was not very good for it. Come, we must take care of Khalid, and then I will have a look.'

There was a tremble in his voice that did not surprise Gabe. The second time he'd been caught out by a snake was similar to Amin's experience. Halfway down a pump column when he spied two beady eyes glistening at him from a nook in the dirt wall, a mere fifty centimetres from his face. Needless to say, Gabe had scaled that pipe hand over hand like a monkey on cocaine.

'Go and sit down while I pack this up,' he said. 'There's another Coke in the fridge behind my seat if you want one.' Amin started towards the vehicle without a word. Gabe called after him again. 'Amin!'

The man turned slowly, painfully, and Gabe could see he was beginning to tire.

'That took balls.'

There was a reluctant admiration in Gabe's voice. Amin paused, accepted the praise with a slight nod and turned back to the ute. Gabe wasn't sure why his praise was so hesitant. Not many people would have volunteered to climb down that well, even with Amin's perfectly sensible explanation as to why he should be the one to do it. Gabe had seen plenty of station hands, new and old alike, flat out refuse to enter the dark, damp confines of an earthen well. How the first settlers had ever dug them was beyond him. He had a feeling that his reluctance came from the knowledge that, had the situation been reversed, Gabe doubted he would have done the same.

He watched Amin limp around to the rear of the LandCruiser and wash before disappearing into the darkness. A few moments later he heard Amin's hushed voice murmuring and assumed it was another round of prayers. Considering the man had nearly ended up falling down a very deep hole, Gabe didn't begrudge him this time.

Save for the glow of the moon climbing the sky in the east, it was dark now. Gabe packed his equipment in the canvas winching bag, and, shining his torch down the hole, he could just make out the shirt of one of the corpses, partially obscured by the wood and dirt that had fallen to the bottom as Amin scrambled out. He knew the bodies would float for some time, but the likelihood of anyone stopping here, or realising what lay beneath the muddy water if they did, was pretty remote. There was nothing more they could do, so Gabe laid the tin back over the opening and replaced the timber, weighing it down, adding a couple of heavy stones for good measure. *Leave no sign, leave no trace.*

He stowed the gear and turned his attention to the last remaining body. Khalid. A small voice in his head suggested he should just chuck him down the hole while Amin prayed, but he told it to piss off. Yes, it was frustrating he couldn't just do the same as they'd done with the other two, but he understood the reasoning against that. He had no idea what might happen over the next few days, but Amin was determined to track down his family, and there was every chance that would lead to Khalid's by default. The thought of explaining to a new widow her beloved now sat in the bottom of a well with the two dogs that had killed him, tossed down there like a bag of unwanted kittens, did not appeal to Gabe at all.

Amin finished his prayers and joined Gabe by Khalid's body. 'Where shall we bury him?'

'Not here,' Gabe said. 'Ground's too hard still, and I don't reckon putting him so close is a good idea. A fresh grave is a bit more obvious than what's down that well.'

'True enough. And I would like to think someone would be able to honour him with a proper burial. Once we are out of this shitshow, as you call it.' Gabe saw a weak smile appear on Amin's face and hoped he was right. 'And I do not want to return here again.' Fair enough, by Gabe's reckoning.

'Let's get him back in the Rodeo, and we'll head up to that last creek crossing. Ground looked a bit lighter there – might be able to scratch out some sort of a hole. If we have to, we'll lay some rocks over it to stop the dogs and bungarras digging him up.'

Lifting the body proved much more difficult than the first time. Amin was struggling with his arm, and Gabe's hip was threatening to go on strike. Usually by this hour he'd be sitting by a fire, not lugging corpses around.

His discomfort did not go unnoticed by Amin, despite the man's own troubles. 'You are hurt?' he asked, as Gabe propped the stiffened body against the Rodeo's tailgate.

'Dicky hip,' he replied.

'From an injury?' Amin held onto the shirt collar to prevent Khalid's body from sliding back to the ground as Gabe prepared to lift it into the ute.

Unbidden, his hand touched the scar running down his temple. 'Something like that.' Gabe grasped the legs and heaved. 'C'mon, you bastard, get in there,' he swore at the dead weight threatening to topple back out of the ute again. It never looked so awkward in the movies. He shoved again and closed the tailgate against the legs.

He didn't bother to cover the tray. Instead he tucked the tarp into the back and instructed Amin to follow him once more. After another inspection of the area to make sure they'd left nothing behind, Gabe climbed into his LandCruiser and the two vehicles set off. Gabe had a rough idea of where they should go and began to follow the track away from the abandoned well and the morbid secret it now held.

FOURTEEN

Half an hour later, the two men used the tarpaulin to carry Khalid to his resting place in a sandy creek bed. Gabe had trapped here once before. It was far enough away from the well for his liking and suitably distant from the track that any passers-by wouldn't be inclined to call in for a look. Best of all, it was easy digging – a good thing considering Amin hadn't been of much help. The man was exhausted, and Gabe knew he needed food, rest and his bullet wound checked again. He wasn't feeling very optimistic about that. His own first aid kit was better stocked than the small one they'd used earlier, but Gabe was worried about infection. Dead bodies and old wells weren't exactly the best way to look after yourself after getting shot, and Amin had been neck-deep in them all afternoon.

They laid Khalid and the tarp in the shallow grave, killing two birds with one stone – getting rid of any evidence remaining in his ute, and protecting the body a little if someone were to reclaim it. However, Gabe had no intention of being involved in that little exercise, should it come to that.

There was an abundance of loose granite stones around the creek's edge, and under the light of the full moon they soon had the body well covered. Even the most determined scavenger would struggle to get close enough for a lick. Gabe was somewhat concerned that the finished mound in front of them was an obvious grave, but he told himself they could only be so careful, and it was extremely unlikely anyone would set foot here anytime soon.

The two men stood in front of the pile of rocks, both breathing hard. Gabe shuffled uncomfortably as Amin stared at the cairn, perhaps contemplating how close he'd come to joining the dead man.

Amin turned to Gabe. 'We can do no more for Khalid. Let us go.'

This posed a problem. Where exactly should they go? Being so focused on covering their tracks, he'd been unable to think that far ahead. They began walking back to the vehicles. 'Got any ideas which way we should head?' he asked.

'For now, somewhere to rest. I am not feeling so good,' Amin said. He held a hand to his bandaged arm.

'We'll go back the way we came a bit, away from here and set up camp. Get some food in you.' *And some whisky in me,* he thought. *Christ knows I need it after today.*

'I think that is a good idea,' said Amin. 'I will follow.'

When they arrived back at the vehicles, Gabe pulled out his GPS and marked the point. He saw Amin watching. 'For later,' he said. 'You know, to find him again.'

'Thank you. That is very thoughtful.'

Gabe grunted, and eased himself into his ute, cursing at the twinge in his hip.

They drove off. After a couple of kilometres, Gabe pulled into a small clearing. It looked like a good site, and he began setting up for the night, working quickly under the white glow of his floodlights, which were fast attracting a bevy of insects. He opened the driver's side of the canopy and cage, the gas struts hissing as they extended, and pulled out his camp chair, offering it to Amin.

'Give us a minute to get organised then you can have a shower if you want,' Gabe said, which seemed to surprise Amin.

'You have a shower?'

'Only cold water, but out here that's not usually a problem. Got a pair of jeans and a shirt you can borrow. Reckon we should get rid of these stained clothes.'

'Thank you.' The gratitude in Amin's voice was plain to hear. So was his discomfort. Gabe retrieved a couple more drinks, passing his last can of Coke to Amin and opening a beer for himself.

'I'll get a fire going, try and keep some of these bugs away, then get some grub on.' At last he was beginning to feel hungry.

'Do you think that is wise?'

'You worried about your buddies seeing us?'

'A little, maybe.'

Gabe shrugged. 'Think we're okay. We're miles from that hole, and covered our tracks pretty good, plus we got off that road quick too.' He looked up at the moon, now high above them. 'It's fairly bright tonight. Fire won't give off much light and once I get sorted the floods will go off. Reckon we'd be hard to spot.'

'If you say so,' Amin replied. 'I trust your judgement.' He leaned back and gazed upwards. Even with the moon out, the stars littered the sky. 'Your night sky reminds me of home,' Amin said.

'Best seat in the house for star gazing,' Gabe said as he readied the table. 'On a night with no moon, you can see everything.'

'My wife's family lived in a small village, far from city lights. Sometimes, when we visited, we would sit out at night and watch the stars dance.'

Amin's voice wavered slightly as he recalled the memory, and Gabe suddenly felt uncomfortable. He used to do something similar, once upon a time. He cleared his throat and set off to collect wood for the fire, leaving Amin alone with his memories, and possibly his imagination as to what almost happened to him today. Gabe was never quite sure what was worse to dwell on – what had been or what might've been.

It didn't take him long to get a good fire going. He helped Amin up and took him around to the passenger side of the LandCruiser. When the canopy frame and surrounding cage were first built, he had set up a shower head on a flexible hose that could clip to the overhanging cage door. It was fed from the main water tank by a twelve-volt caravan pump; his theory being, were he unlucky enough to spill poison on himself, a shower close to hand would be a good thing. Fortunately, he hadn't needed it for such a purpose yet, but it was still handy for knocking the dust and sweat off when it got too much to bear.

'Here,' he said, passing Amin the handheld shower. 'That clips up there, and that' – he pointed to the switch fitted just inside the canopy – 'turns the pump on. Soap's in that bottle. I'll find you a towel and some clothes. Won't be much, but it'll be better than what you're wearing now.'

He opened the passenger door as Amin began to undress and rummaged through his bag of clothes stowed inside, eventually finding a pair of jeans and a light blue long-sleeve drill shirt. Amin was about the same size as he was, maybe a bit wider in the waist, but Gabe always preferred a loose-fitting pair of pants so figured there would be enough slack in them. He held them up to Amin.

'These should do. I'll leave them on the seat. Chuck what you're wearing over there, and I'll burn them with mine.'

'Again, thank you.' Amin was now shirtless and beginning to remove the bandages around his arm. Gabe drew closer for a better look. When the cotton swabbing came away, Amin winced.

'That looks like shit,' Gabe said.

'Yes. And that is also how it feels.' Amin tossed his shirt and the bandages to the side. 'But I have seen men survive worse.'

'Yeah and I bet men have died from a lot less too. I'll get my kit. That could turn septic real quick. Another dead Arab is the last bloody thing I need right now.'

Amin glanced at Gabe and must have seen the humour in his eyes. 'Why not?' he said. 'You have had much practice at hiding dead Arabs, as you call us.'

'You're not Arab?'

Amin gave him a wry grin. 'Are you English?'

'Course not,' Gabe scoffed, a little taken aback. 'I'm Aussie, born and bred, so's my parents. But Mum's family came from Ireland, and Dad's was Welsh. What's your point?'

'Afghanistan is made up of many different ethnic groups. Pashtun, Tajik, Uzbek, Hazara; it is a long list. My own family is Pashtun.'

'Yeah, well, Arab, Pashtun or English, I don't want to do that again.' Gabe started back to the fire. 'Sing out when you're done. And go easy on the water; it's not the bloody Hilton here.'

While Amin cleaned himself up, Gabe started thinking about food. From his larger Engel he pulled a couple of potatoes, some onions and a loaf of bread. Then he stared at the various trays and bags of meat in the freezer section. *Crap, now what?* He knew enough to realise pork chops were out of the question, and so was the bacon, obviously. He did have some cutlets from a young goat he'd shot last trip. Would that be too condescending, offering the Middle Eastern man a feed of goat? He recalled Bobby joking with him one evening as they dined on roo-tail stew. 'Kangaroo is good alright, but only 'cos we got no Uber Eats round here.'

'Ah, fuck it,' Gabe cursed and grabbed a pack of lamb chops. He dumped the food on the table just as he heard the water pump stop. Gabe retrieved another beer, and, after a moment's thought, his open whisky bottle. He sat the whisky next to the food and sipped his beer while he waited for Amin to finish. He would ask about the meat then. If it was too much bloody trouble, the man would have to stick to bread and vegetables and watch him eat the lamb chops by himself. No way was Gabe going vego.

Amin appeared, wearing only Gabe's jeans and the pair of boots he'd had on before. A few beads of water still clung to his beard and dripped off his hair. He held his hand to his arm as he walked over to the table, blood weeping from under his fingers.

'Come here, under the light.' Gabe had already opened the kit and pulled out some cotton wool, passing it to Amin, who began wiping away the blood while Gabe withdrew what he needed from the plastic chest.

'Ready?' he asked. Amin removed his hand, and Gabe couldn't help but suck in his breath. The gouge had turned a deep crimson and ugly yellow bruising had appeared around the edges. He wiped down the area with an alcoholic swab, then, unconvinced by the tiny cloth that looked just like a repackaged KFC towel, grabbed his whisky bottle and held it up to Amin.

'Last chance,' he said. 'This is going to sting a bit.'

'I do not require it,' Amin replied. 'Nor am I allowed it.'

'Suit yourself,' Gabe said. 'Hope you appreciate this. Bloody good whisky, this is.'

It wasn't, but he wasn't about to admit that. To his surprise, Amin gave him a wry smile.

'Gabe, that bottle you hold looks very much like the cheap whisky sold on the black market to the American troops in Afghanistan.'

In reply Gabe took a swig and then poured a splash from the bottle onto the gash, eliciting a sharp hiss from Amin.

'*Padar-nalat!*' Amin glared at him. Gabe did not know the words, but understood them all the same.

'Sorry about that.'

He wiped away the excess alcohol and squeezed antiseptic ointment onto the wound and the surrounding skin, doing nothing to improve Amin's current disposition, and began attaching adhesive suture strips across the gash. Satisfied it was as closed as he was going to get it, Gabe pressed a cotton pad to the injury and wrapped fresh bandages around the arm.

'Best I can do.'

Amin inspected his work. 'You did not do too badly,' he admitted with a smile. 'Though your bedside manner is lacking.'

Gabe made a wide gesture towards the vast horizon. 'Feel free to get a second opinion.' He closed the kit and returned it to the LandCruiser.

Back at the table, he picked up the tray of lamb chops and the tomato sauce bottle. 'I'm going to have a wash, then cook up some tucker. You hungry?'

'Yes, I am.'

Gabe paused, not quite sure how to broach the subject. In the end he decided the direct approach was the best. 'So, can your lot eat this or not?'

'My lot?' Amin had a slightly bemused look on his face.

'You know, Muslims. Don't you have to say *Allah Akbar* or some shit when it's killed? Make it halal?'

Amin laughed. 'That is a very simple way of describing it, but yes, more or less. Since the smugglers did not care very much about our requirements, I have become used to avoiding meat. Thank you for the offer, Gabe, but do you have anything else?'

Gabe glanced at the meagre accompaniments. 'Hope you like bread, taters and onion then. I'm not much of a cook.'

Amin seemed genuinely surprised. 'You have no other vegetables?'

'That's not food. That's what food eats,' Gabe said, deadpan.

Amin shrugged. 'So long as no pork has touched them, it will be very welcome, thank you.'

Gabe scratched the back of his head and shifted uncomfortably as he pointed to the Engel. 'There is bacon and some pork chops in the fridge, but everything is wrapped up.'

'That will be fine. Not all of us are so strict – or terrorists, as you feared earlier.' The good humour shone through, and Gabe grinned.

'Can't really blame me though, can you?'

Amin smiled as he sat down by the fire. 'No, it must have been quite a shock. I can assure you, I was just as surprised as you.'

Gabe set the meat back down on the table. 'Right then, I'll go get cleaned up, get this grub on, and then you can start telling me how the hell you ended up here and just what we're going to do about it.'

He left Amin sitting by the fire and headed for the shower. It would be good to get out of these bloodied clothes. Blood on his shirt and pants was nothing new, but it was different when it was another person's. *Still,* he mused as he undressed, *could've been worse. Could've been mine.* And with a shudder at that last thought, he threw his clothes with Amin's discarded outfit and began to wash.

FIFTEEN

Hunched over their plates, Amin in Gabe's chair and Gabe on an upturned milk crate, they ate with relish and in total silence. If Amin had any concerns about the rough meal Gabe had offered he didn't show it, although Gabe did notice him make a small prayer beforehand and supposed it was a sort of religious insurance policy. Safer than being turned away from the Gates of Heaven because some bushie offered you a chop. Not a bad idea, considering the day, but Gabe wasn't too concerned with such things. He had no doubt as to which Gates he'd be rolling up at.

After the meal, Gabe offered Amin a hot drink.

'Do you have tea?'

Gabe did and quickly set up his tripod and hung the billy over the fire. He poured himself a whisky, and the two men watched the flames dance under the steel vessel as the water slowly heated.

'So,' Gabe said, after a sip from his cup. 'How does an Afghani wind up out here?'

'Afghan,' Amin said.

'What?'

'I am Afghan. The Afghani is our currency.'

'Okay,' said Gabe, not quite understanding why that fucking mattered. 'How does an *Afghan* end up here?'

'Very unexpectedly.' Amin poked the coals with a stick, sending a cloud of sparks into the sky. Shadows flickered across his face as he spoke. 'When you asked if I was a terrorist, for a brief moment I almost laughed,' Amin began. 'For they are the very people who have led me here. My brother was a teacher and translated for the Americans during the war, but when they started to withdraw, he was no longer required.' His face hardened. 'They abandoned him to his fate, and somehow the Taliban learned of his treachery, as they perceive it. They found him and killed him. And as punishment and a warning to others, they hunted down anyone else in his family.'

'Bloody hell,' Gabe breathed. 'I thought the Yanks won the war and got rid of them all.'

'Nobody wins a war, Gabe. Though the American-led forces did remove them from power, and many fled to Pakistan. But many have since returned, biding their time. It is going to be very bad when all the international forces leave.'

'So they came after you?'

'We feared they would, yes. I am also a teacher, and they would have suspected me as well. We sold everything we had to afford safe passage via people smugglers into Pakistan.'

'Couldn't you ask the Yanks? Go to their embassy, tell them about your brother?'

'It is not that simple. Before he was killed, my brother had been trying to get an American visa. He knew it would be dangerous once they left, but for two years, nothing. And then it was too late.'

'Bloody seppos,' Gabe said.

'Sep . . . po?'

'Americans. Seppos.' A blank expression greeted him, and he sighed. 'Full of shit, like a septic tank. Tank rhymes with Yank. So we call them seppos.'

Amin gave a confused laugh. 'That is . . . very strange.'

Gabe pointed at the tomato sauce. 'You want to know what we call that?'

'I don't think I do. But I can see why my brother found your Australian soldiers so amusing. He did spend some time with them. But mostly it was the Americans.'

'You'd think they'd have helped him out.'

'Yes, you would think so.' Amin stared intently at the fire. 'When his wife and two sons were killed in an explosion meant for an American patrol, he volunteered to help rid our country of the Taliban.'

'Bloody hell.' His responses felt a little inadequate for such a tale, but Gabe didn't know what else to say. The rattle of the boiling billy drew his attention. He removed it from the fire.

'How do you have it?' he asked, grateful for the brief distraction.

'Black, thank you. Sugar, if you have some.'

Gabe mixed the brew as requested and passed Amin the tin cup. 'Watch it, that'll be hot.'

Amin took it with thanks and resumed his story. 'I did not try the embassy because it is said Taliban insurgents watch those who enter. We believe that is how they found my brother, and I was not willing to take that risk.'

'Fair enough,' said Gabe. 'But how did you end up *here?*'

Amin didn't reply, and Gabe saw his hands had begun to tremble, almost spilling the near boiling tea over the rim onto his bare skin.

'Hey,' he said, reaching for the cup again. 'Careful.'

Amin looked down at the pannikin, gathered himself and waved away Gabe's hand.

'It's okay.' He stared at the flames again, and then began to speak. 'After many months of waiting in Pakistan, we received our new passports and flew to Indonesia. Again, we waited, until one day I was told to board a fishing vessel. Aamena and Jawad, my wife and son, were not permitted to come. They would follow in a few weeks, I was told, once I had reached Australia and been given a job, which the smugglers said they could arrange.'

Amin's voice quavered a little as he continued. 'I did not want to leave them, but we did not have any choice. None of the men with me did.'

Gabe frowned. 'I thought the boats usually aimed for Christmas Island? Only a short trip. I'm no bloody sailor, but Indonesia to the WA coast would take weeks, wouldn't it?'

Amin held up three fingers. 'Longest three weeks of my life. I had thought hiding in trucks to cross the Pakistan border was bad.' He shook his head. 'We were crammed in like cattle, only allowed above deck at night. I think one man died, but I could not be sure. I pray my family's boat was better. And to answer your first question, yes; I do not understand the laws here, but it seems people such as myself cannot make it to Australia if we are discovered before we reach the mainland.'

Gabe could vaguely recall old news reports, images of people in the water. 'The pollies were pretty pleased with stopping the boats a few years back.'

'And I think that is why they bring us here now.' Amin blew on his steaming tea. 'It seems the boats only stopped for a short while.'

'So, what happened next?'

'We changed vessels one night. This one looked new, made from aluminium, and very fast. There were three Australians on board, and one of the men we shot today to translate. We were sent below deck again.'

'And the first boat?' This was all sounding a little far-fetched to Gabe, and yet somehow it made sense at the same time. He poured himself another drink.

'I believe they sank it. The driver came with us. I think that was his payment for passage. Then, after two days of very fast travel, we came ashore at night by a small boat and onto a bus that took us to a camp site in the bush. I stayed for a week until they sent me to another camp site to work from. They made us wear hoods so we did not know where it was.' Amin looked around. 'Although I do not think it would have mattered. All this land looks the same.'

Gabe chose not to correct him. He'd heard the same remark from many people passing through who knew no better. 'How long ago was all this? Where's your wife and kid now?'

'I do not know.' Amin sighed. He reached into the front pocket of his shirt, withdrew a tattered photo and held it out.

Gabe hesitated, already knowing what it would be. He didn't need to see Amin's family. He didn't want to. That would make them real. He knew damn well Amin was going to try and find them, come hell or high water. Jesus, who wouldn't? But it wasn't *his* family. Gabe wasn't about to embark on a doomed rescue mission like some sort of bloody action hero. All he had to do was get Amin to the nearest town, point him in whatever direction he needed to go and fuck off out of there. Forget about the entire thing as best he could. And he had plenty of experience in forgetting things – or at least trying to.

You can be such an arsehole, said that little voice. *Might as well have cut that winch cable and been done with it all. Valerie would be so proud.*

Gabe swore silently to himself, and took the photo. It was as he'd expected. Amin, his wife and son, standing outside a house in a typical family portrait. The kid, maybe five or so, looked bored and sullen, clearly having been taken away from something far more enjoyable than posing for a photo. The parents beamed, proud and happy, perhaps showing off their new family home. The clothing was different, the solid building nothing like the fibro cottage Gabe had once stood outside as a child, but he'd seen this exact photo a few times over, in one form or another. He handed it back without a word.

'I thought I would be seeing them today,' Amin said, giving the picture one last glance before carefully tucking it away again. 'I have been in this country for nearly three months, working for the smugglers. That is, working on fruit farms, which the smugglers organised. I work, they get most of the pay, with a little bit left over for me. This is how I could afford the passage. It was arranged before I left.'

Gabe blinked. 'Hang on a minute – you mean to say you've been in the country for three months, working, and nobody has picked you up? No one's realised you're here illegally?'

'I think the farmers believe we are legal workers. We do not deal with them, the smugglers do. Australian men take us to work and back again. They provided the necessary papers, which I suspect were fake. I do not know all the details, except that I have been picking fruit.'

'Then where did you stay?'

'There is a small camp in the bush, with removable houses – *dungas*? Very much like the ones they took us to when we got off the boat.'

'Dongas,' Gabe corrected.

Amin dismissed the correction with a wave. 'We went by a bus, smaller than the one that took us from the boat. We all worked on different farms. People come and go all the time. In my time here, two more groups have arrived.'

'But not your family?' Gabe asked.

'No. Not my family. Nor Khalid's, which is why we were angry and threatened to speak out if we did not see them soon.' Amin put his head in his hands. 'That was three days ago. Yesterday they said we were to be taken back to the first camp to see them. We were so happy, neither of us suspected anything. Maybe it was all a lie and they are already dead.' He stared out into the darkness, his pannikin beginning to tremble again.

Gabe sat, drink in one hand, smoke in the other, trying to make sense of it all. It seemed inconceivable that such an operation could take place without anyone noticing. Or was it? Backpackers came and went up and down the coast all the time. Fruit growers, grain farmers and station owners constantly screamed out for workers. And he remembered there used to be a stream of refugees coming in by boat until little Johnny Howard stopped it, which had since been backed up by the current revolving door of prime ministers. Was it so impossible that someone had spotted an opportunity and combined the two?

He caught Amin staring at him with pleading eyes. 'Please, you have to help me.'

Gabe looked away. 'Shit, Amin, I don't know what I can do, even if I did want to help.'

'Do you have children?'

'None that I know of.' It was his usual response, a jest to cover the annoyance that question always brought, and it slipped out before he could stop himself. Amin's face twitched, either unsure of the joke or not approving of the implications.

Gabe shifted a little on his milk crate. 'No,' he said quietly. 'No kids. Was always careful about that, back when it mattered. Never exactly considered myself good father material.'

'And a wife?'

Gabe's hand rose to his face, thumb tracing the soft puckered line down his temple and cheek as he looked into his drink, as if the answer lay at the bottom. He knew damn well it didn't but that had never stopped him checking before. 'Sort of. Once.'

Amin didn't reply, perhaps sensing this was not something he wished to discuss. Gabe cleared his throat and used the awkward silence to bring the conversation back to a more comfortable subject. Well, more comfortable for him anyway.

'Look, if half of what you say is true then you're in the shit, big time. Sounds like a massive operation, and you said the cops are in on it?'

'Yes, I heard one of the Australian men talking. Possibly they did not know I could speak English.'

'You speak it pretty good,' Gabe observed. 'You understand me alright. Can't say that about everyone around here.'

'You are not always easy to follow, my friend.' Amin gave an apologetic shrug. 'But I get most of it. My brother and I had good teachers, and we in turn passed on our knowledge.'

'Your brother, he show you how to use a gun too? Noticed you knew your way around them.'

'Yes. After he received his training, he showed me what he could. The way things are, it is not bad knowledge to have.' Amin stared down at his hands. 'We spent some time practising, on targets and the like, though I have never had to use one for real until today.'

'Don't beat yourself up. Those buggers would've shot you and me both and chucked us down that hole,' Gabe said, kicking another branch onto the fire. 'And that's the other thing. I don't know how common they are in your neck of the woods, but over here a handgun is pretty hard to get hold of. Got to know the right sort of people, and people like that also know people. The kind of people you don't want to piss off.'

'I must know what happened to my family, and I will take whatever risks I need to.'

'I get that. Just not sure what we can do. You don't even know where you were being kept.'

Amin threw out one arm, pointing at the smugglers' Rodeo. 'Then I will drive until I see something I recognise.'

'Might be doing that for a while. It's a big place. You won't have enough fuel left to get too far in that thing.'

'Then I will walk.' Amin stood, and his eyes flashed in the firelight. 'Perhaps instead of telling me what I cannot do, you might tell me what I can do.'

The awkward silence settled once more. Low flames danced between them, sending sparks skywards to join the stars. No breeze blew, no sound, and the stillness was something almost tangible, wrapping around the two men like a heavy fog. Gabe usually found it comforting, embracing it as a child would a favourite blanket, but not tonight. Tonight it felt heavy and oppressive, bearing down on him, the weight of expectation.

He raised a hand in resignation. 'Alright, just pointing out the facts. Settle down and take a seat.'

Amin sat, but looked no calmer.

'Guess the first thing we want to do is figure out where you were working. Remember anything special about the place?'

Amin shrugged. 'We worked on different farms. Always at night to avoid the heat. I think there was a town nearby, but I have never been there. It was a long journey each day from our camp, down many dirt roads, and on some nights I could smell the ocean.'

In his mind Gabe reeled off which town that could be. Geraldton was by far the largest, an actual city, and he'd seen plenty of fruit and vegetable sheds around that area. But it also had the biggest port, meaning Fisheries and Customs officers, and a substantial police presence in town, none of which would be very appealing to any smuggling gangs. Plus, it was a fair way from here. The little coastal towns of Horrocks and Port Gregory also seemed unlikely. Locals would notice something odd, even with the influx of summer tourists, and, so far as Gabe knew, there was no horticulture in the area. Kalbarri was the more obvious choice. Reasonable size, plenty of regular tourists coming and going, and a good number of vessels based their operations out of the wharf. The same could be said for Carnarvon; they had a few fishing vessels anchored there.

Something clicked. 'The boat you changed to, what was it like?'

'Very big,' Amin said. 'Very long. I think it was used for fishing. There were some wooden cages stacked at the back. I saw them before we went below deck.'

'Cages?' Gabe smiled. He held his arms apart. 'About this long? This high?'

'Yes, I think so.'

'And the boat, the back deck would've been flat. Cabin and wheelhouse up the front?'

'Yes, yes.' Amin leaned forward in anticipation. 'You know this boat?'

103

'Don't know exactly which one, but it sounds like a cray boat.' Gabe scratched his head, thinking.

'Cray boat?'

'Cray fisherman.' He saw Amin's perplexed look. 'Rock lobsters. There'd be hundreds of those boats all up and down the coast. Jesus, more I think about it, the more it makes sense.'

'How so?'

'Some go out for days. They'd have all the gear for a trip like you said. Drop you blokes off and then pull back into a wharf as if they'd just returned from pulling pots. And they can fish all year now, no season anymore, just quotas. They could leave in the dark, get home in the dark a week later, and no one would say boo. Wouldn't even have to be a cray fisherman. Plenty of old boats for sale – some people buy one to use for fishing charters.'

'I may be able to recognise it?' Amin suggested, though his tone didn't sound convincing.

Gabe shook his head. 'Waste of time. They all look the same for the most part. Unless you saw a name?'

'No, I didn't.'

'Anyway, they could be based down in Fremantle for all we know. That would be the smart thing. Busy port like that, people wouldn't notice much, I reckon.' He changed his line of thought. 'See anything when they dropped you off on the beach? Lights? Roads?'

'There was nothing. A man was waiting on the beach, and we followed him over to a bus, then we were told to put on the hoods. It was a dark night, no lights, but I could make out many sand dunes, some with small shrubs and plants on them.'

'Not very helpful. You just described most of the WA coast, though they'd have to pick the right spot to avoid tourists. They crawl up and down that coastline like bloody ants.'

'I am sorry – I was not paying too much attention. I was just grateful to be on land again. I think I fell asleep during the bus trip, so I cannot say how long the drive was either.'

'And then you arrived at, what? A camp site with dongas?'

'Yes. There were some other buildings too. Some made from stone, others with tin. There was a motor running, for lights, I think.'

'Sounds like a bush camp alright. Then they took you to another one? Closer to the work?'

'Yes. I think the first one was some sort of holding place for when people first arrive, and from there they are taken to other places. There were some who were on the boat with me, but they were not working on the same farms as I was. I can only assume they were sent elsewhere.'

'Or they're in that hole,' Gabe pointed out.

'Maybe. But I do not think so. Many were still working to pay for passage.'

'You said you were picking fruit. What was it?'

'Tomatoes. And then we started on mangoes.'

'Mangoes?' Gabe sat up straight. It was all becoming clearer. 'See any bananas?'

'Yes, though I did not pick any.'

'Carnarvon. You were in bloody Carnarvon.'

He had no doubt, thinking back to the last time he'd driven through the coastal town. It had everything Amin was talking about – masses of plantation farms, fishing boats, people coming and going – and backed straight onto the bush. He knew that a couple of pastoral stations came right up to the town boundary. *Shit, what if they were in on it too?* Amin said there were stone buildings; that could be a homestead, and the tin ones the sheds. This was getting bigger and bigger.

'That name sounds familiar,' Amin said. 'You know where this place is? How to get there?'

'Yes to both. It's about a three-hour drive from here, give or take.'

Amin immediately rose to his feet. 'We will leave at first light.' It was not a question. The man was going to find his family, with or without Gabe.

Gabe also stood. It had been a long day to say the least, and he felt exhausted, but still worried. 'You sure you don't want to get the cops in? The whole thing sounds pretty big.' He was beginning to think involving the police might not be such a bad idea. This was some serious shit Amin was talking about now. International people trafficking, forced labour camps and God only knew what else. Now, with the benefit of hindsight, Gabe wasn't sure that throwing those two bastards down a well was the wisest move, but surely they could argue self-defence and self-preservation if it came to that. Amin was adamant, though.

'No. I do not know how many police are working for them, or from where.' He must've noticed Gabe's hesitance. 'If we find this place and it is not possible to learn anything of my family on our own, then we may have no other choice. *Insha Allah*, we will not need to.' Amin placed his empty cup on the table. 'Thank you for your kindness, Gabe, but I must sleep. I hope tomorrow will bring us some good fortune.'

Gabe stretched and watched the man as he sat on the camp bed Gabe had set up for him. He didn't know what tomorrow would bring, but it was no use worrying now. He dropped his own cup next to Amin's and climbed the ladder into his rooftop tent, kicking off his boots and placing them in the corner before lying down on the mattress. It was a comfortable enough bed, but the tent limited the breeze a little – when there was one – and his view of the stars.

Amin's whispered tones carried up towards him. The man was praying again. Gabe sighed and rolled over. With any luck he'd awake in the morning and realise it was all just a bad dream.

SIXTEEN

The trickle of water on dirt awoke Gabe with the rather disappointing confirmation this was not a dream. He lay in silence as Amin washed, and soon afterwards he again heard gentle murmurings as his new companion began to pray.

'Jesus Christ,' he muttered, slipping on his boots and clambering down the ladder. 'How does this bloke get anything done?'

It was not quite dawn, with a soft glow beginning to show in the east. The air was crisp, still and silent, broken only by Amin's quiet prayers. He could just make out the figure, standing with his back not quite to the dawning sun, reciting those strange words that meant nothing to Gabe. He shook his head and fetched a toilet paper roll from inside the ute cab. A good shit, a coffee and a smoke were about the extent of Gabe's morning ritual, and he set off to find a suitable spot for the first part.

When he returned Amin had finished, waiting for him by the ashen remains of last night's fire.

'Morning,' Gabe grunted, placing the toilet roll on the table. 'Help yourself if you need it.'

He began assembling his small gas burner. The fire was a pile of cold ash and charred chunks of wood, and he didn't have the time or the inclination to get it going again.

'Good morning, Gabe,' Amin answered, after a moment. There was a quaver in his voice that made Gabe glance up. Amin looked ill; his face was clammy and sweat beaded on his brow. The day wasn't hot enough just yet for weather to be the explanation for that.

'You alright?' he asked.

Amin put a hand to his injured arm. 'I do not know. This arm aches and burns. I think maybe it is becoming infected.'

'Shit. Hang on a second.' He filled his kettle and placed it on the burner. 'Come over into the light and give us a proper look.'

Amin did so and held up his sleeve while Gabe unwrapped the bandage. The moment the cotton padding came away, Gabe knew Amin was right. The edges of the gash had turned a bright pink, and his arm was hot to the touch.

'Fuck's sake.' Gabe rewrapped the arm, brushing away the flies that had miraculously appeared. 'That changes things.'

'Perhaps it will be okay?' Amin asked with questionable optimism.

Gabe didn't think so. 'That'll get nasty real quick. You need to get it cleaned out and stitched up properly, get some antibiotics or something into you.' From Amin's reaction he could see the man already knew this. 'You need a doctor, but he might recognise that as a gunshot wound. He'd have to report it, and that would lead to questions.'

'No doctor then,' Amin said. 'We will get drugs from a store on our own.'

'Dunno how it works in your country, but here you need a prescription. From a doctor.' Gabe prepared a coffee for himself and a tea for Amin as he spoke. The sun was rising rapidly now, bathing their surrounds with an eerie lustre, and already the heat was starting to build. 'Looks like we're shit out of luck, unless . . .' He paused as the idea grew.

'Yes?'

'Maybe the nurse at Jakob's River would take a look.'

'Which nurse? Why should she be any different?' Amin asked.

'I dunno. Those remote nurses are probably used to all kinds of shit, and I reckon she'd have some drugs in the clinic. No pharmacies out here. Might be worth a shot.'

'Do you trust her?' Suspicion tinged the question.

'Don't even know her. Only met yesterday. New girl – seemed okay, I suppose. Not like the cranky bitch before.' He saw the indecisiveness on Amin's face. 'Look, we need to get you fixed up, otherwise you'll be no use to anyone.'

After a moment's consideration, Amin relented. 'You are right. How far away is she?'

'About an hour back that way. And from there we can head up to Carnarvon. Won't be much further that way anyway. Road might even be a bit better.'

Gabe sipped his coffee and began packing up, then realised Amin might be hungry, though he supposed bacon and eggs were out of the question. 'You want something to eat?'

'No, thank you. I think we should get moving.'

'Right you are.' Gabe continued stowing away his gear. He was in two minds as to what to do with the smugglers' Rodeo. If they abandoned it, only for it to be found later, suspicions might be raised, but driving the thing around might risk being recognised by Amin's captors should they pass through looking for them. In the end he decided to take it back to Jakob's River and leave it in the makeshift car yard that had grown on the town's outskirts, a mixture of rusted shells and newer additions that became a sort of one-stop auto shop for the more mechanically inclined residents. It was a common enough vehicle and would blend in with the assortment of four-wheel drives parked around the community too.

Before they set off, Gabe washed out the Rodeo's tray using soap and water from his own ute, until he was happy that all traces of blood were gone. As he did so, he wondered what the new nurse would make of Amin, and whether or not they'd be able to convince her he'd been injured through innocent means. What would happen if she suspected something? Would she report it, call the cops? Gabe wasn't sure if she would, and if doing so would be such a bad thing.

SEVENTEEN

Through the dried, twisted branches of a fallen wattle tree, the dingo watches the Man. She does not move, save for her eyes following the figure as he walks back and forth, sometimes crouching to inspect the earth. Too many Men had come this way of late. Only yesterday there were more, and they were very loud. She had watched those ones too, and almost ran when the thunder claps started, but stayed her ground. This is her territory, her den nestled up high in the granite outcrop. For now, it is empty, but when the days cool and the rains return, she will fill it with a new litter. She will not leave unless forced to do so, and it seemed those previous Men had been too busy fighting among themselves to worry about her. They left blood behind when the noisy machine finally moved on, carrying them all away. Only two were still breathing, and the air was heavy with scent – sweat, fear and blood. Her tongue flicks around her muzzle at the memory, but her eyes do not leave the Man.

This one is different. He is alone, arriving in another machine that alerts every creature within earshot of its presence. It smells of death, kangaroo blood, oil, and of the thunder smoke. She does not like that smell, because that smell and the booms that precede it carry fear and pain. She has a scar on her left flank to prove it. So she stays hidden.

The Man walks to a tree, looks around and begins brushing at the soil where she saw the other two Men sit. One was bleeding, and she had sniffed at his blood once they were gone. The new Man picks something up, holds it between two fingers and inspects it. He smiles and walks back to his machine.

It carries him towards the creek, where she had smelled the pungent odour of foreign dog on one of the banks during last night's hunt, drawing her in to inspect. Among the strange scent there was the faint whiff of Man and, even fainter, cold steel. She knew that smell, remembering the snatching, biting jaws that bit at her front paw two seasons back. She had escaped those jaws, but one toe did not. And so she backed away, ignoring the scent, and continued her hunt.

Now she waits for the sound of the machine to disappear, and emerges from her hiding place. She paces to where the Man stood, sniffing for any sign of those same steel jaws, or anything else that might signal danger. There is none, save for a damp patch of dirt where he'd relieved himself. She does the same, covering his scent with hers. This is, after all, her territory.

EIGHTEEN

They stopped at the nursing post after abandoning the smugglers' ute at the rubbish tip. Gabe was pleased to see the small gravel car park was empty, hoping this meant no one else would be inside save for the nurse. *What was her name again? Caroline?* He couldn't remember, but thought it was something like that. He felt his apprehension grow as he glanced at Amin, and suddenly the cover story they'd concocted for his injury seemed ridiculous. *Tripped and fell against a sharp branch? Well, that's the old 'I walked into the door' just reimagined, isn't it?*

Sitting in the passenger seat, Amin leaned forward, and before Gabe realised what he was about to do, he opened the glove box to stow his handguns in there. Gabe saw him look with some surprise at the roll of yellow notes sitting on top of the toilet paper and service logbook, but he said nothing. They exited the vehicle, doors slamming.

'Let me do the talking, alright?' Gabe said as they approached the fibro building.

'Of course. My English very bad.' Amin spoke with a slight grin as his words faltered under a new, harsher accent.

Gabe grunted his approval and pulled the door open. The

escaping rush of freezing air sent a brief shiver down his back as they walked in, setting off a buzzer in the next room.

'Grab a seat, I'll be there in a minute!' called a female voice.

The reception area was small, tidy and decorated with a mixture of Aboriginal artwork – mostly done by the school children, Gabe assumed – and Health Department posters. A door marked *Toilet* was off to one side. The room was empty, much to his relief. They sat and waited while the nurse's voice drifted out to them, and Gabe's relief soon disappeared as it became clear she was in there with a patient.

'And how did you manage this, then?'

'Dunno,' came a young man's reply. 'Just sort of fell over, I guess.'

'I see. Just fell over. Night before last, you say?'

'Yeah.'

'And you didn't notice your wrist was swollen until this morning?' The tone was pleasant, but Gabe knew an inquisition when he heard one.

'Nah. Thought it would come good, but woke up and it was like this.'

Gabe could picture the nurse shaking her head at the patient in mild frustration.

'It's not broken, but I'll strap it for you and get you some anti-inflammatories. Here, keep it elevated with that cold pack on it while I see who our other guests are.'

A moment later she emerged from the consultation room and Gabe saw the recognition on her face.

'How nice to see you again,' she smiled. 'Gabe, isn't it? I wasn't expecting you back so soon. What can we do for you today – nothing serious, I hope? You haven't shot your friend here by mistake, have you?'

The joke's closeness to the truth startled him, and it must've shown on his face because Courtney – Gabe could now read the badge clipped high over her right breast – immediately apologised.

'I'm sorry, that was a bad joke. Forgive me – sometimes my mouth runs off before I can catch it.' She walked around to the reception desk and Gabe motioned for Amin to follow as he approached. 'Now, what brings you here?'

'This fella's hurt his arm. Got a gash and looks like it's getting infected.' To highlight this, he raised the sleeve of Amin's shirt.

Courtney eyed the dressing. 'I see. And what is your friend's name?' She withdrew a form from a drawer, attached it to a clipboard and poised a pen, ready to take notes.

'Amin . . . um . . . how'd you say your last name again?'

Amin feigned confusion, and Gabe repeated his question. 'Name?'

'Oh. Amin Tahiri. Sorry. English very bad.'

Courtney, halfway through writing, stopped and looked up as he spoke, either from confusion at the pronunciation or curiosity at the very un-Australian voice in what was a very Australian location. Possibly both.

'I'm sorry,' she said. 'I'm going to have to get you to write that down for me.' She passed the clipboard over the counter to Gabe, who handed it to Amin.

Amin shook his head, pointing at the form. 'I no English.'

Gabe suspected Amin's writing would be as good as his speaking, but it was the ideal excuse to get around the paperwork side of things. He wasn't sure how the health care system worked in Afghanistan, but he was fairly certain boat people didn't come with Medicare.

'Can we do away with the form?' he asked. 'He's not from around here . . .' Courtney's eyebrows raised in a mock 'You don't say?' gesture. 'And we're in a bit of a hurry. He's meeting friends in Carnarvon and is already late.'

Courtney stood and approached, eyeing them both very carefully. 'And he's your friend, you say?'

'Dunno about friend. Found him on the side of the road last night with a flat tyre and a nasty scratch on his arm, so I helped him out.'

'I see.' She inspected Amin's bandaging, smiled and said to him, 'Lucky for you he came along then, isn't it? Not the best place to be getting flat tyres. Can't exactly call RAC, can you?'

Amin gave her a puzzled grin in reply, and Gabe was certain this time it wasn't an act. He doubted they had RAC in Afghanistan.

Courtney handed Gabe the clipboard. 'Fill that out as best you can for him. Put down your details if it's easier, while I have a look at his arm. Now, sir, follow me please. You too, Mr . . . ?'

'Just Gabe is fine.'

They entered the consultation room. It housed two hospital beds with a computer desk and chairs between them. Courtney patted the paper-lined mattress of the second bed, signalling Amin should sit there, while Gabe shot a hurried glance at the patient in the first bed, raising a finger to his lips as Courtney rummaged in the overhead cupboard for some examination gloves.

The young man propped up on the bed scowled at him, but said nothing.

'You'll have to excuse Darren over there,' Courtney said as she pulled on the gloves. 'He's had a bit of a tumble.'

'He should be more careful,' said Gabe, glaring back at Bobby's nephew.

'Must have been a full moon the other night,' sighed Courtney. It was, but Gabe suspected Darren's wrist had nothing to do with lunar cycles. 'Now, let's have a look at that arm. And don't forget the form please.'

Gabe took a seat while Courtney unwrapped Amin's bandage. 'Oh my, you have done a number on yourself. Not having a good start to your holiday, are you?'

You've got that right, Gabe thought as he stared at the form, wondering what to put down.

'I fall,' Amin said, somewhat sheepishly. 'On tree.'

'Really?' Courtney leaned over, inspecting the wound. 'Bit of that going on around here lately.' Across the room Darren continued to stare out the window, saying nothing.

'It's very bruised, and you're right, it's definitely getting infected.' She peered even closer. 'It's an odd looking wound for a scratch. A stick, you said?'

Amin feigned confusion, leaving Gabe to reply. 'That's what he said. Or at least I think that's what he said. More charades than words, but pretty sure I got the gist of it.'

'Well, either way, your friend is in luck. Dr Woolford is due here around lunchtime, so he can prescribe some antibiotics and have a look at that arm for himself, and stitch it up if need be.' Courtney gave Amin another friendly pat on the leg, but Amin was looking at Gabe with concern. Gabe knew what he was thinking.

'That's still a few hours away. There's no way you can give him the drugs now?'

'No, I'm afraid I can't,' Courtney said. 'I'm a registered nurse, not a nurse practitioner. You'll just have to wait here until then.'

Gabe tried again. 'It's just antibiotics, not painkillers or anything.'

'Sorry, I really can't.' The nurse rose and headed towards a large cabinet. 'But I can have everything ready for when the good doctor gets here. Save you a bit of time. If you're in such a hurry, why didn't you go straight to Carnarvon? The surgery there could've sorted you straight away, and a few hours wouldn't have made much difference to his arm.'

Gabe said nothing for a moment as his overloaded mind tried to come up with some sort of excuse to answer this perfectly reasonable question. Despite her bubbly disposition, the young woman was no fool.

'I'm not going to Carnarvon for a while yet, and wasn't real keen to send him that way alone with a dicky arm and no spare tyre. You were closer.'

Courtney eyed him again as she unlocked the cabinet, and Gabe gave what he hoped was a pleasant smile. She retrieved a small box and returned to the desk.

'I'll leave these out for Dr Woolford. Save him rummaging through my cabinet and messing everything up again. I swear he is the most unorganised man I've ever met.'

Courtney scribbled a note and stuck it on the packet. For a fleeting moment Gabe considered distracting the nurse, grabbing the drugs and hightailing it out of there with Amin in tow. The idea of hanging around didn't appeal to him at all, but he quickly dismissed it. Nicking drugs was a sure-fire way to draw more attention to them. He glanced at Amin, and the resigned shrug he received told him the man had accepted this. There wasn't much else they could do.

'Alright, we'll hang around till the doc gets here,' he said, giving Amin an apologetic look. He could only imagine what the man was thinking.

'Excellent,' Courtney said. 'I'll give that wound another clean, and you two will be on your way in no time.'

Gabe was about to say he hoped so when a melodic mobile ringtone rang through the medical centre. It was coming from Amin's back pocket.

NINETEEN

Amin's eyes went wide as he retrieved the phone.

'Don't answer it,' said Gabe quickly. Amin just stared at the noisy device in his hand that was demanding to be answered. It rang a few more times, and then was silent. Courtney watched on. If she had any previous suspicions, Gabe was fairly certain this little episode wouldn't have helped allay them.

'It's his phone from back home,' Gabe explained, thinking fast. 'Silly git never got a new one for here, so it'll cost him a fortune to answer it. Cheaper to text them for now. Probably his mates wondering where he is.' Gabe figured he was half right. Someone was definitely wondering where Amin was, but he doubted they'd be considered mates.

'Right,' Courtney said. Gabe couldn't read anything in her reply. 'You're lucky it worked at all; we're right on the edge of range in here. The tower's up by the mine, apparently. But if they get through again, you can tell them you'll be a few hours away and to soak up the sun in Carnarvon while they wait. Now, I'm going to clean and dress this arm. You're welcome to stay and watch, Mr, er . . . Gabe, or you can leave your friend here and wander about town.'

'I might go find a coffee,' Gabe said. 'Amin, you want a tea?' He mimed drinking from a cup.

Amin, now lying back on the raised bed, gave a thumbs up. He looked pale, whether from his arm or the phone ringing, Gabe wasn't sure.

After asking Courtney if she wanted anything, to which she politely declined, he left the medical centre and walked across the road towards the store. A white LandCruiser ute, clearly a roo-shooter's judging by the steel frame on the tray, was parked out the front with the driver sitting at the wheel talking into his phone. Gabe noted the 'FUCK OFF – WE'RE FULL' sticker among the assorted tags plastered across the back window. The irony of such a claim in a place as empty as this made him smile. He didn't recognise the man, but that wasn't surprising. With the big dry, shooters were travelling further afield to catch their quota. As he passed the ute, the driver gave him a nonchalant wave, which Gabe returned as he continued on to the store.

The bell dinged as he entered. Melissa looked up from the counter, surprised to see him again.

'Back so soon?' she asked. 'Missed me, did you?'

'Something like that,' Gabe said. 'Got caught up.'

'So, who's your new mate?' Melissa laughed at Gabe's own surprised look. 'Saw you two pulling in. You pick up a stray?'

Bloody Melissa, she didn't miss much. 'Lost tourist. Flat tyre, hurt his arm.'

'A regular good Samaritan, aren't you?'

'Wouldn't say that. Pain in the arse is what it is.' *And you've got no idea just how big a pain,* Gabe thought. 'Can I get a black tea and a coffee please?'

'Sure thing.' She set about preparing the order as Gabe grabbed another packet of jerky, opened it and chewed on the dried meat while trying to figure out what the hell they were going to do now. Amin had shown remarkable restraint so far, but he knew that wouldn't last. Gabe doubted he would be so patient if things were reversed and it had been Valerie in trouble. But of course, that scenario was impossible now.

'Bit of a ruckus the other night,' Melissa called over her shoulder to him. 'Boys got up to some mischief.'

'Yeah?' He placed a carton of Coke on the counter. Seeing as Amin didn't drink beer, better get him something, he supposed.

'Yeah. Grog came in from somewhere. Nothing too bad, bit of whooping and hollering, few skids down the road. Nothing you wouldn't see anywhere else on a weekend.' Melissa carried over his drinks. 'Heard young Darren went tits up though. Bloody idiot, thought he knew better.'

'Any idea where it came from?' Gabe asked.

'Dunno, not really. Don't get that many people passing through here this time of year.' Melissa eyed him slyly. 'Maybe it was you, hey?'

Gabe chuckled in what he hoped was a friendly, innocent manner. 'If I had a ute-load of grog, I wouldn't be bloody sharing it. Too bloody hot out here – a man's got to keep hydrated.'

'Not here you won't. And tell you what, whoever it was, I wouldn't like to be in their shoes if Elsie finds out who done it. No one's saying anything, but I reckon she'll work it out soon enough. Got the coppers coming back out here today too. Have a look around, see what they can find out.'

'The sarge?'

'Suppose so. And his young mate, I guess. Sarge is alright, for a copper. Dunno about that new fella though. Bit too much city in him, I reckon.'

'Parker will thump it out of him,' Gabe said, paying for the beverages and the snack. 'Thanks.'

He pushed through the door and saw the roo-shooter standing by his back wheel, leaning against the side of the tray. He was dressed in faded jeans and a blue cotton drill shirt with the sleeves cut off, and he looked about forty or so. A tall, lean streak of a man in a broad-brimmed hat – your typical roofing nail type bloke.

'G'day, mate,' the man said as Gabe went by. 'Haven't got a smoke, have you?'

Gabe thought about suggesting the stranger take five steps into the store and buy his own, but then remembered the ridiculously high price tag that came with smokes – or anything else for that matter – in this remote little town.

'Sure.' He placed the cup tray, the carton of Coke and the open packet of jerky on the ute's bonnet, fished out his tobacco and handed the man one of his pre-rolled durries. Gabe took the opportunity to fashion another for himself.

The man inspected the rollie and gave a little smile. 'Cheers. That your rig?' he asked, nodding across the road towards Gabe's own khaki ute.

'Yeah.'

'Nice. A dogger then, ay? Reckon there's probably a bit more of your game around than mine at the moment.'

'Probably,' Gabe agreed. 'Harder to catch, though.'

'Cunning bastards, aren't they?' The man stuck out a hand. 'Chase. Chase Fowler.'

Gabe must've shown his amusement at the odd name, because the roo-shooter smiled. 'Not what my mother called me, but boarding school nicknames tend to stick.'

Gabe gave a chuckle. He knew a few people whose Christian

names were an absolute mystery. 'Gabe. Don't reckon I've seen you around.'

'Nah. Usually run north of Carnarvon, but slim pickings up there, so I came down here, get a bit closer to the cropping country, you know?'

'Pretty thin out here too. Haven't seen that many roos, but then I don't drive much at night.' Gabe flicked his butt to the ground and grabbed the drinks. 'Better get these delivered. Nice meeting you. Happy hunting.'

'You too,' Chase said, smiling at him again, and pointed at the bag of jerky. 'Good stuff that. Careful you don't get it mixed up with your baits, hey?'

Gabe laughed and held out the packet. 'No, that wouldn't be good at all.'

Chase took a couple of pieces and popped them in his mouth. 'Cheers. Be seeing you around, dogger.'

Gabe crossed the road while carrying the hot drinks, which had barely cooled in this midmorning sun. He loaded the Coke into his Engel and headed into the medical centre. Just as he reached the door, he felt a prickle up his neck and turned to see Chase still watching him. Nothing unusual in that, he supposed. Not much else to look at around here, but all the same Gabe felt uncomfortable. *You're being paranoid,* he told himself. *Just a fellow hunter being friendly.* He raised a hand to Chase and then went inside, still feeling those eyes on him as he did so.

Courtney was back at the reception desk scribbling something in her notes when he entered. He gave her a brief, awkward smile and went through to the consultation room to deliver the tea. There was no sign of Darren, so he took the chance to have a quiet word with Amin. 'Did they leave a message or anything?'

'No, nothing, but it rang again,' Amin whispered. 'And I think she suspects something.'

'Not surprising, the whole thing is pretty suss, but you were the one who didn't want to go to the hospital in Carnarvon.' Gabe eyed the drugs on the table again. 'We could grab them and bolt, but then she'd get the cops onto us for stealing. Already found out they're going to be back here soon enough.'

A look of alarm shot across Amin's face and Gabe raised a hand. 'Nothing to do with us.' *Well, not exactly us,* Gabe thought. 'But I think we're best to wait here, get the doc to sign off on you, and then we'll head to Carnarvon and have a look around. Maybe you'll recognise something.'

'Perhaps,' said Amin. 'I hope those pills will work; my arm feels like it is on fire, but she has already given me some aspirin.'

The buzzing of the door alarm sounded in the consultation room, and the two men heard Courtney greet the newcomer in her cheery fashion. 'Hello, sir, and what can we do for you? My, it is a day for strangers, isn't it?'

'So it would seem, love.'

Gabe's guts tightened upon hearing Chase's voice. 'Something's up,' he whispered. 'Don't know what, but I don't like the sound of that bloke.' And then he saw Amin's face. It had gone even paler.

'I know that man,' Amin whispered fiercely. 'From the camp.'

'Shit, I bloody knew he was off.' Gabe looked around. There was no back door, and the only window was barred. 'Fuck it. Now what?'

From the reception Chase continued talking. 'Just here looking for a mate. I heard he might've come in. Arab-looking fellow, 'bout yay high? Been trying to call him, but it keeps ringing out.'

Gabe's heart sank as he heard Courtney's reply. 'Why yes, he's just through there. You can go on in if you like.'

Amin slid off the bed as they heard the footsteps approach. Chase entered, and his face lit up in a disconcerting grin when he spotted his quarry. Gabe didn't like that look at all.

'G'day, mate,' Chase drawled in a low voice. 'Been looking for you.'

Amin started towards him. Gabe wasn't sure what he was planning, but whatever it was, Chase put an end to it when he drew a handgun from his belt, with what looked to be a silencer, going from what Gabe had seen in movies.

Chase held a finger to his lips. 'Ease up there, bloke. Nice and easy, nothing stupid now. Keep it quiet, like.' He jerked his head back over his shoulder. 'For her sake, yeah?'

They could hear Courtney still chatting on the phone. Amin eased up.

'You've already made quite the mess of things, haven't you? Don't know when to quit. And looks like you've had some help.' Chase gave another grin, this time to Gabe. 'You should've stuck with dogs, mate. Kept your nose out of things. Now you're in the shit too.'

Gabe said nothing. His mind raced, trying to find a way out, some escape, some sort of plan. This was the second time he'd had a gun pulled on him, and he enjoyed it no better than the first. Less so, given he was now lacking one of his own.

Chase stepped closer. 'So, here's what we're going to do. You two are going to leave with me, no fuss, no noise, not if you want that pretty little nurse to stay out of it, and then we're going for a bit of a drive.'

'Back to that hole then?' Gabe grunted.

'So you found that?' Chase almost looked impressed. 'Of course you did, man of the bush such as yourself. No, not to the pit. There's a couple of folks who'd like a quiet word with you, Amin. Friends of your two escorts. Want to know what happened to them. I reckon they're in another hole somewhere, with that mate of yours. Sound about right?'

Gabe said nothing, and Amin stared at Chase defiantly. 'Where is my family?' he hissed. 'I will go with you, but where are they?'

'They're being looked after. How well and for how long kind of depends on you, doesn't it?'

Gabe felt Amin tense beside him and rested a hand on his arm. It was no good getting shot, and something in Chase's eyes told him this man would not hesitate to fire.

Without warning, Courtney appeared in the doorway. Her soft shoes made almost no noise on the linoleum floor. 'I've been speaking with Dr . . .' she trailed off, suddenly realising Chase was holding a gun, which he now waved at her.

'Oh, love, you should've stayed put,' he said. 'Over there, with those two.'

'What . . . I . . .' Courtney was momentarily lost for words. *No small feat,* Gabe mused, despite the situation.

Chase took her arm, pulled her into the consultation room and directed her over to where Gabe and Amin stood. 'No sudden movement and no noise.'

Courtney recovered from the shock and turned to Chase, her eyes blazing. 'What the hell is going on here?'

Gabe was both a little surprised and impressed at her apparent lack of fear.

'Just a conversation between friends, that's all,' Chase said, jerking his head towards Amin. 'Me and this fella here have got some talking to do, and you pair got caught in the middle.'

'Let them go,' Amin said. 'They know nothing. They have nothing to do with any of it.'

Courtney spun around. 'You *can* speak English! I knew it!'

'Not now,' whispered Gabe, keeping his eyes on the gun.

Chase shook his head. 'Nah, I don't reckon that's true. No way would a goat-fucker like you be able to find a good dumping ground for bodies out bush, then make it here. Not to mention covering your tracks like that. You did some good work back there, dogger. I bet you catch quite a few mutts, hey?'

'I go alright.'

'Missed a smoke butt, though, didn't you? Little rollie, just like the one you gave me.' Chase grinned again, this time with smug satisfaction. 'Saw where you crossed that creek too, then lost you. Figured anyone who knew enough to hide themselves like that might end up back here, to call for cops or something. Found our ute in that rubbish tip too. Still got its wheels, so it can't have been there too long.'

Chase gestured with his free hand. 'First things first – give us that phone. I know you've got it.'

Amin held out the device, taking a step forward. Chase reached out to take it . . . and then everything went to hell in a hurry.

TWENTY

Amin dived for the gun.

Christ, not this again, Gabe thought, shoving Courtney behind the desk. 'Stay down,' he growled, thinking of the flying bullets last time this happened. He rose to assist, and was halfway to the struggling pair when Chase struck a powerful blow across Amin's head, sending him reeling back.

'You stupid fuck,' Chase spat. 'I ought to shoot—'

He never finished. A metallic thud echoed through the room and Chase staggered forward, falling to his knees. Behind him, holding the fire extinguisher that had been mounted in the reception area, stood Darren.

'Who's this bloody joker then, hey?'

'Go, quick!' Gabe grabbed Courtney's arm and almost threw her towards the door. She barrelled into Darren and the two fell back into the reception area. Amin recovered his senses and again made for the gun, but Chase raised himself to one knee. Gabe saw his eyes beginning to refocus and recognised the rage that was burning in them. He pushed Amin through the doorway, following him as a muffled crack sounded from behind and something thudded into the door frame.

Louder than I expected; Hollywood is full of shit, Gabe thought, even as he ducked instinctively. Next to him, Darren still carried the extinguisher and he hurled it at Chase with all the precision of a pro bowler. The red cylinder cannoned into Chase's shins and sent him toppling forward again with a curse.

'Fuckin' bowled him!' Darren hooted, and then scarpered after the others as all four raced outside, tipping the small table covered with magazines behind him as he went.

'My ute, go!' Gabe looked around, hoping to see Sergeant Parker pulling up, but the street was deserted save for two children on bikes down the far end. Hopefully they would stay there.

'My God,' breathed Courtney. 'I had no idea he was carrying a gun. But you, I knew there was something up with you, I just knew it. Are you on the run?'

'We are now,' shot Gabe, opening the rear door for her. 'You and Darren get in the back. Squeeze in!'

'We won't fit,' Courtney protested, but Darren scooted up and clambered onto the bench seat, shoving Gabe's belongings to one side and wedging himself hard against the Engel.

'Get up here, miss,' he called, holding out a hand. 'He'll be out here in a minute. Reckon I just pissed him off.'

Courtney took the offered hand and pulled herself in, and Gabe was grateful it was her and not the former rotund matron; he might have considered leaving that old biddy behind. He slammed the door with the young nurse barely clear and looked around to see Amin standing outside adjusting his seat, trying to make more room for the pair.

'Fuck's sake, let's go!' Gabe roared, firing up the engine just seconds before he saw Chase stagger out of the medical centre door and limp down the steps. Amin was only halfway inside when Gabe dropped the clutch, shooting the heavy vehicle backwards and reefing hard on the steering wheel. The ute lurched as it swung around, and Amin barely managed to get the door shut. Gravel sprayed as Gabe pressed the accelerator to the floor, thankful he had splurged on the V8 model. In his side mirror he saw Chase limping across the road, no doubt heading for his own vehicle. Gabe hoped the roo-shooter only had the six-cylinder version, or things could get very interesting shortly.

'You boys in some trouble, hey?' Darren said. He had one arm resting on the Engel's lid, the other around Courtney's shoulder, which was fair enough as there was very little room back there with all of Gabe's gear. 'This something to do with the—'

'No.' Gabe cut him off. He glanced at Courtney in the rear-view mirror, unsure if she'd heard Darren, or knew what he was referring to. If she had, she gave no indication. Instead, she was trying to peer through the back window, but soon gave up. Gabe's canvas had clear plastic panels on the front and back, but they were clouded from sun exposure and almost impossible to see through.

'Do you think he's following us? What does he want with you? And why didn't you just tell me you could speak English?' The rush of questions came from Courtney with breathless excite-ment. And she was excited, Gabe could see it. Silly girl, she should be scared.

Gabe checked his mirrors, but their dust obscured everything. 'He's following, but his ute looks a bit slower than mine, hopefully.'

Amin strained around to look at Darren. 'Thank you. It could have gone very badly back there.'

'You blokes're just lucky I needed a piss when I did, or we'd all be in the shit.' Darren pointed to the two-way mounted in the radio console. 'You gonna call the cops or what? They're coming out here today, I heard. Might be able to get them on that thing.'

'No police,' Amin said firmly. 'They are working with that man, and the people smugglers who brought me and my family to Australia. They have my wife and son, and we have to find them.'

'What? Bent coppers? Bastards.' Darren didn't seem overly surprised, but seemed to think about it some more. 'Parker would be alright though, unna? Not much gets past him, but I don't reckon he's bent.'

'My God,' Courtney said before Gabe could answer. 'No wonder you didn't want to fill in that form. So where are we going now?'

'As far away from that Chase fellow as we can,' he said. 'But Carnarvon is the plan still, right, Amin?'

The man in the passenger seat nodded grimly, his eyes staring straight ahead at the wide gravel road. Gabe set his eyes on Darren in the mirror again. 'I reckon you're right about Parker though.'

Darren leaned forward and pointed ahead. 'Up here, go right, down that little track. You stay on this main road, all that fella has to do is follow your dust. Turn here, he might miss it if he's sootin' hard trying to catch us, 'specially if the dust hangs about. He'll drive right past it.'

After a moment's thought, Gabe agreed it was a good idea. He slowed and turned, squeezing the ute under an acacia branch, and headed into the scrub.

'Here, how about this, then?' Darren said. 'You drop us off up ahead, and I'll run back to town and find the sarge. Tell him face to face what happened. They're gonna be looking for me anyway, and if you're missing, miss, they'll get nervous and might bring out more coppers.'

Gabe continued to drive, but much slower than before. There was no sign of their pursuer and the road verge had disappeared behind them. He hoped Darren's theory was right.

133

'That might be a good idea,' he said, and held up a hand to Amin, who looked like he was about to protest. 'Parker's alright – he's been a bush cop for most of his career, and he knows me. Helped him track down a lost kid a few years ago, and some old prospector before that. I'm not saying he's gonna be happy about things, but he's not always completely by the book either. If anyone is going to believe us, it'll be him.'

Amin didn't appear convinced.

'Look,' Gabe continued, starting to think he'd feel a whole lot better if he had a beer in him. Just one, just to settle the nerves. 'I don't know how far we'll get on our own. We've got that clown behind us, and now we're out of town he might not be so slow to use that gun. Least if Darren can get the sarge on the case, he can look into a few things for us.'

Courtney raised a hand. 'I still have no idea what's going on. Did you say people smugglers?'

'Yes,' Amin said. 'They brought me here and promised to bring my family once I'd worked to pay them.'

'Oh, wow,' Courtney breathed. 'And you think the police are involved?'

'Some, yes. That's how they know when to bring the boats to shore, to avoid sea patrols.' Amin looked skyward for a moment, palms of both hands turned upwards, and sighed. '*Tawakkaltu Alallah*, we will do as you say.'

'Righto.' Gabe grabbed one of his business cards from the pile jammed into the console and handed it to Darren. 'Give him this to get hold of us. Tell him to use the sat-phone number. I'll pull up just ahead. You get ready to bolt. Take Courtney with you.'

Darren eyed the nurse. 'No offence, but how fast can you run?'

'Not very,' Courtney admitted. 'And even less so in this bush.'

'I reckon she's better off with you, Gabe,' Darren said. 'If I gotta wait for her, I might miss the copper. He was supposed to be coming this morning.'

'No, I have to go back,' she insisted. 'Dr Woolford is coming, and if I'm not there he'll wonder where I am.'

'Fine, go with him,' Gabe growled. 'Grab a couple of water bottles from that fridge, Darren. I'm going to stop up here. Amin, I need you to give me a hand with something, real quick. I think I've got just the thing for Chase if he follows us down here, but everyone needs to move. Right? Here we go.'

Gabe brought his ute to a halt, careful not to let the tyres skid. He leaped out and ran around to the passenger side. Working quickly, he opened up the canopy and the upright toolbox, and after a moment's searching emerged with a small mallet and something else, something that he only ever used in the most deserted of areas.

'What is that?' Amin asked, following Gabe to the rear of the vehicle.

'A little trick I picked up in Queensland,' Gabe said, passing him the mallet and a large spike with a loop at the end. Fine fishing line was tied through the loop. 'Go whack that in at the track's edge, behind that shrub there. Make sure you can't see it from the road, got it? And you two, get moving!'

Darren waved and set off into the bush. Courtney called back to Gabe as she followed, 'I left you boys a present. Good luck!'

Gabe barely acknowledged her. He ran across the road, uncoiling the fishing line as he went. Behind him he heard Amin hammering in his stake. On this side of the road was another similar shrub, which was why Gabe had stopped here. Amin joined him, having finished his task.

'What are we doing?' he asked, glancing the way they had come. They could hear a vehicle in the distance.

'Hopefully slowing him down,' Gabe said, as he took the hammer. 'He'll soon work out he's shot past us and backtrack. If he found our sign at that pit, he'll find our tracks down here.'

Gabe hammered in his bit of gear. It was an old-fashioned rabbit trap with a steel picket welded to the bottom. Once in the ground, the trap stood about a foot high. He threaded the fishing line around the catch of the trigger plate, pulling it tight enough so the line hung clear of the dirt across the width of the road. With practised ease, he squeezed the spring assembly, and one of the steel jaws fell open, the other tacked rigidly in place. Gabe loaded a single shotgun shell into a small piece of pipe welded to the fixed jaw. The free jaw had a small piece of thin rod protruding from it, which lined up perfectly with the primer in the back of the shotgun shell held in the pipe, pointing over the track.

'Don't stand in front of that, it's live now,' Gabe said, as he set and latched the trigger plate. 'Right, let's go.'

The two men jumped back into the ute, and Gabe accelerated away. 'With any luck, he'll come down there shortly, hit the line and it'll take out his front tyre.'

Amin gave him an approving look. 'Very clever, my friend.'

'Entirely illegal, but it's a handy bit of gear if there's a dog pad and the thing is trap-shy. Dog trips the wire, and I find him dead on the track. Of course, I can't use it anywhere a bloody tourist might wander or station worker drive their motorbike over. Blow his friggin' leg off. But in this case, I reckon old Chase will be the first to go near it.'

'I think the Taliban would be very impressed.'

'We'll see soon enough,' Gabe said. 'This track is pretty rough, so any speed advantage we had is gone.'

'At least we have one less thing to worry about.'

'What's that then?'

Amin reached forward and grabbed the box of antibiotics from the dash. 'Our nurse friend did indeed leave me a gift.'

'Shit, she must've grabbed them as we rushed out of there.' Gabe was impressed. 'I was too busy hightailing it for the door to even think of them.'

'I as well,' Amin said. 'I think she is quite a brave young lady.'

'Even if she does talk a mile a minute. Hopefully she can keep up with Darren okay and they can find the sarge.'

'You had better be right about your policeman friend.'

Gabe hoped so too. Things were getting way out of hand now.

TWENTY-ONE

Chase Fowler shoved the fire extinguisher out of the way, ignoring the throbbing pain blooming at the back of his head and the sharper, fresher one erupting on his shin. Where the hell had that little bastard come from? He must've been in the toilet or something. This was supposed to be a simple pick-up and disposal. And how the fuck had that Arab escaped in the first place?

No time for that now, he thought, struggling to his feet and catching a glimpse of the young Aboriginal man disappearing out the door. A wave of dizziness washed over him as he rose, forcing him to grab the desk for support. Lucky the prick didn't brain him with that thing. Just wait until he caught up with them. And he was in no doubt he would, though he hoped his head would be clearer and his leg a bit more functional than it was right now. He looked around the medical centre. Shit, he'd have to clean this up or it might raise suspicions.

With some difficulty, Chase picked up the extinguisher, hooked it back onto the wall, and righted the upset table and magazines. The unmistakable rumble of a LandCruiser firing up grabbed his attention. He lurched to the door, hoping the place looked normal enough, and shoved it open, almost tripping down the steps of the transportable hut as he hurried outside, only to spy the dogger's vehicle spinning out of the car park, the passenger door still open with that damned refugee battling to climb in. How easy it would be if he'd just fall out and get run over.

For an instant he considered letting off a few shots, but decided against it. That shop was just over the road, and if the girl in there was as nosey as most other shopkeepers he knew, she'd be watching, or if not, the shots would draw her attention, suppressor or no suppressor. Letting that one off inside had been foolish, but he was angry. Was still angry. No, better to catch them out in the bush, where there was no one to hear such things.

Chase half skipped, half ran towards his own ute, still hampered by his sore shin. They had made it to the end of the bitumen by now, clearing the town outskirts and raising a billowing cloud of orange dust as they sped away. At least they would be easy to follow, even if that ute of Gabe's had a few more horses under the hood than his old girl. No matter. He had tracked them here with no more than a discarded cigarette butt, a few well-disguised drops of blood and his own intuition. He would find them again. And even if he didn't, Chase was fairly certain of where they were going, or at least trying to find.

He crossed the road, giving a friendly wave to the two children pedalling down the street towards him, and entered his vehicle. He quickly checked his phone. No calls, so that was good. Plans were still running smoothly. He was certain the old dogger hadn't called the police, or his contact would have let him know, and he wondered why that might be. Surely the police would be the first priority, but he supposed the Arab must've talked him out of it, perhaps fearing he would be taken by Immigration if authorities became involved. That might change with the nurse running off with them, but he would worry about that if the time came.

As Chase pulled out from the store car park, he glanced around, checking there was nobody watching. There wasn't, or no one that he could see. Seemed his single shot hadn't garnered that much attention, so maybe that silencer hadn't been such a bad idea after all. Gregory, the guy with all the connections, had procured it for him only a month ago after Chase admired the one he sported. Homemade of course, but it certainly looked the part, and when he screwed it to the barrel he felt like James fucking Bond.

He drove hard, leaving Jakob's River behind in a cloud of his own dust as he followed his quarry. The fine orange particles hung in the breezeless air like an early morning mist, obscuring his vision ahead. His eyes flicked left to right, checking for any sign they had veered off the road, mainly because, if he were the one being followed, he'd be heading bush at first chance, and that Gabe fellow seemed like a cunning sort of bloke. He must have come across the Arab and the others just at the right moment – or wrong one, depending on your perspective – and somehow intervened. The fact that the other one wasn't with them suggested he'd been too late to save him. Which was fine by Chase. That pair had been more trouble than they were worth, especially with the next delivery being so close.

He knew it had been a bad idea to involve the families. What was it they said in show business? Never work with children and animals. Well, in the people-smuggling game you could say the same about women and kids, so far as Chase was concerned. Too much emotion involved. If he had his way they'd only be dealing with single men, men who only wanted to get out of whatever shithole country they came from and work to send money home.

But no, the powers that be decided more profit could be made by offering to bring the wife and kids over too – the perfect fucking family holiday.

Chase had been on enough shitty family holidays years ago to know travelling with little snot-nosed shits such as he had once been was far from perfect. No wonder his old man had gotten blind drunk most the time. And just like back then, he was dealing with the fallout, only now he wasn't a skinny prepubescent teen standing between his mother and his father's drunken fists, although his head currently rang as though he had. Chase rubbed it ruefully. First thing he was going to do was pistol-whip that smart-arse little prick, see how he liked it. *See who bowled fuckin' who, hey?*

But then what? The refugee and that kid were easy enough. Down the hole with the both of them; no one would notice the refugee, and a missing blackfella might raise a bit of an alarm, but not one that would be paid much attention to by the authorities. Gabe might be more problematic. He might have to make that one look like an accident. Maybe an unfortunate poisoning by strychnine? That could be feasible; Chase had no doubt there would be plenty of the poison in the dogger's ute somewhere. That left the nurse, and she was going to be the sticking point. A missing blackfella in the outback might not cause too much concern, but a pretty young white girl absent in an Aboriginal town? He could almost see the stream of news vans traipsing out to cover the story already. It'd make national news for sure. He'd have to come up with something special for her, and the beginnings of a plan started to form in his mind, eliciting a slight smile. *Yes, that could work.*

His planning was cut short when he realised the dust was thinning with no sign of any vehicle up ahead. Shit, they had turned off somewhere and he'd been too busy plotting to notice. Chase spun the ute around and drove back the way he'd just come, slower this time, completely focused on the verges on either side of the road. After about a kilometre he saw it, a narrow-gutted track that was no more than two bare strips of dirt heading north, with a fresh set of tread marks turning up them.

Chase grinned to himself. 'Almost lost me. But you didn't.'

He pushed on, bouncing his vehicle over the dry washes and occasional ant hill as he weaved his way through the scrub. It was a winding little track, and the ground was very hard in places. He lost Gabe's wheel marks twice, but picked them up again moments later. The track wasn't really that well defined, and it would be easy enough to veer off the path, but Chase had spent years driving down similar tracks at night plying his trade, and his eyes saw the way as clearly as if it were marked with cat's eyes and a white line painted down the middle.

A shimmer of dust far ahead caught his attention and he strained to see it clearer. *Gotta be them,* he thought, and he accelerated marginally, still being cautious not to strike a sharp rock or broken-off mulga stump. There was a flicker of something strung low across the road, and he had just enough time to wonder why the golden orb spiders were out so early, only to realise if it were a web Gabe's ute would've already passed through and destroyed it, before he drove straight over the top.

An explosion came from the passenger side and his ute lurched to the left. Chase skidded to a halt.

'What the fuck?' He climbed out to inspect, cursing again when he saw the damage. His left front tyre sported a thumb-sized hole in the sidewall and was flat as a tack. *What the hell caused that?*

Chase walked past his ute and spied the contraption staked into the dirt, partially obscured by the shrub. 'Oh well done, dogger,' he muttered as he studied the modified rabbit trap. 'Very clever. Deadly bit of gear, that. Don't reckon that one is on the list of approved dogging methods.'

Despite everything, Chase was impressed. 'You're one to watch, for sure.' He pulled the trap out of the ground and followed the line to the other side, removing that stake as well. As he did so, he saw something else. In the coarse dirt on the track's edge two sets of shoe prints headed into the scrub, one large, one small with a fine tread.

'Gone back to town,' Chase muttered, crouching down for a closer look. 'The nurse, and . . .' he thought about it, 'the black-fella.' He rose, walking around the site further. 'Stopped here to drop them off and leave that little surprise for me. But why?'

He stared up the track, wiping sweat from his brow. With the way the main road curved, and then the little detour down here, Chase guessed they would only be ten, maybe twelve kilo-metres from town as the crow flies, and he was in no doubt that black kid knew exactly which way the crow flew. *But again, why go back?* He thought some more as he prepared to change the shot-out tyre. It was fortunate the bullet had only hit the rubber. From the look of the hole, they'd used a heavy slug shot. If that had hit a brake caliper he might have been in some real trouble.

It finally came to him as he was working the jack. The nurse had gone back for the same reason he hadn't been sure what to do with her – to avoid raising suspicion. The other one had gone with her to show the way. Chase worked quickly as he began to plan his movements from here. He would turn back and wait for them at Jakob's River, maybe even park up on the town edge. He'd hear them coming for certain, and nab them before they even reached the community. And that would make his plan for getting rid of them all that much easier.

TWENTY-TWO

In the heat of the midmorning sun, Courtney ran.

She ran as fast as she dared. Not so fast that she would be winded before they arrived, but enough to keep up with Darren, who despite his sore arm was moving steadily. He kept looking back, perhaps expecting her to fall behind, but she hadn't been entirely honest in her assessment of her running skills, because although it was true she couldn't run very fast, she could run for a reasonable amount of time, having regularly made a morning jog part of her fitness routine. After all, as a nurse you couldn't very well preach the benefits of a healthy lifestyle if you didn't live up to them yourself, right? Plus, the sunrises out here were so beautiful, and being the coolest part of the day, it was the perfect time for a run. Night was still too hot for such activities in the seemingly endless summer they were going through.

Ahead of her, Darren held up a hand. 'Wait up, I hear something.'

They stopped, both breathing hard. Courtney took a sip from her bottle and realised she could hear the rattle of a vehicle from behind them.

'Reckon he's found the track,' Darren said. 'Hope whatever Gabe was doing slows him down. You okay?'

'I'm fine,' Courtney said. 'Let's keep moving.'

They set off again and didn't get very far when a shot rang out, followed by the grinding crunch of skidding tyres.

'Sounds like Gabe's plan worked,' Courtney said, between breaths.

'Yep. He's a tricky old bugger alright.'

Another twenty minutes of steady jogging passed. They didn't hear any more noise, and it occurred to Courtney that Chase might have found their trail and was following them on foot. She kept throwing glances over her shoulder, but the low wattles and sparse mulga didn't allow for a very long line of sight. Ahead was the same, and she hoped Darren knew where he was going.

'Pull up for a minute,' Darren said, stopping under shady mulga. Courtney did so, casting another look back as they both listened.

'You think he's following us?'

'Nah, don't reckon so,' Darren said, opening his bottle and taking a mouthful of water. 'Reckon he wants that other fella more. Gabe's mate.'

'Amin?'

'Yeah, him.'

'He said he came on a boat. Do you think he *is* a refugee?'

'Dunno.' Darren recapped his drink. 'What's a bloody boat person doing way out here? Maybe he's making it up. Maybe he's got some other reason he's running with Gabe.'

'Like what?'

Darren stared at his feet, then the sky, and finally at his fingernails. 'We better keep moving. Or the doc might be wondering where you are.'

Before Courtney could question him any further, Darren set

off at a steady jog. She followed, shaking her head and wondering just what the hell was going on.

It took another hour before they reached the town's edge, and they were both breathing heavily. Courtney was glad there was no further to run. Morning jogs or not, this had knocked the stuffing out of her, and it was only the thought of Chase trudging along behind them, gun in hand, that kept her going.

Darren looked just as blown. 'I haven't run like that since playing footy in Gero,' he gasped, hands on his knees.

'How's your wrist?'

'I'll be fine.' He grinned at her. 'I only came in to stop Aunty nagging at me, or I wouldn't have bothered you.'

'Glad you did,' Courtney said. 'Things might have been a lot worse if you weren't there.'

'Yeah, that was all a bit crazy. You okay?'

'I think so,' Courtney said. 'I don't think it's really hit me yet. Feels sort of like a dream, you know? It all happened so fast; one minute I'm treating you guys, the next we're sprinting outside and into that dogger's ute and that crazy man with a gun is after us. How about you?'

'Same, I guess.'

They were walking along Main Street and she could feel heat radiating up from the black bitumen. Yep, they sure didn't want to be running for much longer. Courtney had emptied her water bottle half an hour earlier, and the first thing she was going to do was shower and change. Her quarters were attached to the back of the medical centre, but she would check in first, make sure no one was waiting for her there. She was sure she could explain away her flushed face and sweat-soaked scrubs using her city constitution as an excuse. She'd already heard more than one passing comment about her ability to cope with the outback extremes. Well, today she'd coped just fine, thank you very much – crazed gunman, desperate boat people and all.

Ahead, parked by the Cultural Centre, was a blue and white troop carrier that could only be the police. She tugged at Darren's arm. 'Is that who you're looking for?'

'Reckon so,' Darren said. 'Don't see many other coppers out here other than the sarge.' He pulled Gabe's card from his pocket, checked it, and then stowed it again. 'I hope we're right about this. That boat fella didn't seem real sure.'

'He's probably been through hell,' Courtney said. 'I think he's supposed to be dead, and it sounds like once he is, he's got a family who's going to be just as dead. I don't know if I'd trust anyone either. Who knows what he's gone through back home. Was it Afghanistan he said? I don't follow the news much, but I've heard that place is dangerous.'

'Bloody dangerous here too lately.' Darren veered towards the troopy, then stopped. 'Shit. I bet they're in there talking to Elsie about . . .' He trailed off. 'About stuff.'

'About the grog coming in?'

'Grog?' The innocence on Darren's face was almost comical.

'Oh, come on, Darren. I know you didn't hurt yourself playing football or something.'

'Don't know what you're on about.' He pointed towards the Centre. 'But I might just wait outside there for the coppers to finish. Elsie, she's not real happy with me right now. Not real happy with anyone,' he added.

'Because they won't say who is bringing the grog in, I suspect. Do you know?' She studied him. 'You *do* know. It's all over your face.'

'I gotta go. You better go too, clean up that clinic in case someone comes in. I'll catch up with you later.'

Courtney said nothing, watching Darren cross the road and take a seat by the glass-doored entrance of the Centre. She was certain he knew who had brought the grog in, but supposed if he turned informant he might not be very popular with some of his friends. He would be very popular with the community Elders, she was sure of that. *But that's not quite the same thing, is it?*

On one hand she was annoyed about the grog, having heard past accounts of the troubles it caused, troubles that made Darren's sprained wrist seem a trifle. But she could sort of understand his reluctance. Courtney wasn't what she considered to be a big drinker – most drinkers probably thought that, she supposed – enjoying the occasional glass of wine after work in the city, and she had woken up with quite the hangover more than once during her uni days. There had been some small disappointment when she was informed this posting was to be in a dry community, and the rules applied to everyone, but it had been okay so far. Actually, it got her started on this current health kick, and hadn't all that jogging paid off in spades today?

She reached the medical centre and trotted up the stairs, preparing an excuse for her absence should there be someone impatiently waiting. She didn't really expect there to be. No appointments were booked, and except for a brief busy period yesterday thanks largely to the grog Darren didn't want to talk about, it was generally pretty quiet. And even the busy period wasn't really that bad. She'd done a stint in the Emergency Department of Royal Perth Hospital prior to coming out here. Now *that* had been busy, mostly due to drunken idiots finding new ways to hurt themselves and others. And yet anyone could buy a drink from any venue they liked down there. *Go figure.*

The wave of cool, crisp and oh-so-sweet air-conditioned air hit her as she entered. There was no one in the waiting room, and she was surprised to see the area was actually quite tidy. No sign of the earlier carrying on at all. The extinguisher was hanging in its proper place on the wall, and the table she had heard Darren tip over on his way out was upright with the magazines tossed on the top. *Had someone cleaned it up?* She thought further. Maybe it was Chase. It would make sense for him to cover his tracks, otherwise someone might raise an alarm if they came in and saw she was missing and the place looked like a bomb had hit it.

The answering machine's blinking light caught her attention. She played the message, just in case it was an emergency. Sweaty scrubs or not, she would go if needed.

'Hello, Courtney. I'm very sorry but I've been delayed in Geraldton and looks like I won't get out there today. We had no appointments booked so far as I know, so I will see you next week. If anyone is waiting please pass on my apologies and give them an appointment for next time.'

Courtney sighed at the doctor's message. Typical, really, but in today's case it meant one less thing to worry about. She headed for the consultation room to check everything was tidy in there. Then she would go for that shower, wash away the sweat and the dust, and try to make some sort of sense of this crazy day. Things always seemed a little clearer after a good wash. She was so busy thinking about her planned shower that she almost ran into the figure emerging through the doorway.

Chase Fowler gave her a murderous grin. 'Hello, love,' he said.

TWENTY-THREE

Sitting with his back to the rammed earth wall of Jakob's River Cultural Centre, Darren was just about to go and find a drink of water when the door opened. A pair of navy-blue trousers that could only belong to a police officer strode past. It was the young constable, and Darren debated staying quiet, but he needed to find Parker. He scrambled to his feet.

The officer turned and Darren's eagerness tempered. 'Uh, hey. Is the sarge around?'

Darren felt the constable's eyes glance up and down over him, taking in his dusty jeans and sweat-soaked T-shirt. If this were the city, he'd be politely asked to move on for loitering, and if he refused, not so politely. Darren knew from firsthand experience.

'Can I help you, sir?'

'Looking for the sarge. Got some information for him.'

'He's inside conducting interviews regarding some disturbances the other night. Is your information about the grog running, by any chance?'

Darren shook his head. 'Nah, don't know anything about that. But it's important.'

The officer scratched the side of his face, chasing away the flies that had decided to take up residence under his sunglasses. 'What's your name, sir? Perhaps I can help.'

Darren studied the young man, who didn't appear much older than he was. Sweat beaded under the rim of his police cap, and his cheeks were red and flushed. Could he trust this newbie with what had just happened? This new guy would want to go by the book for sure. They always did, their eyes lighting up at the prospect of filling a monthly quota of fines in a single weekend just by glancing at the old station vehicles driving around the place. Eventually they calmed down, usually after their superior pointed out it's pretty hard policing an outback town when everyone has you pegged as the overzealous wanker with a ticket book. Probably better to find Parker.

Perhaps sensing his uncertainty, the constable shrugged. 'Or you could go inside and wait. He's talking to Elsie. I just came out to grab another notepad.'

The idea of being in the same room as Elsie did not appeal to Darren at all. He knew if he went in there she might ask him something about the grog, and while he had bent the truth for the nice young nurse, the less he said to Elsie, the better.

'Name's Darren.'

The officer stuck out a hand. 'Constable Matthew Jefferson. Good to meet you. Nice little town you got here.'

Darren took the offered hand, deciding that while this fella would probably be all set to call it in, he would also want to tell Parker first.

'You're not going to believe this,' Darren started.

'Try me,' Jefferson said, giving him a warm smile, and he pointed to where a park bench sat under a flooded gum in front of the Centre. 'Over there?'

Darren nodded. Jefferson first retrieved a notepad from the police troopy, checked his phone, and then returned.

'So, what's up?'

Darren gave the officer a quick rundown of the morning's events, starting with how he had been taking a leak in the medical centre's toilets when he heard the muffled conversation coming through the transportable building's thin wall and just knew something wasn't right. How he had crept into the waiting room and spied a lanky stranger standing in the doorway with his back to Darren, saying something about bodies in holes, and so he had taken it upon himself to nut the fucker right on his head with the fire extinguisher there and then. He relayed their hurried escape in Gabe's ute, finally finishing up with his and Courtney's run back into town.

'So I reckon he's still out there, after old Gabe and that Amin fella.' Darren was getting worked up now. Telling the story, saying it out loud suddenly brought home to him this was in fact real. Not some half-dazed daydream. He'd thumped a bloke carrying a gun, and then lobbed the extinguisher at him like he was knocking down pins at the Geraldton bowling alley, some-thing he'd only done once before during a school camp. It had never occurred to him in any real sort of sense that it would not have taken much for Chase to raise that gun and fire it in his general direction. Not then, anyway. It did now, and the thought made him go cold.

'Holy shit,' he said, shaking his head. 'He had a bloody gun, and I whacked him anyway.'

Constable Jefferson eyed him with a slightly bemused expres-sion on his face, the way one might look at a five-year-old who was telling you in no uncertain terms that the bogeyman was indeed living under his bed, and if you were to turn the lights out that would be the end. He had stopped taking notes very early on, but Darren hadn't noticed until now.

'Hey, don't you want to write this down?'

Jefferson gave him a friendly smile. 'Oh, I don't think that's necessary. Quite the story you've got there.' He leaned forward and gave an almost inaudible sniff. Darren recoiled, knowing exactly what it was. It had happened to him before, and was just as unwarranted then as it was now.

'You think I'm drunk? Think I'm making this shit up?'

'Not at all,' Jefferson said, raising a hand in placation. 'But now that you bring it up, when did you last have a drink?'

'Can't drink here, officer. Dry community.'

'Dryish,' Jefferson said. 'That's why we're here.'

'Yeah, well, not me. I'm not making this up. That roo-shooter bloke is after that dogger bloke, and you're standing here not looking too worried about any of it.' He fished out Gabe's card from his pocket and handed it to Jefferson. 'He said ring him on his sat-phone number.'

'It's a lot to take in,' said the officer, pocketing his notebook and, after a cursory glance, the card. 'Boat people, here? We're miles from the coast, and anyway, the boys in Border Patrol would pick them up before they swung past Christmas Island.'

'Not this one they didn't, and if I followed his story right, he's got family stuck somewhere, and if that Chase fellow does what he's planning, they're cactus too.'

'Perhaps I should call it in then.'

Darren's eyes went wide. 'Shit, no, you can't. He reckons some of your boys are in on it. Part of the . . . the . . .'

'Syndicate?'

'Yeah, I guess. Syndicate. That's how they know to dodge the boat police and shit. He wasn't really happy about me coming back to get you guys, but me and Gabe reckon the sarge is alright.'

Jefferson raised an eyebrow. 'Oh yeah. Parker's a good guy. Straight as, no doubt there.'

Darren scuffed the dirt. 'Look, this shit is real. Go and ask that nurse, Courtney. She'll back up everything I just told you.'

'Has she told anyone?'

'Doubt it. She came back so no one would miss her, and we agreed to tell Parker only.'

'But you told me instead.' There was a wry grin on the young officer's face.

'Yeah, well, figured you were alright too, you know, because . . .'

'Because I'm too new to be bent?'

Darren shrugged. 'Pretty much.'

The constable surprised Darren by laughing. 'You're right there, Darren. Thought I was ready for the outback, but never quite realised just how big and hot the place was. I mean, you see it on TV, but it's not the same, is it?'

'Guess not. Hey, so you gonna tell Parker or not, cause if you're not, I'll go and tell him myself.'

Jefferson shook his head. 'Oh, no need to bother him just yet – he's pretty busy in there at the moment. That Elsie is fired up.' He stared at Darren. 'I'd hate to be anyone caught up in this whole grog-running business.'

Darren looked at his shoes briefly before the officer's voice brought his gaze back up.

'I'd like to go over your story with this nurse Courtney. Get all the facts down. Then I can take it to Sergeant Parker, and he can decide where to go from there. If what you say about corruption is true, then this is a pretty big deal, even without the idea of illegal immigrants making it to the mainland. And that in itself puts the whole offshore detention thing in jeopardy.'

Now this was more like what Darren had been hoping for. He stood, heading towards the medical centre. 'She's over there, in the clinic. Reckon she'd be having a shower or something. She was pretty hot and sweaty. I'm impressed she made it back without me having to carry her.'

'Sounds like quite the girl,' Jefferson said, rising to follow.

'Yeah, she didn't lose her shit at all. Reckon most girls might have screamed, or fainted maybe.'

'Maybe so. I'll be interested to hear what she has to say, and then we can deal with this roo-shooter fellow.'

Darren nodded, pleased this policeman seemed to be finally taking him seriously. With any luck, he and the nurse could wash their hands of the whole thing, and get back to life in little old Jakob's River.

TWENTY-FOUR

Courtney Drage's entire world shrank down and focused onto a single point – that point being the muzzle of Chase's pistol. It wasn't an overly big gun, she knew that, and yet right now it looked like a friggin' bazooka.

'Where's your mate, the blackfella?' Chase asked.

She took a moment to answer. She knew very well where he was, but decided to play dumb. 'I don't know. I came in here to get cleaned up. What do you want with me?'

'Just a few words, that's all.' Chase grinned. Under different circumstances it would've been quite the friendly grin, the grin she might expect before he offered to buy her a drink at a bar, except the closest thing to that here was a coffee from the store, and wouldn't that get Melissa going?

Oh, for God's sake, girl, she thought, *he's got a gun and you're worried about small-town gossip?*

'Take a seat over there.' He pointed to the chair between the beds. She did as he instructed, not taking her eyes off that gun.

'I don't know anything.'

'Maybe, maybe not.' He sat on the edge of the closest bed, the one Amin had been lying on earlier that morning. It felt like an age ago. She had thought today was going to be an interesting one when Darren arrived, what with Elsie on the warpath, but that had turned out to be the understatement of the century.

'You seem like a smart girl,' Chase started. 'So why don't you do the smart thing and tell me what you do know.'

'Okay,' Courtney said slowly, while her mind raced. If Darren did manage to tell this Sergeant Parker guy everything, wouldn't there be a good chance he'd want to come and see her too, to get her version of the story? And if so, maybe they'd be on their way over right now. She had to keep Chase here, keep him occupied until that happened. Because like he said, she *was* a smart girl. She knew there was no way he would just accept her story, give his thanks and then waltz on out of here, leaving her behind. Well, she had always been told she could talk the leg off a wooden chair. Time to put it to good use.

'I think that Amin is a refugee, one of those boat people you see on the news, only instead of being picked up by Customs or the Navy or Search and Rescue and shipped off to Manus, he made it here, and I think you had something to do with that. Why else would you be after him? He seems like an okay kind of guy, doesn't say much, but I suppose that's understandable, seeing as he was coming down with an infection. He had a pretty deep scratch on his arm, said he'd fallen onto a sharp stick, but now I'm not so sure. Anyway, he'll be fine, because I gave him some antibiotics. Not prescription, because I can't do that, not yet anyway. I will be able to after a couple more years of practical work, though. But I had them ready for Dr Woolford, the doctor from Geraldton. He was supposed to come out today, but cancelled. Probably lucky for him, hey? Anyway, I grabbed the antibiotics when we ran away from you earlier. Amin said his injury was from a tree branch he fell onto, but now I think maybe there was some sort of fight.

That's how Gabe must have found him. He's a funny old man, doesn't say much either. Surprised he didn't just drive on past but—'

'Christ's sake, woman, would you stop yabbering on?' Chase shook his head in disbelief. 'Jesus, I never heard someone blather so much.'

Courtney gave him a sweet smile. 'You asked what I knew. I'm telling you.'

'I asked for what you knew, not your fucking life story. So where were they headed?'

'I don't know.' She glanced away as she spoke, and Chase pounced.

'Yeah, you do. I can tell. Don't lie to me, little missy, or you might just see a side of me you don't like.'

'Haven't seen one I like yet, either.' The retort was out of her mouth before she could stop it, and for an instant she thought he might slap her. If he was okay with holding a gun on her, then he was most likely the slapping type.

Instead, Chase's face wore a grin. 'I'll give you that one, but don't think I won't teach you some manners next time round. Now, where were they headed, and where's your mate?'

As if on cue, the door buzzer sounded. 'Anyone home?'

Chase pointed to Courtney, then the doorway, and indicated she should call him in. She shook her head, and his eyes narrowed as he looked at his gun then at her. His eyebrows raised. *Really?* She relented.

'In here, Darren.'

Her heart sank as she watched the young man enter alone, then leaped up again as she glimpsed the familiar blue of a police officer's uniform, only to sink once more as she spied the skinny officer who looked barely out of high school.

Here we go again, she thought, getting ready to dive for the floor before someone started shooting. She figured Darren had filled in this new recruit – obviously the older, more experienced sergeant wasn't available – and he'd brought him in to get her side of the story. Perfectly reasonable, because as far as stories went, this one was quite the tale. But in doing so, the young constable was about to be mowed down as he saw Chase, realised that Darren was in fact telling the truth, and reached for his gun.

'Shit, that's him!' Darren pointed to Chase, who was staring at the both of them with stunned surprise. 'That's the fucker I belted!' His eyes darted around, perhaps seeking another fire extinguisher to lob, but it was too far away.

To Courtney's amazement, Chase dropped his gun on the bed and raised his hands. 'Don't shoot. You got me, fair and square. I give up.'

The officer moved closer, and she saw that his hand rested on the butt of his service pistol. Darren darted to her, and she was touched by the concern on his face. 'You okay? He didn't hurt you, did he?'

'No, just asked some questions. You found a policeman then?'

Darren never answered. His eyes suddenly bulged and he went entirely rigid as a strangled moan came from his clenched mouth. Courtney could hear a strange, sharp buzz, almost like the sound a particularly large moth would make when it flew into the bug zapper mounted in her kitchen.

He collapsed in front of her. Actually, he didn't collapse – that would involve bending the knees. He toppled, like a sapling going down under the weight of a bulldozer's blade, and hit the ground with a sickening thud, both hands balled into fists so tight the tops of his knuckles shone. Behind him stood the constable, arms outstretched, gripping his freshly deployed taser, its two fine wires leading straight to the back of Darren's shirt.

Courtney shot to her feet, but her scream was cut off in an instant by Chase's hand reaching around and covering her mouth. His other hand gripped an arm and forced it behind her back. 'Quiet, love, remember?' Still holding her, he gave Darren a vicious kick in the side. 'That's for my head.'

Darren grunted in pain – extra pain, to be more accurate – but barely moved. Courtney had seen enough taser victims in the ER to know he might have trouble moving very well in the near future. If they got that far, she thought, staring at the approaching police officer. No wonder Gabe and Darren had given absolutely no credit to the idea this kid was in on Amin's troubles. If Courtney had still been working her part-time job pulling beers in Perth, she would've sent him home to his mother.

'What happened?' Jefferson asked, looking around.

'Wheldon sent me to suss things out when the boys never returned.'

'I got the message. They escaped? How? The whole point of that hole is no one's around and there's nowhere to go.'

'Only one did, I think. Had some help, too. There was an old dogger – reckon he was working in the area and heard the racket,' Chase said. 'If he hadn't stuck his nose in, no one'd be any the wiser.' He nudged Darren with his toe. 'Like this little shit, or our nurse friend here.'

'Stuck our noses in?' Courtney couldn't hide her indignation. 'You came into my clinic and started waving that gun around.'

'Ah, well,' Chase said, 'can't help bad luck, can we, Jefferson?'

The officer swore. 'You were supposed to take care of it.'

'I was about to, but they bolted on me, then the bastard set a friggin' booby trap and took out my front wheel. So I came back here to tie up loose ends first. Reckon I'll have to get rid of these two now, then track the other pair down again. Done it once, can do it twice.'

Chase's words sent a cold bolt of dread into Courtney's belly. *Get rid of them.* But surely they couldn't do that. If she went missing, alarms would be raised. That was the whole point of her coming back in the first place. If she'd even suspected Chase would be waiting for her, she'd have stayed cramped up on the back seat of Gabe's ute and trundled off to wherever it was those two were going.

'Right,' Jefferson said. 'I haven't got much time, I'm supposed to be meeting our man tomorrow morning. We weren't due back here until next week, but that grog brought us out early.' The constable unclipped the spent taser cartridge, shoved a new one in and reholstered the weapon. 'And Parker will be wondering where I am.'

'Think you can get back to Carnarvon?'

'Possibly. Parker's keen to follow things up here, but there's not much to go on. Everyone's staying quiet. No actual offences were reported, so maybe.'

'See how you go, and if you can't, you can't. Don't push it too hard with Parker – he's not stupid. You carry on as planned, and I'll track down those other two.'

'Maybe you won't have to track them.' Jefferson pulled a card out from his pocket and opened his phone, dialling the number as he spoke. 'I'm about to bring them to you.'

TWENTY-FIVE

Gabe pulled over on the crest of a hill and opened his door.

'What's wrong?' Amin asked as he climbed out.

'Nothing, I hope. Just want to see if we're still being followed.'

It was just after midday and the sun beat down with relentless force, sending shimmers across the horizon and sweat into Gabe's eyes. The elevated position gave him a good view of the landscape, and to the south he could see the sparkle of tin roofs on the buildings that made up Jakob's River.

The track they had been following was not so easy to see, weaving in and out of the low mulgas and gums, around fallen curaras and the rocky piles of granite and ironstone. The air was crisp and still, save for a lone eagle soaring on the thermals above them, and the ever-present bush flies. There was no sign of any vehicle other than his own.

Reaching behind the driver's seat, Gabe grabbed his binoculars and trained them on the area where he thought Chase should have hit his trip-wire. Again, he couldn't see him, but he might be looking in the wrong place, or his view was obscured by the vegetation. Either way, there was no tell-tale cloud of fine red dust that signalled Chase still trailed them. So where did he go? Did he miss the turn-off and keep driving? Perhaps he figured they'd be looking for Amin's family so decided to carry on ahead and lie in wait. Or he'd followed them down the side track, hit the trip-wire and was busy repairing his wheel. But Gabe was certain if that were the case he'd be able to see him, even just the top of his ute. They weren't that far ahead, were they?

Another thought hit him, one that he really didn't like. What if Chase had seen where Courtney and Darren took off into the scrub? Gabe kicked himself for not taking the time to cover those tracks, but then time wasn't really something they had much of, was it?

He heard a door open and Amin joined him. Gabe had his smokes out by now and rolled one for each of them.

'Do you see him?'

Gabe shook his head and passed the binoculars to Amin. 'No. You have a look. My eyes are getting old.'

As Amin scanned the landscape below them, Gabe pondered his earlier thought. Would Chase follow those two back? It would make sense to get rid of any witnesses, though how would he do that without raising suspicions?

Amin handed him back the binoculars. 'I do not see him either. I think he has gone elsewhere.'

'That's what worries me. What if he's gone back after those two kids?'

'Would they not be safer in the town? With this policeman you are so sure is not corrupt?'

Gabe ran a hand over the harsh stubble on his chin. 'You'd hope so, but that Chase fella is a cunning one, I reckon. Found us, didn't he?'

Amin didn't respond. Gabe knew he was agonising over what to do. If it weren't for Darren, they could very well be in much deeper trouble than they already were, but to go back meant delaying the search for his family yet again.

Amin sighed, dropped his finished cigarette and ground it out with his boot. 'I think it is certain we are not being followed anymore, so if you can bear with me for five minutes, I must say my prayers.'

Gabe shrugged. 'Suit yourself. I'll get some lunch organised. How's your arm feeling?' Amin had already taken two antibiotic pills, along with a couple more Panadols from Gabe's well-stocked first aid kit. Morning headaches were nothing new to Gabe, so he always carried a good supply of the cure, as well as the cause.

'Better, thank you. I shall not be long, and then we will be on our way again, though I am torn as to which direction to take.'

'Perhaps you could ask your God for advice?' It was a jibe, but a friendly one.

'Perhaps,' Amin said, as he began to wash from the water tank below the tray. 'Would you like to join me and ask Him yourself?'

Gabe scoffed, but didn't reply. He'd stopped asking God for favours just over four years ago.

When Amin returned, Gabe handed him a roughly made cheese sandwich. 'Hope you're not one of those dairy-free, gluten-free types,' he said. 'Or you're gonna bloody starve. So, what did you decide?'

Amin accepted the sandwich but took a moment to answer, and when he did, it was in a slow, cautious tone. 'I would like to press on. I worry for my wife and child.'

'I can understand that,' Gabe said. 'If it makes you feel any better, I think they'll be okay as long as you're wandering around out here. Without them, you've got no incentive to keep your mouth shut, right? We keep you out of that Chase guy's hands, they won't touch them.'

'What you say makes sense, but what about our friends?'

'Once they find the sarge they'll be okay. He was due out there around the time we left, so he's probably arrived already, and Chase isn't going to do anything in public, if he did go back there. Darren seems like a smart kid – he'll give the sarge my card and we can explain everything and make sure Parker knows it needs to be kept quiet.'

'Do you think he will?'

'Honestly, I've no idea. But this is getting too big for you and me alone, and now with Courtney and Darren involved . . .' He trailed off, again looking back down the track expecting to see a cloud of dust as Chase tore up to catch them. There was none.

Another sigh from Amin. 'I agree, though you will have to forgive my mistrust of the police. My home has a very large problem with corruption, and I was not surprised to learn it was happening here also.'

'Don't blame you for being jumpy. Come on, let's keep moving.'

Gabe had just started the engine and was about to get rolling when an unfamiliar ringing filled the cab. For a moment he had no idea what it was, and then realised. The sat-phone. He rarely used it, if ever, as the charges were too exorbitant for anything except the most urgent of calls, and were it not for being a safety requirement of Parks and Wildlife, he wouldn't bother with the bloody thing. He'd gone a lifetime in the bush without one, and as this thought went through his mind, another immediately followed: *Would've been handy that one time, though, wouldn't it?* He shoved the thought away.

Taking a deep breath, Gabe removed the handset from its cradle and glanced at the screen. The number calling was marked as private, which he supposed was fair enough for a police phone.

He had no doubt it was the police. That phone hadn't rung since he'd bought the thing.

'Looks like the kid came through,' Gabe said, and answered the phone tentatively. *No going back now.* 'Hello?'

There was the usual delay that came with satellite phones as the signal bounced about the atmosphere. 'Hello, Mr Ahern? This is Constable Matthew Jefferson. We met on the road a couple of days back.'

Gabe remembered the young man, out of place and keen to impress, but why was he calling? Darren was supposed to speak to the sarge, and no one else.

'Yeah I remember. What can I do for you?'

'I've been talking with a Mr Darren Anderson. He's got quite the tale.'

'Is that so?' Gabe was feeling just a little suspicious. *Where was Parker?*

As if reading his mind, the constable went on, 'Sergeant Parker is interviewing Darren and also the young nurse, Miss . . .' A pause, as if he were checking notes. Gabe supposed he was, recalling the little notebook in his pocket. 'Miss Courtney Drage. He asked me to make contact and arrange a meeting. If what Darren and Miss Drage are saying is true, these are some very serious allegations.'

'Bloody serious,' Gabe agreed. 'That's why we weren't real keen on getting the coppers involved.'

'It was a good thing you did. We also have your pursuer in custody. He had come back and was waiting for Miss Drage in the medical centre.'

Gabe paled, held his hand over the phone and relayed this to Amin, who looked to the roof. '*Alhamdulillah,*' he whispered.

'Can you give me a brief rundown on what happened?'

'Pretty simple. Came across two men trying to shoot another, and stopped them. They'd already shot someone, damn near shot me, and winged Amin. That's why we went back to town.'

'And where did this happen?'

'Near a large granite breakaway on the Reserve, couple of hours north-east of you.'

'We'll need to inspect the scene. Perhaps you could meet us there?'

'I think so. Or we could come back to town first.'

'No, I don't think that is necessary. We'll finish up here and head out.'

Gabe saw the concern in his companion's eyes. 'You understand Amin's very worried about some in your mob being involved, right? You two will keep this to yourselves until you've got a handle on things?'

'Absolutely. I'll be honest with you, Mr Ahern, there've been rumblings within the Force that something is going on up here. Just whispers, but people have been turning up in Perth without any explanation. They haven't come in by plane or overstayed their tourist visas. They've just appeared, and it's got the Customs boys stumped. I think you might have stumbled upon something big, and, until we know more, the sarge wants to keep it under wraps too. Neither of us like the idea that someone has turned, but from what Darren and Courtney have said, it makes a lot of sense.'

Gabe began to feel a little better. 'Alright. We'll meet you there. I've got some GPS coordinates for you. Give us a second to pull them up.' He fished out the unit from the overhead console and began to retrieve the data. As he did so, Jefferson kept talking.

'Very smart to get the location,' he said. Was there a slight change in his tone? Gabe thought there might have been, but couldn't be sure. He finally pulled up the position. It wasn't the exact site of the granite ridge, he hadn't thought to mark that point, but it was the spot where his illegal trap lay buried in the creek bank. He moved the cursor to about where he thought was the correct place and pressed the button. It displayed the coordinates and he relayed these to Jefferson.

'Excellent,' the constable finally said. 'Our plan is to convince Mr Fowler to cooperate, make a statement and take us to the scene himself.'

'Make sure you watch that bugger, he's slippery.'

'Don't worry, Mr Ahern, we will. We will see you out there in a couple of hours. Good luck and stay safe. We don't know if there are any others looking for your friend.'

Gabe ended the call and told Amin what had transpired. 'We were lucky,' Gabe said. 'If Chase had found those kids before they spoke to the cops, I reckon they'd be headed for that hole right now.'

'Yes, I think you are right,' Amin said. 'I am sorry for getting them involved, and you also. I thought I could do this without the police, but I see now I might have been wrong. I think it is best we go and meet them. *Insha Allah*, they will be able to help and my family will be safe.'

'Hope so too.' Gabe also hoped they wouldn't frown upon the dumping of the bodies. It could certainly be argued they had killed in self-defence, but hiding evidence? Could they argue that? Gabe *thought* they could. They were panicked, afraid others would follow. Maybe that would work. It was certainly the truth. Gabe decided that no matter how it went, it was better than their current situation of not knowing who to trust and when Chase would turn up next. At least he was in custody.

He was about to set off when the phone rang again. It was Jefferson. 'Just thought you'd like to know, Chase has agreed to lead us to the crime scene. Parker will ride with him in his vehicle, and I'll follow in ours with Mr Anderson and Miss Drage. They don't need to be there, but Parker doesn't want them out of his sight.'

'Makes sense,' Gabe said. At least they were taking this seriously. He would worry about the finer details later, but for now he was just glad he would be able to wash his hands of the whole thing in the very near future.

TWENTY-SIX

Darren stirred at Courtney's feet and sat himself up with some difficulty.

'Fuckin' pig,' he said, sounding a little dazed. Courtney let out a muffled cry as he received another kick from Chase, who still had his hand across her mouth.

'Right, you follow all that?' said Jefferson, pocketing his phone. 'Take them out through the nurse's quarters and get going before anyone sees. I've got to get back to Parker and work out some way to ditch him.'

Chase whispered in Courtney's ear, 'I'm going to let you go now, and you're going to help your mate there. No noise. No trying anything stupid, okay?'

She nodded, and he released her. She immediately knelt by Darren and helped him to his feet, glaring at Jefferson.

'Shame on you,' she said.

The police officer ignored her. He seemed to be studying the cupboards. He opened one, rummaged around, then moved on to the next, eventually retrieving a bottle of something with a smile. She couldn't make out what it was as he dropped it into a pocket. Whatever it was, it wasn't an opiate; those were locked away.

'You'd better get going,' he said to Chase. 'I'll meet you up there tomorrow, depending on what I learn in town.'

'What about the sarge?'

'Hopefully he'll be indisposed by then, but if I can't get away, I'll let you know.'

'Righto.' Chase gave Darren and Courtney a rough shove into the reception area. 'Out the back, both of you. And not a bloody peep.'

He led them through her quarters, the two of them half carrying Darren, who was still recovering from the kicks and the taser – which was worse, she had no idea – and down to where Chase's ute was carefully parked out of sight behind the medical centre. If only they had seen it when they jogged back into town, but he'd been too clever, not taking any chances on being spotted.

'You drive,' Chase said.

'I can't drive a manual,' she replied. This was a lie, her father had been particular about her learning to do just that as a teenager, but denying it slowed down their progress to wherever they were going, so all the better.

Chase's face darkened briefly and he pointed at her little RAV4 parked under the carport attached to the side of her quarters. 'I suppose you get chauffeured around in that thing then, do you?'

Goddammit, he didn't miss a trick, did he?

'Fine,' she said. 'But I haven't driven anything as big as yours.'

He leered at her. 'Oh, mine's a big one alright,' and Courtney rolled her eyes.

Still leaning on her, Darren raised his head defiantly. 'Put that shooter down, and we'll see how big you are. Big man with a big gun. Bigger the gun, smaller the—'

He never got to finish because Darren's head snapped back as the gun barrel whipped across his mouth, mashing his lips.

Courtney swayed as she fought to support his weight, feeling his knees weaken under him.

'You bastard,' she hissed.

Darren spat out blood. 'Try that again, without the gun,' he sneered, but his voice was slurred, and with the way he rocked on his feet Courtney felt sure it had been bluster.

'Get in the ute,' Chase said. 'And no fucking about or I'll pop you both and hang you from the back like a couple of big boomers.' He pointed to the rack mounted on the rear tray, its fearsome array of sharp carcass hooks glinting in the sun. Images of bodies hanging from them flashed through her mind, and they weren't roos.

She shuddered and helped Darren up into the cab. It was all starting to sink in. Everything leading up to now had happened so fast, with no time to think. But now, driving the roo-shooter's LandCruiser, Darren barely conscious beside her and Chase threatening them both with his gun, she began to feel truly afraid.

They drove for an hour or more, turning down tracks that were less and less defined the further they went. Chase pointed out the sharp gullies and told her when to shift the ute into low range to get through the sandy creek crossing. *He really knows the area,* she thought. *We're in the middle of nowhere, yet he knows exactly where we are.* That made her wonder what in the hell Gabe was doing out here when he found Amin? Whatever it was, he had been lucky. Or unlucky, depending on your point of view. In their case, they were most unlucky. This was not how the day was supposed to go.

She glanced at Darren from time to time, his head lowered, rocking back and forth with each bump and sway. Occasionally, blood dripped from his mouth down onto his T-shirt. He really looked a sorry sight. Just as her concern for him was growing, he caught her eye and gave her the smallest of winks, out of Chase's field of view. Her heart quickened. He was putting it on, planning something, but what? What could he do?

It was just after two when Chase told her to slow down. 'Up ahead is another sand wash. We get through that, then you stop.'

'And then?' Part of her didn't want to know the answer, the other part suspected she already did.

'We wait.'

She drove through the wash, almost stalling the engine in the deep sand, but managed to power through and, at Chase's direction, pulled up alongside a mulga that threw down a smattering of shade.

'Out.'

As they exited, Chase reached back and unclipped the scoped rifle mounted high on the rear wall of the cab, then he too climbed out.

'Over there.' He pointed to the base of the granite ridge, some thirty metres in front of them. Resting at the base, a large jagged slab of granite pointed towards the sky, and at the foot of it lay the dried remains of some sort of tree.

Chase called to them as the two began to walk towards the rock. 'And don't even think about running.' She looked back to see him patting his rifle affectionately. 'I can ping a roo's head from a hundred metres with this baby, so your fat arses won't be a problem.'

She watched him over her shoulder as he walked around the idling vehicle to the driver's seat and got back in, propping his rifle on the shooter's rest bolted to the door frame. It was with some dismay that Courtney realised that even if she and Darren were brave enough to risk bolting, there was nowhere

174

to run. From his position, Chase had a good line of sight over the clearing. If they could make it past the granite outcrop, she felt sure the scrub was dense enough to cover their escape, but getting to it was the problem, especially given she had no idea how well Darren actually fared.

'You okay?' she whispered, not taking her eyes off Chase.

'Yeah,' Darren said, also whispering. 'He hits like a girl. No offence.'

'What are we going to do?'

'Dunno. But whatever we do, reckon we should do it quick.'

She shuddered. The breeze was blowing now from the west, but still hot and dry, as though she'd stepped into a giant kiln, so why had she started to feel cold? The reason called out to them from the comfort of his ute.

'Grab those branches and drag them out the way.'

'Jesus Christ, we're fucked.' Darren's face hardened as he came to a decision. 'I'm gonna run at him. You leg it for the trees.'

Courtney opened her mouth to protest, but somebody beat her to it.

'Don't be fuckin' stupid.' That voice, a gruff whisper, dried and hardened from a lifetime in the bush. 'Do as he says, but get ready.' Gabe's voice, coming from behind the granite slab. 'Don't let on I'm here. Get ready to run.'

Courtney was too stunned to reply, but Darren spoke out of the side of his mouth, half turning as though he was speaking to Courtney. 'Where to?'

'Christ, I don't know. Anywhere that's not towards him.'

Behind them Chase called, 'Hurry up, or I'll make it slow and painful.'

Darren bent to grab the first of the dead branches. 'When?'

'You'll know when. He's coming.'

She was about to ask who was coming, but never got the chance, because by then Chase had started shooting.

Later, once the dust – and her nerves – had settled, Courtney couldn't quite remember when she first heard the approaching vehicle. Was it before or after the gunshots started? She didn't know. But when that first crack sounded, she felt such a flood of combined terror and adrenaline hit her stomach that for a moment she thought she had actually been shot, or had shat herself. Thankfully, it hadn't been either. Chase was firing into the scrub, sitting square to the open window of his ute with the rifle's barrel tracing an arc as it followed whatever he was shooting at. She heard three shots, all in perfect time as the professional roo-shooter fired, worked the bolt, fired, worked the bolt, his eye never leaving the scope. Above it all she heard the roar of an engine being gunned to within an inch of its life.

Darren gave her a great shove, so hard it almost toppled her.

'Move, miss! Move!'

She moved, tearing her eyes from Chase and the glimpse of khaki paintwork and canvas flashing between branches that could only be Gabe's ute. She turned and started to run, and, from behind the boulder, out stepped the dogger, shouldering a fearsome looking rifle.

'Go!' he yelled, as he too began to fire. The roar deafened her, she was so close to the barrel, and her head rang. Noise everywhere. She heard glass shatter, the crash and crackle of dry shrubbery being crushed under tyre and bull bar. Something exploded against the granite to her left and she felt a blow on her cheek. Courtney staggered, about to fall, and Darren was there again, grabbing her under the shoulder and lifting her with such force her feet almost came off the ground. Noise enveloped her, so much noise. Something hot ran down her neck, and the world turned grey as she ran, led onwards by Darren. A tremendous crash came from behind them, yells and gunfire. Darren half pushed, half carried her, branches whipping past, tearing at her blue scrubs. *These will need a good wash,* she found herself thinking, right before she blacked out.

TWENTY-SEVEN

Chase had been using his scope to admire Courtney's butt as his two captives bent to drag away the branches that would reveal their final resting place. It was a shame he couldn't have some fun with her first, but the others wouldn't be too far away, and he didn't want to be literally caught with his pants down. *Oh well, plenty more fish in the sea.*

He expected them to bolt as soon as they saw the dumping hole. Most did. It never made much difference. At this range he didn't even need the scope, and in fact had to adjust his aim to allow for the closeness. The result was always the same – it was only the distance he had to drag the bodies that changed. Once, he'd even managed to nail one, a middle-aged Pakistani who dropped to his knees begging to be spared, right into the hole. No dragging required. But he didn't think that would happen today. These two knew what was coming. Hell, even he would attempt to flee if the roles were reversed.

He adjusted the scope's zoom, widening his view, and saw both Darren and Courtney stiffen. *Here we go,* he thought. *They're about to leg it.* His finger came to rest on the trigger, and he applied a fraction of pressure, waiting for a slight drop in the wind. Too late, he heard the oncoming vehicle.

His head whirled, and he saw the glint of a steel bull bar crashing towards him. He brought his rifle round with practised skill, lowered his eye to the scope and began to fire. *Cunning sod came up into the wind to cover his noise,* and even as he sent the first bullet through the windscreen, he couldn't help but be impressed. He worked the bolt and sent another round into the windscreen and then a third towards the radiator, but just as he fired his own windscreen exploded. Someone else was shooting at him.

He cast a look to his left and saw the dogger walking towards him, firing down an open-sighted rifle that was shooting far too quick for his liking. *Where the fuck did he come from?* Chase swung in his direction, working the bolt as he went, and sent a shot towards him, but between the ute bearing down on him and Gabe sending round after round into his cab, his aim was off. The dogger ducked, but kept advancing as the bullet went wide, ricocheting off the granite. Chase had two shots left, but didn't think he'd get to use them. He reached for his pistol with his left hand.

To his right the bull bar of the oncoming LandCruiser loomed large, and now he could see Amin behind the wheel. *Jesus fuckin' Christ, he's going to go all suicide bomber on me.*

Chase flung the ute into gear and dropped the clutch, sending his vehicle forward with a lurch. Ahead of him and darting past Gabe were Darren and Courtney. *More than one way to skin a cat,* he thought, lining all three of them up dead centre and raising the pistol, preparing to shoot through his own windscreen if needed.

For a moment, he and Gabe stared at each other, one looking down his steering wheel, the other down the barrel of his rifle. *If he's got one left in there, I'm fucked.* And then the LandCruiser hit him. The massive five-poster bull bar slammed into the rear pillar of Chase's cab. Had it struck the door, his rifle and the arm supporting it would have been crushed, but as it was the end result was bad enough. He was hurled to the left, the gear stick digging hard into his leg. His neck made a horrible cracking noise and he felt tingles run down his spine. And then his ute began to tip.

TWENTY-EIGHT

Gabe was right to trust his gut. As he and Amin drew closer to the site where he first became involved in this whole nightmare, he'd grown more and more uneasy. Something wasn't right. He didn't know what, but while the conversation with the constable had made him feel better at first, the more he thought about it, the more his reservations grew. Why bring Courtney and Darren out here? They had nothing to do with it. Wouldn't it have been better to leave them with the rookie and just have Parker and Chase come out? That was the other thing – Chase giving up, spilling his guts like that, seemed too ... convenient.

'I don't like it,' he'd finally said.

Amin had been staring out the window in deep thought. 'Neither do I, my friend.'

'It's too neat, too easy.'

'Yes.' Amin rubbed his chin. 'But what makes you say that? Why is it too easy?'

Gabe thought for a moment. 'When I set a dog trap, if I do it right, there's no sign of it. No trace, no giveaway it's there. But to get a dog to go near it, I need a lure.'

'I understand. Bait.'

'Exactly. A drop of scent or piece of dog turd in just the right spot catches his attention, he comes over to investigate and bang, got him. But if I make the bait too obvious, it becomes the opposite. A roo leg hanging from a tree, or if I use too much lure, they know something's not right. Occasionally you might get a young one, but the older, wiser dogs stay the hell away.'

Amin smiled. 'Forgive me for saying so, Gabe, but I think it has been some time since you were a young dog.'

'Don't I know it,' Gabe replied, his hand going to the dull ache in his hip.

'And you believe this lure is all too much.' Not a question.

'If it weren't for those kids being involved, I'd turn this ute around and disappear. The more I think about it, the more I'm sure Parker would've wanted to talk to me. This is a big deal, no way would he let a junior officer make the call.' He pointed his finger down the track they were following. 'Maybe I'm wrong, maybe I'm jumping at shadows, but what we're driving towards feels like the equivalent of a roast beef dinner sitting next to a dog trail with a dirty great Jake trap under it and two Bridgers on either side.'

'I don't know what any of that means, but a shadow only exists if there is something to cast it,' Amin pointed out. 'What do we do?'

And so the plan formed. Gabe would climb the ridge and wait to see who or what turned up, while Amin stayed with the LandCruiser some way back. There was no foliage dense enough to completely obscure Gabe's vehicle, but he hoped the fact that any arrivals would be focused on the immediate area around the outcrop would limit the risk of it being spotted.

'Park downwind where you can see the top of that ridge,' he instructed, grabbing the binoculars as he climbed out the vehicle. 'I raise one arm, shit's about to go down. If I don't, shit might still go down, but I'm not expecting it. Either way, stay ready.' He leaned in and retrieved his M1 from the overhead console, and pointed at his Ruger. 'You know how to use that?'

'Yes.' Amin swapped to the driver's seat and unlatched the rifle. He opened the breach, worked a round in and clicked the safety over. He also rested one of the handguns on the dash. '*Bismillah*. God be with you, my friend.'

'Hopefully we won't need Him,' Gabe said, and set off up the rocky slope.

After half an hour of waiting, he had seen the faint rising of dust in the distance. The wind was picking up steadily, blowing in from the west but not yet doing anything to cool the day. It made his eyes water and he squinted through the binoculars. Chase's ute was visible, sun glinting off the white paintwork like a mirror. What wasn't visible, however, was the police troop carrier that should have been following it.

Maybe Parker decided to come on his own, he thought, and then immediately dismissed the idea. They would've come in a police wagon if that were the case. He glanced over to where Amin was waiting, saw his own rifle trained on himself and for a moment his heart did a backflip, until Amin gave him a wave. *Just using it as binoculars.* Gabe made driving motions with his hands and raised one finger. One vehicle. He hoped Amin understood his impromptu charades. They really should have worked something out beforehand.

He searched for Chase's ute, caught sight of it again and watched as it drew closer. He would wait until he knew for certain things weren't as they should be. Five minutes later, when the vehicle was only a hundred metres from the clearing, he could make out the three occupants. He lowered his glasses, raised one arm in a frantic wave motion, and then skidded down the hill. Five minutes after that, the shooting had started.

TWENTY-NINE

Gabe was about to leap clear of Chase's oncoming ute when the whole vehicle was shunted violently to the side and tipped. The sound of breaking glass and rending metal screamed through the air. He watched as his LandCruiser ploughed into the other, charging from the scrub like an enraged mickey bull, and winced, hoping it would be okay to drive afterwards. They still had to get out of here.

He ran towards Chase's upturned ute. The vehicle lay on its side, and through the haze of its splintered windscreen, he could see the roo-shooter up-ended in the cab. Then he saw a hand stretched out on the hot earth, wedged under the edge of the cab's roof. Chase's pistol lay on the ground nearby.

Amin had joined Gabe's side, brandishing his handgun and breathing hard, but when he saw Chase and the position he was in, he tucked it away in the back of his pants. 'I don't think he will be shooting anyone,' he said, picking up Chase's gun.

'Bet that tickles,' Gabe agreed, and looked mournfully at his own ute, still idling away. Two bullet holes marked the windshield where the driver's head should have been, and he assumed Amin had leaned over once the shooting started. 'You couldn't have just shot him? Did you have to ram him?'

'He has information we need,' Amin said. 'I could not risk it.'

From inside the cab, Chase banged his free hand against the frayed glass. 'You fucks!' he roared. 'You're all fucked!'

Amin said nothing, but placed one foot on the splayed fingers. A scream of pain bellowed from the cab. Amin released the hand, stood on his toes and peered down through the driver's window. Gabe heard the unmistakable sound of Chase spitting vehemently at him, but Amin gave no reaction and spoke calmly.

'We will free your arm. And you will tell us what we want to know.'

'Fuck you,' Chase hissed. He sounded short of breath, not surprising considering he was wedged upside down. *Can't be the most comfortable position,* Gabe thought, *even without the trapped arm.* The all too familiar sight of the tipped LandCruiser shook him, but he held it together – just.

Amin repeated his statement, this time moving one foot back over the hand. 'You will tell us what we want to know. Or we will leave you here.'

A gasp of pain. 'I can't. They'll kill me.'

'You are going to die anyway.' The coldness in Amin's voice sent a chill through Gabe. 'How you do that is up to you. You can stay like this and slowly cook in the sun, or you can tell me what I want to know, and you will not suffer needlessly.'

Another gasp signalled Amin had reiterated his threat with further pressure on the outstretched fingers. 'Alright! I'll tell you. Just get me out of here!'

'Very well, but understand, should you not cooperate, it will be very bad for you.'

Without warning, Darren appeared next to them, making Gabe jump. 'You wrecked his day!' He grinned, but it was a sickly grin, through badly cut lips. An ugly welt ran down one side of his face.

'You alright?' Gabe asked. 'Where's Courtney? What happened?'

'She's okay. Got a cut on her cheek, and fainted there for a bit. She's under a tree around the corner. Told her to stay put until I knew it was safe.' Darren kicked the windshield. 'Fucking cop tasered me.'

'The young one?'

'Yeah. He's in on it with this bastard too.'

'What about Parker?'

'Didn't get to see him. The constable got me to tell him instead, then tricked me into going to the medical centre to talk to Courtney, then next minute, fuckin' zap!' He rubbed the middle of his back. 'Me cousins reckoned it hurts. They weren't bloody wrong. Copped a couple of whacks too.' Darren squatted down and yelled into the window, 'You hit like shit. Not so tough now, hey?'

Meanwhile, Amin had backed Gabe's ute away from the rolled vehicle. A quick inspection of the front told Gabe the vehicle had stood up well, save for a smashed indicator and more scratches to the khaki paint. The heavy-duty bull bar had done its job, much to his relief. Using it as a battering ram hadn't been his plan, but things seemed to have turned out okay.

'Got anything to drink?' Darren asked, and jerked a thumb over his shoulder. 'She could probably do with something.'

Gabe pulled a water and a Coke from the Engel and passed them to him. While Darren set off to deliver the drinks, Gabe found his winch gear and attached it to both vehicles. As he tied the free end to Chase's roof rack, he peered in through the driver's window. 'This isn't going to be a soft landing,' he said. Chase didn't reply, but his face was turning red.

The electric motor whined as the cable grew taunt. Gabe let it reel in, watching as the ute was slowly righted. The rear wheel blew out as all the weight went to its sidewall, and then the body of the vehicle came down with a crash. Amin reached in and threw out Chase's rifle. He ran around to the other side and proceeded to extract its owner with just as much force, ignoring his cries of pain. Amin propped him up against the front tyre and stood over the man.

'Where is my family?'

'Oh man,' Chase gasped. 'You guys are in deep shit. You've no idea what—' A blow from Amin cut him off.

Amin repeated the question, slower this time. 'Where is my family?'

Gabe was surprised at how calm Amin seemed, but it was the sort of concentrated calm a dog gets when it spots prey.

Chase spat blood. 'They'll get you. The others. They'll come looking for me.'

'And they will find a dead man,' Amin said impassively. 'Or pieces of him. For the last time, where is my family?'

There was something in his eyes that made Chase look away for a moment. 'Give me a cigarette first,' the roo-shooter said. Amin raised his eyebrows and gave Gabe a questioning look.

Gabe sighed and fished out his packet. 'I'm just the bloody baccy shop, aren't I?' He rolled three smokes and passed one each to Amin and Chase. The injured man took it, allowed Gabe to light it for him and leaned backed against the tyre, cradling his arm. It was already an ugly purple colour. He looked past Amin and eyed Gabe with a wry smile.

'You've no idea what you've got yourself into, dogger. What were you doing out here in the first place? No one comes out here.'

'Doesn't matter why. I'm in it now, like it or not.'

'You know,' Chase panted, his face streaked with sweat, 'I reckon you were being a bit naughty, doing a bit of illegal trapping. That'd be the only reason I could think of. Maybe running some grog too. Heard that's been going on.'

Gabe tried to keep his face neutral, but Chase's pained grin told him he hadn't. 'Guessed right, didn't I? Well, between you and me, I couldn't give a fuck, except that you got in the way. And here we are.'

'Enough of this.' Amin stood with his arms folded, glaring down at Chase. 'Tell us what you know or we will leave you to the crows and continue on.'

Chase stared at him for a moment, took a deep draw of his cigarette, and said nothing.

'Where are they?' Amin demanded.

'Fuck off,' Chase spat. 'Find them yourself.'

'If you will not talk, then we have no need of you.' Amin raised the pistol slightly. Chase flinched, but remained silent, staring doggedly at the ground.

Gabe shifted uncomfortably next to him. 'Amin,' he began, but was cut off with an abrupt gesture as Amin flicked the safety and levelled the weapon at Chase's head, and the roo-shooter's eyes went wide.

'This is better than you deserve.'

THIRTY

'Wait!'

Courtney's scream made all three of them turn. She hurried over, still a little unsteady on her feet and supported by Darren.

'What the hell? You're just going to shoot him?' She reached them, and then saw Chase's arm. 'My God, what did you do?'

'Saved your bloody life,' Gabe said. 'Or didn't you notice the bullets flying around earlier? Dunno why you wouldn't have, one bloody near took your head off.'

'I don't care,' Courtney said. 'I mean, I do, but you can't kill him. Makes you no better than him.'

Gabe, who wasn't entirely comfortable with the whole idea either, glanced at Amin. 'She's right, you know.'

For a moment it appeared Amin was going to ignore them both, until he sighed and lowered the weapon. '*He* would not have been so forgiving.'

'I know,' Courtney said. 'Thank you.'

'He should be the one thanking you.'

Chase grinned up at them, any sign of fear now gone. 'Thanks, love.'

'Call me love one more time and I'll break your other bloody arm. Don't think I didn't consider letting him do it. How many have you killed? How many people are lying at the bottom of that hole?' When she received no answer, Courtney turned to Gabe and Amin. 'I have to splint his arm.'

Now Gabe did protest. 'Dammit, girl, we don't have time for this. His mates might be on their way already.'

'Then you'd better find me some bandages and a splint quick.' She stood there, arms folded, and he knew there was no use arguing. He'd seen that look before. It was the same one Valerie would adopt whenever her mind was set on something. It was easier to just go along.

'Fuck's sake,' Gabe muttered, and he went to fetch his first aid kit while Darren scouted for a suitable splint. Amin kept watch over Chase, though it didn't appear the man was in much shape to try anything. Gabe returned with the kit.

Courtney knelt beside Chase and reached for his arm. 'This is going to hurt.'

He shrugged, and she began tying the makeshift splint against his wrist. He hissed a few times as she tightened the knots, but said nothing. It was only as she began wrapping a bandage around the arm that he spoke.

'No hard feelings? Just doing my job.'

Courtney did not look up. 'So were the guards at Auschwitz. Think that excuses them?' Chase didn't say any more after that.

She finished and rose. Gabe motioned for the group to follow him out of earshot.

'Right, if you're done playing doctor, we need to get going.'

'Where to?' Amin said. 'He gave us nothing.'

'Fuck, I don't know,' Gabe replied. 'Anywhere that isn't here, for a start. First thing is to get these kids back to town.'

191

'Pig's arse,' Darren said. 'No way, not with that crooked cop about. I'll end up dead in a bloody holding cell or with six warning shots in my back.'

'Well, you can't stay here,' Gabe pointed out. 'His mates will be coming.'

'Damn right. That's why we're going with you.'

'Christ, Darren. This isn't a bloody game or some action movie.'

The young man gave him a broad grin. 'No shit. If this were a movie, the black guy would've died already.'

Courtney gave a burst of shocked laughter, then gasped as though realising just how close to the truth it was. 'That's not funny, Darren.'

'Funny because it's true. Safest place right now is with you blokes.'

Amin glanced at Gabe. 'Maybe they can help?'

Gabe shook his head. 'What are we, the four fucking High-waymen?'

'Four is better than two,' Amin pointed out. 'And a nurse might be useful.'

'Darren is right,' Courtney said. 'You didn't see that police-man. He might be young but he's nasty. I don't think he'll stop at anything to clean up this mess.' She paused, thinking for a moment. 'They were talking, back at the clinic. Something about Carnarvon. He had to be back there to meet someone.'

'They say anything else?' Gabe asked. 'Anything about Amin's family?'

'No,' Courtney said slowly. 'But they mentioned a name though. Winston something? Wheaton? Did you hear it, Darren?'

'Wellston, maybe?' Darren said. 'Dunno, my head was ringing pretty hard.'

'Wheldon?' Gabe asked, incredulous.

'Yes! Wheldon,' Courtney said. 'He was the person who sent Chase.'

'You know him?' Amin asked.

'Only by reputation. Pair of brothers, dodgy fuckers. The kind who like to muster their neighbours' paddocks when no one's home and help themselves to anything not bolted down. You say he called Chase?'

'That's what he said,' Courtney replied. 'I'm sure of it.'

'Last I heard, they were still on Brigadier Station,' Gabe said. 'Maybe that's where your family is?'

Amin gripped his gun. 'Let's go ask.'

'You two stay here,' Gabe said. 'Keep an eye out for anyone else coming.' Courtney made to protest, but Gabe cut her off. 'We're not going to shoot him.'

Amin and Gabe strode back to Chase, who was still sitting against his ute's wheel, legs splayed out in front of him. His face, a pale shade of white, was caked in sweat.

'Finished your little powwow, then?'

Gabe ignored him. 'Brigadier,' he said, and was rewarded with a look of surprise. 'They there? Amin's wife and kid?'

Chase remained silent until Amin drew back a boot and readied a kick. 'Alright!' he groaned. 'Fuck's sake, alright. Yeah, far as I know, that's where they were.'

The relief on Amin's face was palpable. '*Alhamdulillah,*' he murmured.

Gabe blew out a breath. 'How the hell did the Wheldons get wound up in all this?'

'Ask them yourself,' Chase spat.

'And you?' Gabe asked. 'How'd you get involved?'

Chase winced as he adjusted his position. 'Guess I'm what you'd call a troubleshooter. Any trouble, I shoot it.' He grinned up at Gabe. 'If I hadn't been called down to Gero that day, it would've been me you ran into, dogger. Not those two damn amateurs. Wonder how things might have turned out then.'

'Be about the same,' Gabe growled. Inwardly, he wasn't sure. Those shots into his ute's windscreen would've taken Amin's head off had the man not been ducking. And the one that bounced off the rock hadn't missed him by much either. Not bad considering the shot was taken under fire and with a ute charging at him.

They left the injured roo-shooter and returned to Darren and Courtney.

'And?' Courtney asked.

'Brigadier,' Gabe said. 'That's where they are. Guess we go there first, suss it out.'

'What about the copper?' asked Darren.

Amin shook his head. 'We get my family first, that is the main thing, then we deal with him.'

'What if we went to the media?' Courtney asked.

'Couldn't do that until we had his wife and kid out,' Gabe said. 'Or we'd lose their only reason for keeping them alive. Without them, Amin has no incentive to keep his gob shut.'

Darren nodded over towards Chase. 'And bugalugs?'

'Leave him here.' Amin raised a hand as Courtney was about to protest. 'We have no choice. We can't take him, and his vehicle will not drive with the tyre like that. We will leave some water, check he has no satellite phone or radio to warn his friends, and leave him. If God wills it, he will be found. With luck, long after we have done what we need to.'

Gabe could tell Courtney didn't like this at all. *Goddamn soft-hearted women, why did they have to make things so complicated?* His mind dredged up images from the past; Valerie urging him to turn back and drive the one hundred kilometres to Geraldton with the winged eagle someone had hit and abandoned on the Mount Magnet road. Valerie berating him for shooting a doe kangaroo that turned out to have a young joey in its pouch. Valerie making him run down and catch the lamb with the busted leg so she could splint it. Given Courtney's efforts with Chase, that last memory almost made him smile.

'He's right, Courtney. We have to get moving. Chase already said people would be looking for him. Might even be that Jefferson cop, and we don't want to be here when that happens.'

Her reluctance was plain to see, but she agreed in the end. They went back to the two vehicles.

Chase grimaced as they approached, and Courtney looked concerned. 'Are you alright?'

'Just fucking fine and dandy,' he said. 'So, you decided to finish me off, or what?'

In answer, Gabe rummaged through the cab and placed Chase's large blue water cooler and an unopened packet of jerky on the ground next to him. 'Keep you going for a bit. By then your mates should be here.'

'We should move him to the shade,' Courtney said, but before Gabe could protest Chase cut him off.

'Go on, piss off, all of you. Been in worse spots before. Won't make much difference either way. You're all dead, you just don't know it yet.'

They stayed a second longer, and then did as he said.

With Darren's help, Gabe removed the Engel and his other belongings from the rear seat of his ute and loaded them into the canopy. Amin retrieved Chase's rifle from where he had discarded it earlier, and a box of bullets he found in Chase's cab.

'This might come in handy,' he said. Gabe nodded, and stowed it in the spare clip next to his own .223. His M1 returned to its usual hiding place.

'Ready then?' he asked.

'As I'll ever be,' Courtney said as she climbed into the back seat, Darren following.

Gabe started the ute. As he headed down the track, towards the way Amin and his companions had come from only yesterday, he looked in his side mirror and saw Chase waving them away, still propped up against the tyre. Gabe returned his eyes to the road, hoping to never see that man again.

THIRTY-ONE

'Where are we?' Courtney asked, breaking Gabe's thoughts. In reply he pulled a battered country road atlas from his door pocket and passed it back to her.

'Show her, Darren.'

He saw that she had cleaned herself up as best she could, given the circumstances. A splinter of rock from the ricochet had cut her temple, but it was only a small injury, though a little more to the left and she might have lost an eye.

'So, what's the plan?' the nurse asked, thumbing through the pages.

'Your guess is as good as mine, love,' said Gabe.

'Don't call me that.' Fire blazed in her eyes. 'You sound like him.'

'Sorry, habits of an old man.' And just like that, the fire was extinguished. God, she was so much like Valerie. 'I know where Brigadier Station is, but what we do when we get there is beyond me.'

'Chase will warn them we are coming,' Amin said. 'His friends will find him, and he will tell them. And they will be waiting. We should have killed him.'

'That would have been easiest, I agree,' said Courtney. 'But I stand by what I did.'

'You were right,' Gabe admitted, somewhat reluctantly. 'Shooting a bloke when he's trying to shoot you is one thing, but when he's defenceless on the ground like that?' He shook his head.

'What's done is done,' Amin sighed. 'So Courtney's question is a good one. What is our plan?'

'I'm open to ideas,' Gabe said. 'Casing the joint would be my first suggestion. But like you said, we don't have much time. I dunno how long Chase will be stuck there, but once they find him they'll be expecting us.'

Darren, who had been tracing his finger along the road nearest to where they were on the map, suddenly piped up. 'That a sat-phone you got there?'

'Yeah,' Gabe said. 'Why's that?'

'I've got some cousins in Carnarvon. You want to case the joint? Reckon I could give them a ring, they'll go for a drive. Brigadier is only an hour or so from town, hey?'

Gabe thought about it. 'I dunno if we want any more people involved, Darren, but it would be safer than us trying to do it. Save time, too.'

'It'll be alright. I'll just tell 'em I got some guys looking for work.'

Courtney seemed a little confused. 'Wouldn't someone just ring if they wanted to know if there was work?'

Darren gave a laugh. 'Bit harder to tell a blackfella he's not wanted face to face. Nah, these boys often do a loop around stations. Probably been there before, might even be able to tell us stuff without even going.'

Gabe handed him the phone. 'Keep it short. That thing's expensive.'

Darren dialled the number and after a very brief conversation handed it back. 'Justin's gonna go check it out, but he reckons

Brigadier's been real quiet for the last year or more. Said we could get work on Quobba though.'

'Good to know,' Gabe said. 'After all this shit is settled, I reckon I'll be needing a new job.'

'I thank all of you.' Amin turned his head to look at each of them. 'For doing this. For helping me.'

Darren grinned. 'Just doing it to piss the government off. Only thing they hate more than a blackfella on their land is a brown fella on a boat.'

This elicited a shocked gasp from Courtney. 'You can't mean that?'

'Why not? True, isn't it?'

Amin chuckled. 'Whatever your reasons, my thanks again. I hope God looks down on you all with favour.'

'Say,' said Darren. 'You're Muslim, yeah?'

There was a slightly bemused expression on Amin's face.

'Don't think I've ever met a Muslim before.'

'How do you know?' Amin asked. 'Despite what some may think, we do not all walk around with a bomb vest strapped to our chests.'

Stunned silence filled the cab for a moment, until Darren roared with laughter. 'Ha! That's exactly right!' He high-fived Amin. 'We'll get your mob back, you bloody wait and see!'

Amin settled back into his seat, smiling weakly. Behind him, another question came from Darren. 'You guys really don't eat bacon or drink?'

'Correct, though not all are so observant.'

'Man,' Darren breathed. 'That's some commitment.'

'I thought you didn't drink, Darren?' An innocent smile adorned Courtney's face, and Gabe suppressed a grin of his own as he watched the young man in his rear-view mirror.

'I don't. It's the bacon I'm talking about.'

'Of course.' The knowing tone in her voice was apparent to all, and they drove on in silence for a while.

'How far away is this place?' Amin finally asked.

Gabe glanced at the dash clock. 'Another hour to the Junction, then almost two to Carnarvon and another to Brigadier.' He tapped his punctured windscreen. 'But we're not going anywhere near Carnarvon or the highway with this, so could be a bit longer.'

'Allah,' Amin sighed. 'Your country is so large. Back home we could be halfway across Pakistan by then.'

'If you survive the road blocks, land mines and booby traps,' Gabe pointed out. 'Worst thing you got to worry about out here is kamikaze kangaroos.'

'Yes, I suppose you are right, though none of those things you mention are of our doing. First it was the Persians, then the British, then the civil wars that resulted from that, followed by the Russians, then the Taliban, and finally the Americans themselves and their *freedom*.' He spat the last word out as if it were a curse. 'And now that their withdrawal is underway, many fear it is only a matter of time before the Taliban return in full force.'

'No wonder you got on a bloody boat,' Darren said.

'Yes, it was not in my future plans when we married, that is for certain.'

Amin turned as Courtney placed a hand on his shoulder. He glanced down at her hand and shifted a little in his seat. Courtney withdrew, perhaps realising she may have crossed some sort of cultural line. 'What's your wife's name?' she asked.

'Aamena.' Amin seemed to exhale the word. 'And my son is Jawad.'

'They are lovely names. I hope to meet them soon.'

'I hope so too. I hope so very much.'

Courtney smiled and gave him a reassuring thumbs up. 'We'll find them.'

To Gabe's surprise, Amin laughed.

'What?' the nurse asked, clearly as confused as Gabe.

'That gesture. I know here it means "okay", but to Afghans it is more like your middle finger.'

'Oh,' Courtney said, quickly lowering her hand. 'Sorry. But I meant what I said. We'll find them, and somehow we'll make sure those people smugglers are put behind bars.'

This promise did not receive the reaction she might have expected. Instead of agreeing with her, Amin stared straight ahead.

'That *is* what you want?' she asked.

'My family, yes. But if we bring an end to the smuggling, many people will be stranded.'

'But . . .' She was puzzled, clearly not expecting this line of thought. 'But it's dangerous. Illegal. And they're killing people.'

'All bad things,' Amin agreed. 'But we would not take such risks if there were any other choice. In all likelihood, had we not fled when we did, my wife and my child and I would be dead.'

Courtney flushed red. 'That bastard was about to shoot me and Darren, and the both of you if he got the chance. You can't seriously think he's one of the good guys.'

'Not a good guy,' Amin agreed. 'Not at all. But maybe part of a necessary evil, given your government and other western countries' attitudes to refugees.'

'I can't believe you're saying such things,' Courtney said. Gabe could see the anger flickering behind her eyes like embers of a dying fire, ready to flare again on the first hot wind. 'They're going to murder your wife and son.'

'If they try, they will die,' Amin said. He turned and stared at her. 'But, understand, I was part of a group of forty men.

When I first left the camp, to supposedly meet my family, those other men were still working. Still in a country that was not theirs, still alive and sending money home, or working to bring their own families here, where it is safe—'

'Safe? You call this . . .' She waved her arm in a broad gesture, and finished by tapping his wounded arm. 'Safe?'

Amin did not flinch at the touch. 'This is not my first gunshot wound. You did not let me finish. Where it is safer, I was about to say. Yes, they have killed others. Yes, they would have killed me. I don't deny such things. But what will happen to the others when we expose these men? Will they be allowed to stay? Will they be detained, or will they, as I suspect, be flown back to their homelands without a single regard to what persecutions they may endure on return?'

Courtney didn't reply. Gabe watched her face as she wrestled with these questions. They were questions he had not considered himself, either. Up until a few days ago, he never gave much thought to refugees or wars and was of the opinion they should keep their shitty problems confined to their own shitty countries. Not his problem. Only now it was, and Amin raised a good point. What were they going to do once they located his family?

THIRTY-TWO

Courtney runs through the open scrubland, branches tearing at her clothes and face. Behind her, Chase laughs over the roar of his ute, but she dare not turn her head, knowing she would see his wild eyes and his mad grin.

'Hey.'

Gabe's voice cut through like a dull blade, and she rose up out of the dream. Somehow she had fallen asleep, knees tucked up under her as her head rested against the door's window. Her mind cleared, glad to be out of that nightmare, but also wishing she could return to it. At least she knew that was a dream. The alternative was frighteningly real.

She had played over the past day as they drove. She couldn't think about it too much; it was too crazy. Somehow, she'd gone from giving Darren a lecture in the clinic about falling over while drunk, to running for her life alongside him, and then the both of them escaping execution by the narrowest of margins. Her guts felt sick with the thought, so she focused on their destination instead. Not that that made her feel any better. *What a bloody mess.*

And what was their destination? A sheep station where desperate asylum seekers were being held. Then what? She didn't know, and suspected her companions weren't overly sure either. Studying each of them, she'd seen they all were lost in their own thoughts. Amin was clearly thinking about his family. Darren, who didn't say much at the best of times, could well have been thinking about his tasering at the hands of the policeman. His reaction was intriguing. Angry, sure, that was only normal, but the lack of any real surprise was a little disconcerting, as though he had expected it. Maybe he had at some level.

Then there was Gabe. What to make of him? He was unlike anyone she'd known before. Her own father was jovial, open and inviting. Played Santa at every Christmas party. She tried to imagine Gabe doing that, and the closest she could come to was that movie *Bad Santa*. She got the distinct impression he'd be glad to be rid of them all and carry on his way. There was something going on she wasn't aware of, and she suspected his motives weren't purely out of the goodness of his heart. Yet he'd saved Amin, brought him to her when his arm needed fixing, and he'd intervened before Chase could finish them off. And then there was the way he looked at her sometimes, almost in recognition. Which was crazy, because he had at least thirty years on her and they'd only met yesterday.

She watched him climb from his seat, saw the twinge of pain flash across his face and a hand go to his hip. Arthritis, maybe? Probably, given his age, but it could be an old injury too, perhaps from when he got that scar on his face. He looked like someone who had worked hard his whole life and been in a few scraps along the way. Those hands, tanned deep brown, hard and calloused, stained yellow around the fingertips from his smokes and touched with a slight tremor. Hands of an outdoors man, an old bushie, never happier than when he's sitting by himself around a camp fire, gazing up at the stars. Had he always been by himself? She couldn't tell. She might've asked under different circumstances, but right now it was not important.

Courtney extracted herself from the cramped cab, winced at the pins and needles in her legs and almost fell over as they buckled. She grabbed the door for support and glanced around. They were in a small town, parked under a white gum growing next to a grassed rest area.

'Where are we?'

'Gascoyne Junction. Need fuel and I don't want to do it in Carnarvon, just in case eyes are about.' Gabe turned and studied them all. 'Might be better if you lot stay out of sight. Graham is bound to notice if I've got company, and I'd rather not have to explain. Be hard enough if he sees these bloody holes in the windscreen.'

Courtney followed his eyes. They were a ragtag bunch to be sure. Her blue scrubs were stained with dust and sweat, Darren's get-up was no better, and Amin's clothes could almost stand up on their own. In fact, Gabe looked the most presentable of them all, something she suspected was not usually the norm. 'Who's Graham?'

'Roadhouse owner. It's not exactly busy around here these days. He'll come out for a chat for sure.'

Amin finished gulping down two more antibiotic pills, tucked the tablets back in his pocket and waved his empty drink bottle at Gabe. 'If you think that is the best thing, that is what we will do. Do you have any more water?'

'Grab the last one out of the Engel and I'll get some more from the store. There's plenty of Coke in there though.'

'And a feed too, hey?' Darren suggested. 'Getting shot at works up the appetite.'

'Don't suppose any of you brought your wallets?'

Courtney gave him a wry smile. 'Sorry. Slipped my mind as we left.'

'Looks like I'm paying, then,' Gabe said. 'That'd be bloody right.'

'Won't that policeman be able to track your card?'

'I'll use cash.'

Courtney raised her eyebrows. 'A full tank of diesel at outback prices? Do you always carry that much cash around the bush?'

She saw Darren give him a quick look, then avert his eyes, as though they knew something she didn't.

'Call me old-fashioned,' Gabe growled, a little too defensively. 'All very well using cards for everything, but out here cash is king when the power goes out.'

'Lucky for us,' Courtney said. 'I'm going to go for a walk to stretch these poor legs of mine. Come with, Darren?'

Darren didn't look as though he felt like walking, but joined her nonetheless. They left Gabe and Amin under the tree and set off across the lawn. It was ridiculously hot; even the green grass radiated heat up at them, but she didn't care. She needed to work some blood into her legs and clear her head. Beside her, Darren trudged along, hands in his pockets.

'How you holding up?' she asked. 'That taser must've really hurt.'

'Sore,' Darren admitted. 'Achey, like I've had a bad cramp all over. I'll be alright though.' He stopped and looked around. Gabe had just driven off, heading for the roadhouse. 'But honestly, I'm shitting myself.'

'Me too.'

At this admission, Darren seemed to relax a little. 'Whole thing's nuts. But I dunno what else we can do except go along. We tried getting out of it earlier and look what happened.'

'True,' Courtney said. 'Are we really going to do this though? We don't even know Amin, and I only just met Gabe yesterday. There's something he's not telling us.'

Darren said nothing, as if unsure how to reply, so she continued. 'And Amin, I mean, I get why he doesn't want the police involved, but surely they can't all be bad. Isn't there a big station in Carnarvon? We could ask to see the captain, or superintendent, or whoever it is in charge.'

'We could,' Darren said slowly. 'But I'm with Amin on this one.'

'You don't trust the police either?'

'It's not that simple.' He stared up at the sky, then back at her. 'Look, what if everything Amin says is bang-on true. That's huge. It means people have buggered up big time, and when that happens cops protect their own. Even if it's only that little prick who's bent, how keen d'you reckon his bosses will be to say they didn't know smugglers were operating right under their noses with one of their own helping?'

'Even so,' Courtney said, a sinking feeling starting to well in her gut, 'they can't sweep it under the carpet.'

Darren laughed. 'They can bloody try, wouldn't be the first time. Nah, I like your first idea better – go straight to the media, but we can't do that until his wife and kid are safe.'

They reached the end of the grass and sat under another smaller white gum. Courtney leaned against the smooth trunk and closed her eyes, trying to ignore the flies determined to find their way into them. 'So we're doing this?'

'Reckon so.'

She sighed. Three months ago, when she had applied for the position of Remote Area Nurse, she knew there would be challenges and unexpected adventures, but this was far beyond what she could have ever imagined.

THIRTY-THREE

Gabe watched Courtney and Darren walk across the park, then turned back to his ute and found Amin eyeing him cautiously.

'You are the one bringing in the alcohol,' he said. 'That is how you know Darren and why you have that money in the glove compartment.'

It wasn't a question, and Gabe didn't bother with a denial. 'So? What of it?'

'I don't know enough to judge, but I think this would not be in your favour if others found out.'

'It'd cost me a pretty penny,' Gabe admitted. 'And I wouldn't be travelling through Jakob's River anytime soon.'

'Then why?'

'Seemed like a good idea at the time.'

'And now?'

'I dunno. Mate of mine asked, and I helped him out.' His hand went to the scar at his temple. 'I owe him.'

'You don't think there might be consequences?'

'Don't give two shits about consequences,' Gabe retorted. 'World's already fucked, and I'm done with it. Bad shit happens. If I didn't bring the grog in, someone else would, so might as well be me pocketing the cash. Anyway, if I hadn't been camped up overnight waiting for the boys, I would've been long gone by the time your little party started.'

'And I am grateful, though I think perhaps our young nurse might not look on you so favourably. After all, she was the one dealing with the fallout.'

Gabe said nothing, returning to his ute and leaving the man sitting under the gum. But he couldn't help but ponder over Amin's words. What fallout? Courtney said she had been busy, but never specified. Darren had obviously gone tits up at some stage of the night. Nothing unusual there, he'd been guilty of that himself a few times. And Bobby said the real problem drinkers had left pretty early on in the piece, gone on to Gero or Carnarvon, where the booze flowed freely. Or was that just something he said to keep Gabe happy?

Gabe didn't know, and to be honest he didn't care. That wasn't his problem. In all his years, he'd never raised much ruckus as a drinker. A few brawls as a young bloke, but nothing wild. And later, after he had found Valerie, the idea of any violence towards her was unfathomable. Truth be told, had he done such a thing, he had no doubt she would've left him the next day, possibly even used his skinning knife to render him cockless. No, if somebody caused problems on the grog, that was their own fault, not his.

He drove around the corner and pulled up at the bowser. As expected, his was the only vehicle, and he didn't think that would change anytime soon. The summer heat kept any tourists away, and even the locals were wise enough not to venture from their air conditioning if it could be helped. He pumped the diesel, wincing as he watched the litre counter tick over ever so slowly compared to the dollar one. There was a time when it used to be the other way around. Back when things were simpler. Easier. Happier.

'Back again?' a voice called. As he'd guessed, Graham Jones had come out for a look, though somewhat reluctantly. That's the trouble with air conditioning; spend too long in it and stepping outside becomes even harder.

'Be there in a minute,' Gabe called. 'Go back inside before you melt.' Graham didn't need to be told twice.

Gabe finished up and entered the public bar attached to the service station. It still smelled new. Clean, crisp and nothing like the original he had spent so many hours – and dollars – at. But that one was long gone, washed away in the floods of 2010 and replaced with this sparkling version with all the mod cons, not to mention the swimming pool and caravan park that went with it. He was sure the tourists and probably even the locals appreciated it, but Gabe preferred the old one, with its leaning walls and sagging timbers, and the names of various shearing and mustering teams that had passed through over the decades etched onto walls, doors and benchtops. Who knew, maybe in fifty years this one would have that feel about it, but he suspected Graham would not look favourably on anyone leaving their mark on the new furnishings. Which is why Gabe had carved his own moniker with his Leatherman on the underside of the new bar top while the bartender was occupied elsewhere. He'd tell him one day, maybe.

'Usual?' Graham asked.

'Just one,' Gabe grunted. 'And two to go.' He tossed the wad of notes on the counter. 'For the fuel. And grab us four burgers and chips, and a pack of water bottles, cold ones if you've got them. And make one of those burgers vegetarian if you can.'

'Hungry today?'

He'd already thought about the answer to this obvious question. 'Calling out to Bidgemia. Crew put an order in, guess they didn't feel like cooking.'

Graham laughed, placing a freshly poured pint in front of Gabe. 'Usually they'd come get it themselves and run me dry while they wait.'

Gabe shrugged. 'Bad luck for you, I guess.' He drained half the glass in one go. It was cold enough to send a spike of pain through his back teeth and up to his temples, but it was good. 'Shit, I needed that.'

'Rough day?'

'You've got no idea.'

Graham took the required notes and headed round to the shop till. 'Someone been shooting at you?'

Gabe looked up in alarm, seeing the publican peering through the storefront window at his ute windscreen. 'Stupid fuckin' tourist shit themselves coming past me,' he called out, hoping Graham's eyes weren't too good. 'Veered off the track and sent a couple massive stones my way.'

'Must've been bloody big stones.' Graham returned, handing Gabe his change. 'Don't let the Carnarvon coppers see that, they'll sticker your vehicle in a heartbeat.'

'Don't worry. I'm steering clear of cops for a while. I'll get it fixed in Gero.' He finished the pint, considered the empty glass for a moment, and shrugged. 'Give us another – burgers will be a while, I guess.'

Graham obliged, and as Gabe started the second glass a thought occurred to him. 'Hey, there's no bacon in those things, is there?'

'Yeah, there is, why's that?'

Gabe thought fast. 'They've got a Muslim backpacker out there. Could your girl do that vego one in a separate pan or something?'

Graham's face twisted a little, but he passed the food order on, and Gabe returned to his beer. Through the opening in the kitchen he could see a young blonde woman bustling about, preparing the food. *Most likely a backpacker,* he thought, wondering if the girl ever expected to find herself flipping burgers in the middle of nowhere during a scorching summer. Probably about as much as he and his companions had expected to find themselves in their current situation.

As he sipped away he cast his eyes about the new bar. At least they had tried to preserve some of the history. Photos of the old place adorned the walls, along with station memorabilia, but something else caught his eye. A T-shirt hung from one wall, designed with the discerning tourist in mind and emblazoned with a cartoon signpost showing just how far they were from everywhere else. The caption read 'I Got Lost at the Junction'. Gabe grinned and pointed at the shirt.

'Give us one of those too.'

'Big spender today.' Graham looked a little surprised, but he was an astute enough businessman not to ask any questions lest Gabe changed his mind. He fetched the requested item, collecting another note from the pile.

Gabe made his beer last the distance, and upon seeing the four packs of food being carried out to him fifteen minutes later, he drained the final dregs and rose. Graham placed a brown paper bag with two stubbies on the bench. 'Happy hunting. Many wild dogs out there?'

'More than you know, mate,' replied Gabe, scooping up his order and heading for the door. 'More than you know.'

THIRTY-FOUR

The heavy rumble of Gabe's ute made Courtney open her eyes, and she saw it pull back into the rest area. 'Looks like dinner is served.'

'Good,' Darren said, helping her to her feet. 'I'm bloody starved.'

Thinking about food made her realise that she was too. As they walked back, she saw Amin had left the shade of the white gum and was now kneeling at the edge of the grass, some distance from where Gabe had parked.

'What's he doing?' Darren asked.

'Praying, I think,' Courtney said. 'Can't say I blame him.'

'Hope it works.'

They were halfway to the LandCruiser, where Gabe leaned against the bonnet, lighting a smoke and watching them approach. 'What about what he was saying?' she said. 'About not reporting anything? We can't let the smugglers keep bringing people in. We have to tell someone eventually.'

Darren was silent, and by the time he answered they had reached the ute. 'I dunno,' he finally said.

'Dunno what?' Gabe asked.

'About not reporting those smugglers,' Courtney said.

Like Darren, Gabe said nothing, instead throwing them a cold water bottle each.

'You both agree with him?' She was stunned.

'No,' Gabe answered, and then scratched the back of his head in thought. 'Not entirely. I don't know. Look, three days ago I'd have said anyone coming here on a boat is a bloody queue jumper and should go back where they came from. Keep their shitty problems to their shitty countries.'

Darren gave a little snort and grinned. 'Good plan. Maybe we should've done that a couple hundred years ago.'

Gabe ignored him. 'Part of me still thinks that. Look at the shit we're in because of it. But he's just trying to keep his family safe. What would we do in his shoes? Guess I never really thought about how bad it could be in other places.'

'But smugglers are evil,' Courtney protested. 'Look at what they tried to do to us.'

'I agree, but they're only there because there's a demand. Shit, I even voted for the Libs, and they're the ones who started the whole "Stop the Boats" thing. Not that it matters much now – both bunches of arseholes are the same these days. Anyway, this is all theoretical. We might not have a choice either way.'

'What do you mean?' Courtney asked.

'I doubt they're just going to let us walk in, grab Amin's wife and son and walk out again. Maybe we can sneak them out, but most likely it'll be a snatch and run. We might have to head straight for Carnarvon to the cop shop. I doubt every cop there is bent.'

'What will be, will be,' Amin said, returning the group. 'But I think you are right, we will have to involve the authorities at some stage. But not until we achieve what we came for.'

'Sounds fair,' Gabe said. 'Happy with that?'

Courtney thought about it for a while and finally agreed. She didn't understand all the complexities of what was going on, but knew it was much larger than she'd first suspected. Before she could say anything, Gabe threw something else at her, which she caught by reflex.

'Put that on,' he said. 'You look a little out of place in those scrubs.'

'Great, so now I'll look like a dopey tourist instead?' She grinned, inspecting the cheesy slogan on the shirt.

'Better a dopey tourist than a lost nurse.' He handed out the burgers, which were accepted with relish, and nodded at Amin's. 'No meat in that one, and they cooked it in a clean pan, away from the bacon.'

Amin smiled. 'Thank you, my friend. It was good of you to think of that.'

Courtney left her burger on the bonnet and headed for the ablutions block. 'I'll change into this shirt first.'

Inside the block she whipped off her filthy scrub top and, using the last of the paper towels by the sink, gave herself a quick wipe all over. God, she stank, but then her companions were no better. She put on the new shirt and inspected herself in the mirror. The shirt was ridiculous, but at least it smelled clean. Who knew, maybe the smugglers would take one look at her and die laughing. She shrugged and entered a cubicle. No paper. Typical of how the day was going. The second stall wasn't any better, and as Courtney headed back outside she told herself that if they got out of this mess she would let the Shire know to lift their game.

Gabe smiled at her new top when she approached, and she held out her arms and did a little spin for them. 'Better?'

'Much,' he said through a mouthful of burger.

'There's no paper in there,' Courtney said.

'Bloody tourists,' Gabe grunted. 'They'll take anything not bolted down. Hang on, I'll grab you a roll.'

She followed Gabe to the passenger side. He opened the glove box and to her surprise a large wad of notes fell out, which he caught and tucked back into the compartment. He handed her the toilet roll. 'Don't trust the banks. Never have,' he said, but his voice held a cautious edge.

'No wonder you could pay cash,' she replied, and headed back to the ablutions block. Why was he being so defensive? He had already told her he carried cash out here. *That old man is definitely hiding something,* she thought.

Courtney returned to finally enjoy her burger. She fished out the patty and bacon and held it up. 'Anyone want this?'

Darren did, and added it to what was left of his burger.

'Don't eat meat?' Gabe asked Courtney, his face tinged with mild curiosity and a touch of scorn.

'Nope,' she said, chowing down on the remains. It was good. The others had already finished theirs, but with the exception of Amin no one seemed in any hurry to get going again. She couldn't really blame them.

'How's a bloody vego survive in Jakob's River?' Gabe asked. 'And why didn't you say so? I could've got you the same as Amin, or a sandwich or something.'

'Didn't want to be a hassle, and I'm not that fussy. And to your first question, with some difficulty. Not much in the way of fresh veg in the shop.'

'No,' Gabe agreed. 'I saw that. Must be hard trying to eat healthy when the delivery truck's always late.'

The harsh tone of the satellite phone cut through the air, startling them all. After some hesitation, Gabe reached through the open door to answer it, listened for a moment and handed it to Darren.

'That was quick. Your mates.'

Darren listened, asked a couple of questions and then ended the call, passing the phone back. 'Justin said they went out there, but were sent away pretty quick.'

'Did he see anything?'

'Yeah, said there were four or five workers wandering about – mustering crew, he reckoned. Also said there were some new dongas out behind the old shearing shed. Reckons they might be going into tourism.'

'Guess they are, in a way,' Gabe mused. 'Anything else?'

'Said there was a bus parked nearby. Figured it might be a shearing crew, but they had no sheep in the yards. And that was it. I couldn't ask him to look for anything special or he'd want to know why.'

'Fair enough. Been a while since I went through there, but there weren't any dongas there then. Might be where the families are kept?'

'It would explain the bus,' Amin said. 'Could be the one they use to pick up new arrivals from the boat.'

'How long until we get there?' Courtney asked, scrunching her burger wrapper and tossing it into the bin.

'About three hours, but we're not going straight there.' Gabe raised a hand to placate Amin. 'We're going to circle around, park up and case the joint first.'

Amin sighed. 'That is the wise thing to do, but our time is getting short.'

'It'll be even shorter if we just turn up unprepared,' Gabe pointed out. 'Got to get the lay of the land first. See which way the wind blows.'

'Wind?'

'Just an expression. See what's what.' Gabe shook his head as he explained, and Courtney wondered how many other colloquialisms the old bushie had to explain to Amin, then realised she would probably have just as much trouble understanding him if they spent long enough together. He had a way of speaking that was unlike anyone she'd met, even out here.

She took a long drink from her water bottle. It had already started to warm. 'So what's the plan?' she asked, wiping the last of the burger's sauce from her chin.

'Find a camp spot away from the station and get some rest,' said Gabe. 'It's dawn around five, so we'll sneak up for a look before then. Might have to walk a ways if the wind's in the wrong direction. From there, we'll see. You two should probably stay at the camp while Amin and I go check things out.'

'Fuck that,' said Darren. 'What if they see you? Then we'll be stranded out there on our own.'

'Goddammit,' Gabe swore. He'd already started back to his ute and wheeled around to face them. 'And what if it turns bad? I don't want to be babysitting two kids if shit goes down.'

'Can look after myself,' Darren said.

'Me too,' Courtney added, though she didn't know what would be more terrifying, staying put or tagging along.

Gabe threw up his hands, then went and retrieved something from his larger Engel. 'Fine, do what you want,' he said as he returned. Courtney noticed the beer stubbie he was carrying. He saw her looking at it.

'Don't start,' he said. 'If things turn to shit tomorrow, this could be my last day to have a beer, and I'm not going to bloody waste the chance.'

She said nothing, but decided she would count his drinks from now on, beginning to suspect where the slight tremor in his hands originated.

He cracked the top and swallowed, then raised the bottle questioningly at Darren, who shook his head.

'Don't drink,' he said. Courtney noted the doubtful look on Gabe's face. She had heard Darren claim this before, but she had assumed he was lying. Now she wasn't so sure.

'At all?' Gabe asked. There was a sceptical tone in his voice, as though he had reason to think otherwise.

'Never touched the stuff,' Darren said defiantly, and then looked around at the others. 'That so hard to believe?'

'No,' Courtney said. 'It's just . . .'

'Just what? You thought I fell over pissed and that's how I hurt my wrist?'

She didn't answer, suddenly feeling like she had wronged him. Because that's exactly what she had thought.

'I strained it catching Uncle when he nearly toppled into the camp fire,' Darren said quietly. 'He always loses his footing eventually when he's on the grog.'

Courtney watched as Gabe swallowed the rest of his beer. He did not meet her gaze, but she saw Amin glaring at him.

Gabe returned the glare, his face darkening. 'You can keep those looks to yourself,' he said. 'If I didn't bring it in, someone else would.'

'You?' Suddenly it all made sense. She had known there was something not quite right with Gabe, but she hadn't expected grog running, though it did explain the roll of notes. That's why he called through Jakob's River. That's how he knew Darren. And that's why he was so keen to leave the police out of this whole mess.

'Yeah, me,' Gabe said, and pointed to Darren. 'With some help from Mr I-Don't-Drink over there. He was more than happy to help the other night.'

'You think I like grog coming in?' Darren snapped, mirroring Amin's glare. 'Best thing Elsie did was get the town dry. But it's not that simple, is it? People still want a drink, so they get blokes like you to bring it in. You know the first time you did, Bobby nearly shot his mate by mistake? They decided to go roo-shooting after knocking off a bottle.' He shook his head. 'I hate the bloody stuff, but at least if I'm there I can keep an eye on him and the others.'

'Christ, if he's got a problem he should get help,' Gabe said, indignant.

'Where?' Darren shot back. 'He's lived in Jakob's River most of his life. He was born there, in the back room of his aunty's shack. There's no AA meetings in town, and even if there was it's not going to be anonymous with the place the size it is. He'd have to move to Gero, and then what? He'd get lonely and down, and drink himself to death.'

'Fuck's sake,' said Gabe. 'Should've just kept bloody driving instead of sticking my nose in. This is what I get.'

'And why were you there anyway?' Darren asked. 'You were heading up to Mount Augustus, you said. If you found Amin at that hole, you hadn't even left the Reserve.'

'You want to know what I was doing?' Gabe's voice was beginning to tremble with barely contained rage. 'Setting bloody traps to cull some of the dogs that breed up there. Doing the place a favour. Your mob isn't very popular with the neighbours, so I get them before they reach the station boundaries.'

'But that's illegal,' Courtney said. 'It's a Reserve.'

'It's a bloody breeding ground is what it is,' Gabe said. 'No one making the damn rules sees what I see. None of them drive around the stations, finding dead calves and sheep torn to shreds. None of them have to listen to the station owner who had eight thousand sheep last year say he's down to four because what doesn't get eaten is run ragged by the dog packs.'

'What else aren't you telling us?' Courtney could feel her own fury building up again. 'We're about to do something that could get us killed, and we deserve to know who we're following. Do you run drugs too?'

'Fine,' Gabe spat, staring at her with an intensity that was frightening. 'You want to know what else I've done? Where do you want me to start? I run grog. I trap illegally. I shot two blokes with a rifle that should've been handed in years ago, and I dumped the bodies down a well to cover all that up. Not because I give a shit about some fuckin' refugee, but to save my own skin. I am not a good person.'

As if to emphasise this last statement he hurled his empty bottle past Courtney. It slammed into the steel bin and exploded. 'So you're right, you shouldn't be following me. In fact, you don't have to anymore, because I'm going to do what I should've done in the first place. Already got Val's death on my hands and fucked if I'm adding two kids and a refugee to that too.'

Courtney watched in stunned silence as Gabe stormed by, pushing past Amin, who rose to stop him.

'Don't you bloody touch me,' growled Gabe, shoving the man back. He clambered into the ute, fired the engine and sped off before anyone realised what was happening. Blue metal chips sprayed up, causing them all to turn their heads and raise their arms. By the time they looked back, Gabe was gone, with nothing but the roar of his engine reverberating back to break the uncomfortable silence that followed his departure.

THIRTY-FIVE

Gabe drove hard, gripping the wheel with one hand, the other clasped around another stubbie so tightly he feared he might break it. He did not look back, had no intention of looking back. He was going to do what he should've done all along – wipe his hands clean of the whole affair, then bury it away in the back of his mind, where he kept all the shit, the shit you did not want to remember, the shit you tried to wash away, or at least dilute down. But that's the trouble with shit; it bubbles up to the top, and no amount of beer, whisky or any other liquor can ever get rid of the stain permanently.

The glint of the setting sun bounced off his side mirror and into his eyes, and once again his mind replayed that day. It never really stopped replaying, stuck on a perpetual loop like a skipping DVD. All Gabe could do was try and look away, or blur his vision a little by staring at it through a beer glass or whisky bottle. Not that it ever helped, and even as he drove now, he could see it again. The road. The rise. The sunset in his eyes, reflecting off his steel bull bar, the bar designed to smash through any animal unfortunate enough to get in its way, be it fox, dog, kangaroo, cow or . . .

*

Courtney found she was trembling. 'What did he mean, Darren?'

The young man was hunched over, head in his hands. Next to him Amin stared out past the single row of houses into the low scrub that stretched on forever, broken only by the trees running along the Murchison River.

'Darren? He . . . he killed her?'

Darren rose. Sadness spread across his face. 'He did.'

The dusty windscreen is almost opaque in the setting sun, but he doesn't worry. He could drive this road with his eyes closed, and he is in a hurry. The day has been hot and hard, and he's had no offsider. Valerie's on the stores run, but she should be back by now, and among her load of shopping will be his beer. She will have packed some in the Engel for him before beginning the long drive from Geraldton, and they will be cold and like cool nectar on his parched throat. Yes, they will look for some different work. Even with a pneumatic drill, digging strainer holes is no job for someone of his vintage.

His ute crests the rise. The sun, partially hidden behind the horizon, now flares with all the intensity of a welder's flash. The impact is so sudden, so out of the blue, he thinks he has strayed off the road into a tree or spoon drain. Something rolls over the bonnet, blots out the sun and smashes into the windscreen. He is hurled forward, his head striking the wheel and sending a cloud of blackness over his eyes. Far, far away, something screams.

'He and Valerie used to call in to Jakob's River all the time,' Darren said. 'I didn't really know him, but we all knew who he was. He was different then. Like, still a grumpy old bugger, but cheery at the same time, if that makes sense. He'd always be growling at her to hurry up, leave them kids alone, but his eyes smiled while he did it. I don't think they had children, I think they met later in life. Valerie would have her horse with her. Sometimes when they called through, she would unload him and lead the kids around town. Elsie reckoned Gabe and Valerie were more popular than the delivery truck, and that thing brought ice creams to restock the store.'

Amin stared out after the long-gone vehicle, its roaring engine slowly fading away. 'There is a sadness about him now, though. What happened?'

'They were contract fencing, can't remember where. Those two were made for that sort of life. All set up, like he is now and just part of the country. They'd work side by side. Most times he'd stay out working while she went to Gero or Carnarvon to get supplies, depending on where they were.' Darren shook his head. 'She got back to camp one afternoon and decided to ride out to meet him. He normally never left until dark, something about not wasting daylight, but on this day, he headed back early.'

A hammer pounds relentlessly against his skull. The right side of his face is wet, warm. He opens his eyes but everything is dark, save for the kaleidoscope swirling in front of him. He is on his side, and he becomes aware of a searing pain in his hip. *Jesus Christ, what the fuck did I hit? A cow? Must have been, but where the hell did it come from?*

He twists his head very carefully. It seems to work okay and he looks around. Fading sunlight filters through the passenger window, which is now pointing skywards. Thank Christ Valerie hadn't been sitting there; she'd have ended up on top of him, or worse, through the bloody windscreen. *Shit. Now what?* It'll be a while before she comes looking, and that's if she is even back yet, which he doubts. Probably still yapping with Elsie or playing with the urchins at Jakob's River, doing bloody pony rides. No, he is going to have to get out of this by himself.

He pulls himself up the cab of the smashed ute. The windscreen and frame around it are pushed back, and a red smear marks the point of impact with whatever it was he hit. The glass is a fractured haze. *Lucky it didn't smash into the bloody cab with me,* he thinks, grimacing as a bolt of pain shoots down his leg. Something is really not right with his hip; he can feel bits grating as he moves, but continues to climb out of the cab. Diesel ute or not, he has seen enough trucks burn to know that lying in a hot, tipped vehicle is never a good idea.

His legs come free. He tries to stand, but the left one gives way, almost sending him crashing back down in a heap. One hand catches the door frame and he stays upright. He hoists himself halfway through the open passenger window and looks around. In the eerie light of dusk, he can make out the cow behind the ute, but there is something odd about it. It is too long, too narrow. Dread begins to gnaw at his belly. He pushes it away. It's a cow, just a skinny strung-out station cow that jumped off a passing cattle truck, that's all. The animal lets out a piercing scream, kicks, and he sees the outline of a saddle.

'Oh Jesus Christ, no.' The pain in his hip is gone. He flings himself out the window and collapses onto the dirt, knocking the wind out of him. He stands, gasping, hauling himself up by the bent chassis, and staggers forward, his left leg dragging behind him. Tools and fencing gear are scattered all around. A steel picket has pierced the back windscreen, directly in line with the driver's seat, but had been stopped by the backrest. He doesn't give it a second thought, too focused on the horse.

Rohan. The horse lies on its side, bellowing great gasps of breath. Red frothy bubbles spray out in a fine mist that hangs in the air, catching the setting sun's orange hue, while eyes bulging in fear and pain roll in their sockets. One front hoof kicks feebly, the back legs shattered almost beyond recognition, and a second star picket protrudes from the animal's belly. The air is thick with the smell of hot blood, diesel and dust. Another scream, weaker, that of a dying animal refusing to give in. It rouses him.

'Valerie?' he roars, drowning out Rohan's pained cry with that of his own. No answer. He looks around, jerking his head side to side, fighting to stay upright, to remain conscious. Blood is in his eye, and he wipes at it with a sleeve. *Where is she?* Another wild scan of the roadside. *There!* A boot, under that acacia.

'Valerie!' Panic fills the cry. He lets go of the vehicle, makes to run to her and topples as his hip gives way. He doesn't feel anything this time and drags himself across the hard gravel surface. Stones cut at his belly, scrape away at his hands as he scrambles to her. She is on her back, not moving.

He reaches her, freezes, afraid to touch her lest he makes things worse, but when she moans, he softly cradles one cheek streaked with blood. An ugly graze runs down the other side of her face.

'Oh Christ, Valerie!'

'Gabe?' Her eyelids flutter, the eyes behind them vacant, unfocused.

'I'm here. Don't . . . don't move.' He sees the shape of her body, bent at a horrid angle. Shallow breaths escape her lips, intermittent and weak.

'Rohan,' she sighs. 'Is . . .'

'Shhh,' he whispers, the tears flowing now. Always thinking of others. 'He'll be alright.'

'Liar.' A weak smile. 'I got your beer.' And then she shudders, and closes her eyes.

'Bobby found them around nine o'clock that night,' Darren said, feeling the ache in his chest as he remembered the way his little sister squealed in delight each time the horse float rolled through town. 'Just plain dumb luck he did, because the muster job he was on had finished a day early. He doesn't talk much about what happened when he got there, and all I know is it was a bloody mess. Gabe was lucky to survive, though I'm not sure he feels that way. Wasn't long after that Bobby started his drinking for real. He'd always had a beer before, but after that accident, he got worse.'

'You think that is why Gabe brings the alcohol in?' asked Amin.

'Maybe,' Darren said. 'Started off as just a few bottles for Bobby, but then word got around that Bobby could get grog, so orders started coming in. I helped with the last lot, mainly to make sure he didn't try and keep it all for himself. Gabe seemed pissed off. I just thought it was because I was there, but I dunno – could be he doesn't actually want to do it, but feels like he should. When we became a dry town, Bobby never drank at home. But after that accident, he took it up. Guess Gabe thinks that's his fault too.'

'And he blames himself for his wife's death.'

Darren nodded. 'Wouldn't you? Gabe did nothing wrong. It was an accident, the sarge and the ambos could see that. All just bad timing and bad luck, but imagine walking around knowing if he'd set off five minutes later, he might've seen her coming.'

To his left Courtney stood stock still, stunned. 'He's just left us?'

'Looks that way,' Darren said, trying to decide if he was relieved they weren't going to be heading out to Brigadier, or concerned they were now stuck at the Junction with no money.

Amin's face was a mixture of sympathy and despair. 'That is a tortured man,' he said. 'But it changes nothing. I must get to that station.'

'How exactly?' Courtney asked, looking around the seemingly deserted town. 'He took the phone, the guns, everything. What are we supposed to do?'

'No, not everything.' Amin reached behind his back, withdrawing Chase's pistol, and from his front pocket pulled out the mobile phone. He waved it at Darren. 'Perhaps your friends can help?'

Darren wasn't so sure. 'I can try, but I don't know how we'll go. What do we want to do?'

'The plan remains,' Amin said firmly. 'We arrive, look around, and if the opportunity arises, we grab my family and go.'

'And if it doesn't?'

'Then I think Courtney's idea about the media is the best. Or maybe we have no choice but to go to the police in Carnarvon. But we have to try to get my family first.' Amin's eyes pleaded with them. 'I won't be happy until I hold them both.'

He started to sob, the events of the past two days finally catching up with him. Darren exchanged glances with Courtney as she put her arm around Amin. 'We need to help him,' she said quietly. 'If it looks too risky, we go with plan B, or C.'

'What if Gabe comes back?'

'Then he'll have a fair idea of where we've gone, won't he?'

Darren sighed and stuck out his hand. 'Alright, give the phone here then.'

He dialled, hoping he wasn't going to regret this later.

Gabe hit the brakes, bringing the ute to a sliding stop. He breathed hard, trying to clear his head, trying to push the memory of that night back down. It was so clear, still as fresh as the day it happened, and deep down he knew it always would be, no matter how many beers or bottles of whisky he drank. His hands resting on the steering wheel trembled, and he raised them to his eyes, studying the calloused surface of his palms, the tobacco-stained fingertips. He could still see Valerie's blood on them, still feel it, as though it had seeped into his very flesh, never to be washed away.

He fumbled out his tobacco pouch, rolled a smoke and lit it. This familiar action, performed without thinking, gave his hands something to focus on, and the trembling began to subside. Gabe lowered the window and watched the smoke dissipate into the searing heat. He began to breathe slower, calmed down a little and assessed the situation. *Now what?*

He had made the right call, even if it was for the wrong reasons. The whole plan had been fanciful from the get-go. Jesus Christ, mount a fucking rescue? Who did they think they were, the A-Team? A for amateur, more like. What a bloody joke. It was time to handball the whole thing, and Gabe knew to who. Parker. Despite the senior officer's offsider being corrupt, Gabe had dealt with the old sarge enough in the past to be sure he could be trusted, and he would know how best to handle the situation. After all, that was the original plan, wasn't it? And up until Darren had inadvertently told the wrong cop the story, it had been a good one. He supposed he could just turn around and head to Carnarvon, but someone there had to be tipping Jefferson off. Maybe they were in with him, maybe they didn't realise, but either way Gabe didn't want to risk it.

But how to do so? He could ring Parker on the sat-phone, but what if Jefferson answered? The officer already knew his number and would know it was him calling. No, it would be best if Gabe went there in person. Would Parker believe him though? It'd be his word against Jefferson's, at least until he got Darren and the others to back him up.

The thought of the other three brought a pang of guilt, but he brushed it aside. Darren knew the Junction, and he could take them to wait inside the roadhouse. Old Graham might get a bit dark on them for not buying anything, but stingy travellers were nothing new. They would be fine – just had to sit tight until he got back.

He flicked the finished cigarette butt out the window and pulled back onto the road. The best way to convince Parker would be to bring him some proof, and Gabe knew just where to find that. Chase. He would return to the site where it had all started, pick up the injured man and escort him straight to Parker's little police station, even if he had to hogtie the bastard to the roof rack. Maybe Jefferson would be there, maybe he wouldn't, but he didn't think the kid would do anything stupid in front of Parker. Probably try to talk his way out of it. Jefferson had to have some sort of plan to explain Courtney's disappearance, and maybe he was just sitting there waiting for Chase to return with good news. Gabe didn't think Chase's mates would have found him yet. It had only been a couple of hours since they left, and Gabe was sure he could reach him before anyone came looking. But he drove hard just in case, thankful for the well-kept Shire road he was travelling back down.

Although he had to slow once he turned off the main road, it was just after four by the time the granite outcrop came into view. *Back here already,* he thought. *After this I never want to see the bloody place again.*

Gabe guided his ute around the base, his senses on high alert. Chase would've heard him coming and he hoped the man assumed it was his friends. Although they had checked Chase's vehicle before leaving him, Gabe knew better than anyone that a weapon could be hidden easily enough. He rounded the corner and was momentarily stunned by what he saw, or rather by what he didn't see.

Chase, along with his vehicle, was gone.

THIRTY-SIX

Chase Fowler seethed, barely feeling his fractured wrist as he struggled with the wheel spanner. Changing tyres was never the easiest job, but doing it mostly one-handed could get fucked. Lucky it was his left arm out of action. He'd managed to set the jack and loosen the wheel nuts, but the hardest part had been winding over the poxy winch that held his spare under the tray. Chase rarely bothered with it, instead opting to use the second tyre mounted on his shooter's frame since it was easier to get to, as he'd done that morning. As a result, the seldom used winch chain was seized with dust and dirt. A mild annoyance at most times, but it was infuriating when trying to operate it with a busted wrist. The splint that nurse had put on kept jarring against things, sending bolts of pain through his arm, but he persevered and finally succeeded in lowering the spare tyre through sheer bloody-mindedness.

In truth, it wasn't really the tyre he was angry at. He was angry at himself. That old bastard had outsmarted him again. He'd read the sign, laid the trap and caught him by the balls as though he were just another stray dog to be put down. That did not sit well with Chase, and he planned to do something about it. He knew where they were headed, and what they were planning.

He had no doubt that if they did manage to get hold of Amin's family, they would make for Carnarvon. They had to; where else could they go? The sheer isolation of the place was why the operation had been set up there. You could run away, but to where? Not that many did. They must've come from some real shit spots in the world to prefer Brigadier. And the occasional troublemakers were dealt with. No one seemed to miss them. Chase guessed everyone just assumed they'd been moved on. All in all, it had been going pretty smoothly, right up until yesterday.

But he would fix that. The plan remained the same. Get rid of the four of them. This time he would not wait, there would be no warning. Just as Gabe had trapped him like a dog, he would return the favour, but in his line of work there was no need for traps. Just a second or two to get the shot in the scope. And he would do so, broken wrist or not. They hadn't found his other rifle locked away in the toolbox bolted to the tray. He would have to check it over first, make sure the sights were still okay after the ute tipped. As for the ute itself, it was horribly bent and the driver's door took some effort to open, but it would do. If not, he could circle back to the tip at Jakob's River and take the Dual Cab Gabe had left there. By now Jefferson should be well on his way to Carnarvon to meet their informant in the morning, and if his plans for the old sarge had worked, the man wouldn't bother him either.

He would stick to the station tracks and avoid the main road. He knew where to go. To one of the many flat-top hills scattered through the Gascoyne rangelands. There were three that overlooked Brigadier, and from that vantage point he could wait and observe. If they tried to grab the family and were caught, so be it; he would arrive and mop up. But if they succeeded, if they began to make their way back to town, he would be waiting for them.

*

233

Gabe parked in front of the small transportable building that served as the community's police station. Upon discovering Chase missing, he'd debated what was best to do, but decided to continue with his plan. The sooner Parker took over the better, figuring Chase was on his way to Brigadier, though he must've taken the back roads as Gabe had not passed any vehicles since leaving the Junction. There were a million tracks crisscrossing the pastoral country, some better than others, and somebody like Chase would know them all, just as Gabe did.

He took a deep breath and made his way towards the front door, only to find it was locked, with a notice in the window. *CLOSED. For Emergencies Call 000.* Gabe gave a wry laugh. What bloody good would that do out here? He looked around the back. The police troopy was gone. *Shit, now what?*

Maybe Melissa knew where they were. She seemed to know every other bloody thing that was going on in this town. Maybe she'd know when they'd be back. He didn't hold much hope, but there wasn't much else he could do.

He drove down the street towards the shop. School was out and uniformed kids wandered about. Some of the older ones waved, recognising him. He gave them a curt nod, but focused on his destination. There seemed to be quite a few people milling around, not unusual for this time of day he supposed, but when he entered the store, Gabe was shocked to see the place was a mess. Upturned display shelves were scattered across the floor, and it looked as though someone had hurled the last pack of overripe tomatoes against the far wall. By the counter he saw the diminutive frame of Elsie with Melissa, who had her back to him, and beside them stood two men Gabe did not know. They all appeared to be standing over someone lying on the floor.

'What the hell happened?' he asked. Elsie looked up in surprise, saw who it was and gave a little scowl.

'Your bloody friend, that's what's happened.'

'What?'

Elsie jerked her head towards the two men, who stood with worried expressions on their faces. 'Bobby. Gone off the rails. Came in drunk, looking for more beer. Melissa here tried to get him to go home, and he started smashing the place up.'

'Christ.' This was the last thing Gabe needed right now. He was about to ask Melissa if she was okay when she turned and he saw the towel she held to her forehead. 'Shit, did he hurt you?'

'I'm okay, shelf caught me as it went over.'

Elsie banged her hand on the counter. 'This is exactly why we've got to keep the grog out. Good people do dumb things.' She took Melissa by the elbow. 'We need to get you over the road, get the nurse to have a look at you. And where's Darren? Someone tell him to come get his uncle.'

Gabe swallowed, hard. There was no way to explain everything to them all – not here, not now. He needed to find Parker.

'Gabe?' A weary voice came from the opposite side of the checkout counter. 'That you? Hey, I need a drink. You got any more?'

Gabe strode around to where the two men were standing over Bobby, ignoring the accusing look from Elsie. Bobby was slouched down on the floor with legs outstretched and his back against the wall. His head lolled, and upon seeing Gabe a grin erupted across his face.

'Hey, brother.'

'You dumb shit, what do you think you're doing?'

Bobby shrugged. 'Ran dry already. Forgot they don't sell it here no more.'

'Jesus, Bobby, you wrecked the joint.' Gabe stared down at his friend. This was all his doing.

'I saw her again,' Bobby mumbled.

'What?'

'Valerie. Saw her in my sleep. Always see her in my sleep, lying there, all broken like that horse of hers.'

Gabe's anger dissolved in an instant, and he knelt down beside him. 'Yeah, me too, mate. All the time.'

'I didn't want to see her no more.'

'Me either, not like that.'

'I keep thinking, you know? Maybe if I got there sooner—' Bobby started, but Gabe cut him off.

'Wouldn't have made any difference, Bobby, I keep telling you. You gotta stop thinking like that. She was too far gone, mate. Nothing anyone could do. And if you didn't come by when you did, maybe I'd be dead as well.'

Bobby didn't reply, placing his head in his hands. Gabe squeezed his shoulder and rose, addressing the two men. 'You know where he lives?' They nodded. 'Good. Take him back home and get him cleaned up. Darren isn't around, but he'll be back soon.' *If things go according to plan,* he thought. Then he noticed Elsie. She'd come around the counter and had been listening in.

'It's been you.' It was not a question. He said nothing, keeping his eyes lowered. 'Gabe.'

Something in the old lady's voice made him raise his eyes. She did not look angry. She looked disappointed, and somehow that was worse. 'What would Valerie say?'

'Valerie's not here,' he retorted. 'Just her memory, and it's not a bloody good one. You never saw her, Elsie. He did. I did. I still see her every time I close my eyes, and I reckon he does too, so I don't blame him for needing a drink. Christ knows I do.'

Now it was Elsie's turn not to reply. Gabe wanted to be angry, to blame Bobby, blame Elsie and her stupid bloody dry community, deflect the blame from himself, but looking around at the smashed shop and the shaken Melissa, he could not. Instead he focused on what had brought him to the store in the first place. 'Where's the cops?'

To his surprise, Elsie shook her head gently. 'No coppers, Gabe. We'll handle this ourselves. I thought it was a stranger bringing the grog in. I'm still not happy about it, and you and I, we got some talking to do, but we don't need the coppers.'

'I appreciate that, Elsie, but I need to speak with Parker anyway. Station's closed, though.'

Melissa spoke up from the other side of the counter. 'Parker's crook,' she said. 'Came in couple hours back looking for something for an upset stomach. Told him to see the nurse, but he said she wasn't there.' She gave Gabe a quizzical look. 'Weren't you in there this morning with that tourist fellow?'

He ignored the question. Maybe one day he'd explain, but right now he needed Parker. He'd never thought to check the living quarters that backed on to the station. 'So he's home then?'

'Far as I know,' Melissa said. 'The constable left not that long ago, in one hell of a hurry. Think he was heading to Carnarvon.'

Gabe's heart skipped a beat as he realised he must've only just missed meeting Jefferson on the road when he turned off to find Chase. That might have been interesting, to say the least.

'Right, look, I got to go,' he said. 'Sorry about the mess.' Gabe paused, watching Bobby being led outside and leaning heavily on the two men. 'I didn't realise he was this bad.'

'He needs help,' Elsie said. 'But that's not easy to find out here.' Without her realising it, Elsie had repeated Darren's earlier sentiments, and Gabe felt his guts twist.

237

He left the two women, returned to his ute and sat for a moment as his mind went over what he'd just seen. *What would Valerie say?* Oh, she'd give him an earful, that was for sure. But Valerie wasn't around anymore, it was just him. He banged a hand against the steering wheel, swearing to himself, then reached over and retrieved the roll of banknotes from the glove box.

'Fuck's sake,' he said again, storming back into the shop. He tossed the roll to the surprised Melissa and Elsie. 'Here. For . . . damages.' He turned and left before either of them could say anything.

Gabe knocked on the door to the old police quarters. The station was never permanently manned, only running part-time on certain days, which always struck Gabe as strange, like somehow the bad guys only operated on a set schedule. He could hear movement from inside, and the door opened to reveal a very pale Sergeant Parker.

'Gabe? What are you doing here?' the sarge said.

'Need your help.' Gabe was suddenly feeling very nervous. 'In a bit of trouble.'

Parker's face immediately grew concerned. 'What's up? Though I don't know if I'll be much help. Must have had some bad food; it's going right through me. Reckon I could shit through the eye of a needle.' He moved aside and waved Gabe in. The apartment was tidy enough, but it was obvious two men lived here.

'Where's your apprentice?' Gabe asked, looking around.

'He's had to shoot up to Carnarvon, something about an appointment he had booked for tomorrow. Doctor, I think. We were pretty much done here anyway, and I would've gone with him, but, well, let's just say I'm not moving far from the loo right now.'

This was almost too convenient to be coincidence. 'I need you to come with me,' Gabe said. 'There's been some serious stuff go down in the last couple of days, and I'm done trying to sort it out on my own.'

This got Parker's attention. 'What sort of stuff, Gabe? What have you got yourself into? Is it the grog?'

Gabe gave a dry laugh. 'If only that's all it was. But we need to move. Your boy isn't who he says he is, and I think he's heading off to do something that's going to get a lot of people hurt.'

'Wait, you mean young Matty? What the hell are you talking about?'

He could see Parker wasn't going to go anywhere without some sort of explanation. 'Alright, here's the quick version. There's people smugglers operating off the coast up here. Yesterday I came across two about to shoot an Ara—' he caught himself. 'An Afghan called Amin. We got away and went to find his family, but this nutter roo-shooter came after us, nearly shot us both in the medical centre over there and we bolted, with young Darren and the nurse Courtney as well.' He paused, seeing the look of incredulity grow on Parker's face.

'Don't look at me like that, I know how it bloody sounds,' Gabe growled. 'I haven't even got to the real crazy bit yet. Your boy is in on it. Amin says there's bent cops working with people smugglers. That's why I never came here first. Look, Sarge, we've got to get moving. I'll tell you everything on the way, but we need to get to the Junction. I left the others there, and if we don't get back soon, they're likely to do something stupid.'

'Gabe, this is a lot to take in. And I can't just head off with you like that. Jefferson's got the troopy.'

'I know, and right now he's probably heading straight to Brigadier Station, not Carnarvon like he said, and Chase is doing the same. That's the roo-shooter who tried to do us in. We left him stranded in the scrub, but I went back to bring him here and he was gone.'

He could see the sergeant still wasn't convinced, standing cross-armed while Gabe paced back and forth. 'Here, come have a look at this.'

Parker followed him outside. Gabe pointed at his windscreen. 'That's from Chase. He was about to drop Courtney and Darren down a very deep hole before we stopped him.'

The sight of the bullet holes seemed to galvanise Parker a little. 'I need to call this in,' he said.

'You can't!' Gabe almost shouted. 'Not yet. Get the others safe and then make a call. You don't know who to trust, and we can't risk Amin's family like that.'

Parker shook his head. 'Jefferson?' he said again. 'But he's just a kid.'

'Yeah, well, that kid left two taser marks on Darren's back and busted his lip pretty bad too.' Gabe watched Parker wrestle with his thoughts. 'We reckon someone has to be feeding him info out of Carnarvon. Border Control or Customs maybe, maybe without them even realising it. Sarge, I'll tell you everything, but we have to move.'

The police officer said nothing, continuing to stare at the windscreen.

'Look, you know me,' Gabe continued, almost pleading now. 'You know all I want is to be left alone out here in peace. Do you really think I'd be running around like a headless chook if it wasn't serious? And that I wouldn't handball it to you boys in a heartbeat if I could?'

Parker studied him, weighing up his arguments. 'You're not making this up, are you?'

'Think I even could?'

'Shit,' Parker breathed. 'Alright, I'll come with you. Give us a minute to get dressed. But you've got some serious talking to do, Gabe. Starting with how the hell you got involved in all this.'

The sarge disappeared inside and returned shortly afterwards in full uniform. He still looked pale and sweat ran down his cheeks, but his face was set with grim determination. Gabe was pleased to see the service pistol sitting in the holster on his belt, just in case they ran into Chase or Jefferson. He wasn't sure which would be worse.

THIRTY-SEVEN

'Remind me,' Parker said through gritted teeth, one hand clinging to the grip above his door window, the other braced against the dashboard, 'never to engage you in a police pursuit once this is all over.'

Gabe smirked as they raced down the gravel road. He veered around a kangaroo, who seemed determined to attempt suicide by LandCruiser, and pushed his foot down harder. Parker sucked in his breath, regained his composure and tried to recap what he had just heard.

'So instead of calling the police, you and this Amin fellow decided to dump the bodies and set off to find his wife and kid?'

'Well, yeah. When you put it like that it sounds pretty stupid,' Gabe admitted. 'But Amin was sure we couldn't trust anyone, and I dunno, we sort of panicked, I guess.'

'But dumping bodies? Bloody hell, Gabe, how stupid could you be?'

Gabe took a deep breath. This was to be expected. 'Look, we weren't thinking, alright? You didn't see those bastards, or how shit-scared Amin was about police. We knew people would come looking, and that if they found their dead mates, his family would be in even more danger. Christ, he was so wound up, he might've even shot me if I tried calling it in.'

Parker considered this. 'How'd you even find him?'

Crap, Gabe thought. *Well, I'm already fucked.* 'I . . . I wasn't supposed to be in the area. I'll come clean. Only reason I crossed paths with Amin is because I was setting traps on the Reserve when I heard the shot that killed his mate. So not calling you guys kept him happy and my nose clean.' He decided to keep quiet about his rifle, for now. No point giving everything to Parker on a platter. 'Just wanted to get out of the mess I found myself in soon as possible. Anyway, you guys would've been who we went to, and turns out he was right about your constable.'

'I'm still finding that hard to believe,' Parker said. 'He seemed a good sort. Bit overzealous at times, but all the young ones are.'

'Well, you better believe it if we run into him. Scared the shit out of Courtney, and, according to her, he was working pretty close with Chase.'

'Bloody hell,' Parker said. Gabe wasn't sure if it was at the statement or at the pothole they'd just bounced over. When this was all over, his ute would need some serious attention. 'So what happened to Chase? You said you left him at that ridge?'

'Fuck knows. He had a busted arm. Courtney patched him up and we left him there.' Gabe also decided not to elaborate on how Amin was all set to shoot the man in cold blood. Bit hard to argue self-defence on that one, even if Gabe might have considered doing the same if it were Valerie in danger. 'He had enough water for a few days, and he said others would come looking for him, so we figured he'd be fine, and we'd be long gone by the time they did.' Gabe pointed at the open bag on the dash. 'Gave him a packet of that jerky too. Help yourself, by the way.'

Parker screwed up his nose. 'Horrible stuff. Might as well eat roadkill. So, by these "others", you mean the people smugglers?'

'Smugglers, bent cops, whoever. We didn't hang around long enough to find out. But either he got himself out of there or someone came to help him real quick.' He shook his head. 'I dunno, maybe we should've taken his keys, but it never occurred to me. Not exactly used to this sort of thing.'

'Neither am I,' Parker admitted. 'Breaking up fights, chasing up on stolen livestock, keeping tourists safe and generally keeping the peace pretty much sums up my career.' He studied Gabe. 'So why the change of heart? Why'd you come back, and more importantly, why'd you leave the others behind?'

Gabe was silent for a moment. 'We had a difference of opinion on a few things,' he said finally. 'And I realised what a stupid bloody idea it was to try and rescue Amin's wife and son on our own. So I left them at the Junction and scarpered to find you. Figured you'd know what to do, and that was the original plan anyway, before things went south.'

'I know what I *should* be doing,' Parker grunted. 'And yet here I am.'

'I told you, we can't risk it. If they get wind the cops are coming, they might do something drastic.'

'Clean house, you mean?'

Gabe nodded. 'They were all set to shoot Amin and his buddy, and Courtney, Darren and me just to keep things quiet. Who knows what they'll do to the wife and kid.'

'You know I'm going to have to call it in sooner or later.'

'I know, but I'll be happier once we get everyone somewhere safer first. Then you can call in the bloody army for all I care.'

'There's going to be some blowback if this all turns out to be as you say,' Parker mused. 'People smugglers, illegal workers, murder, attempted murder.' He looked at Gabe pointedly. 'Tampering with evidence.'

Gabe coughed and focused on the road.

'Police corruption, police violence,' Parker continued. 'All the current catchphrases in one go. You sure know how to pick them.'

'Tell me about it,' Gabe grunted. 'I reckon it won't just be smugglers or bent coppers wanting to keep this quiet.'

'You might be right,' Parker said. 'More I think about it, the more I'm starting to agree with you. Get people safe, then blow the whistle.'

'And what if some of your other mates in Carnarvon or elsewhere are in on it too?'

Parker's response was abrupt and to the point. 'Then they are no longer my mates.'

Gabe nodded in appreciation, feeling a lot more confident he'd made the right choice, though this was clearly going to come back and bite him in the arse if they ever got out of it. No way would they let him off, not with everything he'd done leading up to this point.

His passenger gave a groan. 'You're going to have to pull over for a second.'

Gabe did so, handed the officer the toilet roll and watched as he hurried off behind a tree. Despite the situation, Gabe couldn't help but grin. Shit really was going sideways now.

By the time they pulled alongside the Junction roadhouse, Gabe was sure Parker had left clench marks in the seat cushion. The setting sun made it an uncomfortable drive but he'd managed the trip in record time.

'Reckon they'll be in here,' Gabe said.

The two men made their way to the door, entered, and the handful of patrons who had arrived since he left only a few hours earlier turned to inspect the newcomers. It was the usual crowd – a couple of station hands, a small road crew still in their high-vis workwear, and two ladies Gabe recognised as the Shire clerks reclined on the lounge as they chatted.

Parker made a beeline for the toilet while Gabe approached the bar. Graham saw him coming and gave a puzzled look. 'Thought you went to Bidgemia.'

'Change of plans,' he said.

'Usual?'

He wanted one, Christ knew he did, but shook his head. 'Not now. I'm looking for a group, three of them. They might've come in here. A young blackfella, a girl wearing your T-shirt and another guy, Middle Eastern type.'

Graham nodded. 'Oh yeah, they came in a couple of hours ago. Used the toilets and stuff. Didn't buy anything though. Sat on the lounge making phone calls, and then a car came to pick them up.'

'What?' Gabe felt his stomach flip. 'A car? What sort? Who was in it?'

'Whoa, ease up. I don't know. It was an old troopy, bit clapped out. There was another car with them, but I don't know who was driving it. The ones you're talking about took the troopy, and its driver got into the second car.'

'Shit!' Gabe swore loud enough to make others turn their heads.

'What's this about?' Graham asked. 'That girl was wearing the shirt you bought here. How do you know them?'

'Doesn't matter. When did they leave? Did you see which way?'

'I don't know, hour, hour and a half ago.' Graham's eyes left

Gabe, focusing on someone behind him. Gabe turned to see Parker approach, conspicuous in his uniform.

'Well, where are they?'

'Not here,' Gabe said. 'C'mon, we need to find them.'

Bartender and patrons alike watched him leave, police officer by his side, and Gabe knew all sorts of stories would be flying around within minutes.

Back in the ute Gabe banged the steering wheel. 'Stupid bloody bastards. Where the hell do they think they're going?'

'What happened?'

Gabe relayed the story, and in doing so formed an idea. 'I bet Darren called his mates with the phone Amin took from the smugglers and said to come get them.'

'Where do you think they went?'

'One of two places, I reckon. Either to Carnarvon to alert the media, or out to the station to get Amin's family.'

'You know them best. What's your guess?'

Gabe thought for a moment. There was something missing, he knew it, but couldn't nail it down. They made a phone call, and someone ran a vehicle out to them. Darren's mates, most likely. *Darren's mates.*

'Wait a minute,' he exclaimed, reaching for the sat-phone. 'I'll bet you anything he called the same mob he rang on this phone.' He scrolled through to the call list, which wasn't hard, as calls on that phone were few and far between. 'You got a pen?'

Parker pulled out his notebook and scribbled down the number as Gabe read it out. The officer retrieved his own phone and began to dial but Gabe held out his hand.

'Reckon I'd better ring,' he said. 'Not sure his mates will be real keen on telling a cop where he's going, not if Darren has filled them in on everything.'

Parker considered this, shrugged and handed him the phone. It rang briefly before someone answered. 'Wattup?'

Gabe got straight to the point. 'You Darren's mate?'

'Maybe,' came the cautious reply. 'Who's asking?'

'Gabe. I was with him earlier.'

'You the grumpy old prick who dumped them at the Junction?'

It was a fair assessment. 'Yeah, but it wasn't like that. Came back to get them but they're gone. You know where they are?'

A pause. 'Dunno if I should be talking to you. Darren was pretty shook up.'

'I bet, but that's not why,' Gabe said, trying to keep his voice calm. 'He's in some serious shit, all of them are, and I'm trying to stop them doing something stupid.'

'Says you.' But the reply sounded unsure.

'Look, I just need to know where they are.'

'I don't know. All Darren said was, if we didn't hear from him by tomorrow night, to call the cops out to that station, Brigadier.'

'Shit!' That was all the confirmation Gabe needed. They weren't heading to town. They were going to attempt a rescue on their own.

'Hey, what's this all about—' Darren's friend started to ask, but Gabe ended the call. There was no point talking any further. He needed to get moving, and fast. He started the engine and drove out of the Junction, explaining to Parker as he went.

'They're going to try and mount a rescue themselves.'

'Shit.' Parker mirrored Gabe's own sentiments. 'How are they going to do that?'

'I've no idea, but Amin's no fool. I reckon they'll sneak in, try to grab his family and sneak out.'

'Tonight?'

'How would I know? Makes sense to do it in the dark. I guess Darren knows his way there. Wouldn't matter though – all the stations are signposted along the roads anyway.'

Parker took up his grip on the cab's handrail once more. 'You'd better put your foot down then.'

THIRTY-EIGHT

By the time Darren switched off the engine of his cousin's troopy, Courtney had almost fallen asleep again, though she didn't understand how that could be, even as she felt her eyelids droop. Now that they were actually here on Brigadier, and only a few kilometres from the homestead, the reality of what they were attempting broke over her like a wave. How could she possibly be tired? It had taken all of the three hours Gabe said it would to get here. Darren drove much more cautiously than their former companion, but whether that was because he wasn't sure of the way, didn't know the roads as well or was merely trying to delay their arrival, she couldn't be certain. Each scenario was just as likely.

'Where are we?'

'We should be a kay or so from the homestead,' Darren said. 'Sign on the road said forty kilometres, and, so long as the troopy's meter is right, we came about thirty-eight.'

In the moonlight she could see Darren had turned off the gravel road and parked some way into the scrub. 'Now what?'

'We go for a walk,' Amin said. He was determined to get going, that was plain to see. He held the pistol in one hand. 'Lead the way.'

Darren shrugged and set off. Courtney and Amin followed, side by side. The air was still, dry and carried the remains of the day's heat. Silence enveloped them like a blanket, making their footsteps seem to echo under the cavern of stars persisting through the moon's glow. In different circumstances it would have been a gorgeous evening.

They had only gone a short distance, creeping through the low scrub, when Darren spoke. 'Hey, Amin?'

'Yes?'

'Your wife, she a Muslim too?'

'Yes.'

'And there's other Muslim families at this place?'

'I would think so, yes. Why do you ask?'

A pause, an awkward one. 'Just that, if they're all wearing those burqa things, how are we supposed to know who is who?'

Courtney listened in with humorous curiosity, awaiting Amin's reply. It began with a chuckle.

'If you mean the full face veil, we call it the chadari. But not all women wear those, my friend. Aamena chooses to wear just a head scarf, though she was made to wear a chadari during the Taliban's rule. They were not good days.'

'Is that why you came over here?' Courtney asked.

'Not so much the chadari, but it was due to the Taliban. No, my brother was killed for helping the Americans, which made us a target.'

'That's terrible,' Courtney said. 'I'm so sorry.'

'Thank you. It is what it is – though I did not ever expect to find myself walking through the Australian bush with two young people such as yourselves, on the way to rescue my family.'

'If it makes you feel any better, it's not how I was planning to spend my Thursday night either,' she replied.

They walked on in silence after that, but to Courtney every footstep sounded like thunder, and each time she pushed through one of the low wattles she was sure the rustle must have carried towards the homestead, alerting those residing there. They reached a plain wire fence and climbed over it, entering what looked to be a small holding paddock. *So far, so good,* she thought, threading herself through the rusted wires. The occasional squeak of a windmill turning in a stray breath of wind was the only noise. A faint glow rose into the sky ahead of them. The homestead lights, she assumed.

Darren held out an arm to stop Courtney and Amin, and he pointed at a tank stand on their right, partially obscured by a large white gum growing beside it. He made a climbing motion. She nodded, and they headed towards the structure. The steel framework of the stand had seen better days, as had the tin tank atop it. Water dripped down on all sides, and the ground below was damp.

'I'll go,' Darren said, and before anyone could protest he scampered up the rickety ladder. The platform's timber boards, white and fuzzy with water rot, creaked as he inched his way around the tank. Courtney half expected the wood to give way. After a few minutes he climbed back down.

'What did you see?' Amin asked.

'Not much,' Darren said. 'But the dongas are around there, to the west past the workshop. You both should go and take a look.'

'Will that platform hold me?' Courtney asked. As much as she hated to admit it, she probably weighed a touch more than the young man next to her. She didn't like the idea of climbing up there, but she wanted a better view.

'Reckon so.'

She took a deep breath and started up the ladder, feeling the metal rungs flex under her with each step. Thankfully, they held, and once atop the wooden platform she sneaked around the side of the tank and took in the view under the bright moonlight.

Brigadier looked like many other outback stations, she supposed. The old homestead, once a magnificent example of the boom times when the country rode on the sheep's back, had seen better days. The tin roof was a patchwork of rusty sheets, one gutter hung off the side and a few of the weatherboards had come loose and dangled down. An assortment of additions had been tacked on to the building over the years, resulting in a hodgepodge of colonial architecture and modern-day design melded together.

The workshop didn't look much better, nor did the usual array of outhouses and quarters that made up the rest of the complex. If the Wheldon brothers were making any money out of their involvement in this venture, they weren't spending it on maintenance. In fact, the only things that looked reasonably new were the three white dongas nestled behind the dilapidated workshop.

She counted the vehicles illuminated under a large floodlight that lit up most of the area. Three utes, a station troopy and a coaster-style bus. The bus was interesting, new looking and well set up for outback travel, with high-lift suspension, and appeared to be four-wheel drive. Her eye caught the outline of motorbikes nestled under a lean-to that dangled precariously from the workshop wall.

So now what? There didn't appear to be anyone stirring. Could they sneak in, grab the two captives and scarper? She wasn't sure that would work, but every moment they waited risked them being discovered. And had these people found Chase yet? Possibly. If so, what would they do knowing this ragtag band were heading for them? Move Amin's family elsewhere? Lay a trap?

The last one seemed the most likely. After all, Chase and that horrible policeman had already tried that once.

She descended and gestured to Amin. 'Your turn.'

Amin returned a few minutes later. 'Looks quiet,' he said.

'Yeah, so what do we do?' Darren asked.

'I do not know. Every bit of me wants to run to those buildings and search for my wife and son, but that would not be wise. We do not know how many are in there, and we may cause alarm to the others. And they may wish to follow us – we cannot allow that.'

'But we can't just leave them there either,' Courtney said.

'There's the bus,' Darren said. 'Load 'em up in that.'

'Then what?' Amin asked, growing agitated. 'I do not think they will just allow us to drive out of here.'

'What if they're busy doing something else?' Darren asked.

'Like what?'

'Dunno yet. Got an idea, but I need to go check something out first. Back in a minute.'

Courtney was about to protest, but Amin spoke first. 'Take this.' He handed Darren the pistol. 'You might need it.'

Darren stared at the gun, shrugged and took it. Amin showed him the safety and how to cock the weapon. 'Aim for the chest,' he said. 'But don't think that silencer will muffle the sound completely. You heard it go off back in the medical centre.'

'Shit, I'll be lucky if I can hit that bloody shed.' He smiled, a broad grin that was tinged with nerves, and then he was gone.

'What the bloody hell are you doing?' Darren whispered to himself. He had just darted across the holding paddock and was pressed up against the side of an old tin shed, breathing hard.

Still no sign of any people, and he hoped there weren't any dogs roaming about. Hadn't thought of that when he first set off.

His plan was simple enough. Check the vehicles to see if the keys were in them. If this place was like most other stations, they would be, but he also supposed if people were being held here against their will, then an assortment of escape cars ready to go might not be the smartest thing to leave lying around. Which was why he'd wanted to check, but now, standing with his back to the still warm tin wall of the shed, he was beginning to think this wasn't such a good idea. Too late now though.

He snuck a quick look past the shed. No one to be seen. Fifty metres ahead of him were the bikes, parked under the lean-to attached to the workshop. He was sure they would have keys, but if the bus didn't, then there was no point. His plan needed that bus.

Darren took a deep breath, gripped the pistol a little tighter — though he had no idea exactly what he would do with it if spotted — and ducked across the yard in a low run, aiming for the side of the bus. Never before had he felt so naked and exposed, certain there were a dozen eyes watching, waiting for him to draw just a little closer. Any second now he expected to hear a shot and feel a red-hot pain. Or would he feel the pain first? He didn't know and didn't care to find out.

He reached the bus and squatted by the driver's door. Looking over his shoulder, he could just make out a figure peering out from behind the water tank high on its stand. Okay, so they could be seen from here. Good to know if shit turned south. Darren checked through the door window and was relieved to see the keys were in fact there, dangling from the ignition. He opened the door, wincing as it creaked on its hinges, and removed them. They would need these later.

Darren pocketed the keys and closed the door with a click. Now for the bikes. He was halfway to them when the unmistakable screech of a flyscreen door almost froze him in his tracks. Almost. He sprinted on, dived behind the nearest Yamaha, and peered through the cowling towards the homestead. A figure silhouetted by the glow from inside the building stood on the verandah, lighting a smoke. They didn't seem to have noticed anything, instead staring out towards the east, sipping from a mug. Darren hoped whoever was up the water tower had seen the door open and had hidden. *Now what?* He looked around. He might be able to get back to the water tank if he circled wide.

Keeping one eye on the smoker, Darren gave the bikes a quick once-over. Selecting the newest looking Yamaha, which didn't look very new at all, but in comparison to the other three it was practically fresh off the production line, he turned the key. A green light shone on the instrument dial. He turned the key to off. So there was power; that was a start. There was also fuel, oil and a faint wheel track where the bike had been ridden in. Darren felt confident it was usable. He was no stranger to them, having done more than a few musters for stations. His only concern was that some bikes could be temperamental bastards to start, but hopefully this one wouldn't be when the time came.

As satisfied as he could be, Darren stole out of the rear of the lean-to, scanning in all directions for people, and making sure the smoker on the verandah continued facing the opposite direction. Apart from him, there was no one, but something did catch Darren's attention. A newish looking extension had been tacked on to the back of the workshop, and light emanated from under the door. He wondered what it was for and decided to have a look. Any and all information could be valuable later on. Peering in through the window yielded little result as the glass was covered in tinfoil. He crept to the door, listened closely and, not hearing any noise, tried the handle. It opened, thankfully with no creak. He peeked inside and instantly recognised what he was seeing.

A single bench ran down the centre of the room. Everything appeared exceptionally clean and dust-free, in stark contrast to the rest of the place. Stools were placed on either side along the length of the bench, and at each seat was a silver tray, scales and small piles of plastic bags, the resealable kind used for coins . . . or drugs.

In his mind, Darren pictured it all. Rows of women sitting at the bench, measuring out portions of drugs into the little bags, ready to be sent off all over the state, or perhaps even the country. Shit, was this why they kept the families separate? Keep the men working in what they thought were legit jobs, earning money to bring their families over, all while the women and children had already been brought here and were packing drugs in a far-flung station, miles away from the nearest drug squad?

The creak of the flyscreen roused him from his thoughts, and he closed the packing-house door. Risking a quick peek at the verandah, he saw the smoker had returned inside. He glanced at the three dongas, saw the light and shadows moving around in them and could hear muffled voices. Women, and . . . little kids? He briefly considered having a closer look, but decided against it. Last thing they needed was a bunch of scared folk seeing his face and screaming.

Darren wasted no more time and made his way back to the tank, taking the long way around in case anyone else felt like an evening stroll. He reached the tank just as Amin finished climbing down the ladder.

'What did you see?'

'Oh man, we are in some big shit,' Darren said. 'They're packing drugs there. Just like in the movies, they've got a room all decked out with scales and bags and shit. Only thing missing was two guards with machine guns standing over a bunch of women working.' He faced Amin. 'I'll bet that's what they're doing with all the women. Making them break down big packs of drugs. I dunno what though. Could be dope, but probably meth. Who knows? Might be anything and everything they can get their hands on. But there's definitely women and kids in those dongas. I didn't see them, but I heard them.'

Amin took all this in. 'What you are saying does make a lot of sense. Afghanistan grows much opium, and the two men we killed, Gabe and I, they were from Afghanistan also. Perhaps it could all be linked?'

'Perhaps,' said Courtney. 'But it doesn't really matter right now. What matters is how we get your family out.'

'Here's my plan,' Darren said. 'We go back to the troopy and get some sleep. Then we come back real early, before dawn, and wait. You two search for your family, Amin, while everyone is still in bed, then I'm gonna grab a bike, start the bastard, make as much racket as possible, and piss off outta here real quick. I reckon they'll take one look at me, see some dirty blackfella pinching their gear and be after me.' It sounded so simple when he said it.

'What happens when they catch you?' Courtney asked.

Darren grinned, hoping it didn't look as fake as it felt. 'Ain't been a scrubber bull or wild ram that's caught me yet. Don't reckon those wadjela will have a chance.'

'Bulls and rams don't carry guns,' she said, matter-of-factly. It was a good point, and one he didn't really want to think about too much.

'Nah, but I'll be riding a lot harder too. Anyway, when I get their attention I reckon you will be able to load up the women and kids into that bus and hightail it out of here.'

Her brow furrowed, clearly still concerned. 'To where, exactly? I don't know if I could even drive it.'

'You'll be okay, it's automatic, and not that much bigger than Chase's LandCruiser,' Darren said. 'You drove that fine. Make a beeline for Carnarvon. I reckon you wheel into the cop shop with a load of refugee women and children, you'll get someone's attention.'

Amin looked concerned, and Courtney placed a hand on his shoulder to reassure him.

'They can't all be corrupt, and we agreed to tell them sooner or later. They might believe us now, but like Darren said, we arrive with a busload of refugees and they'll have to do something.'

'Very well,' Amin sighed. 'But this is the last night I spend without them.'

Darren hoped he was right, because otherwise it meant tomorrow's plan had gone horribly wrong.

THIRTY-NINE

Courtney stretched out on the bench seat of the troopy, peering out of the window up towards the stars. She doubted she would be getting much sleep, not sure what to expect tomorrow. There was a part of her that refused to believe what was happening, thinking it was instead some sort of bad dream, disassociating her from the reality of the situation. If she wasn't careful, she would get lost in that train of thought, going along in blissful ignorance, confident everything would turn out alright. Reluctantly, she pushed those thoughts further back. The realities were much scarier. What would they find? And what would they do when they found it?

She glanced around the cab. Amin was somehow already asleep and snoring faintly. In front of her she could make out Darren's bushy hair, lying in the reclined passenger seat, and she suddenly felt guilty. She had misjudged him yesterday, made an assumption based on . . . what? His age? His skin? Surely not; she was better than that, wasn't she? Courtney didn't know anymore. She had assumed he hurt himself while drunk, and then hadn't believed him when he denied it. But that was a fair call, wasn't it? It had seemed so at the time, but now, thinking about it, things were no longer so black and white.

Through the open rear doors of the troopy, a satellite blipped across the sky, barely discernible against the backdrop of stars. She watched its trajectory, wondering if it was staring down at her this very moment, and she suddenly felt extremely small. Silence overwhelmed her, broken only by the rustle of branches in the soft breeze. She rolled to her side and closed her eyes, willing herself not to think about tomorrow, not yet. Somewhere far away a dog howled, and it was a long time before Courtney finally drifted off to sleep.

She awoke to somebody shaking her. At first she didn't want to come up out of the dream. It was safe there, pleasant, but the shaking persisted. She opened her eyes and found it made little difference to the darkness. She grimaced as her back twinged. The seat was not the most comfortable of beds. Glancing out of the window, she saw the moon hanging low in the sky, its glow outlining Darren standing at the rear of the troopy.

'We gotta move,' he said and flicked on the cabin light.

'What time is it?' she mumbled, wincing at the sudden brightness.

'Four. Did you get any sleep?'

'Yeah, surprisingly. You?'

'Some,' he said. 'Not real comfortable, but better than lying on the dirt, I suppose.'

She laughed, and then remembered her thoughts from last night. 'Hey, Darren,' she said, keeping her voice low. 'I want to apologise, for yesterday. You know, thinking you'd hurt yourself while drinking.'

'That's alright,' Darren said. 'You wouldn't be the first one.'

'Maybe so, but that doesn't make it okay.'

'Thanks, Courtney,' he said, and she realised he had just used her name for the first time. 'Appreciate it. Now come on, we gotta go.'

She climbed out, just as Amin emerged from the scrub. 'I would understand if you have changed your minds.'

'Not bloody likely,' Darren said, and Courtney nodded too. Amin looked relieved.

'Thank you,' he said. '*Ba khair,* with luck, all will go well.'

By the time they reached the tank stand, the day was already well lit. *Sun rises fast out here,* she thought. A lone kangaroo drank from the puddle at the stand's base. It stared at them for a moment before bounding away, disappearing into the scrub. Part of Courtney wished she could do the same, but she held her resolve. Things would be okay. *We can do this,* she told herself. Told herself? More like lied to herself. But there was no going back now.

Darren scaled the tower, then returned. 'Can't see anyone,' he said. 'Probably still too early.'

'Good,' Amin replied, checking over his weapon for what seemed to be the hundredth time.

He's just as nervous as the rest of us, Courtney thought. Unsurprising, but given his background she'd thought he would be used to this sort of thing. *Stop making assumptions. Look how that turned out with Darren.*

'Okay then,' she said, taking a deep breath. 'Ready?'

They crept closer until all three of them were hiding behind the same tin shed Darren had used for cover the previous night. Courtney wasn't overly sure what they were going to do next, and she was about to suggest they inspect the dongas when she heard voices. All three of them froze, eyeing each other. The day was heating up, and in more ways than one.

Courtney peered around the corner. There were eight women, all in long dresses and head scarfs, walking into the room Darren had described as the packing shed. Two men walked with them, but as far as she could see they weren't armed, although they could always have handguns tucked away. But they certainly weren't packing AK-47s like she'd expected. Maybe she'd been watching too many Hollywood movies.

Amin was by her side, watching the women intently. 'She is not with them,' he said coldly, once they returned to their cover behind the shed.

'Are you sure?' Darren asked.

'I am sure,' Amin said, a hint a desperation in his voice. 'What if Aamena and Jawad are not here, what if they have been moved, or—'

'Hang on, mate,' Darren said. 'Don't get ahead of yourself. She might not be on packing duty, she might be looking after kids.'

A thought occurred to Courtney, one she did not like. 'What if she's in the house? If they know we're coming, that would make sense, wouldn't it?'

Amin grabbed her arm. 'You and I go find the children. Once we find them, we will return here and plan the escape. You will have to guide them once we do, Courtney, for I do not think many of the children will speak English, and I will have to translate to find out where Aamena is. Hopefully those two men will be after Darren.'

'And if they aren't?'

'It will be their bad luck.' Amin held up his gun.

An unfamiliar voice startled them. 'I don't think that is a good idea.'

263

All three of them whirled to see a police officer at the end of the shed wall. His gun was drawn, but he held it lowered. Beside her Amin began to raise his weapon.

'Christ, Amin, hang on,' hissed a second voice, familiar, harsh and dry. 'Don't do anything stupid.'

Relief flooded through Courtney as Gabe rounded the corner. She fought the urge to cry out in joy, and embraced him, hard. 'You came back!'

He was carrying a rifle, with a second one slung over his shoulder, and stood next to Sergeant Aaron Parker.

'Where have you been?' she hissed, slapping his shoulder, a wave of nervous frustration washing over her. It quickly passed as she remembered. 'I'm so sorry about your wife. Darren told us what happened.'

He looked embarrassed and pushed her away. 'Course I bloody came back, except you clowns pissed off on me. Couldn't find you last night, so we circled back and camped up till dawn. Parker saw you hiding here as we got closer. What the hell are you planning to do?'

Amin gave him a curious look. 'What we always planned to do, my friend,' he said. 'Get my family.'

Parker stuck out his free hand. 'You must be Amin. Do I have some questions for you.'

Amin looked Parker squarely in the eye, not taking the offered hand. 'And I will tell you everything, once we have completed what we came here to do. Can we trust you?'

'You can,' Parker said. 'Gabe has told me everything. There's going to be a lot of questions about your actions.' He raised a hand before anyone could speak. 'But I can see why you were reluctant to involve the police.' He gave the group an appraising look. 'I hope you all understand the seriousness of the situation.

If everything is as you say, we are dealing with some massive issues that will upset some very powerful people.'

'All I care about is getting Aamena and Jawad out before they come to harm,' Amin said, still holding the police officer's gaze. 'And I will not be stopped.'

Courtney could feel the tension build even further, until Parker raised his hands in a conciliatory gesture. 'I'm not here to stop you. I agree with you. But we must be careful.'

Amin visibly relaxed. All of them did, and Courtney realised she had been holding her breath. She sighed and gave what she hoped was an optimistic smile at Amin.

Parker took control. 'Tell me your plan.'

The police officer and the dogger listened intently as Darren ran them through what he had found the previous night and his theory about what the women did here.

'This keeps getting better and better,' Gabe muttered, but when Darren explained Courtney and Amin's plan to inspect the dongas, Parker shook his head.

'Too dangerous,' he said. 'I'll go with you instead, Amin. Besides, I'll need a look inside that shed.'

Courtney felt relieved and annoyed at the same time. Why couldn't she do it? Typical men trying to protect the little girl.

'I do not think that is wise,' Amin said. 'These women, they will not trust you. They will be wary of me. You can't understand what they have been through. But . . .' he gestured to Courtney, 'they may trust another woman.'

Parker considered this for a moment, then nodded. 'Very well. I'll accept your judgement, but be careful. Learn what you can and get back here as soon as possible.' He pointed at Amin's pistol. 'You can use that?'

'Yes.'

'Try not to if you can help it,' Parker said. 'You two are in enough trouble as it is.'

Courtney heard Gabe swear to himself, and gave him a reassuring smile. 'We'll be alright,' she said.

'Better be,' he muttered. 'I don't like this one bit. Amin, how's the arm holding up?'

'It is fine,' Amin said, not taking his eyes off the dongas. 'It will not bother me, if that is what you are thinking.'

Courtney scanned the area and saw no one. The women and two men had already entered the packing shed, but, for all she knew, there could be eyes inside the house, just waiting for their arrival. Surely Jefferson or Chase must have warned them by now.

A hand rested on her shoulder. It was Darren. 'Be careful,' he whispered.

'I will.' Courtney steeled herself and glanced at Amin. 'C'mon then. Let's do it.'

The two stole around to the back of the shed, darting between buildings, old tanks and anything else that gave some semblance of cover. She followed Amin, who stopped her at every break, checking ahead to make sure no one was in their way. They had followed the old plain wire fence that ringed the complex and were now hiding behind a rusted horse float that clearly hadn't carted anything for some time. Ahead she could see the three white dongas mounted on concrete blocks.

'We must check them all,' Amin said.

They darted to the first one, running in a bent-over stoop, and crouched behind it. The hum of an air conditioner was the only sound coming from the building.

'Look in the window,' Courtney whispered. 'I'll keep watch.'

The two of them crept around the side, and while she searched for any sign of movement coming from either the house or the packing shed, Amin peered through the dirty glass window of the donga.

'Blind is closed,' he whispered, and before Courtney could answer he had opened the first of the four doors that lined the front of the building. The click the latch made sounded disconcertingly like the cocking of a gun. She held her breath as he ducked inside, waiting for the scream of alarm that would ring out and alert the smugglers of their presence. It never came, and he reappeared.

'Empty.' He tried the next three doors, with the same result. Courtney's heart sank. What if they weren't in the next ones?

The second donga yielded the same results, and they crept to the last donga. This one was different, with only two doors at the front instead of the usual four. Courtney stood and peered in the window. A young woman's face stared back out at her, wide-eyed with surprise.

'Shit. Amin, someone's in there.' Courtney held a finger to her lips and hoped the woman inside would understand. The expression on her face had gone from shock to one of fear, and she stepped back, pressing herself against the room's rear wall.

'I'm going in,' Amin said. 'Get ready to run if she screams.'

Courtney nodded and tried to look as friendly as she could through the window. Inside the donga were half a dozen chairs and a small table with some very basic cooking gear. It appeared this woman was in the process of cleaning up the morning's meal. Courtney saw her cower as Amin entered, and decided to follow him into the building.

Amin holstered his gun in his belt, held both hands out in a conciliatory gesture and spoke something that Courtney did not understand, but the tone was gentle, calming. The woman still looked fearful, but appeared to relax ever so slightly. Her eyes kept going to a door in the wall that divided the two sections of the donga. She replied, and the two spoke back and forth for a minute. Courtney kept checking out of the window, but still saw no sign of movement.

Finally, Amin turned to her. 'This is Mojda. She is in charge of the children, who are in that room.' He pointed to the door.

'How many?' Courtney asked.

'Five, but Aamena and Jawad are in the main house, as we feared.'

'Shit. Does she know how many men are in there?'

'Three, she thinks. Plus the two with the women in the shed.' He spoke again to Mojda, who shook her head and replied urgently.

'Their husbands are in the work camp, though she is not sure where it is.'

'Worry about that later. We need to let the others know. Tell her I'll come back for her and the children, and she should get them ready to run for the bus with me.'

Amin relayed this, and they left. Courtney was relieved to see a more determined look in the woman's eyes, and she hoped that when the time came it would still be there.

FORTY

'What's taking them so long?' Gabe hissed. He clenched and un-clenched his hands around the rifle. Darren and Parker squatted beside him, their eyes darting from building to building.

'Dunno, but if they're not back soon, I'm going to go find them,' Darren declared.

'Goddammit, this whole thing is a bad idea. Should've just taken him straight to the cops when I had the chance.'

'And why didn't you?' Darren asked.

'You know why. Between the grog, the traps and my rifle, I'd have been in real shit.' His eyes darted to Parker. 'Not that it matters now, I suppose.'

Parker raised an eyebrow. 'That the only reason?'

Gabe considered it, then finally shook his head. 'No, I guess not.'

'See?' Darren grinned. 'You're not the grumpy old prick you pretend you are.'

'Don't bet on it. I'm plenty grumpy, and today's not helping.'

Amin and Courtney skidded in from around the corner, both breathing hard. 'Well, it's not about to get any better, my friend.'

'Course not,' Gabe scoffed. 'What's wrong?'

Amin pointed to the house. 'Aamena and Jawad are in there. The men must be expecting us. And we found a woman looking after five children, but she thinks there are also three men inside the homestead.'

'Fuck's sake. What do we do?'

'I will have to go get them,' Amin said simply.

'You'll get shot.'

'Not if I shoot them first.'

'This was supposed to be a snatch and grab,' Gabe snarled. 'Not a bloody shoot-out.'

'It may not come to that,' Amin said.

'Yeah,' Darren piped up. 'A couple are bound to follow me.'

'Or they'll know it's a distraction,' Gabe pointed out.

'Enough of this. I am going to get my family.'

Amin made to rise but Gabe pulled him back down. 'Hold your horses. We'll get them. Just trying to work out how to do it without us all ending up dead. Sarge, any ideas?'

'Yes,' said the police officer, who had remained silent as the others discussed their plans. 'But you're not going to like it. Not sure I like it myself.'

They waited for his explanation.

'Right. Gabe, you take that scoped rifle of yours and climb that water tower. I don't want you taking pot shots at anything, but if someone is in real danger, deal with it. We'll worry about consequences later.'

Gabe gave a dry laugh. 'Probably already going to jail as it is.'

Parker ignored him. 'Darren, you stick with your plan with the bikes, while Courtney and Amin get the women and children, but not until Gabe gives the signal.'

Gabe rubbed his chin. It felt like sandpaper. 'And what exactly are you going to do?'

'I'm going to knock on the front door,' Parker said. 'Tell them my vehicle broke down a little way back and I need to make a call. Try and get inside, see how many we are dealing with, see how nervous they all are. With any luck, they'll play dumb and be very helpful. I might even be able to confirm the location of Amin's family. But if I'm not back out in ten, Gabe, you get Darren to do his thing. It's risky, but it may give them enough of a shock to throw them off.'

'They may just shoot you on the spot,' Gabe said.

'I doubt that,' Parker said. 'Hiding a dead cop is a bit different to hiding a general citizen, or in your case, Amin, someone who nobody even knows is here.'

'Yeah, well, they may not be that bright,' Gabe said. 'You're just announcing our arrival. I don't like it.'

'Told you so. But I'm also giving them pause for thought in case they do decide to start shooting. Got a better idea?'

'I can't see any other way,' Courtney said. 'You and Darren distract them, Amin gets the women while I get the kids and Mojda, then he finds his family and Gabe keeps an eye out for trouble from that tower.'

'Then what?' Darren asked.

'Courtney,' Gabe said. 'Could you find your way to Carnarvon from here? All you have to do is follow that road until you hit the bitumen, then turn left.'

'I think so,' she replied. 'That was kinda our plan already. But what about you two?'

'We'll be right behind you. Once you're gone, I'll grab my ute, find Darren and meet up with you.'

'How are you going to find him?'

'Easy. Just follow the noise. But in case I can't, Darren, where's your troopy?'

Darren pointed west. 'Back that way, off the road. We walked in this morning.'

'That's why we couldn't find you last night,' Gabe said. 'Head there if you don't hear me coming up behind you.'

He took a pistol from his waistband, the one Amin had taken from the dead smugglers, and held it out to Courtney.

'Oh, hell no,' she said.

'Just take it,' Gabe said. 'Most likely you won't need it, but just in case you do, better you have it than not.'

She took the weapon from him cautiously, as though it might go off by accident. 'Great,' she replied, with all the enthusiasm of a steak lover being handed a salad. Or in her case, the opposite.

Parker gave her a quick rundown on the gun. 'Only use it if you absolutely have to,' he said. 'Aim for the chest and don't stop shooting until they go down.'

Gabe passed Amin his M1. 'Don't lose it,' he said. 'Bloody good gun, that.'

Parker gave a little cough, and Gabe shrugged. 'Not that I'll have the thing for much longer.'

Earlier, the police officer had looked on in mild surprise as Gabe retrieved the illegal rifle from its hiding place in his ute. Gabe could've brought Chase's rifle, but given how useful the old M1 had already been, he'd decided to risk it. In for a penny, in for a pound.

He hoisted his own rifle, the one Parker hadn't questioned. 'I'd much rather be doing this at night, but reckon we've pushed our luck enough with time. Right, give us five minutes to get up that tower, then do your thing, Sarge.'

The policeman nodded. 'You keep a good eye out.'

'I will,' Gabe said.

He set off, not looking back, telling himself the looping sensation in his guts was from missing breakfast and his trembling hands were due to the lack of whisky last night, not anything else.

Within minutes he was at the water tower and scaled the rickety ladder, cursing again as his hip gave a sudden twinge. *You better hold up, you bastard thing,* he thought as he rested against the tank and peered through the rifle's scope. From his position he could see his four companions crouched behind the shed. He swung around and scanned the house. No sign of anyone. He adjusted again. The packing shed was obscured behind the workshop, but past that he could just make out the roofs of the three dongas.

He felt the wind. Almost no breeze, which was lucky. It was about a hundred and fifty, maybe two hundred metres to the house. Well within the .223's range, should it come down to that, but while he had dropped plenty of kangaroos at that distance, the consequences of missing had not been so high.

Gabe swung back to see Courtney, Amin and Darren dart away to their respective positions, then disappear out of view. Parker circled around in the other direction and approached the homestead's front door at a brisk walk, all business and official-like. His stomach gave another twist. Parker was only here because he'd brought him in. If something happened to the officer, it was on Gabe. *Christ,* he thought. *Enough with the guilt.*

Through the magnified scope Gabe watched the sarge walk up the crumbling concrete step onto the front verandah, raise a hand and rap on the door. Gabe gripped his rifle a little tighter as the door opened. He could just make out the figure standing in front of Parker. It was the older Wheldon brother, a scruffy looking man of about forty. The two men talked for almost a minute, before the officer was led inside. Ten minutes. Gabe had ten minutes, and if there was no sign of Parker by then, he would signal Darren to do his thing. Gabe knew these were going to be the longest ten minutes of his life.

Courtney ran to the dongas, gun in hand and the bus keys jangling in her pocket. She reached the buildings, hid behind the second one and looked around the corner. Amin was crouched below the window of the packing shed, Gabe's rifle at the ready. She caught his attention. He gave her a smile, raised his eyes towards the heavens and clasped both hands together. *May God favour us.* The gesture looked a little odd considering he still held his weapon, but Courtney could appreciate the sentiment. They were going to need every bit of help they could get.

The sharp rapping of fist on door broke the otherwise silent morning, and Courtney hoped Amin's prayer had been heard.

Darren stood astride the Yamaha, thumb hovering over the starter button, head turned back and eyes fixed firmly on the distant tank stand. He could make out Gabe pressed up against the rusty tin, watching the goings on through his scope, and Darren waited for the signal, should it come. He figured ten minutes was going to feel a lot longer than it really should, and suddenly wished he wore a watch.

The worst thing about waiting was it gave him time to think. What if it went wrong? What if it didn't? Bloody hell, which one was worse? There was going to be a hell of a lot of explaining to do after all this. It seemed Parker knew about the grog, and if the sarge knew, Elsie probably did too. That was almost scarier than the prospect of dodging bullets on a motorbike. At least he had half a chance here.

The bike pointed towards the far opening of the lean-to, and he couldn't see the homestead from his position. He waddled it back just a little, trying to get a glimpse of the house, but not wanting to risk sticking his neck out too much. He already felt exposed enough, like a rabbit caught in the open while the eagle soared above, and it was not a particularly pleasant feeling. He didn't see anything on the verandah, so he moved back under the lean-to's shadow and studied the two bikes on either side of him. They looked pretty rough, but still had the keys in them. Probably didn't want anyone using them to run him down. He reached over, pulled the keys from each one and flung them into a bungarra hole in the back corner of the lean-to. One less thing to worry about.

Darren's stomach rumbled. Nerves more than hunger, but it had been a while since that burger at the Junction, though he didn't expect to be eating anytime soon. A sudden dark thought occurred to him. What if that had been his last meal? He pushed it away. Shouldn't think like that, but that was easier said than done. Besides, as far as last meals go, it was pretty disappointing.

Gabe did not like this one bit. Minute by minute dragged past. There had been no movement from the homestead since the sarge went inside, and as each second ticked by he grew more and more nervous. Every possible scenario played through his head as he waited, and none of them were good. Sarge being clocked from behind as he walked in. Sarge with a gun to his back. Sarge lying in a pool of his own blood on the kitchen floor.

'Fuck's sake,' Gabe spat, checking his watch. Six minutes. Bloody well close enough. He shot out an arm and waved it furiously back and forth at Darren. Almost instantly the splutter of a motorbike engine being kicked within an inch of its life rattled up towards him. Gabe shouldered his rifle, took up aim against the tank wall and stared down the scope towards the verandah. *Here we fucking go.*

FORTY-ONE

The bike coughed, choked, but didn't start. The starter motor had refused to wind over, so Darren was kicking down on the starter with all the force he could muster.

'C'mon, ya bugger,' Darren hissed, working the throttle. Another cough, a splutter and finally a roar as it burst to life. He flicked the throttle a couple more times to be sure it wasn't going to die, switched off the choke and slammed the bike into gear.

He shot out of the lean-to and swung hard to the right, sending a spray of gravel rattling against the drug shed. He caught a glimpse of Amin crouched behind the back wall, waiting, hoping for the two men inside to take the bait. Then his view disappeared as he veered around the lean-to and into the open yard. So far he saw no one else, but figured that would change soon. Darren planted one foot and sent the bike into a hard three-sixty spin, gunning the throttle as red dust and grey smoke billowed around him.

Through the roar of the engine and grinding gravel he heard yells, saw the homestead's flyscreen door swing open and took that as his cue to get moving. The bike lurched forward, its front wheel coming off the ground as Darren gave an exhilarated holler, his fear having been temporarily swallowed by a rush of adrenaline.

'Come catch me, ya bastards!' he yelled in his best blackfella voice. *Might as well play to expectations,* he supposed. He shot between two fuel bowsers, wondered briefly if they could blow them up somehow, then reminded himself this was not Hollywood and not only would bullets not ignite diesel, any that came his way were likely to be lethal.

As he followed the fence along the edge of the homestead yard, bouncing over assorted rubbish and dead branches, he stole a glance towards the house. Two men were now on the verandah, pointing and yelling. One of them started running towards a ute. *Shit, where was the sarge?*

Darren jigged to the right and tore around the far side of the house. One more lap of the yard, then he was heading bush. He saw Courtney opening the door of the last donga and disappear inside. He saw the packing shed, its side door open and two more men running towards another ute, thankfully not noticing Amin in his hiding position. And he saw the guns they carried.

He twisted the throttle, picked up speed and shot around to the shed where all five of them had been crouched only a few minutes ago. As he came out the other side he heard a ute engine – his signal to get scarce.

Courtney entered the donga and came face to face with Mojda holding a toddler, with four other very frightened looking children. From outside came the roar of Darren's bike as he raised hell, and it was no doubt scaring them all. She gave her best 'friendly nurse' smile, although inwardly she was dismayed to see just how young some of them were. One looked no older than two.

'Hello,' she said, in a voice to match her smile. 'Are we ready to go on a bus ride?'

They all stared at her blankly, but Mojda seemed to get the gist of what she was saying and pointed at the door. Courtney held up a hand. 'Soon.' She squatted and smiled at a young girl carrying a small bag. The girl smiled back shyly and hid behind Mojda's skirts.

She rose and gestured to the toddler. 'May I?' Mojda considered her for a moment, then passed the child over. Courtney spoke gently, cooing at the toddler who, while too young to realise what was happening, had certainly picked up on the nervous vibes in the room. Courtney blew a raspberry on the child's forehead, which raised a squeal of delight, and some laughter from the other children. Mojda gave her a grateful smile.

From outside came the stutter of a ute engine winding over. Courtney's demeanour grew serious. 'Get ready,' she said and opened the door just enough for her to keep an eye on what was happening out there. She saw the man still on the verandah and motioned for Mojda to stay put. The door of the packing shed flew open and two more men raced out, thankfully turning and running straight through the lean-to towards the other ute, failing to see Amin crouched down against the back wall, gun raised in one hand. She opened the door a little further. He spotted her and beckoned for them to come to him. Courtney signalled for Mojda to wait, handed her back the child and darted across the ground, skidding down against the wall next to Amin.

'Okay?' she asked.

'So far,' he said. 'I am going in to get the women. You watch for me.'

Courtney just had time to agree and he was gone. Almost instantly a babble of women's voices rose within the shed, and above it she could hear Amin talking. She waited for a gunshot, but none came. Across from her, still standing in the doorway of the donga, she could see Mojda watching on nervously, the group of children huddled behind her.

Amin appeared back at her side. 'They will come, but they are afraid.'

'Not the only ones,' Courtney said. 'Now?'

'Yes, now. I will help you get them to the bus, and then I'll go to the house. I do not know where our policeman friend is.'

'Still inside, I think.' Which was not a good sign. 'Ready?'

Amin nodded, and she signalled Mojda to come to her. After a moment's hesitation, she did so, toddler on her hip and four children following closely. At the same time, Amin called in through the door of the packing shed and the eight women emerged. The mothers scooped up their children as the two groups met, and Amin barked an instruction, then turned to Courtney.

'Lead the way.'

Gabe watched the whole thing unfold in front of his eyes. Darren had certainly got their attention, but where was Parker? The two men from the packing shed were already at one of the utes. A third was running from the house towards the other vehicle, while the last man remained on the verandah. That left the older Wheldon brother inside with Parker. Where was the younger one? Gabe hadn't seen him yet, so did that mean he was still inside, or elsewhere? He didn't like not knowing; there was enough that could go wrong as it was.

Darren did one more screaming lap of the yard and shot out over the cattle grid down the road. The two utes spun out from their parking spots and took off after him.

'Good luck, kid,' Gabe muttered.

The remaining man on the verandah seemed to scan the yard for a moment, then headed back inside. Moments later, a flash of colour caught Gabe's attention. It was Courtney, in her white 'I Got Lost at the Junction' T-shirt, running out from the lean-to, heading straight for the bus. Behind her trailed nine women, one with a toddler on her hip, some leading a child by the hand, and all looked extremely frightened. *Christ, they're just bloody babies.* Amin followed with his gun held at the ready.

Gabe searched the grounds again. The two utes were long gone, and the dust and smoke from Darren's efforts wafted gently towards the scrub. From off in the distance came a guttural throbbing of all three engines revving. It sounded like the bike was circling back. He wasn't sure if that was a good idea or not, but before he could think about it any further, the house door opened again, and his heart sank. This time the man held a rifle and began to raise it towards the group of women and children, who had just reached the bus.

There was no time. Gabe squinted through the scope, placed the crosshair on the man's chest and fired. The retort was deafening, amplified by the steel tank he was resting the rifle against, and his ears rang. A dull thud broke through the ringing, and he saw the man stagger back and collapse. Gabe worked the bolt as the metallic taste of spent gun powder sat heavy on his tongue. He was fairly certain he would be tasting it again soon enough.

Courtney ducked as the shot rang out. Women screamed and flattened themselves against the ground. Two turned as if to flee but Amin caught one by the arm, yelled something at her and pointed at the bus. All around Courtney the air was filled with children's cries, and past that she could still hear engines revving and the crunch of branches.

Gathering herself, she darted to the driver's door and climbed up into the seat. Her hands fumbled the keys, but she managed to get the right one into the ignition and turned it, then scanned the dash, found the switch she wanted and pressed it. The side doors swung open, and women and children poured in like water, huddling into seats, keeping their heads down and hunching over the children's faces. Amin followed them in and leaned over beside her.

'If I am not back shortly, or if there is danger, leave,' he ordered. 'Get these people to safety.'

'I can't leave without you,' Courtney protested, but Amin was saying something to the women. They listened intently. Courtney saw their eyes switch from her to Amin before nodding, but they still looked very afraid. Finally, Amin turned to her.

'Good luck, Courtney.' And then he was gone.

Gabe watched Amin leave the bus and head towards the house, torn as to what to do next. Should he stay, keeping overwatch, or run into the house as well? The first idea had its merits, the main one being that up here he was less likely to get shot, but unless someone ventured outside again, he wasn't going to be much use. He had no way of warning the others should anyone return from chasing Darren, who could still be heard tearing around on the bike, and nor could he be of any assistance to Parker or Amin in the house. The longer they took in there, the greater the chance of everything turning to shit.

'Fuck it,' he swore and began to climb down the ladder. It was no good standing up there just watching anymore. With an ear tuned for any oncoming vehicles, he skirted around the buildings again, making his way towards the house. Off to the side he saw Courtney sitting in the driver's seat of the bus. She had the engine idling, ready to go. A brave girl that one. He thought back to their first encounter. Never in a million years would he have suspected she was capable of all this.

He decided to let her know his plan. Plan? What plan – go into the house and hope for the best? Not really much of one if you thought about it too closely. He made his way to the passenger door, keeping the bus between him and the house, and rapped on the glass. Unsurprisingly, Courtney let out a little scream, then saw who it was and lowered the window.

'My God, you trying to give me a heart attack?'

'Sorry.' He couldn't help but grin, and then pointed to the house. 'I'm going in there.'

'Be careful. Amin said to go if they aren't back soon.'

'Good plan. Don't wait for us. Might have all turned to shit in there. I told him it wasn't a good idea.'

'Where's Darren?' she asked. 'Did you see him?'

'Reckon he's alright. He had that bike fairly moving. You be ready to do the same with this thing.'

She hesitated. 'But what about you?'

'Don't worry about an old bloke like me,' Gabe said.

She nodded, breathing deeply, and he smiled at her, then left.

Gabe moved towards the side of the house, deciding the front door was probably not the best option, and crept alongside the faded weatherboard wall. He stopped under a window and snuck a quick look through the dusty glass, darting back down once his eyes took in the scene. He didn't like what he saw.

The room was a large dining area with a rectangular table in the centre. Parker sat on a wooden chair, his arms behind his back.

Two men stood over him, while a third paced back and forth around the room, talking into a cordless phone. That one seemed agitated, with good reason Gabe supposed. He wondered who he was talking to and realised, had he thought things through a little, cutting the phone line might have not been a bad idea. Easy enough to do; out here the phones ran through radio repeaters and the signal tower was only fifty metres from the house, but it was too late now.

The man on the phone was clearly not happy. Gabe recognised him as Garrick Wheldon, the older of the two brothers. Where was the other one – what was his bloody name again? Troy? Trevor? Something like that. And where the hell was Chase, or Jefferson?

'I'm fucking telling you, they're bloody onto us. There's a cop here, someone's pissed off on a bike, and Karl's been shot.'

Gabe continued moving, trying to form some sort of plan. There was no sign of Amin, who he'd last seen running around the back of the house. Was he inside already? Probably searching for his family.

He reached the corner and peered around, looking down the back verandah. A rickety wooden table positively sagged under the weight of empty beer bottles and overflowing ash trays. Windows ran down the side of the house, and a flyscreen door hung ajar in the middle. Gabe made his way along the wall, peering through each window. They were bedrooms, but all were empty. He decided to check the other side of the house before risking going inside, but just as he was about to round the corner he collided with a figure coming the other way. Gabe raised his rifle butt to strike, but had to duck as Amin's own weapon swung past where his head had been moments earlier.

'Shit, watch it,' Gabe hissed.

'I have seen them.' Amin's eyes were wide and teary. 'They are inside that room, but I cannot open the window.'

'We'll go get them,' Gabe said. 'But Parker's still inside. They've got him trussed up. Three others are in there with him, and I don't like it.'

'First we get Aamena and Jawad ready to go, then we get the policeman.'

Gabe could tell there was no arguing with Amin, so he merely nodded. The two men approached the flyscreen door. 'Ready?'

Slowly, very slowly, Gabe opened the door, waiting for the telltale screech that every spring hinge seemed to make, no matter how new or old. This one was no exception, and both men winced. With any luck it wouldn't carry to the dining area, or the men in there would be too preoccupied to hear it. The doorway opened to a central hall, with the bedrooms branching off either side. Amin pointed to the second door on the right.

'That one.'

Gabe could feel the man's anxiousness and placed a hand on his shoulder.

'Easy, mate,' he whispered. 'Take it easy, we'll get them.'

Amin didn't take his eyes off the door. They crept forward, the wooden floorboards under their feet creaking with each step, despite their best efforts to tread lightly. Muffled voices sounded through the hall and Gabe expected someone to come charging down the corridor any second. They reached the door.

'Don't let them make a sound,' Gabe said.

'I will try.'

'That goes for you too. Save it for later.'

Amin gripped the door handle, and after one single, deep breath, opened it.

Aamena was sitting on the bed, pulling a shirt onto a slight, dark-haired boy of about seven or eight – Jawad, Gabe assumed – and he watched her expression change from apprehension to shock, and finally to stunned relief as her eyes fell on her husband. She jumped to her feet, her hand stifling a cry as Amin raised a finger to his own lips.

'*Subhanallah*,' she managed to say, and then Amin embraced her, gathering the boy between them, the family reunited again. They spoke in low voices, barely above a whisper, and tears welled in their eyes.

Gabe watched in silence, touched by what he was witnessing. This was right. It felt right, felt good. It was with some shame he recalled the times he'd considered abandoning Amin. Hell, hadn't he done just that yesterday, stranding them all at the Junction in a fit of anger? The plan to involve the sarge only came later. *Shit, the sarge.*

He touched Amin's shoulder. 'We need to move.'

The man turned, wiped his eyes and motioned for his wife to come forward. He spoke something to her. Gabe caught his own name.

Aamena gave him a grateful smile and spoke in halting English. 'Thank you, Gabe, sir.'

Before he could reply, footsteps and the sound of protesting floorboards carried through the door. Gabe grabbed Amin and pushed him against the wall. Aamena turned, sat back on the bed and made as if she was still dressing Jawad. The boy played along. Gabe was amazed at how well the young lad was handling everything, and then he recalled Amin's account of their travels through Afghanistan and Pakistan on covered trucks, and his voyage from Indonesia. Aamena and Jawad's own boat ride probably would have been similar. Gabe doubted the kid was a stranger to this sort of thing.

The footsteps grew closer, and Gabe tensed, raising his rifle stock, as did Amin. A figure entered the room and Aamena jumped to her feet, clasping Jawad to her in a mother's protective embrace.

'What are you—'

The man never got to finish. Gabe's rifle butt crashed into the back of his head the moment it appeared around the open door. It sent a shock through his wrists and made a dull thud as the rubber-backed stock connected with skull. The man collapsed to his knees and fell forward onto his hands. Stunned and dazed, but not unconscious. That did not last very long, as Amin stepped up and mirrored Gabe's actions. The stock of the older M1 he carried had no rubber shoulder guard – such things deemed superfluous by the US military back in the day – and a sharp crack resounded this time. The body slumped to the floor and did not move, blood already pooling on the dull floorboards.

'Parker,' Gabe said. Amin said something to Aamena. She made to protest but he cut her off with a sharp word, though his expression was gentle. She sat back down, her face a mixture of fear and sadness.

'We'll be back,' Gabe said, as gently as he could. He didn't know if he was right or not.

FORTY-TWO

The hallway was empty, but they could still hear voices up ahead.

'What's the plan?' Gabe whispered.

'Surprise,' Amin said. 'Run in shouting, waving our guns. Perhaps they will give up.'

'And if they don't?'

Amin's eyes hardened. 'Then they die.'

Gabe took a deep breath, just as a voice called out from the room ahead. 'Westy, hurry up in there!'

'Ready?' Gabe asked.

'Ready.'

'Here goes nothing.'

The two of them exploded through the doorway, rifles raised.

'Don't fuckin' move!' Gabe yelled, hoping he sounded more intimidating than he felt.

Parker was the first to react, launching himself and the chair he was strapped to shoulder-first into Garrick Wheldon. Gabe saw the two bodies crash to the dusty wooden floor. The sergeant was a big man and pinned his would-be captor under him, ignoring the blows raining down around his ears, and Gabe was reminded of a similar scene only a few days ago.

The second man did not hesitate either. He flung up his arm, the barrel of his pistol trained on Amin, but he never managed to fire. The crash of the M1 exploded through the room, once, then again. Behind them Gabe heard a scream from Aamena. The man slumped back against the wall and slid down, gun falling from his hands.

Gabe strode over and placed his rifle against Garrick Wheldon's head, who was still struggling with Parker. 'Quit it,' he said. Wheldon quit, dropping his arms to the floor, and stared blankly up at Gabe.

Sergeant Parker half rolled, half fell off the prostrate man and Gabe saw his wrists were handcuffed behind the seat's backrest. The officer gave him a pained grin.

'Took your bloody time.'

'Told you it was suicide. Where's the keys?'

'On my belt.' He craned his neck around and looked at Amin. 'Did you find them?'

'Yeah, we did. Amin, come watch this prick for us while I get the sarge loose.'

At that point Gabe heard footsteps, and saw Aamena emerge with Jawad from the hallway and survey the room, clearly concerned the gunshots may have been directed towards her husband. As he rummaged around Parker's waist, searching for the keys, he noticed Jawad glance at the collapsed body against the wall. The boy barely seemed to register it and merely stood with his mother, clasping her hand as she watched Amin stand guard over their captive. Gabe again wondered what he had seen in his short life, and decided he would rather not know.

He released Parker and helped him up. The police officer immediately hoisted Wheldon to his feet, spun him around and snapped the handcuffs over the man's wrists.

'I'm arresting you for assault of a public officer, possession of illegal firearms and a metric shit-ton of other charges we don't have time for now.'

While Parker dealt with Wheldon, Gabe peered out the window. The bus was still there.

'We need to move,' he said.

Parker gathered his service pistol from the table, checked it over and holstered the weapon. He shoved Wheldon towards the door. 'The bus. Go.'

They filed out, Wheldon and Parker first, followed by Aamena and Jawad, with Amin and Gabe in the rear. They stepped past the body lying on the verandah, and Gabe stooped for a closer look. As he straightened he saw Parker also looking at the dead man.

'You?'

Gabe nodded. 'He was about to take a ping at Courtney.'

'Shit. Anyone else?'

Gabe didn't get to answer. Engines could be heard in the distance, and they were growing louder. 'Go!' he yelled. 'They're coming back.'

They were halfway across the yard when he saw them. The two utes raced over the cattle grid, almost launching into the air across the sharp rise. Gabe immediately fired at the first one, but to no effect. Amin and Parker did the same, and the windscreen became a mat of cracked glass. The driver spun his vehicle in a broad skid, coming to a rest near the fuel bowsers, but the second ute roared towards them. Amin fired again. Parker shifted his aim too, but the vehicle kept coming. It was going to bowl them over like skittles if they didn't move.

Gabe grabbed Aamena's arm, yanking her back towards him and, by default, Jawad with her, held in a vice grip by his mother.

Parker shoved Wheldon in the opposite direction, still heading towards the bus, firing his last shots at the oncoming vehicle as he ran. Only Amin remained where he was. He fired twice more, but the second shot was followed by a sharp ping as the clip ejected.

With the party split three ways, the driver kept his line on Amin. Gabe pushed Aamena and Jawad towards the workshop.

'Run!' he yelled. 'Behind the shed!' He had no idea if she understood him or not. He worked his bolt and sent a round towards the ute, more in hope than anything else. To his utter amazement, the front tyre exploded, and the ute veered to the right. Just a little, but enough to allow Amin to dive in the opposite direction, dropping the rifle as he did so. Gabe ducked to catch him, just as something struck the dirt near his feet. The occupants of the first vehicle were firing at them from behind the safety of its body.

The second ute skidded alongside the waiting bus, almost crashing into it and the driver began to climb out. Gabe hauled Amin to his feet, expecting at any moment to feel the thud of a bullet. He shoved Amin in the direction of Aamena and Jawad.

'Around there! Move!'

Amin ran to his wife and child, placing himself between them and the firing men, and the three of them disappeared around the corner of the workshop.

Gabe flicked the bolt through its motion as he backed away, sent a wild shot towards the fuel bowsers, which, as far as he could tell, missed everything and flew harmlessly out into the scrub. Through the raised dust he could make out the figures of Parker and Wheldon entering the bus.

'Courtney!' he yelled. Somehow she heard him, turning her head through the open driver's door window. 'Go!' He saw she was about to protest. 'Christ's sake, girl! Drive!' He sent another shot towards the first ute, all while backing away towards the side of the workshop. They locked eyes, and he pleaded with her. 'Go!'

She was torn, he could see it, but just as he ducked behind the workshop, the bus lurched forward, almost running down the second ute's driver who was about to open the door and drag Courtney out.

Amin had joined his family and Gabe saw they were ready to run past the packing room and around the opposite end of the shed, where the lean-to stood.

'This way,' he called, making for the dongas and the fence that stood past them. Amin started to protest but Gabe cut him off. 'Bus is gone. She had to leave. We're running from here.'

He saw the look of concern flash across Amin's face, but it quickly turned to grim determination as he redirected Aamena and Jawad to follow Gabe. The four of them sprinted past the dongas, stepped over the plain wire fence and melted into the scrub.

Courtney heard Gabe's order, knew she must do as he said, but hesitated. How would he get away? Another shout, and she saw him begging her to go. She also saw the driver of the second ute leap from his vehicle and make a beeline towards her door.

'Hang on!' she called over her shoulder. Parker had just sat Wheldon down on the seat behind her and was about to climb into the front passenger seat when she shot the bus forward, sending the officer tumbling back.

'Sorry!' she shouted, seeing his upturned feet in the rear-view mirror, hoping he heard her over the chorus of screams and wails coming from the rest of the passengers. In the side mirror she could also see the ute driver lose his grip on the door handle.

The bus accelerated quickly, and she headed straight for the cattle grid leading out of the homestead's yard. *Follow the road and turn left.* She remembered Gabe's instructions and was struck with guilt as she realised driving over that grid would mean leaving him, Amin and the very reason they came here behind. In the mirror she saw the huddled women and children in the back. So many, and she had Parker and one of the smugglers with her too. Dammit, this wasn't how it was supposed to go.

So much was happening around her. The screaming. Dust. Gunshots. *This is fucking nuts!* And then Sergeant Aaron Parker's voice cut through it all.

'Fast as you can, Courtney. They'll be okay. The dogger will look after them.' He was panting hard.

She set her jaw, gripped the wheel and pushed down on the accelerator. Ahead, leaving the protection of their vehicle, the two gun-wielding smugglers, or drug dealers – either way, she didn't care, they were the bad guys – had started chasing Gabe. Courtney swung towards them and sent the men scurrying back behind their vehicle. The bus shot past, bouncing off the ute's side and sending a shower of sparks skywards as they squealed by. Her passengers screamed. Seconds later they cleared the grid and careened down the road.

'I don't think they are following us,' Parker said. He had regained his footing, leaning into the front compartment as they rattled down the narrow gravel road.

'What about Gabe?' Courtney asked. 'We just left him, and Amin.' Another thought. 'Oh God, where's Darren?'

Parker gripped her arm. 'I don't know. We need to get back to Carnarvon, or at least close enough that I can call the station.'

'But—'

'Courtney, we have no choice,' Parker said. 'I can't risk leaving you alone, and we can't take everyone back there. Just get to town fast as you can.'

From behind them, the chorus of nervous chatter continued.

'Maybe you should try to calm them down,' Courtney said. She watched in the mirror as the sarge turned to the women and children, raising his hands.

'Does anyone speak English?' The chatter quietened, but there was no response. 'English?' he repeated. Again nothing, but Courtney could see all eyes were on the policeman. She focused hers on the road again.

'We're taking you somewhere safe.' His tone was warm, friendly, but there were sudden intakes of breath, and a few of the bolder women started berating him. Courtney turned her head back to see the perplexed officer giving the women a cheery double thumbs up.

'Put your thumbs down,' Courtney hissed. 'To Afghans that's like flipping them the bird.'

Parker stared at his hands, then at the distressed women. He quickly raised his palms again, shaking his head in apology. 'Sorry,' he kept repeating as the group quietened down. A few of the woman must've realised his rudeness was unintentional, and they gave him an understanding nod.

'We will be alright,' Parker said, sounding a little sheepish.

'Um, Sergeant?' Courtney swallowed hard. 'You might have spoken too soon.' She pointed ahead. A vehicle rushed towards them, sending a cloud of white dust high into the air like fine talc. It was a troop carrier. A police troop carrier. Constable Matthew Jefferson had arrived.

There was nowhere for them to go. The scrub on either side of the road was too thick to drive through.

'What do we do?'

The police vehicle broadsided to a halt, effectively blocking the road. Jefferson leaped out, brandishing what appeared to be a shotgun. Courtney gasped as she saw the second vehicle pull alongside the troopy, recognising the white LandCruiser with its steel rack, spotlight, matted windscreen and bent door frame. Chase.

'Goddamn little bastard,' swore Parker. Behind them, Garrick Wheldon gave a guffaw of laughter.

Courtney thought about crashing through, but didn't think the bus would be strong enough to survive the process, and the fearsome looking weapon the young policeman was pointing at their rather large and clear windscreen didn't help. Parker must have come to the same conclusion.

'Pull over, Courtney, we can't get through.' He slotted a fresh magazine into his service pistol, and holstered it again. She noticed he did not flick over the restraining strap.

She stopped the bus a few metres from the road block, her stomach sick with dread. Jefferson motioned for them to exit, and after exchanging glances with Parker, Courtney opened her door, leaving the bus running. Just in case.

The two of them walked slowly towards the young police officer and his companion.

'You should've stayed in bed, Sarge,' Jefferson said as they approached him.

'What the hell are you playing at?' Parker demanded. 'What have you got yourself involved in?'

'Nothing that concerns you,' Jefferson replied. 'Or you, Miss Drage.'

'Hello, love,' Chase said, that big shit-eating grin stuck to his face.

A shout came from the bus. 'Oi! Get them to uncuff me!'

Jefferson looked past them and saw Wheldon leaning over the seats. 'Where are the others?'

Neither of them answered, and Jefferson shrugged. 'Sorry, Sarge, but can't have you carrying. Chuck them over here. Nothing funny, or the nurse will be busy.' Chase waved his gun at her, and Courtney took a step back.

Parker slowly removed his service pistol and taser, throwing them at the constable's feet.

'Good. Now, go and release Mr Wheldon please, and he can return those ladies to work.'

Courtney watched as Parker walked back to the bus. She could sense his frustration; the man was positively radiating rage. He returned with Wheldon, and removed the cuffs. Wheldon grinned, rubbing his wrists. 'You two know when to show up,' he said.

Jefferson held out his own set of handcuffs. 'Restrain them both, then take the bus back to camp. The women have got work to do, and we need to find the others, before they can get back to town.'

Courtney felt the cold steel snap over her wrists and heard the click repeat as Parker was also cuffed. Jefferson picked up Parker's gun and taser from the dirt and tossed them to Chase, then pointed at the bus.

'In the back, you two,' he said.

They clambered inside, and the doors slammed closed behind them. The seated women said nothing, heads down.

'Now what?' she whispered to Parker.

'I have no idea,' he said. 'To think all this was going on right under my nose.'

'To be fair, it's a big place, and they've got inside help.'

'Yeah,' Parker growled. 'Wait until I get my hands on that little bastard.'

Thinking back to the last time they were captured, and the fact they had managed to escape then, Courtney hoped Parker would get the chance. And that reminded her of Darren. Where the hell was he?

FORTY-THREE

From his perch high up on the water tower, Darren saw the two utes he'd managed to lose in the scrub tear back towards the homestead yard, and he didn't like it. They were meant to be still searching for him, but the useless shits had lost him within minutes. He supposed he could have gone a bit slower, but then, they had guns, so fuck that for a joke. He'd doubled back to the tank stand to get the lay of the land. And right now, the lay was going all cockeyed.

Movement at the house caught his eye as Gabe, Parker and Amin rushed out of the homestead with what looked to be Amin's family and a Wheldon brother in tow. So that was good. But his relief was short-lived as the vehicles entered the yard. What could he do from up here? Not much, he decided, and stayed hidden.

His empty stomach tried to climb into his throat as the second ute nearly collided with Amin and then the bus, and almost succeeded as Courtney ploughed past the first ute before screaming through the gate and down the road. He let out a deep breath, swallowing hard as he watched the dust cloud billow behind her. There was just one problem. She was short of five passengers – Darren, and the four others who had just fled around the back of the shed and into the scrub.

He watched on as the three men regathered themselves into a group. He couldn't hear what they were saying, but judging by their gesticulations they weren't happy. Two kept pointing the way Courtney had gone, the other after Gabe. They had run to where the bikes were parked, and Darren felt a small puff of pride as the group started looking for keys.

The man arguing for Gabe's direction must've won, and the three thugs disappeared behind the shed, undoubtedly hot on Gabe and the others' heels. Darren waited for what he guessed was five minutes and descended the ladder. His bike was parked a little way back, but he didn't go to it. Instead, he once again stole across the yard and made his way to what he had dubbed the packing shed.

The door was still open. It had been a mass exodus, that was for sure, and aside from the scattered chairs the shed held one other significant difference from last night. The tables were no longer clear. Four large, plastic-wrapped bundles of what Darren could only assume were drugs were laid out evenly along the tabletops. One bag was open, as though the women had been about to start breaking it down into the smaller sachets. He guessed his little stunt show earlier had put an end to that.

Darren looked around, an idea forming in his head. Whether it was a good idea or not remained to be seen. He found a grey duffle bag on one of the shelves, shoved the bundles into it, threw the bag over his shoulder and left the packing shed, heading for his bike. Insurance, evidence, he wasn't sure which, but if he had something of theirs, that could only be a good thing.

Darren had a rough idea of the area where Gabe said his ute was. They had a good head start on their pursuers, though they did have a kid with them, and Gabe was no fast mover himself, what with that hip of his, but there was nothing much Darren could do. The three men after them were all armed, and he was not, so he decided his best course would be to find Gabe's ute, wait for him and then meet up with Courtney and Parker back in Carnarvon. And if it all turned to shit, at least he might be able to use the drugs as a bargaining tool. He wasn't sure how much he was carrying, but supposed it was no small amount. It wasn't overly heavy, maybe five kilos at the most. A few people he knew dabbled in drugs, and apparently twenty bucks didn't get you much of anything. So yeah, he was carrying a fair bit of coin and was pretty certain they'd want it back.

Darren reached his bike, the sound of vehicles approaching along the road growing louder behind him. *More bad guys? This just keeps getting better.* He mounted the bike, rested the bag on the fuel tank between his legs and fired up the engine. It sounded exceptionally loud to his nervous ears, and he set off once more, heading in the general direction of Gabe's ute and away from whoever it was bearing down on the old station homestead.

'Keep going,' Gabe ordered, his breath ragged and raspy. *Shit, I'm unfit.*

Branches whipped past as they ran. His hip screamed in protest, but he ignored it as best he could. They weren't far from his ute now, just a few hundred metres and then they could get the hell out of this nightmare. He looked back, saw Aamena, Jawad and Amin all following, their eyes on him. Christ, what a bloody joke, him leading them out of the desert like goddamn Moses. He knew the three of them could've easily overtaken his old body had they not needed his directions. But the ute was parked between low wattles and would be hard to spot unless they knew where to look. Bloody scrub through here was thick – both a blessing and a curse.

A cry came from behind him. Aamena had stumbled on a dead branch, but was quickly hauled to her feet by her husband and son. There were other noises too. Gabe raised a hand, motioning for them to stop, and held a finger to his lips. The sharp warble of a motorbike engine cut through the still air, mixed with the snap and crackle of breaking branches as something, or someone, pushed through the scrub.

Amin gave him a worried look. 'Darren?'

'Maybe. Or they got smart and are following us on bikes. Keep moving, not far now.'

They ran on, their speed hampered by the vegetation. Gabe kept expecting to hear a gunshot and feel the bullet, but he told himself that was unlikely for now, with the wattle, curara and mulga offering good cover. But the bike was drawing closer, and he didn't like that. He fumbled fresh cartridges from his pocket and fed them into the rifle.

His khaki LandCruiser came into view. Gabe flung open the doors, allowing Aamena and Jawad to scramble inside onto the bench seat at the rear and Amin in the front, then raced around to the driver's side. The bike was very near, the engine's note rising and falling as the rider weaved their way through the foliage. Gabe leaned his rifle across the bonnet and took up aim. Amin retrieved his handgun and raised it through the open window, also waiting.

'My other rifle would be handy about now,' Gabe said through gritted teeth.

'Would you like to go back and get it?' Amin asked. He sounded as though he was smiling, but Gabe didn't look. His focus was all down the gun's sights.

A blue mudguard flashed through the leaves. Gabe tensed, his finger resting on the trigger, ready. The bike broke through, and Gabe almost fired from sheer nervousness. Darren skidded to a halt and gave him a huge grin.

'Found ya,' he said, clearly proud of himself. 'But you gotta move, they're right behind you and this thing is nothing but a bloody homing beacon for them.'

'Right you are.' Gabe leaped into the driver's seat. 'Follow us.' He noticed the bag in Darren's lap. 'What the hell is that?'

'Insurance. Can I chuck it in the back? Bit awkward and I don't wanna drop it.'

'No time, it's all locked up,' Gabe said, wondering what the hell the kid was on about. He fired the engine and the big V8 rumbled in anticipation. 'Keep up if you can. We'll stop once we're clear.'

'Right, they're on foot so we should be good.' Darren had no sooner said this when shouts came from the direction they had just run from. 'Better piss off quick, I reckon.'

Gabe dumped the clutch and the heavy ute lurched forward. As he swung the wheel hard, he saw figures emerge from the shrubbery, all raising rifles, ready to fire. He heard Darren's bike surge, followed by the crack of rifle shots. Something clanged and whined from inside the canopy, and he figured a bullet had ricocheted off one of the steel toolboxes. Aamena ducked her head, holding Jawad close to her as Amin fired a couple of shots out of the window in reply, letting their pursuers know they could shoot back too. Gabe weaved his way through the scrub, ignoring the screeches of protest from the ute's paintwork as they scraped past branches and crunched over dead wattles. He willed his tyres to hold.

The gunshots receded behind them and he began to breathe a little easier. He could see Darren off to his right, slotting through the scrub with practised ease, as though this were just a normal mustering run, flying bullets notwithstanding. Slowly, ever so slowly, the poisoned knot of dread that had sat heavy in his gut since this whole affair started began to loosen. He turned to Amin. The man had twisted in his seat and was facing Aamena, their foreheads touching, each with a hand on the back of the other's neck. Gabe didn't need to know the language to understand.

He reached over and squeezed Amin's shoulder. 'Another hour or so and we'll be home free, I reckon.'

'*Alhamdulillah*. Thank you, my friend,' Amin said. 'From all of us. I do not know how we can repay you.'

'Come break me out of jail,' Gabe laughed, but he was only half joking. Once the dust settled, he suspected he was in for some hefty charges, but looking at the family next to him now, he decided it was worth it after all. The little boy beamed at him, and Aamena's tear-filled eyes shone with gratitude and relief.

'I would,' Amin said. 'But I suspect I may be joining you – that is, if we are still allowed to stay here.'

Gabe considered this. 'You think they'll deport you?'

Amin shrugged. 'I don't know. It was mentioned many times by the smugglers.' He said something to Aamena, who nodded and replied.

'They threatened to drop the women to the police,' Amin explained, 'saying they would be sent home if they did not do as they were told, and that no one would believe their story.'

'I barely believe the story, and I've seen it firsthand.'

It hardly seemed fair to Gabe, to go through all this and still be sent back to the country they'd fled. But what could they do? Before he could think about it any further, Darren rode over and motioned for him to wind down his window.

'Back to my cousin's troopy?' he asked.

'Guess so,' Gabe said. 'Then leg it into town. Lead the way; I don't think they're following us.'

Darren peeled away, and Gabe followed.

They reached the troop carrier soon enough. Gabe noted Darren had parked it much the same as he had parked his own vehicle, wedged between trees and covered as best he could. They stopped and all climbed out. Aamena said something to Amin, who translated.

'She asks how you can find something in this bush, when it all looks the same.'

'Practice,' Gabe answered. 'Right, Darren?'

'Yep.'

'Now, what have you got in that bag?'

'My retirement plan,' Darren joked. He dropped the bag on the ground, opened it and hefted up one of the packages.

'What the hell is that?'

'Drugs. Meth, I think. They were carving it up into smaller bags when we showed up and wrecked their day.'

'Bloody hell, when did you grab that?'

'Just after you guys bolted into the scrub.' He put the packages back into the bag and threw it into the rear of the troop carrier. 'Figured that's what they were doing in there, and after they left to follow you I shot in and nabbed it. Guessed it might come in handy later, in case something went bad. And if not, a few kilos of crack should get someone's attention in town.'

'Reckon so,' Gabe said. 'Good thinking, though I don't think—'

A sound that was becoming all too familiar cut him off. The satellite phone was ringing again.

FORTY-FOUR

'What do you mean it's gone?' yelled Garrick Wheldon.

Courtney watched in silent fear as one of the lackeys reported to Jefferson and Garrick. The man was obviously as terrified as she was. He looked a mess, covered in dried wattle leaves, sweat and dust. She assumed he had gone after Gabe's group on foot, and if he'd returned empty-handed, that must have meant they'd gotten away.

'We were just starting when shit hit the fan,' the man explained. 'We bolted out to see what was going on, saw that blackfella on the bike and went after him, like you said.'

'I didn't say leave a couple of million dollars' worth of gear lying around for anyone to just walk in and grab!'

'I bet it was that kid,' another lackey said, equally as nervous. 'We lost him at first, came back here, nearly got them but then the bus took off.'

'I know what happened,' Wheldon snarled. 'I was in the fucking thing, remember? How the fuck are we going to explain this?'

Chase stood in the corner of the room. He held Gabe's rifle, the one Courtney saw Amin drop during the earlier confusion, and was turning it over in his hands. If his wrist bothered him, it didn't show. Perhaps he'd taken something for it, something you couldn't get in your local pharmacy, and he looked as though he was almost enjoying the show. Jefferson seemed less enthusiastic. He kept casting glances at Parker, who only returned his looks with a cold, hard stare.

She and Parker were seated at the kitchen table. Courtney didn't know where the women and children were – probably sent back to their rooms, as, from what she could gather, whatever it was they had been working on in that shed was gone. Darren. It had to be; there was no way Gabe and the others had time to snatch something. She kept her face impassive, but inwardly she was smiling. If he had something of theirs, maybe she and Parker had a chance. But another part of her told her that was a little too optimistic. Parker was a cop, and an honest one. There was no way anyone would trust him to keep his mouth shut. They could threaten her and the others, but Parker was too experienced, too much of a risk. Easier just to get rid of him.

'What do we do now?' Wheldon asked Jefferson, but before the officer could answer Chase strode over.

'Easy,' he said, retrieving a card from Jefferson's pocket. 'We phone a friend.'

'That can only be one person,' Gabe said, looking at the number coming up on the screen. 'Should I answer it?'

'Perhaps you should,' Amin said. 'In case . . .'

'In case what?' He already knew what Amin was hinting at, but didn't want it to be true.

'In case the others didn't make it.'

'Shit.' So Amin suspected the same thing. He pressed the button and waited.

'Dogger.'

He knew that voice.

'Chase. Wasn't expecting to hear from you again.'

'Lot of things we all weren't expecting, dogger.' The tone was calm, calculating. Gabe didn't like it.

'Bit like the Carnarvon cops will feel when we rock up with a bunch of refugees and a stack of that shit of yours we nabbed, whatever it is. I guess that's why you're ringing.'

'Smart as ever. Except for one thing. You have something of ours, and we have something of yours. Two things, actually.'

There was a crackle, the sound of the phone being handed to someone else.

'Gabe?' Her voice was tense, fearful.

He punched the ute's door. 'Courtney. You okay?'

'I'm sorry,' she began. 'We ran right into them, we had no choice.'

'Parker there?'

'Yes, we . . .' And then the rustle again.

'So, I'm sure you can work out what we expect,' Chase said.

'I can.'

'Good. Head back here and we'll do a trade.'

Gabe's mind raced. Going back to Brigadier was a bad idea. 'No.'

Momentary silence. 'No? You do realise what that means, don't you?'

'It means we're not coming to you.' An idea floated at the back of his mind. He had the gear. He had the lure. All he needed was the perfect site. 'You're coming to us.'

'Is that so?'

'Damn right it's so,' Gabe said. 'You reckon we're going to believe you'll just let us go once we hand over your drugs? You must think we're fucking stupid. And what about Parker, you think you can convince him to keep quiet if you did let him go?'

'He is a problem,' Chase conceded. 'But there is a lot at stake here, and I think his partner can convince him to keep this to himself.'

'And how are you going to do that?'

'I hear he has a niece and nephew.'

Gabe heard a sudden curse erupt from Parker in the background, followed by the sound of a chair being pushed back, a dull thud, a cry from Courtney, then silence.

Chase spoke again, panting a little. 'So, are we going to trade or do I need to find something else to do with these two?'

'We'll trade,' Gabe said. 'But not at Brigadier.'

'Where then?'

'You know where. The ridge. Back where it all started. But if anything happens to those two, the next time you see your drugs or us will be on the six o'clock news.' And with that, he ended the call.

'What is it?' Amin asked.

Gabe relayed the conversation. 'Seems you've done good, Darren.'

'You know it's a trap,' Darren said.

'Of course it is, just like last time.'

'So, what do we do?'

Gabe didn't answer at first. He rolled a smoke, gave it to Amin. Rolled another for himself, thinking hard. He looked at the troopy and the drugs in the rear, at Darren's motorbike and back to his own ute.

'Easy,' he said. 'We set our own.'

*

Courtney sat in the back seat of the police troop carrier, hands cuffed behind her. She rocked and swayed each time the vehicle jolted over a pothole, and twice her head smacked into the side window. She would've cursed at them, but her mouth was gagged. Seated across from her, Parker was in much the same predicament, worse, even. Blood trickled from a cut on his forehead, courtesy of the blow received when the officer reacted to Chase's threats about his niece and nephew. She caught his eye, tried to give him a weak smile. He responded in kind. There wasn't much else they could do.

'I don't like it one bit.' Garrick Wheldon was staring out of the police carrier's passenger window. 'Why would he want to go back there? And why are we humouring him?' He turned to Jefferson. 'All we have to do is get rid of these two, find the others and get rid of them too.'

'Do you have any idea how much heat a dead cop would bring? We're going to have to be smart about this.'

'Smart thing would have been to never become involved,' Wheldon muttered. 'Fuckin' Troy and his scheming. Should've told those suits to piss off from day one. Stuck to growing dope.'

'Perhaps,' Jefferson said. 'Too late now though.'

They drove on. Courtney caught glimpses of Chase's ute ahead of them through the dust. How he was doing anything with that wrist amazed her, but then she had seen the look in his eyes. The man was running on blind fury, and she doubted any suggestion to let them go would sit well with him.

They drove along for what seemed an age. Courtney noticed they didn't take any main roads. Darren couldn't have known about these back tracks when they drove to Brigadier yesterday. She wondered if Gabe knew of them, or if he'd come up the highway. Doubtful, not with that windscreen of his, but then he had Parker with him too, so she supposed that would be like a free pass.

Parker. What were they going to do with him? Probably the same as her, despite what Jefferson said about the risks. It would be riskier to leave him alive. She could only hope at least one of her companions could get back to Carnarvon and raise the alarm, but could they do that in time?

When the granite ridge near the dumping hole came into view, Courtney realised where they had been heading and shivered. *Oh God, not here again.* She would never forget this place, coming so close to death only yesterday, and here they were facing the same fate once more. Her stomach churned. How in the hell were they going to get out of this? They were going to end up in that hole with a bullet in their heads, regardless of whether Gabe handed over the package or not. There was no way they'd be trusted to keep quiet.

'There they are.'

'Son of a bitch,' breathed Wheldon. 'What's he playing at?'

'Don't know, but keep those two close,' Jefferson said, bringing the police vehicle to a halt. Courtney strained to see what was happening, but all she could make out was Gabe's ute parked in the middle of the clearing near the base of the ridge. She caught Parker's eyes again, and he shrugged, just as clueless as her.

Wheldon opened the troopy's rear doors and dragged her out, beckoning for Parker to follow. She looked around. Chase was climbing out of his ute, along with another man. Behind them was a second vehicle, with two more men. All were armed in some fashion, and it appeared Chase was still carrying the rifle Amin had dropped back at the station. Gabe's rifle.

She wondered how many people were involved in the operation. She also wondered what fate the women and children had met back at the homestead, and felt a rush of guilt. It was stupid to try to rescue them. They should've gone straight to the police.

'Don't try anything,' Jefferson warned as he led her and Parker around the front of the troopy, each gripped by a thug and with a gun barrel shoved squarely against their backs. Courtney gasped. The dogger leaned against his ute. She couldn't believe he was standing there so casually, just smoking and studying the posse that had arrived in a cloud of red dust. He didn't even have a weapon.

Chase immediately raised Gabe's rifle, but Jefferson stopped him.

'Easy,' he said quietly. 'We need the others first.'

She knew it. Once Gabe handed over the drugs they'd be shot and chucked down the hole. He'd better have a plan. He would, wouldn't he, or why bring them back out here? Their little group stopped about ten metres from Gabe's ute.

'Alright,' called Jefferson. 'We're here.'

'Where's the blackfella and that fucking Arab?' Chase demanded.

'Afghan,' Gabe corrected, dropping his smoke butt and grinding it out under his boot. 'Pashtun Afghan, to be precise. He's gone. They all are. Just me left. Now let Parker and Courtney go.'

'First, where are the goods?' Jefferson said, motioning for Chase to shut up.

The dogger waved his hand towards the horizon. 'Somewhere out there. You'll get them once those two are safely away from here.'

'Really?' Jefferson mused. 'What guarantee is there we'll get anything once these two are with you?'

'That's easy,' said Gabe. 'I'm your guarantee. We'll trade. Me for them.'

'And what's to stop us from just getting the information out of you and then disposing of the evidence down that hole over there?' Wheldon called.

Gabe held up something small and black. The sat-phone. 'Amin is waiting for my call. I don't ring him, he goes straight to the Carnarvon cop shop. He's probably in town already. He's not real keen on getting the cops involved, him being a refugee and all, but if I don't make the call, or if he thinks I'm in any sort of stress, he's there in a flash. We might all die here today, but you lot will be done, one way or another.'

'Very clever,' Jefferson said. 'But just how well do you expect him to be able to convince any officer of this story. I doubt he could even find this place.'

'Not without the GPS coordinates, he couldn't,' Gabe replied, rolling another smoke as he spoke. 'Luckily I gave them to him before he left, so I reckon someone will be able to find it. Then, of course, Brigadier's not hard to find either, and I'm betting the other camps he mentioned wouldn't be too far away. I know there's an outstation on the place. That where all the workers are kept? How quick can your boys clean house?'

'So we give you the girl and Parker, you stay with us?' Jefferson asked.

'Yep. And once they're gone, I'll take you to the drugs, then head on my merry way and we can all pretend this never happened.'

'Sounds good in theory,' Jefferson said. 'But why won't anyone just blow the whistle later on?'

'Self-preservation. Amin doesn't want to be sent back home. I don't want people looking into my affairs. And from what I've gathered, you've made it clear to the sarge your mob will do anything to keep him quiet. I'm guessing some pretty scary people are running this show, and you guys are just the hired help.'

'And the others?'

'They'll keep their mouths shut,' Gabe said, staring squarely at Courtney. 'For our sake.'

'Bullshit,' Wheldon spat. 'I say we shoot the lot and find the drugs ourselves.'

Courtney shuddered.

'Good luck,' Gabe said, his face determined. 'Big place out here.'

Jefferson turned to Wheldon. 'You really want to tell your brother you lost the entire haul when he gets back? How the hell would we find it?'

Wheldon quietened down.

'Alright,' Jefferson said. 'I think we can work with that. But I want to search your ute, make sure you're not messing with us. The drugs could be in there, and while you're busy leading us on a goose chase Parker marches straight into Carnarvon. That sort of haul would demand an immediate response.'

Gabe shrugged and reached into his pocket. Immediately guns were raised.

'Steady, boys,' Gabe said. 'Just getting my keys.'

Courtney watched as Gabe opened up his canopy and the surrounding cage.

'Go,' Jefferson commanded Wheldon. 'They're bulky packages, shouldn't be too hard to find.'

Wheldon and Chase approached the ute cautiously and began the search. Chase rummaged through the cab while Wheldon inspected the tray.

'What's this locked box?'

'My poisons and dog traps,' Gabe said, unlocking the lid. 'There's some nasty shit in there.'

Wheldon look suspiciously at Gabe. 'What kind of shit?'

'Strychnine, 10-80. Few other bits and pieces I'd be in trouble for if others found out. But go ahead, poke around if you like. It's probably safe enough.'

Garrick Wheldon peered into the box, and took a quick step back. He continued to rummage around the tray before finally calling to Jefferson, 'It's clear.'

Chase emerged from the cab, chewing on something and holding Gabe's ever-present bag of jerky. *What is it with guys and that stuff?*

'Don't mind, do you, mate?' he asked, shit-eating grin in its usual place.

'Knock yourself out, sport,' Gabe said.

'Move,' Jefferson instructed, shoving Courtney forward, and the group approached the dogger's ute as he closed down the canopy.

'Un-cuff them,' Gabe said. 'And get those fucking gags off.'

'I want you searched too,' Jefferson replied. 'Make sure you're not carrying.'

'Fine. Whatever. Just hurry up or Amin is liable to get impatient.'

At Jefferson's instruction one of the men holding Courtney released her and approached Gabe, who remained where he was, but raised his arms. He was thoroughly patted down and given the all clear.

Courtney felt the cuffs come away and immediately pulled off her gag, preparing to unleash a torrent of abuse at their captors, but a sharp look from Gabe silenced her. She didn't know what he had planned, but the lightning-fast wink he gave was enough for her to trust him.

Gabe threw his ute keys to Parker. 'Get out of here,' he said. Parker made to protest, but the dogger cut him off. 'Sarge, this is the only way we all get out of here alive. For once in your life put aside your bloody morals.'

'He's right, Parker,' Jefferson said. 'We're in a deadlock here.'

'You little bastard,' Parker spat, completely ignoring Gabe's advice. 'Anything happens to those kids, I'm coming for you.'

'Nothing will happen if you keep your mouth shut. So here's what you're going to do, Sarge. You're going to put in for a transfer. I don't really care where, but not anywhere near here. Go south for a change, take in the cool sea air, or go way the fuck up north.'

Courtney saw the expression on the senior officer's face. It was one of cold determination. There was no way he was going to just let things go, let Jefferson get away with it. One way or another, Parker was going to do his job, she could see that.

It seemed Chase could see it too. He raised Gabe's rifle and fired, the retort echoing off the surrounding ridgeline, sending two nearby crows and an eagle flapping into the sky.

Courtney screamed as Parker slumped to the ground, his face one of stunned surprise. He stared up at her for a moment, and even as she dived to his side, pressing down hard on the dark stain welling on his blue uniform, she saw the light fading from his eyes. Somewhere, seemingly miles away, she heard Gabe roar something, an incoherent cry, and then she was dragged to her feet, still struggling until a slap across her cheek silenced her.

She looked around wildly, saw Gabe being restrained by two of the thugs, and then she saw Chase. He was pointing the rifle at her.

'You bastards!' Gabe yelled. 'You're not getting a fucking thing now.'

One of the men punched him in the stomach and he doubled over. Courtney screamed again.

Two quick shots shocked her into silence. Jefferson stood with his service pistol pointed skyward, the barrel smoking. He was staring at Parker's body, taking it in. She could almost hear his mind working. The constable raised his eyebrows to Chase, who merely shrugged at him. Jefferson lowered his gun, rubbed the bridge of his nose between his fingertips, and glared at Gabe.

'Here's how things are going to go,' he said in the silence that followed. The coldness in his voice made her shiver. 'Dogger, you are going to lead us to those drugs. Because if you don't, Nurse Courtney here will suffer the same fate as the sergeant. Now throw me that phone of yours and lead the way.'

Courtney cast a fearful glance at Gabe, who dropped his head in resignation. She saw his hands clench, relax and clench again, and finally he looked up.

'Alright. She stays here though. City girl like her won't make the walk.'

'Of course she does,' Jefferson said. 'Wheldon, you watch her. Let's go, dogger.'

Gabe gave her a smile, full of sadness. 'You're alright, Courtney, even if you are a bloody vego.'

She sniffed, and gave a small laugh that choked on a sob. Wheldon shoved her down to the ground next to Gabe's ute, standing guard over her, and she watched as the group began to make their way up the ridge, led by the dogger, and she wondered if she would ever see him again.

FORTY-FIVE

Gabe fought to remain calm. Every instinct was screaming at him to run, to take his chances and leg it through the bush, but he held firm. He had to, if they had any hope of getting out of this alive. At the very least, maybe Courtney would, but only if everything went absolutely according to plan. But it hadn't gone to plan at all, had it? Parker. He looked behind him, catching Chase's eye, and scowled. *You'll get what's coming, you bastard.*

They walked single file, weaving their way through the bushland, the three nameless thugs behind Gabe, followed by Jefferson and the roo-shooter at the rear, still brandishing the rifle. *His* rifle, the one used to gun down the police officer. Gabe felt a rush of guilt. This was his fault; he'd brought them all here in some crazy, deluded idea of mounting a rescue. Hell, he was the one who got Parker involved. He should've known there was no way they'd let him go. The others, maybe, but a police veteran? He was foolish to even consider it, but what else could he do?

'How much further?' Chase called. They had been walking for half an hour.

'A while yet,' Gabe said, and looked at Jefferson. 'How exactly are you going to explain Parker?'

'It's quite the tragic tale,' Jefferson said. 'We happened upon an illegal grog operation run by a certain dogger. He was none too pleased and put up a fight. Poor Parker was shot in the process, but the dogger was also killed.'

'Convenient,' Gabe said, focusing on the path ahead. Not much further now. 'How'd you know it was me?'

The silence that followed made him look back to the surprised expression on Jefferson's face, which became a grin.

'I didn't. But thank you for making the story more credible. I think once Bobby is told the news he'll confirm you were the supplier.'

'How'd a young copper like you get involved in all this?'

Jefferson hesitated, then shrugged. 'Made me an offer I couldn't refuse, so I transferred up here. Was just supposed to pass on information, harmless enough. Then you came along.'

Gabe said nothing and focused on the trail. The scrub was growing thicker, and he was following the old sheep track he'd found earlier today; further along was a group of low wattles, and the trail led straight through them. Gabe pushed past the first one, brushing the fine green leaves away from his face. His eyes searched ahead and saw what he was looking for. This was it. He gave the sky a fleeting glance, noticing the handful of low cloud that had built up as the afternoon cooled ever so slightly.

Stopped asking You for favours a while back, he thought. *But could do with a few now.*

Gabe did not wait for any indication he was heard, and stepped over the bare patch on the trail.

Leave no sign, leave no trace.

To him, the branches and sharp stones he had arranged around it looked so out of place it wasn't funny. But the question was, would those following notice? The first man was about a metre behind. Gabe kept walking, willing himself not to look back. Every muscle of his old body was tensed, ready. He just hoped he would be quick enough and that his plan worked. The first part had, sort of, but if this didn't come through it would be for nothing.

There was a split second between the snap of the buried rubber-jawed dog trap as his follower stepped onto the only clear bit of ground, and the explosion amongst the dried leaves of a fallen branch. Gabe dived to the side the moment he heard it and began to run for all he was worth. Behind him, a piercing scream resounded as the thin fishing line tied to the buried trap's jaw tightened and triggered the modified rabbit trap hidden off the trail, firing the shotgun shell. Hopefully that scream meant it worked just as well as yesterday's one had on Chase's tyre, but he didn't really want to think what the buckshot had done to someone's leg.

Surprised shouts rang out and the firing began. He darted right, pushing through the thicket as the gunshots cracked behind him. He ran, heading for the rise. He had to get there in good time. His hip twinged yet again, but he ignored it, swallowing down the pain.

The track opened up and he saw the termite mound about fifty metres ahead. Gabe made a beeline for it, not looking back, not yet. He couldn't tell if they were following or not, but was sure they would. They had to. After all, only he knew where the drugs were, or so they thought. He felt exposed in the thinning scrub, but there was no other way. He had to get to that mound.

About halfway to the termite mound, Gabe passed under the mulga. This was going to be close. The sun glinted off the glass jar hanging from one branch, a couple of metres above head height, and Gabe prayed no one would notice it as they followed him. Hopefully they would be too busy looking at the ground for more possible trap sites. Judging by the wails that echoed behind him, it had worked pretty well. Probably took the guy's leg clean off. Gabe did not feel an ounce of remorse, either for what he had done, or for what he was about to do.

He reached the termite mound, skidded around it and grabbed the rifle leaning against the dried red dirt, loaded and ready to fire. He heard shouts and the crash of bushes as they raced after him. He snuck a look around the mound, and saw three of them emerge from the wattles. Two thugs and Jefferson. Dammit. Where was Chase? Had he gone back for Courtney? Too late now; he only had one shot at this.

They saw him and started towards the mound, firing. Gabe ducked back behind cover. Not yet. They had to get closer. He risked another look. *Almost there.* The two thugs were moving forward hesitantly now, perhaps fearing another trap.

'Don't be stupid, dogger,' Jefferson called. 'There's no way out of this.'

Gabe wiped the sweat from his eyes, peeked around the mound again, and his heart rate increased even further as he saw the three of them, crouched under the mulga. Still no sign of Chase, but he couldn't wait. It was now or never. All his years of rifle work came down to this.

He leaned out from behind the termite mound, placed the container dangling above the men's heads squarely in the sights, and fired. Shots rang out. His. Theirs. His hip suddenly seized momentarily and he almost fell, taking a second longer to duck back, but that was all it took. Something hot smacked into his side and he fell, gasping with the pain of it. And just as he toppled, he saw the jar explode in a shower of glass and its contents rain down on the men below.

'What the fuck?' someone shouted, and began to cough fiercely, gagging as the fine white powder reached their lungs. More coughing, harsh and hacking. Gabe dragged himself to his feet and staggered onwards, pressing a hand to his side. Blood seeped through his fingers, but it wasn't hurting too much. He wasn't sure if that was a good thing or not, but there was no time to worry. Once they got over the initial shock, Gabe knew it could take some time before the strychnine began to work. Might be ten minutes, might be an hour, depending on how much they breathed in. Either way, if they gathered their wits quickly enough and set off after him again he'd be in trouble, especially now with this hole in his side.

He lurched away from the mound, trying to keep it between him and his pursuers.

'Dogger!' shrieked Jefferson. Any further words were cut off by another round of fierce coughs. Gabe did not look back, searching the scrub ahead for the motorbike. He had to get back to his ute before Chase or any of the others did.

Chase had known something wasn't right. Why was the old man leading them out here? What was the point of giving them the drugs now? The copper was dead, Jefferson was going to pin the blame on the dogger, so what could he have to gain by handing over the only leverage he had? Did he think it was going to save the girl? But even that was unlikely. No way could any of them be let go now. Not that Chase ever had any intention of letting them go, no matter what Jefferson said. Too many loose ends. Already the young blackfella and the Arab – *Afghan, whatever the fuck* – were in the wind. He would have to see to that. Or perhaps it was just time to move on. Head back to Queensland maybe. Or the NT. Plenty of places to lay low out there. The whole operation had become too big, too unwieldly. Just look at the trouble one washed-out old dogger had caused simply by being in the wrong place at the wrong time.

Trailing at the rear of the group, he saw Gabe glare back at him. Such contempt in the old man's eyes. Strange, wasn't it? Both men made a living from killing and here they were, on opposites sides of the coin. Wait, was that a smirk? What was he up to?

A thought occurred to Chase. Were the Afghan and the black-fella really waiting in Carnarvon, or were they waiting somewhere else? Maybe on that flat-topped hill he could see in the distance, both with a scoped rifle in their hands, just as he had planned to do before he was persuaded by Jefferson to follow him back to Brigadier. He knew they had taken Gabe's weapon, but felt sure the dogger would have another, more legal, rifle somewhere in his ute. As fine a weapon as the M1 he now cradled was, Chase doubted it was Gabe's only one.

He scanned the horizon for any glint from a scope, but the sun was to the west now, in front of them. It was exceptionally bright and hurt his eyes a little. He looked back, but could see nothing. Perhaps he was getting jittery. He was tired and his wrist throbbed despite the aspirins he'd been taking. He supposed he would have to get it looked at eventually. Now was not the time though.

The gunshot startled him badly, and as the first pained cries began he saw Gabe dart into the scrub. He moved pretty quick for an old fellow, despite that slight limp he carried. Chase hoisted the rifle and sent two quick shots after him, but was hampered by his wrist and they were wide of the mark. He hurried to where Jefferson and the others were standing over the unfortunate Jarrod, who was clutching what remained of his right leg.

The sight made even Chase wince. The shell had gone off only a metre away, and the result was gruesome. The man's jeans below the knee were shredded and most of his calf was missing. The pellets, not having time to spread before striking, had shattered his shin bone, almost tearing the leg away completely. Chase could see the jagged white edges of bone as Jarrod writhed in pain. A small, rubber-jawed dog trap still clung to his boot.

'Help me,' the man moaned. Chase didn't know him all that well, or the other two for that matter. He generally stayed clear of Brigadier, instead acting as an escort for the drug packages and refugee transfers. And, when needed, the executioner.

'Think that leg's fucked, mate,' he said. *And probably the owner with it too.* Even if they weren't in the middle of nowhere, the amount of blood he was losing meant it would be touch and go anyway.

'What the hell was that?' asked Jefferson, looking around wildly for the shooter, his pistol waving about.

Chase pointed at the dog trap and the fine line running to the smaller, modified rabbit trap staked in the ground.

'I told you he was a cunning bastard. Used one of these to take out my wheel yesterday. Christ, how many more are out there?'

'Smart,' the police officer said. 'But we need him back. We lose those drugs and we're all screwed.'

Chase spat on the ground. 'I'm going back for the girl. You go find the old bastard, and when you do we'll make her go in front.'

'What about him?' asked one of the other goons, pointing at his wounded comrade. Chase couldn't remember his name. 'Can't leave him.'

'He's fucked,' Chase said. 'Put a tourniquet on him if it makes you feel better, or put him out of his misery. He'll pass out shortly from blood loss. But either way, get after that dogger.'

The man was already incoherent and a horrible, clammy white colour. His companions regarded him for a moment, then set off into the bush.

'Keep your eyes open,' Chase warned as Jefferson followed. 'He's no fool.'

Jefferson nodded and disappeared with his gun drawn.

Chase began jogging back along the trail, heading for the ute, Wheldon and the girl, but after a few metres he considered that Gabe might have left more traps along the path that either he had led them around, or they had been lucky enough to miss. So he stepped off the trail, keeping it on his left.

He heard muffled calls, then gunshots rang out behind him, causing him to instinctively duck. *Shit, now what?* Had they found him, or did he find them? Despite being surrounded by head-high scrub, Chase suddenly felt very exposed. He picked up his pace, grunting every time his arm knocked against a branch as he pushed through the thicket.

Another five minutes of jogging and he was breathing hard. Sweat poured off him. That was when he heard the unmistakable sound of a motorbike, and he suddenly realised Gabe's plan. Lose them in the scrub, either with his traps or by simply outpacing them in the confusion, then double back behind them with the bike he'd obviously stowed somewhere beforehand.

'Shit,' he swore again. It was only Wheldon guarding the nurse, and if Chase had to bet on who might come out on top, based on the last two days, he would put everything he had on the dogger.

The bike was somewhere to his right, taking a wide circle. *He must know I'm not with the others.* Which meant he would be prepared when Chase finally made it back to the ute. Prepared, or simply gone. He took two deep breaths and began to run.

FORTY-SIX

The man hadn't stopped pacing since the others left. Wheldon kept staring at Parker's body and then looking away. Courtney didn't. She couldn't. She barely knew the police officer, but that didn't make it any easier. There was nothing to cover him with, and, considering her hands were cuffed again, that was impossible anyway. So she didn't look, not wanting to see the flies that had already swarmed about the dead man's face and wound.

She blinked, trying to keep the sweat from running down her forehead into her eyes, but to no avail. Her crying had stopped, but the stinging created tears anyway. She tried to wipe them away on her shoulders. It didn't work and more flies gathered about her own eyes. Maybe some of those had been on Parker. Courtney shuddered.

'Can you at least put my hands in front of me?' she asked. 'I'm choking on these flies.'

Wheldon didn't reply.

'What am I going to do? Run away? Attack you? I just want to wipe my face.'

He considered her for a minute, then approached. Courtney shrank back a little, fearing he might be about to refit the gag, but he yanked her to her feet and spun her around.

'Don't try anything,' he warned after recuffing her hands in front of her.

'What's going to happen to me?' she asked.

'Not up to me.'

There was a note of resignation in his voice. Another glance at the dead policeman.

'You won't get away with this,' she said. 'The others will raise the alarm. They'll find us. They'll find you.'

'Shut it,' he warned, without conviction.

A muffled thud echoed towards them, making them both jump. Was that screaming she could hear? There were two more gunshots and her heart sank. What was happening to Gabe?

'Let me go,' she pleaded. 'I'll say you helped me, they'll be lenient.'

'Can't.' He stared into the scrub, towards the noise.

'We can leave. Both of us, now.'

'They'd find us,' he said, shaking his head. 'You seem like a nice girl. I dunno how you got caught up in all this, but I can't help you.'

'How did you get caught up' – she forced herself to look at Parker's body – 'in killing policemen?'

He looked away. 'It was never supposed to be like this.' Two more shots rang out in the distance, rolling across the sky. 'Sounds like your dogger mate is causing some trouble.'

'He's pretty good at killing feral pests,' Courtney retorted. 'I'd be worried if I were you.'

'Maybe,' Wheldon said. 'But so is our man.'

The gunshots had stopped. And so had the cries. She didn't know if that was good or bad. It was definitely screaming she had heard. Didn't sound like Gabe, but at that distance who could tell? Sound travelled out here, even with the intermittent breeze tugging at her hair.

Courtney sat on the driver's seat, half in, half out of the vehicle. She contemplated her options while watching flies buzz around the empty packet of jerky Chase had discarded on the ground. Should she run? But to where? And how far could she really expect to get? What if Gabe had managed to slip his captors and was coming back for her, only to find her gone?

'Can I get a drink from the back?' she called.

Wheldon hesitated, then approached. He opened up the canopy, found the fridge and retrieved two bottles, opening one for her. She thought he might've taken a beer too, but he didn't, and returned to staring into the bush, drinking his water. They said nothing, captive and captor both silent and straining to hear something, anything that would give some clue as to what was happening out there.

Courtney tilted her head, ever so slightly. Was that an engine? She glanced at Wheldon. He seemed not to notice anything. Yes, she was sure of it. A motorbike, riding very slowly off to their left. Her heart quickened. Darren had been on a motorbike the last time she saw him. Was it him, or had Gabe left it hidden some-where ahead, knowing he would be needing it later? Either was possible, and Wheldon still hadn't heard it. She had to distract him.

'How does a guy go from being a station owner to a drug and people smuggler? It seems pretty wild, the sort of thing you might see in a movie. How do you even get the drugs down to the city? It's ages away. Do you use a boat, or a car?'

He studied her curiously as she spoke. 'What's it to you?'

She barely paused to draw breath, speaking a little louder. He'd have to hear the bike shortly, wouldn't he? 'Just curious. It's not like I'm going anywhere to tell anyone and—'

Before she realised it, he had grabbed her and pulled her out of the vehicle. He spun her around and held his pistol to her side, pressing himself hard behind her. *Oh crap, he's heard,* she thought. Wheldon scanned the scrub. The motorbike had drawn closer and sounded as though it had circled them.

'Who's there?' Wheldon yelled. No answer. 'Chase? Jefferson?'

He wheeled, spinning her with him. The steady purr of the engine grew louder.

'I'll shoot her, swear to God I'll fucking shoot her right here if you don't show yourself!'

No response. Courtney didn't dare move. She couldn't see anything ahead of them, and it sounded like the bike had stopped. The engine still idled away, out of view.

Wheldon stared into the scrub, alternating between holding his gun outstretched towards the noise and pressed against her side. She could feel him trembling, his breath hot and heavy in her ear. He stank of sweat, cigarette smoke and fear. His arm straightened again, pointing ahead of them. The breeze dropped and everything went still, quiet save for the idling motor.

It was over before she knew it. A zinging past her ear turned to a horrible wet thud an instant before the gunshot's crack rolled over her. Wheldon went rigid for a split second, and then dropped to the ground. Ears ringing, she staggered forward, stared back at Wheldon and promptly threw up, retching as the water and bile burned her throat. She had seen dead bodies well before this day. Cadavers during her training, and two separate car crash victims who didn't make it. But even those mangled bodies could not prepare her. The left side of Wheldon's head was gone. It was then she saw the blood and grey ooze on her shoulder, and she retched again.

Footsteps approached, shuffling in the red dirt. Worn leather boots entered her view and she stared up at the owner. The dogger stood before her, rifle in hand, his face a deathly shade of grey. He was holding his side, which was soaked in blood.

'Gabe,' she started, forgetting her own distress. 'What . . .'

She never finished. Gabe grunted, swayed and toppled towards her. Courtney caught him, barely managing to hold the man up. Her professional instincts took over.

'Let me see.'

'It's nothing,' he grimaced, pushing her probing hands away. 'Can't do much with those hands cuffed anyway. Where's the keys?'

She rummaged in Wheldon's pocket and found them, swallowing down the bile. Gabe uncuffed her, his bloodied hands shaking. *My God, had they been shaking like that when he fired?*

'We have to go. He's out there, somewhere.'

'Who?' But she already knew. Chase. It had to be. 'The others?' She was almost afraid to ask.

'Slowed them up a bit. Might be for good, not sure.'

She stared at him. His eyes were cold, unyielding. 'What did you do?'

'Nothing less than what they deserved,' he said, wincing as he straightened. 'What any pack of wild dogs deserves.'

His eyes fell on Parker's body, sprawled in the dirt, and the coldness vanished. 'Poor bastard,' he breathed. 'Should never have got him involved.'

'It was his job to get involved. And it's my job to make sure you're okay.'

'No time. Get in the ute. You better drive though.'

Courtney stared at the police sergeant's body. 'Gabe, we have to take him.'

A sigh, but no sign of surprise, as if he'd expected it. 'Just be quick about it.'

331

He dropped down the tailgate while Courtney struggled to drag the dead man behind the ute. Somehow, they manhandled the body into the tray. Gabe grunted with each effort, but did not complain. She had to get him to a hospital, or just far enough away so she could stop and take a look at his wound properly.

Gabe slammed the tailgate closed, took one last look at the body crammed in amongst the gear and rolled down the canopy.

'Let's get out of here,' he said, his hand returning to his side.

'Oh, I don't think so, dogger.'

Courtney spun around to see Chase emerge from the scrub. His shirt was stained with sweat and littered with fragments of dried wattle leaf, his breathing laboured. Clearly he had been running hard. And he still carried Gabe's rifle.

'Persistent little bugger, aren't you?' grimaced Gabe, slumping down to the ground and leaning against a tyre. Courtney could almost see the fight leave him. She went to him, lifted his shirt and gasped at the wound.

'He needs a doctor!' she screamed at Chase, then turned back to Gabe. 'You silly old man, why the hell didn't you let me look at it earlier?'

'You sound just like Valerie,' he said weakly. 'You remind me of her. I think she would've liked you.'

'No doctor, love,' Chase said, coming over to the ute. He grabbed her half-empty water bottle and gulped it down. Courtney stayed by Gabe's side, holding the wound and wiping the sweat from his brow. Gabe held the roo-shooter's gaze.

'Let her go, Chase,' he said. 'Please. You're screwed anyway. Darren will have rung the cops by now. She'll make no difference to the outcome.'

'Maybe,' Chase said. 'Maybe not.'

'Your mates are gone too.'

'So I figured. How'd you manage it?'

Gabe shrugged. 'Doesn't matter, but I doubt they'll make it back here.' He coughed, winced and closed his eyes. 'Sorry, Courtney.'

The snapping of nearby branches and pounding footsteps made all three of them turn their heads. A figure broke through, staggering wildly, taking great gasping breaths of air. Chills ran through Courtney as she saw Constable Matthew Jefferson careen towards them. Even Chase took a step back.

'Help me!' the young man cried, and then a spasm shook his entire body, arching his back so far Courtney expected to hear the spine snap at any minute. She watched, horrified, as he toppled and convulsed on the ground. Blood ran from his mouth, and she suspected he had badly bitten his tongue.

His gargled, incoherent sounds set her teeth on edge. 'My God, what the hell?'

'Looks like strychnine,' Chase said quietly. 'I reckon somehow your old mate here gave him a good dose.'

She could not tear her gaze from Jefferson's face. His eyes bulged, fish-like and unseeing, rolling in their sockets as his head tossed back and forth. An image of the open-mouthed laughing sideshow clowns flashed across her mind. She would never look at them the same way again – if she got out of here, that is.

'Jesus Christ,' Chase said, and shouldered the rifle.

'No,' Courtney yelled. 'You can't!'

Chase never took his eyes off Jefferson, still aiming at the hapless policeman. 'He's fucked, love. Look at him. There's no antidote for strychnine, and we're too far from anywhere even if there was. Kinder to put him down.'

'But . . .'

'But what?' Chase retorted and fired. She screamed again and collapsed in a heap. The constable bucked and jerked as his nerves continued to react to the poison, but mercifully he was silent.

Courtney put her head in her hands and wept at the horror of it all. Parker, Wheldon, and now Jefferson. She wept for Gabe too, knowing he had caused the last two deaths and blamed himself for the first, and for her current situation. As if blaming himself for his wife's death wasn't enough.

'Looks like I dodged a bullet,' Chase said, still breathing hard. His eyes kept darting left to right, and he held a hand up, shielding them from the sun. Sweat positively streamed from the man.

'Pity I didn't,' said Gabe weakly. He coughed, and Courtney saw how much that hurt. To her surprise, he began to chuckle.

'What's so fucking funny?' Chase demanded.

'Nothing. Everything.'

'You won't be laughing when you see what I'm going to do to your little girlfriend.'

Courtney paled and expected the dogger to threaten Chase, to rage at the man, but all he did was give him a knowing smirk.

'I wouldn't be so sure. You need her.'

'What the hell for?' Chase wiped his brow, blinked hard. He was changed, somehow, she could see it now. His cool cockiness gone, replaced by a nervous agitation she couldn't put her finger on.

'How you feeling, son?' Gabe asked, struggling to his feet. Courtney helped him up. He threw one arm around her shoulder and leaned on her. 'You're sweating, hard. Sun seem a little too bright? Bet your heart's racing too.'

Chase stared at him.

'You need her,' Gabe continued. 'Because by my reckoning you've got maybe a couple of hours before you really start to feel it. You might get to Carnarvon by then. You might not. But it'd be better if a nurse drove you there.'

'What the hell are you on about?'

'They've always said 10-80 is odourless. Tasteless. I've had my doubts, especially since they started putting that dye in the brew. I always figured a wise old dog might see it and shy off. Luckily, I keep a few bottles of the old stuff, the clear mix. To use if I think just such a dog is wandering about.'

He paused, the fire returning to his eyes as he stared at Chase. 'But you're not wise, Chase. You're just a pup, running around, thinking he knows everything, thinking he can outwit an old dog with a gammy leg.'

Courtney saw Chase's gaze flick to the empty jerky packet on the ground, saw the realisation dawn in those eyes and watched his face turn from perplexed amusement to one of abject horror.

'No . . .' he said weakly, then promptly jammed two fingers down his throat.

'That won't help,' Gabe said, as the man retched and vomited in front of them. 'Wasn't easy injecting those bits of jerky, but I figured it was worth a shot. And you took the bait.'

'Gabe,' Courtney said stunned. 'You . . . You've poisoned him?'

'Seems so,' he said. 'Knew you wouldn't touch the stuff, and the sarge practically threw up when I offered him some yesterday. Darren and Amin saw what I was doing, so their first job if you made it back was to get rid of it if Chase didn't find it.'

Chase straightened and staggered towards them, raising the rifle. 'You bastard!'

'Been called worse,' Gabe said. 'But I wouldn't dally if I were you. Courtney, take my ute and get him into Carnarvon. There might still be time to save him.'

'You're coming too,' Courtney said, trying to lift him, but despite her efforts Gabe fell back to the ground.

'No, Courtney,' he said, his usually gruff voice surprisingly tender. 'I think I'll just sit here for a bit.' He shuffled alongside the police carrier, sitting against one wheel in the shade. His breathing became shallow.

'Gabe,' she started, tears welling again.

'Get in the ute!' Chase screamed, grabbing and shoving her towards the vehicle. He'd dropped his rifle but that did not make her fear him any less. She turned back as Chase dragged her along.

'Gabe!' The dogger gave her a faint smile.

Chase pushed her into the driver's seat, slammed the door and raced to the other side.

'Drive!' Chase yelled as he climbed in. 'Or I'll make sure you suffer so bad you'll wish I'd killed you here and now.'

She obeyed, throwing the ute into gear and pulling onto the faint track as Chase guided her. Through tears she could see the dogger in the mirror. He raised one hand in a final goodbye, and then disappeared in the dust.

FORTY-SEVEN

She'll be alright, he told himself. He wasn't sure if he believed it or not, but it was out of his hands. Chase was fucked, whether they made it to a hospital or not, but Gabe had sowed the seeds of hope, just to keep Courtney alive. The roo-shooter would deteriorate quickly, he was certain of that much, and if the poison worked the same on humans as it did animals, he'd soon be unable to do anything to her.

He dragged himself to where Jefferson's body lay and searched for the sat-phone. As he did, he regarded the young officer. *How in the hell did you get mixed up in this shitshow?* It didn't matter, and he doubted he'd be around to find out. For such a warm afternoon, he was feeling uncomfortably cold.

While the phone rang, he watched an eagle circling high above. Not exactly a vulture, but the image unnerved him slightly. *You knew this was the most likely outcome,* he told himself.

'Gabe?' Darren almost shouted down the line.

'Yeah.'

'What's going on? Did it work? Everyone all okay?'

'Yes and no,' Gabe said, and coughed, sending a burning pain right through his whole body. 'Courtney's with Chase. The rest are dead.' He paused. 'Parker's dead.'

'Holy shit,' Darren said. There was a muffled voice beside him. 'Hang on, the copper wants a word.'

There was a scuffling sound as the phone was passed.

'Mr Ahern?'

'Yeah.'

'This is Inspector Gavin Turner. Quite the situation we've got here.'

'Don't I know it,' Gabe grimaced. 'How far away are your boys? The nurse is in my ute with Chase Fowler, heading to Carnarvon.'

'They haven't left yet; we were waiting for your call.'

'Get them going!' Gabe ordered. 'Tell them . . . *shit* . . .' He coughed again, wiped his mouth and saw the blood on his wrist.

'Mr Ahern. Are you okay?'

'Don't worry about me. Tell your guys the man she is driving, Chase Fowler, killed the sarge and fuck knows how many others. He's in a bad way himself, and might threaten the girl.'

'TRG are on their way from Perth, but it will be some time before they get here,' Turner said. 'What about Constable Jefferson?'

'Dead.' Then in a moment of inspiration he added, 'Chase shot him.' Silence on the line – hard to tell if it was intentional or the satellite delay. 'Inspector?'

'I'm here. Shit, what a mess.'

'You're telling me.'

'We'll get the officers moving and instruct them to proceed with caution. Darren here tells me you've got the drugs hidden away?'

'Yeah. Darren knows where, he'll show you. Inspector . . . the sarge's body is in the back too. Just let your guys know, before, you know, they open up the canopy.'

'I will. Thank you. We'll be needing a full statement from you.'

'Not sure I'll be around for that.' Gabe coughed. 'Just make sure Courtney is okay. She can tell you everything.'

'Are you hurt?'

'Caught a bullet. Inspector, Amin and his family? What's going to happen to them?'

'I honestly don't know. Quite unprecedented.'

'He's the one who blew this whole thing wide open. Promise me you'll do what you can to let him stay.'

'I know. He's here making a statement. His family is getting checked out at the hospital. We've got a bunch of people coming up from Perth. Immigration, Drug Squad, the works. Brigadier will be raided. From there, I can't say, but I can promise I will do everything in my power to help him. I don't know about the other families.'

'I need to talk to him.'

'Hang on, I'll send someone to find him.' More voices in the background, then the inspector returned. 'Can you hold on, Gabe? Can you get help?'

'No one around. Just get Amin. Put Darren back on for now.'

'Okay. Hang in there. We'll get people to you ASAP.'

Gabe closed his eyes and didn't answer. There was rustling again over the phone.

'Gabe? You alright, man?'

'Been better, Darren. Listen, about Bobby.'

'Yeah?'

'He's not good, mate. Seeing Valerie in that accident, it buggered him up bad. I never realised how bad.'

'Yeah, I know. And I know why you brought that grog in too.'

'Buckley's chance of that happening again,' Gabe said, coughing once more. He felt something tear deep inside. 'For what it's worth, I'm sorry. Thought I was helping a mate, but really I was just helping myself.'

Silence from the other end. 'I dunno what you want me to say, Gabe.'

'Nothing. Just listen. Courtney is going to be a mess. I want you to look after her, alright?'

'Reckon she'll be looking after me,' Darren said. 'Not doing real flash myself.'

'That's not surprising. Just keep an eye on her. Top girl, that one. Top girl.'

'I will. Amin's here.'

'Put him on.'

'Okay. Be seeing you, Old Boy.'

He didn't reply.

A different voice came on the phone. 'Gabe?'

'Amin. How's your family?'

'They are okay. The doctor is looking at them now. But where are you, my friend?'

'Up shit creek, mate. Up shit creek.'

'I don't understand, but I think that is not good?'

'No, not good.'

'Then let me thank you while I can. I could not have done any of this without you.'

'You know I considered dumping you on more than one occasion?'

'I know. I could see it in your eyes. But you never did. That is why you are a good man. Even if you do not believe it yourself. Even if you have done bad things. I think Valerie would be proud of you.'

'I hope you get to stay, Amin.'

'Thank you. So do I.'

'And Khalid. His grave. Darren has the GPS, to find it if you need to.'

'Thank you. Aamena tells me Mojda, the lady with all the children, was his wife. I do not look forward to telling her.'

'Don't envy you, mate. I'm going to hang up now. Look after yourself.'

'Allah be with you, my friend.'

Gabe switched off the phone before the inspector could call back. He'd said all he had to say. The others could fill the police officer in if needed. He leaned his head against the tyre and stared at the horizon. The sun was beginning to turn the sky an orange and purple hue. Low clouds stretched out like ripples in the ocean. Perhaps it might rain soon. He would miss that, miss the scent of an afternoon storm after a hot, humid summer's day. Apparently, there was a special word to describe it. Gabe didn't need special words. 'Bloody wonderful' had always sufficed. His eyes closed . . .

. . . and opened again. For a moment he thought his sight was failing, then realised all that remained of daylight was the dull glow to the west. He must've blacked out there for a bit. That couldn't be good either. He felt tired. So very tired. Each breath caused a stabbing pain to his side, like a bad stitch. Like he'd run a mile at full pelt.

Movement caught his eye, high up on the ridge. He blinked, trying to focus. There it was again. He felt his stomach tighten. In the eerie light of dusk, he saw the familiar outline of what could only be one thing.

Gabe knew he was dying. Part of him was surprised he'd made it this far. Death didn't scare him all that much, not now that he was so close to it. Truth be told, he hadn't really been living since Valerie died, merely existing, and in the darker moments he'd almost put an end to things himself. God knows he had the means. But this, the idea of a dog here, at this very moment? That did make him afraid. Dying was one thing. Being mauled to death and too weak to do anything about it was another. If the dog didn't finish him off, the irony of it all just might.

It slipped silently down the ridgeline. *I was right,* he mused, feeling a small sense of pride. *Must be a den up there somewhere.* He watched it approach, wary and uncertain. It looked to be female, an older one, but it was hard to tell in the fading light. His hands searched weakly for something, anything. A rock, a branch, but there was nothing. His rifle lay in the dirt, well out of reach. He did not have the energy to try and get it.

The animal regarded him cautiously, keeping its distance. He made to cry out, to scare it away, but only a hoarse croak emerged from his throat, and it almost turned into a laugh. How many times had this situation been reversed? How often had he walked up to a trapped dog, rifle in hand?

'Come on then,' he growled as he felt himself beginning to slip away again. 'Come get it over with.'

The dog started towards him, then stopped, sniffing at the empty packet of jerky. It visibly recoiled. *So, it can smell it,* he thought. *Clever girl.* The dog paced towards him again, and stopped once more. It cocked its head, glanced off to the side, and bolted, running back up the ridge while keeping low to the ground. And then it was gone. Gabe stared after it, barely seeing anything.

A roaring filled his ears and his vision was overwhelmed by a great blinding whiteness. *Holy shit,* he thought. *It's really real.*

He saw a familiar figure run towards him, silhouetted by the light, and he smiled. *Valerie.* She would scold him for being so pig-headedly stupid, then she would kiss his cheeks and scold him again for being so rough and stubbly. He would promise to shave, and forget on purpose the following morning. He would get better, and they would carry on, just the two of them, driving through the great outback, doing whatever they needed to get by.

Gabe smiled again as the darkness enveloped him. Everything was going to be alright.

FORTY-EIGHT

Courtney watched the regression of Chase Fowler with a mixture of fascination and horror. She drove as fast as she dared, which was nowhere near fast enough for the panicked man seated next to her, pointing his pistol at her midriff.

The setting sun hampered her vision, especially with the two bullet holes and fretwork of cracks that matted the windscreen, but the harsh glare seemed to affect Chase far more. He would wince and avert his eyes each time a ray peeked through the scrub.

'Faster,' he said. The panic in his voice was clear. Courtney couldn't blame him. If what he was facing was even close to Jefferson's experience, she half expected him to turn the gun on himself.

'I'm going as fast as I can,' she said. 'It won't be much help if I crash.'

He didn't answer. He was busy retching out the window again. He had been doing that regularly since they left, swallowing down great gulps of water and then vomiting it back up again.

'Water neutralises it,' he muttered to himself between bouts. 'Got to get the water in me.'

A shudder ran through him, startling them both. Courtney hoped his finger was well clear of the trigger. Should a real convulsion hit, he might well clench unintentionally, and that would be no good for either of them.

'You have to stay calm,' she said. 'You have to lower your heart rate, slow down the absorption.'

'Easier fucking said than done,' Chase spat. 'Have you seen what this shit does?' He banged his fist on the dash, making her jump again. 'Fuck that old bastard. I should've . . .'

Courtney never found out what Chase wanted to do because the man doubled over and let out a screech of pain, gripping his stomach tightly.

'Do something!' he yelled.

'Like what?' Courtney screamed back. 'There's nothing here!' She didn't add that she had absolutely no idea what to do anyway. Somewhere in the back of her mind she recalled Gabe saying there was no antidote to the poison, but he was talking about pet dogs, wasn't he? There had to be something they could do for Chase at the hospital, even if it was just to knock the man out.

'Bullshit,' Chase hissed through gritted teeth. 'You're waiting for it to do me in, aren't you? Payback, isn't it?'

She swerved past an anthill, steering the ute into a gutter, which in turn sent the two of them bouncing around the cab.

'Goddammit, if I didn't want to help I wouldn't be driving like a maniac,' she shot back. 'And if I wanted you dead, I would've let Amin kill you yesterday.'

His breathing was heavier. She didn't know if that was from the poison or the panic. Both, most likely. Her own breathing was just as bad, and that was definitely all panic. Any second now he was likely to lose his nerve completely, and then anything could happen.

The same questions went over in her mind as they had done so many times before. Should she run? Could she get away in time?

And then a new one. Even if she could, would she? Would she really abandon him to his fate, deserved as it may be?

A kangaroo darted out in front of them, and she slammed on the brakes, just grazing the animal's rump as it bounded past. It teetered for a split second, regathered itself and shot off into the bush without hesitation. Courtney watched it go, wishing she could follow.

'Don't worry about the bloody roos, keep going, woman!'

He was shaking continuously now, and sweat ran in rivers down his face. The gun hung loosely from his hand, but still pointed in her general direction. She considered trying to grab it, but that could just as easily end very badly. She drove on.

They turned onto the main road, the one that would take them past the Junction and on to Carnarvon. She was contemplating asking if there was an ambulance in the little community when the first convulsion hit.

There was no real warning. Chase suddenly arched his back at an impossible angle, and the gun fell to the floor. He bucked in the seat, his arms rigid and eyes rolling, staring unseeingly at the cab ceiling. He made very little noise, just a gurgled moan, which turned to spluttering gasps as white foam began to dribble from his clenched mouth.

Courtney brought the ute to a screeching halt. There was no point racing to the hospital if the man was about to choke on his tongue. By the time she got around to his side of the ute, trickles of blood ran down his chin. She tried to restrain him, to no avail. He thrashed about, almost knocking her to the ground. Twice, his head struck the door frame, drawing blood on the second blow.

A sob escaped her throat, she couldn't help it. Chase's eyes rolled to her, a mixture of fear, pain and . . . pleading? She couldn't tell.

She tried to calm him, to soothe the man, but with no effect. He writhed as she watched on helplessly, and the smell of faeces and urine hit her nose as his bowels let go. A shudder ran through him once more, and then he slumped forward, his breaths coming in ragged gasps.

'Chase?' she asked tentatively. A faint groan in reply. 'Chase? Are you alright?' A stupid question, but what else was there to say?

'Love,' he said in a voice so weak she had to strain to hear it. 'If that happens again, you shoot me.'

'What? I can't . . .'

'You take that gun, you put it to my skull and you end it.' His eyes blazed momentarily at her and then faded again, as though he'd burned through the last reserves of his strength. He picked up the gun and leaned back in the seat, still quivering. He wiped at his mouth. 'Drive.'

They had travelled for another fifteen minutes when the next convulsion hit. This time Courtney did not stop. She drove on, her vision blurred through tears from the sheer horror of it all. The gun remained in Chase's lap, but she did not reach for it. She couldn't. Courtney remembered Gabe's words. *Be kinder to just shoot it there and then.* But that was a dog, an animal, not a human. Regardless of what he'd done, what he had threatened to do, she couldn't just shoot him.

The screaming started. It rose from the very depths of his lungs, welling up into an explosion of pain that hurt her ears. She drove for another minute and could bear it no longer. Courtney slammed on the brakes and veered off the road. She had to get out. She fumbled at her seatbelt, her hands forgetting what to do. Next to her, Chase continued to writhe. She caught his eyes, saw the pain and pleading in them again . . .

As she opened the door, it seemed his screams grew louder, although she wasn't sure how that was possible. One last look over her shoulder as she climbed out. He was watching her, even in his throes. Or maybe he wasn't and it was just her conscience taunting her, telling her she should stay with him, that the kindest thing would be to do what he had asked. Instead she put her hands over her ears and ran, but still those screams echoed inside her head.

'Can't this thing go any faster?' Darren asked from the back seat of the Carnarvon police troop carrier. 'He's got Courtney with him.'

'Going as fast as we can,' said the driver, a young female first class constable named Sarah Cosgrove. Her partner, Sergeant Clinton Banks, sat grim-faced and silent. Behind them, a second troopy followed.

Darren leaned back and shook his head, still trying to digest his conversation with Gabe. The plan had almost come off, only instead of Gabe and Courtney legging it to town, it was her and that bloody roo-shooter, who had taken the bait, but not in the way Gabe had hoped. And the sarge. That hadn't been in the plan at all. *Shit, what a mess.*

'He's not going to be happy,' Darren said. 'I've seen what that shit does to dogs. I've got no idea what he'll be like when we see him.'

'You say this Gabe fellow, he deliberately poisoned them all?' Banks asked.

'He didn't really have any other choice,' Darren said. Part of him didn't want to tell these cops anything, but from the sound of things Gabe was in a bad way. Might not even make it.

'He figured it was the only option. Couldn't win in a shoot-out, couldn't outrun them. He knew Chase would grab that jerky, and he knew if his trap worked and he broke free, they'd leg it after him.'

'Big if,' Banks said. 'Still can't quite believe all this is going down.'

'You and me both,' Darren said.

'So why didn't you and this Amin fellow just bring the drugs back with you?'

'We were going to, but Gabe was worried we might run into others.'

'Other smugglers?'

Darren paused. 'Yeah. Or cops. So we hid them and decided I'd show you where they are only once we were sure there were no more bent coppers around.'

He was about to go on but a glint up ahead caught his eye. He leaned forward, squinted and then almost tumbled into the front of the troopy in his excitement. 'That's it up there. Gabe's ute!'

'You sure?' Banks asked as he grabbed the radio handset.

'Bloody sure. Not going to forget that vehicle in a hurry.'

The senior officer pressed the button. 'Suspect vehicle has been sighted ahead. Proceed with caution.' Someone in the second troopy behind them acknowledged the call.

The two vehicles pulled up some twenty metres from Gabe's ute.

'You sit tight,' Banks said to Darren.

'Watch out for Courtney,' he said, noting both officers had their weapons drawn.

'We will. Just keep your head down.'

He watched the four officers advance with guns raised, their long shadows stretching out in front of them. Darren couldn't make out anyone in the vehicle, but the cracked windscreen did make it hard.

'Chase Fowler!' yelled the sergeant. Darren saw no response. Shit, what if . . . what if the two of them were dead inside, Chase shooting her before succumbing to the poison in a final act of revenge?

'Chase Fowler,' Banks repeated. 'You are under arrest. Put your hands outside the vehicle!'

Darren half expected a hail of gunfire to come from the ute. Chase's final stand. Go down in a blaze of glory. That'd be the sort of thing that redneck fuckwit would probably do. He watched on, holding his breath as two officers kept their guns pointed at the windscreen while Cosgrove and Banks approached from either side. It was when they both looked into the ute and recoiled that Darren knew there would be no last stand. All four police officers holstered their weapons. The constable looked like she was about to throw up.

Darren had seen enough. He leaped out of the vehicle and raced to the ute. 'Courtney!' he yelled, expecting to see her dead body slumped over the wheel. None of the officers tried to restrain him as he approached. Darren looked into the ute and wished he hadn't. 'Holy shit.'

Chase was dead. Darren didn't need to be an expert on such things to know he hadn't died well. The man's eyes were wide open, staring up at the ceiling, face and shirt covered in a mixture of vomit and blood. Darren saw the gun, and wondered if he hadn't tried to do himself in. It looked like it would've been much better than the alternative he was staring at right now. But where was . . .

'Darren?'

He whirled to see Courtney step out from the scrub.

'Courtney!' He ran to the young nurse and, before he realised what he was doing, embraced her. She clung to him and began to sob.

'You alright?' he asked. 'He didn't hurt you?'

She shook her head. 'It was awful, Darren. I couldn't watch. He wanted me to . . . to finish it for him, but I couldn't.' She wiped her eyes. 'I just ran.'

He hugged her again as Banks came over.

'Miss Drage? Are you okay?'

Courtney nodded, and then looked at Darren again. 'Amin? Aamena and Jawad?'

'They're fine. With the coppers in town,' Darren said. 'What about Gabe?'

'Oh God, we have to go!' she cried. 'He's shot. I couldn't do anything for him, he wouldn't let me. Darren, he made me take Chase. He knew I'd have to drive.'

'We'll get there,' Banks said. 'Before we do, you've got something to show us, Darren?'

'Yeah.'

'Careful. Remember Sergeant Parker is in there.'

'I know,' Darren said. He quickly opened up the canopy. He didn't want to see the sarge, but there was no avoiding it. The body lay wedged against the toolboxes on the tray.

'Poor bastard,' he said. The other officers leaned in, stony-faced. Courtney let out a sniffle. It was worse when Darren flicked on the canopy light. It highlighted everything. The blood, the stunned expression on the dead man's face. The flies swarming over him.

'Least that prick in the cab got what he deserved,' one of the other officers said. Darren noticed Courtney looked at the ground at that, and was glad he never saw the man's final moments.

Thankfully when he opened the toolbox the body was obscured from view. Banks peered in, observing the traps, vials and other gear stored in there.

'Thought you said there were drugs in here.'

'Grab that,' Darren said, pointing at the rope handle tucked against the sides. They lifted the false floor to reveal the canvas bag tucked in underneath.

'Bugger me,' Banks said. 'What the hell was he hiding in there before?'

'Doesn't matter anymore,' Darren said. 'C'mon, we gotta go find Gabe. Now.'

Banks nodded and gestured to his vehicle. 'Come with me. Watters, Jonesy, you two stay here, call it in and secure the crime scene. Cosgrove, you're driving again.'

Once they were underway, Banks looked back at his passengers. 'You sure you're alright, Miss Drage?'

'I'm fine, just shook up, that's all.'

They drove on in silence. Darren held Courtney, and she pressed herself to him. Every now and then she would shiver as though cold. He didn't know what to say, so he just stroked her hair.

It was dark by the time they drew close to the ridge. Darren guided the constable along the track, pointing out the gutters and gullies to avoid until finally the ridgeline loomed up in front of them. Darren held his breath, not sure what to expect. Their headlights glistened off the vehicles parked haphazardly around the area. It looked like someone was lying in the dirt? Was that Gabe?

'Stay here,' Jacobs instructed again as the two officers climbed out, guns drawn.

Courtney was having none of it. She sprang from the vehicle and raced towards what Darren recognised as another police troop carrier. He followed, and could see Gabe now, propped up against a tyre. The old man lifted his head as they approached, their shadows dancing around him like ghosts. Courtney reached him first and fell to her knees, cradling him, pressing down on the wound at his side.

Darren arrived just in time to see Gabe raise a hand to her face, smile and whisper something.

'Valerie.'

He smiled, shuddered and closed his eyes.

FORTY-NINE

She had watched them come and go. Men swarming about in their machines with strange strobing lights. She did not know what they were doing. She did not know why they were here. All she knew was that they brought with them the noise, the scents and the fear. The air had been full of it these past days. Full of death, and that strange acrid scent that followed the thunder and the pain. So she lay hidden in her den, high up on the ridgeline, and waited.

She had seen the old Man sitting in the dirt, after the others left. He was hurt. He was dying. He was familiar. Her curiosity had got the better of her, and she'd crept down from her den to inspect this Man, his scent one she caught on rare occasions during her travels. Just a hint, only a faint sign and trace, as if he had passed by long before. It had been on the metal thing still buried in the ground by the dry creek, ever so slight, but there, as a warning.

He saw her, and she smelled his fear. It emboldened her and she drew closer, stopping first to inspect the foreign thing that smelled of dried meat and . . . death. Tainted with something that burned the insides, made her young howl in pain and run themselves ragged before dying. She grew angry and approached again, but then another machine arrived, and so she fled back to the safety of her den.

Now, after many days, she creeps down again, tests the air for scent. The old man is gone, so too the machines and the dead that had been there before. He can still be smelled, along with the others, a heady mixture that puts her on edge. She sniffs the ground where he sat, squats, marks it and then carries on in search of tonight's hunt. Later, she will seek out a new den, somewhere that doesn't have Men coming and going, but not too far away.

This is, after all, her territory.

ACKNOWLEDGEMENTS

I started writing 'The Dogger' in October 2017, and, were it not for the support and encouragement of those around me, it would most likely still be in the drafts folder along with all the other attempts at getting a second novel published.

To Alison, who has read every manuscript and short story I have ever written, and who always provides such great and honest feedback, thank you. We got there in the end!

Thank you to all the readers who took the time to review, rate, or simply comment on my first publication, *Ridgeview Station*. Those kind words really helped lift the spirits and keep me going.

Authenticity is very important to me, and to that end the help of Raihanaty A Jalil, and Nerilee and Bill Bennell of Kooyar Wongi has been invaluable, and greatly appreciated. Thanks, guys; the book is better for your input.

To my amazing agent, Alex Adsett, what a whirlwind this has been, hey? Thank you for taking a punt on an ex-farmer from WA. To my publisher Beverley Cousins and her team at Penguin Random House Australia, your enthusiasm and praise for this story has been unbelievable, and very humbling, thank you.

Every writer needs a good office, and in all likelihood, a real job, so thank you to Spanner, Ash, Deborah, Zoe, Liam and

Hannah for providing me with both at the same time, and not minding too much when I bugger off during seeding or harvest for writers' events and the like. Though the office does bounce a bit.

Another thing every writer needs is a support group. Fellow writers get it, they know what it is to be rejected and what it is to be accepted. The WA writing community and the wider Australian writing world have been amazing since I first entered the scene. So to my tribe, my fellow WA writers, Holden Sheppard, Raphael Farmer, Raihanaty A Jalil, Alicia Tuckerman, Louise Allan, Jess Gately, Emily Paull and Melinda Tognini. You guys. You guys kept me going. And I have never seen so many people lose their collective shit over a single tweet from a potential agent.

Thank you to my family for their unyielding support in everything I've done. I don't say it enough, but I do appreciate you all.

Finally, to my girl, Kylie. You're the best. See? I really was writing all those times locked away at the end of the house ignoring you, and was absolutely not gaming at all. Mostly.

ABOUT THE AUTHOR

Michael Trant is a WA country boy now residing in Perth after a variety of careers ranging from farmer, marine draftsman, pastoralist and FIFO pot washer.

Michael writes with an authentic rural voice, drawing on his experiences to open readers to places and lifestyles foreign to many. He has a passion for farming, writing, gaming and guitar, the order of which vary throughout the year. He still works on farms as a tractor driver, mainly to annoy those teachers who claimed no one would pay him to stare out a window all day.

His debut novel *Ridgeview Station* was published in 2017.